"I loved it! Every nuance. Every turn. Every word. It all holds together. Not one moment of "where did that come from?"

Betty Radford Turcott, teacher, author, workshop facilitator, motivational speaker.

"One woman's journey through a tangled life of family dynamics, romance, love, hate and survival and ending with a revelation that I didn't see coming. All written by an author who knows her craft well. What a treat!"

A. Evans, Documentary Film Maker
Spirit Valley Pictures.com

"I loved it! Each day when I had to stop I couldn't wait to get back to it. The plot flows along beautifully, the characters are well-developed, with strengths and flaws, and sometimes downright humorous. I strongly identified with Cynthia, I guess because of her age, her sidetracks in life, her creative energy, her love of food, and her desire to be loved. The Broken Promise, Book 2, stands alone as a great story, even if I hadn't read The Hidden Vow, Book1, but it sure makes me want to read it again. I look forward to Book 3."

Barbara Heagy, author of "10 - A Story of Love, Life, and Loss," and co-author of"Good Grief People."

The Broken Promise

Dragonfly Series: Book 2

www.spiralpress.ca

 Logo by Ken Coward,
Communication Design Inc. www.holycowcom.com

Cover Design by Robin Ludwig Design, Inc.
www.gobookcoverdesign.com
Cover Photos:brookebecker at istockphoto,com
ID 140819473 Paul Jackson. Dreamstime. com
ID 28599104Beata BeclaDreamstime.com
Dragonfly Brooch made in Scotland by Ladycrow Silks,
www.ladycrowsilks.co.uk
Photo of Dragonfly brooch by Stuart Mccannell
Poems by Ruth Cunningham, www.selftoself.com

ISBN 978-0-9951914-3-3

This is a work of fiction. Other than obvious places (Guelph, London, New York, etc,) names, characters, incidents and places are the products of the author's imagination or are used fictitiously.

The Broken Promise
Dragonfly Series: Book 2

Gloria W. Nye

To Melanie

"I met my Self and then I knew
It's what we each are meant to do
It's up to all to each review
and paint life's canvas hue-on-hue.
Creating and by choice imbue
ourselves—our world to renew."

From Conversations through the Window
by Ruth Cunningham

Note to Reader: This book tells the story of the dragonfly's journey 800 years in the future from *Book 1: The Hidden Vow.* You may have fun guessing who the people are in this book and who parallel those who were in the first one. If you don't want to wait, there is a list of who was who in Appendix 1 at the back of the book. However, this book stands alone and you don't have to read the first book to enjoy this one.

Chapter 1

Cynthia Marshall parked her car in the curved driveway of her mother's house. She got out and stomped up the front steps. A brass knocker hung from bared teeth of a ferocious lion head. Dangling from the trapped circle on a length of butcher twine hung a used envelope with NO FLYERS scrawled in black marker.

"Okay, let's get it over with." She clunked it once with a loud crack, pushed the door open and stepped onto an expanse of black and white checkerboard tiles.

Her mother, matriarch Josephine Marshall, breezed up the hall from the kitchen. A bush of white hair flared around her head, and she clutched a miniature Yorkshire terrier to the bosom of her daisy-flowered housedress. Over the dog's high-pitched yapping, she shouted, "It's about time you got here. I phoned you an hour ago." She turned and strode back down the hall to the kitchen, her clunky charm bracelet clattering.

Cynthia took a breath, closed the front door and followed the raucous duo. "Hardly an hour," she muttered under her breath. *More like twenty minutes.*

Tastefully arranged groupings of framed family photos lined the wide hallway. Between two brushed silver frames, an eight-by-ten glossy of Tippy, the yapper, had been recently, and crookedly, scotch-taped onto the French embossed wallpaper.

Mrs. Marshall's second marriage had made her a rich woman, but it hadn't improved her taste. Her penchant for plastic doilies, orange macramé lampshades and plaid scatter rugs had transformed the once-stylish home into a bargain store basement.

As Cynthia entered the kitchen, her mother pointed to a low plastic-covered stool in a corner. "Sit." She had seated herself behind the table on one of Frank's antique oak pressed-back chairs. She held Tippy on her lap. The dog had stopped his infernal barking but his sharp marble eyes kept a wary lookout.

Cynthia dragged the stool over and sat down. Half a tuna sandwich and a dill pickle lay on a paper plate in front of her mother. Her mother hated washing dishes or housework so Bonnie Baxter, a Scottish widow in her sixties, came every weekday afternoon. She'd shop, clean and chat over cups of teaand make dinner and eat with Mrs. Marshall. In eleven years she had become friend and confidant to her employer but she had a soft spot for Cynthia and served as a buffer between her and her mother.

Her mother pointed to the teapot. "It's still hot."

"No thanks. I only drink herb tea."

"You mean that watery stuff that tastes like dishwater."

Cynthia dropped her purse on the floor. "Why did you call me over here?"

"I need the house."

"You what?"

"You heard me. I need the house."

"What house?"

"Don't play your naive game with me. You know what house. The house you're living in."

"You mean *my* house?"

"It is not *your* house. I hold the deed if you remember." She picked up a plastic fork and stabbed the pickle.

"But I've lived there for twenty-eight years. I've—"

"That's long enough. It *is* my house after all." She bit off a chunk of pickle, spat it into her hand and offered it to Tippy, who sniffed and declined. She flipped her hand toward an upper cupboard. "Go on. Make yourself one of those fake teas. Bonnie bought a box of it for you."

Her mother's words swam in her head, looking for a place to land. *She can't take my house away from me. Can she?* She opened the cupboard, took down a box of lemon-ginger tea and a china cup and saucer—her mother's only sense of refinement.

The dog resumed its yapping and Mrs. Marshall patted it, not looking at her daughter. "Your niece needs a house. You know she's pregnant."

"But she and Mike have a perfectly good house in Kitchener. Why do they want mine?" She pressed the switch on the electric kettle. *Will that obnoxious mutt shut up.*

Her mother's dark green eyes—inherited from her Irish mother —glared at Cynthia. "They need a bigger place, and stop calling it *your* house. It's never been *yours*." She picked up the barking animal. "There, there, my Twiddle Diddums. It's only Cynthia." As the dog settled down, she dug out a piece of tuna from under a slice of mushy white bread. "Here you are, my Tippy Whippums." Its pink tongue curled around the soggy morsel.

Cynthia's mind raced. Her stomach dropped into an old hollow place she thought she had discarded and words floundered in her mouth as if she were a child learning how to speak. "Well—it's— but—twenty-eight years ago you called it a gift."

Her mother took a sip of tea and looked up. "I'm sure I never said that. I must have said, 'I lent it to you.' Frank insisted I do something when that no good man, whoever he was, left you pregnant with Stephanie."

Cynthia poured boiling water into her flowered cup. The tea bag already filled half of it. "Uncle Frank thought it was a gift."

"And that's another thing. Why do you persist in calling your stepfather, Uncle Frank."

"Because he *was* my uncle, not my father."

"Well it confuses people." She pursed her lips. "Every time you say it, I have to explain that I married my dead husband's brother."

Cynthia put the kettle on the counter and sat down. "And here I thought when you phoned me to come over, you were going to give me a present. Some present this is."

"Present?" Her mother stared blankly.

Cynthia grimaced. "Why do you always remember my sisters' birthdays and never mine?"

Mrs. Marshall glanced at a calendar thumbtacked onto the oak trim of the cupboard door. A Dalmatian in a firefighter's hat peered over the April heading. "Well, look at that. On Wednesday, it will be fifty—" She looked up. "Fifty-three years ago when you nearly killed me." She pursed her lips.

That old refrain. "Really, mother. It was hardly my fault."

"After you were born I was so sick. And you cried all the time." Her voice rose in volume. "You were impossible."

"For heaven's sake. I was a baby."

"It wasn't my fault you were born with that ugly mark on your face." Tippy yelped as his mistress's stroke turned into a clutch. "It looked as if someone had splashed wine on you."

Cynthia's hand darted to her right cheek. After a childhood of teasing, a teenage life of humiliation, and constantly tilting her head so her hair would fall over her cheek—the rusty blemish, shaped like a kid's drawing of Newfoundland, had been lasered off. "I never said it was your fault." Blemish free for twenty-two years, she still wore her straight hair bobbed at shoulder length.

Tippy, eyes closed, crouched quietly in his mistress's lap.

Cynthia took a drink of tea. "So my birthday present is you taking my house away."

Her mother stroked the dog several times. "When your sister asked me if I could help Sharon and Mike buy a house, I thought it was quite clever of me to think of giving them yours. I mean *my* house that I've allowed you to live in all these years."

"And where am I supposed to live?"

"You can live in the condom on Speedvale. The tenants are planning to move."

Cynthia groaned. "I wish you'd stop calling it a condom. It's a cond-O."

"Then why is it called a condom—ninny—mum—whatever. I'll call it what I like, and stop correcting me."

The dog lapped at his mistress's tuna wet fingers.

Cynthia stared at her grandmother's porcelain teapot and the matching rose-covered cups. Her gaze moved to the sharp paring knife laying beside her mother's white plastic plate.

Mrs. Marshall continued. "I can give the tenants notice to move on July first." Her tone shifted into her best Baptist Sunday School teacher's voice. "I'm sure you can be ready by then, Cyn."

"For the hundredth time, don't call me Cyn."

"You don't need all that space now with your Stephanie off married. You're rattling around in that house all by yourself."

"Uncle Frank, and for sure Daddy, wouldn't have wanted you to take my house away."

"Well, they're both dead and just because you were your father's favourite, doesn't mean you get everything you want."

Cynthia glowered. "I don't want to get into this now." She stood up grabbed her purse from the floor. "I have to go."

"You haven't finished your tea."

"I've had enough." She turned and stalked out of the kitchen.

The dog's stabbing barks did not block out her mother's raised voice. "Remember. July first. That's plenty of time to pack."

She yanked the door open, stepped out and slammed it shut. The snarling lion's circle clattered and she snarled over her shoulder. "And you shut up too."

Chapter 2

Cynthia stomped down the stone steps and marched to her Honda Civic. She wrenched the door open, threw her purse toward the passenger seat and climbed in. She thumped the steering wheel with the heel of her hand. "Don't let her get the better of you."

The day had started out sunny, but dark borders now crawled around the rumbling clouds, threatening an April shower. She didn't mind rain. Or had she talked herself into it because she had been told so many times to 'accept what the Good Lord gives you.'

"I'm tired of just accepting. She grasped the wheel until her knuckles paled. "Keep breathing."

Dandelions and twitch grass poked through the cracks of the flagstone path. In the neglected garden, a white tulip leaned against the prickly stem of a tall thistle growing amongst a tangle of weeds. Brown leaves and unfurled buds drooped on straggling stalks of her Uncle Frank's once prize winning roses.

A little calmer, she took a deep breath and glanced at her watch. Still time for a couple of hours work. She reached into her purse and scrambling around the bottom, finally uncovered her keys.

Ten minutes later, the overhanging willow on Glasgow Street welcomed her home. She pulled into her parking spot behind her hundred-year-old stucco house, held upright by adjoined, ancient neighbours on each side. Was it ironic, or some Karmic joke, that she, instead of either of her two sisters, lived closest to their mother? Patricia, the eldest (never Pat, Patsy or Trish) lived in Kitchener, forty-five minutes away, and her younger sister, Madison (Maddy) lived in Elora, a half-hour away. *Why don't they have a problem with our mother?*

She opened the back door and walked through the mud/laundry room and into the kitchen. Dropping her purse on the counter, she took a fresh look at the familiar surroundings. *It took me three tries before I found the perfect yellow paint for these walls.* The Mexican tiled backsplash, each tile hand painted, was an extravagant gesture she couldn't resist. *I thought I would live here forever.*

Minou, her calico cat, pushed its head against her leg. Cynthia bent down and ruffled her back. "Hi Minou. What do you think about moving?" She picked the cat up and walked into the next room which used to be the dining room and now her home office. "Surely, my mother can't be serious."

The cat wriggled free and Cynthia sat down at her desk. Having a home bookkeeping business had its plussed and minuses. She could set her hours, but she wasn't a good boss. She took too much time off. However, with tax deadline looming, she had little choice that month. Yesterday, Dr. Brooks had dropped off a shopping bag of his last year's receipts. It was still sitting on the floor beside her desk, and they weren't going to jump out of the bag and organize themselves. With a sigh, she grabbed a handful of papers from the bag and plunked them in front of her.

After several cups of Licorice tea, and a short supper break of warmed up left-overs, she hit save on the computer. Five after seven. *So much for an early Friday.* Minou had taken ownership of the out-tray, squeezed into its not quite big enough space. Tufts of orange, white and black fur spilled over the sides. She twitched an ear when the laptop clicked shut.

"C'mon, Minou." Cynthia stretched and pushed her chair back. "It's time we quit.

Early the next morning, she rescued her slipper from a curled up cat, had a shower and put on jeans and a long sleeved t-shirt. Still a bit breezy for short sleeves. After a smoothy breakfast she grabbed the two string bags off the kitchen door handle and set out on the five block walk to the farmers' market. *Maybe I'll buy myself a birthday present.*

She walked past her neighbours yard, thankful that two weeks ago, four rambunctious children, ages six months to six years, two clattering parents and a gigantic barking dog had recently moved out. Because the three cloned houses had little insulation, the walls allowed shouts, flushes, barking and slamming doors to punctuate her daily life. She had prayed to the God's of Real Estate that a quiet person, or persons, would move in. Preferably not with dog.

She walked up Cork Street, through The Church of Our Lady parking lot, down Macdonell, past the duvet store and the secondhand bookstore on the corner. She slowed down to look in the window. That morning, the display featured houses: renovating, decorating, selling and buying. She bristled. *My mother can't simply take my house away from me? Could she? Would she?*

She hurried past the crowded city parking lot, across the street and under the railroad bridge to the-squatting market building. *The market will take my mind off houses.* At the entrance, a golden lab tethered to a sapling, wiggled its back quarters as she approached. Cynthia patted it and nodded to the bearded young man singing John Lennon's *Imagine*. She dug out a looney and tossed it into the open guitar case at his feet.

Inside, a chaotic bulletin board, with notices haphazardly taped and thumb-tacked over each other, announced a flurry of future events: Bikram's Yoga Class, Craft & Bake Sale at St. Andrews

Church, music at the Shakespeare Arms, and beer tasting at the Wellington Brewery. After a cursory glance, she moved toward the rows of vendors' stalls with their fruits, vegetables, cheeses, or latest petition. Beyond the meat counter, the warm and buttery aroma of crunchy flax loaves and nine-grain buns wafted from the Mennonite table. Cynthia returned the smile of the bonneted women and continued on to the organic vegetable stand. Soon her bags bulged with a bouquet of kale, beet greens, romaine, spinach and carrots. There was barely enough space to squish in a plastic bag of sunflower sprouts from the Living Earth booth.

She bumped shoulders and elbows of shoppers crowding the aisles as she nudged her way past the apple cider table toward the crafts section. She nodded to a vaguely familiar face. *Did I meet her at a workshop or the Bookshelf?*

The first table displayed Native wood carvings, begging to be touched. She scanned the smooth curves of birds and totem animals. *What would my totem be? Perhaps a dragonfly.* She had read Native folklore about how the dragonfly breaks illusions and with its almost three-hundred-and-sixty-degree field of sight, brings visions of power. *It would be nice to have visions of power.*

On the other side, the date-square lady teetered on a tall bamboo stool. A well-used blackened baking pan held the last square of Cynthia's favourite goody. She hesitated, and a racing child smacked into her. By the time she untangled herself, the date square was gone. *Just as well.* A tenacious extra ten pounds had taken up residence and refused to budge no matter how much dieting, cajoling or on-again-off-again exercise she attempted.

Old Mrs. Matheson with her hand-knit baby clothes sat in the next booth, and beside her, a spike-haired young woman lolled in a lawn chair behind a display of wire-wrapped jewellery. She (the young woman) wore a ring in the side of her nose and two in her bottom lip. *That must hurt.* Beside the bedecked young woman, the antique—aka—junk table with its mishmash of undiscovered treasures beckoned to her.

Usually, a brash young man, bouncing from foot to foot, would catch one's attention with his claims of authenticity of vintage coins, spoons, necklaces and tarnished frames. Today, an older man, his round head garnished with a monkish fringe of gray hair, smiled at Cynthia from behind the cluttered table. She nodded and peered at the jumbled array. *What is that poking out from under that oval mirror?* She lowered her bulging bags to the ground.

"Could I see that?" She pointed.

The roundheaded man slid the mirror aside and withdrew an object. "This?"

In his hand, he held an old dragonfly brooch. Its scratched wings spanned three inches. Cynthia's heart skipped a beat and she put out her hand.

The old man, with a protective gesture, cupped one of his hands under Cynthia's and with an enigmatic smile, lowered it. "Pewter—it's made of pewter."

Her gaze followed the dragonfly's flight and when it touched her palm, she shivered. Wavering images from some long forgotten time swirled around her: a nun praying, a child crying, a quill pen, and a dragonfly brooch. *My brooch! I've found my brooch!* Her heart beat faster.

A voice bellowed in her ear. "Are you going to buy that?"

Cynthia pulled her attention through the taffy of time. Market noises—a hum of words, a splash of laughter, a child's shout—replaced the veiled vision. She turned her head and a pair of bold eyes set in a moon face encircled by a red and orange scarf stared back. "I said, are you going to buy that? Because if you don't want it, I do." She reached out her hand.

Cynthia tightened her grasp on the dragonfly. "No. I mean yes. It's mine. I mean—I want it." *What am I saying?*

The smiling fringed man, his hand still cradling hers, said, "My grandson says it's an antique. He wants—" He lifted the dragonfly and turned it over. "Fifty dollars for it."

The dragonfly hovered and landed gently as the old man placed it back on her palm.

The yellow-haired woman stretched pudgy fingers toward it. "I'll take it."

Cynthia pulled her hand back. "No. It's mine." *Am I nuts? What do I want with an old scratched up brooch? Let the puffy lady have it.* She looked at the old gentleman. "Will you take forty?" *Why am I bargaining for this old thing? Let it go.*

"I don't know about that." He scratched his head above a thin line of hair over one ear. "I don't think my grandson would like that."

"What about forty-five?"*For heaven's sake, stop. Am I losing my mind?*

"I'll give you fifty," the other woman said, waving a credit card.

The old man looked at the fifty-dollar woman and at Cynthia. "My grandson said I'm not supposed to lower prices."

Cynthia held her breath.

Still gazing at Cynthia, he said, "But I think this is for you."

The woman humphed and Cynthia's heart fluttered. "Will you take a cheque?"

"We don't take cheques."He waited.

She said nothing. The dragonfly said nothing.

"Are you local?" he asked.

Loco maybe. "Yes." She opened her purse and as she wrote the cheque, he wrapped the dragonfly in recycled tissue paper, and the front page of the Mercury.

The woman at her side leaned toward her. "You've got yourself a helluva bargain. I'm an antique dealer and that's worth plenty. If you ever want to sell it, call me." She pushed a card into Cynthia's hand and strode off.

"Thank you." The Marshall girls were always polite. She tucked the card into her cheque book and squished the newspaper wrapped package between the Swiss chard and the sprouted sunflower seeds.

The early morning sun crept through the half-drawn blinds, bounced over the tables of coffee drinkers and lit up a shelf of golden honey jars and glistening grape jellies. Excusing herself as she zigzagged her way out, she nodded to another familiar face she might have seen at the River Run Centre or the Galaxy.

She passed the cheese counter and the overflowing bulletin board and stepped outside. A feeling of lightness filled her heart.

She walked past the book store and up the street toward the cathedral. Half way up the stone steps, she stopped and tipped her head back. The tall twin spires pierced the blue cloudless sky. Cynthia's gaze travelled up, up, and beyond and she smiled for no good reason at all.

Could it be that an ancient dragonfly, nestled in her shopping bag, had just opened a new chapter in the life of Cynthia Anne Marshall?

Chapter 3

A laughing couple came down the steps and Cynthia gathered her bags and her thoughts and continued upward. In another ten minutes she turned the corner onto Glasgow and stopped and stared.

Parked in front of her house, stretching to her neighbour's, was a gigantic moving van. Its ramp lay open and Hercules walked down, carrying a chest of drawers under one arm and two chairs in the other. Hercules Two emerged from her neighbour's propped-open front door and strode toward the truck. A collection of boxes, lamps, a table, and a six-foot ficus tree in a burnt orange pot crowded the sidewalk.

Cynthia wound her way through the maze of disgorged household goods. Strewn over the front lawn that spanned both houses were mirrors, lamps, a coat tree, and a large weaving loom with a black and purple project in progress.

"Hi, I'm your new neighbour."

Cynthia turned her head.

A woman—somewhere between 50 and 75—faced her. Her voice matched her looks: direct and spirited. Rusty hair, with streaks of gray, flew in all directions. Although tied back in a thick pony tail, with what looked like a shoelace, many strands has escaped and stuck out at the sides like antenna. Friendly green eyes looked out of this forest of red, and with a wide grin, the woman stuck out her hand. "I'm Sara Jane Jenkins."

Cynthia dropped her bags on a nearby parson's chair and took the proffered hand. "I'm—Cynthia." Along with the woman's strong grip came a swell of familiarity. *Have I met her somewhere before?*

The woman grinned and spread her arms with a shrug. "I've sorta encroached on your side of the lawn." Her yellow and lime green poncho fell over a cotton skirt of graduated blues reaching to ankles of black tights which were slid into Mary Janes. She was a stocky woman, who looked comfortable in her body.

"That's okay. Moving can be a drag."*What do I know about moving? I've lived here for twenty-eight years and all I brought with me was a baby and no furniture.*

"I don't mind moving," Sara Jane said. "It's a chance to start new again."She turned and called to the Greek (or was it a Roman) god carrying a wicker wardrobe and a purple lamp. "They go on the second floor. First door on the left." Then to Cynthia. "Gotta go. See you later." She took a few quick steps to catch up with the muscle man. "Careful. That's delicate."

Cynthia picked up her bags and stepped around a two-foot leprechaun to get to her front door.

She set her market bags in the kitchen. The wall phone flashed a message—from her mother. "Give me your room measurements so I can cover up those ugly bare floors." Click.

She slammed the receiver onto its holder. "My floors are beautiful, Mother." She snatched up one of the string shopping bags and plunked it on the countertop .   A quick shake and romaine, endive, and green beans tumbled over the tiles. The celery toppled into the sink.

"She can't do this." She snatched up the plastic package of sprouted sunflower seeds before they careened to the floor.

"Who does she think she is? This is *my* house. *My* living room with *my* plank pine floors and *my* ten foot high ceilings."

Minou flattened her ears and ran from the room.

Cynthia yanked the celery from the sink and shoved it and the other greens into the vegetable bin in the fridge. "I was the one who scraped off four layers of wallpaper and stripped a hundred-and-one years of grime and paint off eight-inch baseboards." She parted the strings on the second bag and yanked out kale, spinach, and radishes, plunking them on the counter. "Canadian pine and an antique dry sink won't fit in any bloody modern condo."

Over the years, she had doggedly replaced the arborite tables and plastic couch and chairs supplied by her mother. "Three rooms of furniture for the price of one," her mother had brightly announced to a wide-eyed Cynthia. "They even included a set of dishes and aluminum pots and pans." Those were the first things Cynthia replaced.

A spinach leaf had trapped itself in the small package wrapped in last week's newspaper. *Whatever possessed me to pay forty-five dollars for an old scratched up dragonfly brooch?* She plucked the leaf off and picked up the package. Again a flutter of images spiralled through her mind. *Bells ringing, a monk's face, a castle, running, children...and dragonflies.*

She held onto the counter until her head stopped spinning. "Am I going crazy?" She poured herself a glass of water, took a long cool drink and slid the package to the back of the counter between the electric kettle and the blender. "I'll open you later."

It was only ten o'clock and tax month meant working Saturdays and sometimes Sundays so she resigned herself to taking the rest of the morning to work on Dr. Brooks' account. Maybe she would take Wednesday—her birthday—off. She made a cup of tea and took it to her office.

It didn't seem long when the Grandfather clock chimed twelve. When she'd bought the clock her sister Madison said the gongs would drive her crazy but Cynthia found the regular chiming of the bells somehow comforting. Minou, curled up in her usual spot in the out-basket, twitched an ear on the first gong. "I suppose it would be nice to offer our new neighbour some lunch.'

The cat opened one eye.

All morning, bangs, scrapes and shouts of, "Where does this go?" and "Put it there, no there," had echoed through the adjoining wall, but the last half hour had been quiet. She went to the front window.

The Hercules twins were closing the back ramp. They climbed into their motorized chariot and pulled away from the curb and up Glasgow Street. Odds and ends of smaller items still decorated the two front lawns.

"Good timing, Minou." She went to the front door and stepped outside. Her new neighbour was standing in her own doorway, hands on her hips and a glazed look in her eyes. Cynthia called, "How would you like some lunch?"

"You're a lifesaver. I'll wash up and be there in a toodle."

Cynthia took out the mayo and the egg carton with 'boiled' printed on the end. Egg salad sandwiches and a green salad would make an easy, quick meal. Still a little too chilly to eat outside, she set the kitchen table. The dining room had long been converted into her home office and the kitchen was plenty large enough for the Quebec pine table she had found at the Aberfoyle Market.

All was ready but her neighbour must have been still toodling. Cynthia reached between the blender and the kettle and picked up the small parcel. *I'll open you later.* She ran upstairs and put it on her bedside table beside the current Alice Munro book she was reading. *Perhaps I'll keep you until my birthday to open you. Or maybe I should phone that antique dealer lady.* But her inner voice yelled, NO.

"Yoo-hoo," a voice called from the front door.

Cynthia ran downstairs. "Come in. You must be exhausted."

A gray sweater, two sizes too big, had replaced the poncho. It sides flapped as Sara Jane, looking like she'd survived a wind storm, blew into the centre of the living room and spun in a circle, her arms spread. "I love what you've done."

"Thank you."*First a strange dragonfly flies into my life and now this dervish. Both on the same day.*

"Your house is a mirror image of mine." She stopped spinning and stood with feet spread. "At least the staircase and the front room are." She walked into the living room and caressed the Mennonite quilt folded on the back of Cynthia's favourite chair. "Did you make this? It's fabulous."

"Bought it at St. Jacob's Market a couple of years ago."

She pointed to the fireplace. "Does that work?"

"Yes, I had a new chimney put in."

"Are you an interior decorator?"

Cynthia laughed. "Far from it. I'm just a boring bookkeeper. My uncle, who was also my stepfather, was an interior designer." *Why did I add stepfather?*

Sara Jane lifted an eyebrow. "Was he your uncle or your stepfather?"

They walked to the kitchen and Cynthia motioned Sara Jane to a chair.

"Both." She took the salad out of the fridge. "When my dad died, his younger brother, Frank, whom we knew nothing about, came to the funeral and eighteen months later, he and my mother were married. She didn't even have to change her name." She peeled the Saran wrap off the plate of sandwiches. "Dig in."

Sara Jane dove into the first half of the doorstep sandwich. "I don't think I had breakfast." After one mouthful, she attacked the salad.

"Herb tea or regular?" Cynthia asked.

"I would love a strong cup of caffeine, but finish your lunch."

"I had breakfast. I'm fine." Cynthia got up. "I'm sure I have some coffee here somewhere and a coffee pot." She scrambled through the bottom cupboard, found a bag of coffee and pulled the coffee maker out.

"So what's the deal about your mother and this uncle/stepfather thing? I have a feeling there's more to the story."

Cynthia busied herself with the coffee making. *Why does this feel so natural to talk to her about my family? My rants about my mother have always been super private.*

"I don't mean to pry." Sara Jane lifted her shoulders. "I have been accused of being a motor mouth." She picked up the second half of her sandwich.

"I don't usually talk about my mother. Even to my sisters. Well, perhaps to Madison. She's my younger sister."

Sara Jane laughed. "The plot gets thicker. The way you say *mother* tells me this story is going to be juicy."

Cynthia took a forkful of salad. Words tumbled onto her tongue, scrambling into sentences, wanting to be spoken. She took a bite of sandwich. Something inside her was prodding her, pushing her to the edge, and urging her to dive off the precipice to tell all to this strange woman.

"There is no greater power on this earth than story," Sara Jane said.

"That sounds like a quote."

"It is. Libba Bray in *The Diviners*."

"Didn't Margret Laurence write *The Diviners*?"

"She wrote the first one," Sara Jane said. "Book titles aren't copyrighted."

"Are you a writer?"

"Good heavens, no. I'm a weaver but I love to hear a tale well woven."

Cynthia teetered on the edge of confession. "Unfortunately, the tale of my mother and me has long been unravelled beyond repair. Too many broken threads to ever be mended."

"Although I talk a lot, I am a good listener." Sara Jane scooped another helping of salad onto her plate. "And I have nothing pressing to do."

Cynthia laughed. She liked this strange, red-haired whirly-gig who had splashed into her life. Was it a coincidence that she and the dragonfly had arrived on the same day—both of them splintering time and tugging her into vague and shadowy memories?

"I just love stories," said Sara Jane. "Don't you?"

Cynthia poured out two cups of coffee. "I don't have any cream."

"That's okay. I take mine black.

Cynthia added a little honey to hers.

"So you were about to tell me about this uncle/stepdad thing."

Cynthia put her spoon down and took a deep breath. "Well, I guess it started at my birth."

"That's a good place to start." A honky tonk piano, playing *Raindrops Keep Fallin' on My Head,* sounded from Sara Jane's sweater pocket. "I've got to take that."

She pulled out a fuchsia iPhone and put it to her ear. "What's the verdict?" Pause. "Can you handle it?" Pause and a sigh. She clicked it and tossed it back into the depths of her sweater. "I have to go. But I want to hear your story. Every delicious word of it." She got up.

"Take your coffee with you."

"Thanks." She picked it up and swept out of the kitchen.

Cynthia followed her to the front door.

Sara Jane lifted a finger. "Remember we have an appointment for storytelling."

"Sure thing." Cynthia watched her neighbour cross the lawn and disappear through her front door. In the middle of the shared lawn, between a large cardboard carton and a bamboo coat tree, sat a child-sized rocking chair. A squirrel leapt to the carved top and sprinted off, leaving it rocking. She smiled. *Everyone has a story.*

She walked back to the kitchen, poured the coffee into the sink, and made herself a cup of herb tea which she took to the living room.

She sat down in her favourite chair beside the love seat, where Minou was sleeping. "A song on a cell phone saved me from spilling my guts." She put the hot cup on the coffee table. "Anyway, no need to rehash the past." The words and tune from Sara Jane's phone ran through her head. *Cryin's not for me. 'Cause I'm never gonna stop the rain by complainin'. Because I'm free. Nothin's worryin' me.*

Cynthia looked at the curled up cat. "What do you think, Minou? Am I free?"

Chapter 4

Cynthia plugged away on Dr. Brook's account most of Sunday. Not a peep or a sound emanated from the vicinity of her new neighbour and the early morning start-up of a car in the lane behind their houses, meant she had gone out.

Early Monday morning, Madison phoned. "So what do you want to do for your birthday, sis?"

"I noticed the Abstract Expressionists Show has opened at the AGO in Toronto."

"Fantastic. I'll get back to you."

She hung up. Madison, her younger sister, was the extrovert of the family, Cynthia, the introvert, and Patricia, in addition to being the eldest, was infuriatingly proper and vied with Emily Post for good manners and decorum.

Cynthia gathered a handful of kale, baby spinach and sunflower sprouts from the fridge and threw them into the blender. As she was about to hit the button, the phone rang.

"The Gallery had two tickets left for Wednesday, the 17th. We have the three o'clock spot and I'll treat you to lunch at Karine's so you can have anything on the menu."

"Thanks. I appreciate it." It was getting easier to eat out as more and more restaurants offered vegetarian.

She worked the whole day with only short breaks to make up taking offWednesday, Any day in April was not a good time to take off if you were a bookkeeper, even if it was your birthday. For most of her clients, she kept monthly books, so it was easy to send summaries to their accountants for tax returns. For others she filed directly to the CRA. However, there were the Dr. Brook's types who, in a mad flurry would drop off their bags, boxes or accordion files of receipts, invoices, and payroll slips. Posting and balancing was still a tedious chore even though software programs made it easier than using the large blue-lined ledger books. She had thought of trying for her CGA exams, but it meant getting a bachelors' degree in accounting or finances first, and she was not willing to devote five years of part-time study to a subject she hated.

Sara Jane had cleared the lawn of boxes and other household items and all afternoon random bangs and the occasional squeal would erupt from next door. At five-forty, the yoo-hoo from her front porch came as a welcome relief from hours of columns and rows of marching numbers.

"Coming," she called. She saved the file and closed the computer. On the way to the front door, she did a few shoulder rolls and head turns.

Sara Jane held a steaming casserole in her hands—the right protected by a lobster glove and the left, a green rubber mitt that reached her elbow. "I bet you haven't eaten. Lentils, chickpeas and vegetables."

"Come right in." Cynthia opened the door wider.

Sara Jane strode to the kitchen and deposited the casserole on the counter.

"How did you know I was a vegetarian?"

"I didn't. I am."

They both laughed and sat down to a scrumptious meal. After devouring several helpings, Cynthia filled a pair of glasses with red wine which they took to the living room. Two stuffed chairs and a love seat formed a curve in front of the fireplace. Sara Jane sat in one chair and tucked her feet up under her wide gathered skirt. Cynthia settled into the more obviously used chair directly facing the fireplace.

Sara Jane took a drink. "On Saturday, when we first met, you called yourself a boring bookkeeper. Why do you do it if you find it so boring?"

"I kinda fell into it and never climbed out."

"But there are kajillion ways to earn a living. Why not pick one you like?"

"You make it sound so easy."

"It is."

Cynthia grunted. "When I was twenty-five I was in a bit of a jam and I didn't think I had a choice."

"Yeah. I know what you mean. Sometimes you feel backed into a corner." She grinned. "I think we've all been there at one time or another But something tells me there's more to your story."

Cynthia jiggled her glass, making ripples in her wine. *Where do I start? An unhappy child, a wretched teenager, a toxic relationship with my mother, and of course my shameful, never-to-breath-a-word-to-anyone, secret.*

"You don't have to tell me anything if you don't want to."

"This feels so weird. I hardly know you and yet I have the strongest urge to confess my most hidden things to you."

Sara Jane zippered her fingers across her lips, turned the imaginary key and tossed it over her shoulder. "I respect the sanctity of a new friendship. I promise to never utter a word."

Cynthia smiled and relaxed.

"And by the way, we have known each other before."

"No, we haven't. I would remember you."

"Not in this life. Another one, or maybe two or three. I knew the moment I saw you."

"You mean reincarnation?"

"Exactly. What other explanation is there for that unmistakable feeling that you sometimes get—good or bad—when you first meet someone? I'm sure it's happened to you before. It sure has me."

Cynthia furrowed her brow remembering her weird experience when she first touched the dragonfly brooch still sitting unopened upstairs. *Were those images of lives I lived many years ago?* "So do you believe in Karma and being punished for our sins from a past life?"

"I don't think reincarnation works quite like that. I think each new life starts with a tabula rasa—a clean slate."

Cynthia raised her eyebrows. "But what about punishment?"

"It depends on your definition of sin and punishment."

"Isn't sin, sin? My mother was a Baptist and she had a long list of sins: no card playing, no lipstick, no washing your hair on Sunday, and that's only the beginning. When she remarried and became Catholic she added a few more. I'm surprised she hasn't looked into Judaism."

"You're a hoot." Sara Jane drained her glass and waved it. "Any more of this?"

"Help yourself. The bottle's in the kitchen."

Sara Jane brought the bottle back and placed it on the glass-topped coffee table between them. "So how many sins or big dark secrets do you have to confess?" She sat down, slipped off her shoes and put her red-stockinged feet on the coffee table. "Do you mind," she said with a wiggle of her toes.

"Not at all. I do it myself."

"So where were we? Oh, yes. You were about to enumerate all your sins."

"Only one. And it's a big one." Cynthia picked up the bottle, topped up her glass and took a sip. The clock chimed a single gong. Half-past something.

"You don't have to tell me anything if you don't want to. She grinned slyly. "We could always talk about bookkeeping."

Cynthia laughed. "I'd rather be scared than bored." She looked into her wine glass and then at Sara Jane. "There's something about you. Even though we've just met, you seem like a sister to me. As close as Madison. That's peculiar."

"Maybe we were sisters in a past life."

"Maybe."Cynthia stared into space for a few moments. She let a breath out and lowered her shoulders. "Twenty-eight years ago I got pregnant."

"So?"

"I wasn't married."

"So?"

"So!" Her mouth dropped open.

Sara Jane lifted her eyebrows as if to say 'so what' again.

Cynthia swallowed and found her voice. "That was a big time sin. A sin worse than death." She took another breath. "Well, I don't know if death is a sin, but you know what I mean."

"Plenty of women have babies without husbands. What's the big deal?"

Cynthia's jaw dropped. "Twenty-eight years ago it was a big deal. At least in our family it was. It just wasn't done. You were a disgrace to yourself and your family. Especially a family with a mother brought up Baptist, recently turned Catholic."

"So what happened? You've talked about your daughter Stephanie, so you obviously didn't take the abortion or adoption route."

"Never. I turned into one of those fiercely protective mothers you read about." She brought one fist up into a boxer's pose. "No one was going to take my kid away."

"What happened when your mother found out you were going to be—" She spoke in a low aghast voice. *"An unwed mother."*

Cynthia set her glass on the table. "Don't make fun of me. It was a scary time. Even though I was certain I would keep my child, I had no idea what I was going to do."

"What did you do?"

"I didn't tell my mother, that's for sure."

"What do you mean? She would soon find out."

"Oh, not that I was pregnant, but that I was unmarried. I made up a story."

"This is delicious. Tell me all about it."

Cynthia couldn't help but smile. Sara Jane had a way about her that lightened any moment.

Sara Jane continued. "And I want to know everything. Who? Why? Where?"

Cynthia picked up her glass and held it up for a toast. "Here's to the unveiling of deep dark secrets."

They clinked glasses and drank.

Chapter 5

Before a word emerged from Cynthia's mouth, Sara Jane narrowed her eyes. "And I want all the juicy details about this most horrendous and grievous sin of yours."

Cynthia plunked her glass down. "Honestly, Sara Jane. You make it sound trivial. It was a devastating time for me." She folded her arms and glared at her new friend.

Sara Jane leaned over and touched Cynthia's arm. "Having a child is not trivial, but I think the whole marriage thing is."

Cynthia picked up her glass. "In my family, marriage before babies was sacrosanct. The 60s revolution and women's lib may have happened worldwide, but not in my house."

"I was never cut out to be married. How can anyone at age nineteen promise to love another 'till death do you part'? She took a gulp of wine. "And what's with all the cleaving and plighting of one's troth? Not to mention the totally ridiculous 'obey' part."

"I think obey has been removed for some time and the medieval cleaving and plighting are definitely out.

Sara Jane laughed. "Why are we talking about marriage vows? I want to hear all about the good stuff." She lowered her voice. "The whole dark and mysterious story."

Cynthia couldn't help but smile. "I wish I'd known you twenty-eight years ago."

"Better late than never. Now get on with it."

"The facts are simple, but first a little bit of a background."

"I hope not too much. Background can be boring"

"Do you want to hear my story or not?"

"I do. I do. Please go on with your most interesting background."

Cynthia shook her head. It was hard to stay annoyed at her crazy new friend. "Well, as I told you before, my father had died, and his younger brother Frank came to the funeral. My father had been estranged from his family for years, disowned and banished at the age of eighteen when he had the nerve to run away to Paris to be an artist. He never spoke of his parents or siblings."

"No pictures? Nothing?"

"Nothing. Oh, we tried to pry it out of him, but he'd just say, 'let sleeping dogs lie.' So when Frank turned up at the funeral, we were all surprised."

"Sounds like a soap opera. 'At Home With the Marshalls'."

"It might well have been if you'd seen my mother. My father had died—heart attack—and he only had a modest insurance policy. He had moved from job to job, so he had no pension."

"Was he a working artist?"

"No. A frustrated one. He tried to be a salesman. He sold everything: cars, insurance, toothpaste, but he hated it."

"I can see where you inherited your job hating history."

"Sara Jane, if you keep interrupting with psychological comments, you can go home right now." She gasped.

"What's wrong?"

"I can't believe I said that."

"No big deal."

"But that's not like me. I'm always so polite."

"Even when you don't want to be?"

"Especially when I don't want to be."

They both laughed, and Sara Jane said, "I've found it's better to be honest and let the chips fall where they may." She took a drink of wine. "I was being a little snarky, so it was your right to call me on it."

Cynthia sat in the unfamiliar feeling of having blurted out her feelings. *The earth didn't stop and I wasn't struck by lightening.* She pulled her shoulders back. "Where was I? Oh, yes. When my mother met Frank, an attractive, rich bachelor from Guelph—rich being the deciding factor—she played the helpless widow. On discovering he was Catholic she quickly abandoned her Baptist upbringing and turned on the charm."

"So what's all this parental stuff got to do with you getting preggers?"

"It happened on the wedding night."

That's quaint? I thought you said you were never married."

'Not *my* wedding night. My mother's."

"Are you sure this isn't a soap opera?"

She glared. "Shall I continue?" *There I go again. Who is this new person inside me?*

Sara Jane tilted her glass. "Oh, please do."

"For my mother's second wedding, relatives we never knew came from England: two of Frank's brothers, a sister-in-law, and a maiden aunt. The Holiday Inn hosted the guests, with the British clan taking up three rooms. Patricia, my older sister, and her husband were in another. Madison, my younger sister, and I were in one, and Madison's fiancé in a room by himself."

"What?" Sara Jane's eyebrows went up. "Didn't Madison and her fiancé share a room?"

"Are you kidding? They weren't married and do not forget, pre-marital sex was a sin."

Sara Jane rolled her eyes. "What about the bridal couple? Where did they stay? Surely they didn't have separate rooms."

"Very funny. Frank was a romantic and he'd booked a suite in Niagara Falls. They left by limo around ten."

"This is getting more mysterious. So who was the scoundrel who did you wrong?"

" Well—"

"Wait. Don't tell me. An old boyfriend?"

Cynthia shook her head.

"A new boyfriend?"

"I was fresh out of boyfriends at the time." She glanced away. " I didn't date much."

"That sounds like another story. All right, I give up. Who was the mystery man?"

"This is the shameful part."

"Don't tell me it was the waiter? Or the butler?"

"Do you want to hear this story or not?"

"Absolutely. Every juicy detail."

"Madison had already arranged for her fiancé Charlie to switch rooms with me so I had a room all to myself."

"Convenient for their tryst. And yours." She waggled a finger. "Naughty you."

"It's hard enough telling this. I don't need your silly footnotes." *This is fun saying what I feel.*

Sara Jane slid her feet off the table and tucked them under her skirt. "Okay. I'll be good."

"I was twenty-four years old and never drank much, so at the end of the reception, after wine, champagne and a vodka, I had a little trouble standing and Evan offered to take me to my room."

"Who's Evan? What did he look like? How old was he?"

"He was one of the guests from England. Handsome and over forty years old."

"Ahh." Sara Jane waved a hand in the air. "A mysterious older man. A stranger from a far away land."

"Sara Jane, you said—"

She put up her hands like stop signs. "Okay, okay."

"Anyway, we stumbled to my room. He'd had quite a bit himself and after I unearthed my room key from my evening purse, I couldn't get it to work. Being the gallant gentleman, he unlocked the door and unsteadily steered me to the couch." She picked up her glass. "I'm empty. Is there anything left in that bottle?"

Sara Jane filled both their glasses. Cynthia took a sip. "Where was I?"

"A gallant mysterious man has steered you to a couch."

"He suggested a nightcap, but I said no, I'd had enough. He mustn't have heard me because he said, 'Good idea,' and weaved his way to the bar fridge where he pulled out two miniature bottles." She stopped talking and stared into space. "It's silly the things you remember. Even though I was in a fog, I still hear him saying, 'There's not enough alcohol in these to drown a flea.' And I'm sitting there picturing a flea doing a backstroke."

Sara Jane chuckled.

"Before long, six of those teensy-weensy bottles lay scattered on the coffee table. After that my recall is fuzzy. I do remember crying. Blubbering about missing my dad and how could my mother marry anyone else." She swirled the red liquid in her glass. "He had his arm around me and he leaned over and kissed my forehead. The way my dad used to. But then he kissed my cheek and my lips. The way no one had ever kissed me." She looked up. "Do you want some crackers or something?"

"Oh, for heaven's sake. Not now. What happened next?"

"I don't remember and when I woke up late the next morning he was gone. Not only from the room but the country."

"What? Where did he abscond to?"

"The whole British entourage had left early. They wanted to see the falls so they rented a car, drove to Niagara and on to New York to fly home."

"And Evan with them."

"Yes."

Sara Jane tilted her head. "So what's the big deal?"

Cynthia gulped, held up her glass of wine and whispered, "Evan was Frank's brother."

Sara Jane leaned forward."What did you say?"

"Evan was Frank's brother."

"But wasn't Frank your dad's brother?"

Cynthia nodded and stared at her glass.

"Let me get this straight. Frank was your dad's brother and Evan was Frank's brother. Ergo, Evan was your—uncle. Oh, my gosh you did it with your uncle!"

Cynthia grimaced. "Now you know the whole sordid truth."

Sara Jane shook her head. "What a story."

"I didn't know I was pregnant when I woke up the next morning. I was in shock that I wasn't a virgin anymore."

"Oh my god! It was your first time?"

"I was a young twenty-four and I never dated much. As I said, the ironic part was, I didn't remember a thing after he kissed me."

"How did you know anything happened?"

"I not only woke up naked, I was sore in places I had only read about." She drained her wine glass. "I can't believe I told you this. The only other person who knows is Madison."

"What did Evan say when you told him?"

Cynthia wriggled in her chair. "I didn't. I've never talked to him or seen him since. Only you and Madison know he is Stephanie's father."

"Not even Stephanie?" Sara Jane opened her mouth wide.

"No.

"Don't you think you should tell her?"

Cynthia stared at her empty glass. "I know I should." She moved her gaze to the fireplace. Behind the screen, cold, half burnt logs filled the grate. "I'm afraid she'll hate me."

Chapter 6

The next morning, Cynthia awoke with a headache. She hadn't drunk so much wine or slept in so late since January 1. She sat up in bed and held her head in two hands. *Did I really spill my guts to someone I hardly know? But it wasn't like talking to a stranger, more like to an old and dear friend. What is it about that woman?*

She threw on her housecoat, and stumbled downstairs. The coffee maker still sat on the counter. "Good idea." She measured out the last of the grounds. The cat pushed her face against Cynthia's ankles. "Give me a minute to wake up." The cat's persistence won, however, and Cynthia scooped a spoonful of chicken pate out of the tin and into the cat dish. She leaned on the counter with her chin in her hands, waiting for the coffee to drip.

"I will really need to tell Stephanie now." The cat munched her breakfast. "Now that I've blabbed the whole thing to a person I've just met."

Stephanie had asked many times about her father and Cynthia simply told her it was a short marriage and that she (Cynthia) had lost track of him when he moved to England. When she and Stephanie searched for him online, nothing turned up, of course, since Cynthia had given a phoney name. She also told her daughter the marriage license had somehow got lost. Stephanie seemed resigned to not finding her father and had moved on with her life into a happy marriage. Even so, guilt pangs never left Cynthia. Maybe she should have given her up for adoption. Even before she was born, Cynthia's heart had staked an unalterable claim to protect and nurture the child at all costs. *But Stephanie is an adult now and she deserves to know the truth.* A jarring series of beeps announced the coffee was ready. She took her cup to the living room and sat in her stuffed chair in front of a cold fireplace. Her mind whirled.

Stephanie would understand the unwed bit. Things have changed in twenty-eight years but what about the incest part? And what if Stephanie tells her husband—or worse, her grandmother. It's enough to be crucified for moral misconduct but what about the legal aspect? Could I be charged after all this time? I wouldn't put it past my mother to report me.

She took her cup to her office and opened her laptop. A Google search brought up a chart on the coefficient of relationships, which stated who it was illegal to sleep with. No dates were given as to when that law came into, or out of, effect. Nevertheless, she quickly scanned the list. In Canada, sex with an uncle was punishable by up to fourteen years imprisonment. She read on.

"Good heavens, Minou. There's no statute of limitations in Canadian criminal law. I could go to jail!" The cat continued her morning wash. Cynthia read on. "Except for treason," she added. "The statute for that is three years." She leaned back in her chair and stared at the screen. "I could have blown up parliament and received less punishment than sleeping with my uncle."

She closed the computer, refreshed her coffee and took it upstairs to her wicker chair beside the open window—her favourite place for her morning quiet time. Sometimes she read, sometimes she sat and looked out the window.

That morning, she needed a distraction from the unruly thoughts swimming through her mind. She put the hot cup on the wide window sill on the pottery coaster that Stephanie had made for her in Grade One

Alice Munro's *The Secrets We Keep* was on the small table beside her chair. "I would be reading that now." Next to it lay the wrapped parcel from Saturday. She picked it up, remembering how the old man had reverently folded the dragonfly brooch in tissue paper before covering it with last weeks news.

"I don't have to wait until my birthday." She unfolded the newspaper and white tissue and lifted out the dragonfly. A gust of well-being wafted over her like a magical breeze. *I have known you before. Where have you been all this time? Were you free to fly or did others dictate your life?*

"Where shall I put you, Dragonfly?" Beside her mug of coffee on the window sill, sat a quartz crystal and a deck of *Angel Oracle Cards* from Madison.

She slid the cards over and placed the dragonfly between them and the crystal. *Are you my oracle, dragonfly?* A nanosecond after the question had flitted into her mind, a breeze puffed the gauzy curtain aside. It was as if the dragonfly had flown in and landed.

A loud ring started her. She jumped and grabbed the phone off the table. Her mother's name glared at her. She set it back to let voice mail get it and picked up her mug in both hands. The phone rang again. Madison's number. She pressed the green talk button.

"Mom's been trying to reach you."

"I know. She rang here."

"And you didn't answer of course."

"You know me too well."

Madison continued. "I don't know what's gotten into her. Why does she want to give your house to Sharon?"

"You know mom. When she gets a bee in her bonnet, there's no stopping her."

"I'm sure Patricia doesn't want her daughter to move out of Kitchener, especially with the baby coming."

"Maybe mom wants to be closer to her first great-grandchild."

"Well, that's no reason to kick you out of your house."

"*Her* house, mom keeps saying."

"She helped Patricia and me with our down payments, so why not give you the same privilege?"

"You know how it is with Mom and me. We've never gotten along."

"At least you were dad's favourite."

"Maybe that's why mom never liked me." Cynthia took a sip of warm coffee.

"Well, it stinks if you ask me. I'll do what I can to persuade her to change her mind."

"Thanks, sis."

"I—er—phoned you for another reason," Madison said.

"That doesn't sound good."

"I feel like crap about this. With it being your birthday and everything but I can't go to the Art Gallery tomorrow."

"Why not?"

"I forgot to check my book. Charlie's doctor's appointment is that day. He could go alone, but I want to keep tabs on him after his heart surgery."

"Of course you have to go with him. We can go to the Art Show another time."

"You can still go. I'll email you the tickets right now. You could take Stephanie.

"Maybe." Cynthia rang off. *Standing in front of a Jackson Pollock or a Kandinsky wasn't the place to confess your sins to your daughter.* "Maybe Sara Jane would like to go."

Chapter 7

A green smoothy and a cup of chamomile tea eased Cynthia's headache. The hum of a radio, accompanied by faint singing, sounding through the adjoining wall told her Sara Jane was awake. She dressed, walked downstairs and over to her new neighbour's and rang the bell.

"Come on in," Sara Jane said. "You don't have to wait on the doorstep. Just ring and come in"

"I can't stay." She followed Sara Jane into the living room. The loom, transplanted from the front lawn, took up most of the space. On the wall adjoining their houses, hung three panels of fabric art, each a riot of colours, shapes and textures. Wool yarn, cotton squares, strands of rope, thread and hemp mixed with silk, burlap and other unknown fibres danced around and through each other. The end result was not spaghetti salad, but a pleasing cohesive whole.

Cynthia smiled. "You should try painting, If it's anything like those, you'd be a master."

"I like the feel of material in my hands. Besides, wool and swatches don't mess up the floor the way paint does."

"I can imagine."

"Coffee's on. Will you have one?"

"Thanks, but no. I have a ton of work to do. I came over to ask if you'd like to go to the AGO tomorrow.. I have tickets for three o'clock."

"I'd love to. The Abstract Expressionists' show is on. If I were a painter, I would definitely be one of those kind. No kittens and puppies for me."

Cynthia nodded to the cascade of colour on the wall. "I can see that. How's one-thirty? That should give us time to find parking."

"Do you want me to drive?"

"No. My dependable Civic is a work horse."

"Why don't we stay for dinner? My treat."

Cynthia hadn't told her it was her birthday tomorrow. "Sure. That would be fun."

The next morning, Cynthia wished herself a happy birthday to her bathroom mirror. Madison phoned and apologized again for missing their date and that she would pop by that evening with a little something.

"You don't have to do that. Fifty-three is no special birthday."

"Maybe not, but you're special."

It was nice having sisters, even though her older sister Patricia and she weren't close. Even when they were kids, Patricia always seemed to hold herself apart and took the role of being the eldest very seriously.

Stephanie phoned and sang Happy Birthday. "Sorry I didn't call earlier. I've been swamped. I have five bowls and three platters to make before the show next week and I'm up to my armpits in clay."

"I'm glad you're doing so well. How's Mark?"

"He's super. The best thing that's ever happened to me."

"I'm happy you're happy."

"I am. Totally. I have to run. Have a great day. We'll celebrate the first minute I get."

After their June wedding, Stephanie and Mark settled in Aurora, north of Toronto. It made sense for them to live closer to

York University where Mark had another year of post graduate work in psychology. And it was only an hour and fifteen minute drive from Guelph, so Cynthia saw her daughter as often as she could. Since several galleries had taken Stephanie's pottery, and her website sales were going well, she could live anywhere.

At one-thirty, Cynthia waited in the back alley where her ten-year-old Civic and Sara Jane's large black Mercedes was parked. *Did she save a long time for that? Or maybe it was a present from her dad, or from her divorce.*

Sara Jane burst through her back gate. A rainbow feather boa swirled around her neck and down a long and flowing black dress.

Cynthia, in a light blue blazer over a white shirt and black slacks climbed into her car. "I like your outfit," she said.

"Thanks." Sara Jane flung the trailing end of the boa over her shoulder. As she got into the car, a blue feather broke free and fluttered to the ground.

In thirty minutes, they reached the 401, the main throughway to Toronto. Traffic and conversation moved steadily and Cynthia learned that Sara Jane had two older brothers and two younger sisters.

"So you were right in the middle."

"Yup. It was great. Brothers to stand up for you and sisters to play with."

"What about your parents?"

"They're glad we're all grown and out of the house. It was bedlam at times with five kids and two active parents."

"What did they do?"

"My dad was an inventor and my mom a social activist. There was always a lot going on in our house."

"Sounds like it. You haven't told me much about you. I've blabbed my innermost secret to you, so your turn."

"Not much to tell. We lived in the west end of Toronto in a teeny-tiny house until one of my dad's inventions took off and we moved to a rambling fixer-upper that my brothers fixed up."

The traffic moved steadily and Cynthia learned that Sara Jane had a degree from York in Art History and Appreciation. Her siblings were a motley mix of creativity and ambition. Each living their own lives. Her brothers fix up old houses, one sister is a lawyer and the other a happy housewife. "So what about you?" Cynthia asked. "Any dark secrets?"

"None, really. I had a brief marriage and several affairs—" Her voice cracked. "One with a woman."

Cynthia didn't delve deeper as she pulled over to merge onto the Gardiner Expressway.

"I forgot to tell you," Sara Jane said. "I have to meet one of my customers before dinner. Hope you don't mind. I told her five o'clock."

"That's okay. It still gives us time plenty of time and we can check out other exhibits as well."

"You'll like her. She's Japanese and collects art."

By 2:35 they reached McCall Street in the downtown core and Cynthia drove slowly past Henry Moore's sensual sentinel at the Art Gallery entrance. As past residents, they both prided themselves on their ability to find street parking, but after four circles around the block, Cynthia resorted to a Municipal Parking lot.

Sara Jane sighed. "I used to know all the alleys and side streets you could park on."

"There was less traffic when I lived here," Cynthia said.

As they walked out of the parking area, Cynthia tugged the edge of her jacket down. "I can do with the five block walk. Maybe it will loosen up those ten pounds that have made their home around my middle."

"You look fine. Stop being so critical of yourself."

"I feel like your maiden aunt in sensible walking shoes."

"I wore mine too." Sara Jane lifted her skirt, exposing flat ballet slippers. "The better to twirl with," she said with a twirl. "As George Bernard Shaw said, 'Life isn't about finding yourself. Life is about creating yourself'."

At the gallery entrance the flying ribs of a gigantic sailing ship loomed high over their heads. When they walked through the front door, Sara Jane's cell phone jangled *Raindrops Keep Fallin'*. Cynthia dug out the tickets while Sara Jane talked. The call was short. She tapped her phone off and tossed it into her turquoise quilted handbag. "You won't believe this."

"Oh, I might," said Cynthia.

"I can't come in with you."

"What!"

"My client is taking an early flight out and if I want to see her, I have to go now." She touched Cynthia's arm. "I have to see her. She's my biggest customer."

Cynthia grimaced. "I understand. You go."

"You're the best. I'll call you when I'm finished."

"I don't have a cell phone."

"What? Get yourself into the twenty-first century, woman. How can you live without a cell?"

"Why don't we meet at the car? Say five o'clock?"

"Okay." She flew around the corner and out of sight.

People jostled by and Cynthia went to the box office to return the spare ticket. There were no refunds, but at least someone else could use it. She joined the three o'clock lineup on the sweeping curve leading to the exhibit. The architecture alone was worth the trip and Cynthia's heart beat a little faster and a happy feeling fluttered in her stomach. The line moved and in a moment she stepped into the crowded room. Pollock, Kandinsky, Klee. Her heart sped up. Colours, shapes and textures leapt off walls, sending a tingle down her spine. Her joy metre went off the chart as she feasted on each huge canvas. Fully absorbed, she leaned forward, stepped back, and tilted her head. Pollock's four-by-three foot *White Light* captivated her attention.

"It's incredible how he defies any line to represent anything." A man's voice on her left had spoken.

Cynthia pointed to a section of the painting. "And when you think a yellow curve is leading to a circle, it disappears."

"There's no inside or outside of his lines or the space through which it moves," the voice said.

Cynthia turned. Two dark eyes—deep blue not black, their corners wrinkled from his broad smile set in a handsome face—stared back. Her heart stuttered and her stomach did a somersault. She grabbed onto a side railing as the room faded into hazy static. Years, decades, centuries tumbled by, blurring into a scramble of memories. She willed her mind to stop slipping sideways and his face and those eyes, those deep dark eyes, slowly came back into focus.

"Arthur Richardson."He held out his hand.

"Er—Cynthia—Marshall." She took his hand and an electric current flashed up her arm, through her heart and landed in her solar plexus where it exploded.

She stared at him, keeping a tight hold of his hand. If she let go, she would surely fall over.

Chapter 8

"Are you all right?"

She took a deep breath and released her grip. "I'm fine. A little dazzled—with all this art—I guess." She took a step toward the next painting and tried to compose herself.

"Twittering Machine," he said.

"Pardon?" *Did he call me a twittering machine?*

"That painting you're looking at is called *Twittering Machine*."

"Oh." She laughed. "I thought—never mind." She turned back to the painting.

He gestured to it. "Paul Klee painted, drew or etched over ten thousand pieces. Can you imagine?"

Cynthia's heart had returned to its normal beat and her face didn't feel as if she had sunburn. They were at the end of the exhibit with others waiting to enter.

They walked out and he said, "Would you like to get a coffee?"

A slanted scar chopped off the end of his right eyebrow. Gray highlights tiptoed through his sandy hair, but it was his dark eyes that commanded her attention. "Yes," she heard herself say.

The cafe was closed but the Espresso Bar in Galleria Italia was open. Arthur ordered coffee and a tiramisu. Cynthia, an Italian soda and a strawberry gelato.

"This is not a line, but have we met before?" he asked.

"That's strange. When I saw you, I thought I recognized you and I've been racking my brain trying to remember from where."

"Where do you live? Maybe we shop at the same store."

"I'm from out of town—Guelph, but I did live in Toronto. Over twenty-five years ago."

"I was in Nova Scotia then."

"Where do you live now?"

"Oakville. But I work in Toronto at Queen and Yonge. I'm an architect."

Cynthia smiled. *Creative and handsome.*

"Why are you smiling? Are you an architect too?"

"Oh, heavens no. Nothing like that." She sighed. "I'm only an ordinary bookkeeper."

Their order arrived, and Cynthia said, "I've never tasted gelato but the name sounded good."

"You're in for a treat. Authentic Italian here."

"Isn't it some kind of ice cream?" *I can't believe how easy it is to talk to him.*

"No comparison. The ingredients are similar but gelato has less fat and it's churned at a slower speed which means less air is whipped in, all of which gives it that rich flavour."

Is this guy a chef as well? She picked up her spoon and tasted. "I see what you mean. Delicious."

"And this is heavenly." He took a forkful of tiramisu. "Would you like a bite?"

"No, thank you." It shouted at least two pounds on her hips.

After several mouthfuls, he said, "The way you said bookkeeper, sounds as if you don't like your job."

She looked away from those intense eyes and took another spoonful of gelato and a sip of soda. He was still staring at her.

"So what would you like to do?" he said.

"I'd love to be an artist." *Why on earth did I blurt that out?*

"Why not go for it?"

"Oh, I couldn't."

"Have you ever tried?"

"I mucked around with water colours once but—"

"But what?"

"Let's talk about you. How long have you been an architect? Do you like it?

"Thirty-four years and I love it. I design ergonomic and environmentally sustainable structures."

"Sounds fascinating." She took another spoonful of dessert.

"It is." He waggled his spoon at her dessert. "Did you know that an architect introduced gelato in its modern form? During the Italian Renaissance, Bernardo Buontalenti, an artist and architect, was commissioned to create an elaborate feast for the King of Spain. And, voilà, gelato."

"Are you also a trivia expert?"

He grinned. "I have been accused of boring my friends."

I feel like I know this man. Intimately. She lowered her head and let her hair swing down to cover her right cheek.

"There are three big differences between gelato and ice cream," he said. "The first, as I mentioned, is the lack of air in the mix. Ice cream is traditionally made up of 50% volume by air, while gelato ranges between 20-35% . . ."

His voice retreated into the background as she peered around her hair and studied his face. *His eyes are remarkable.*

"—butterfat between 4-8%—"

And such a nice smile. He looks to be in his late fifties.

" —sugar content is closely monitored —"

I wonder if he's married. Or has been.

"—which is paradoxical because gelato tastes so much creamier than ice cream."

I must read The Fountainhead again.

He paused. "I think I've bored you? You look a little cross-eyed."

Cynthia refocused her eyes. "I heard every word—but don't give me a test on any of them. "

He laughed. "I do get carried away with minutia. I promise to close the encyclopedia. Do you like movies?"

After a chat about their favourites they ate in comfortable silence for several moments. When they did speak, they both started at once.

He laughed. "You first."

"It feels as if I've known you—a long long time ago." She grinned. "Maybe in a past life."

"Do you believe in reincarnation?"

"I might. Why else do some people know each other right off when they meet for the first time? Like us. Now."

"There's always an explanation. Maybe I remind you of someone." He took a drink of coffee. "Or it's just a coincidence."

"I don't believe in coincidences." She finished her soda and plunked the glass down.

"What do you mean, you don't believe in coincidences? Of course there are coincidences." He frowned.

"A coincidence implies it happened by chance and has no meaning. I believe everything has a meaning and there's no such thing as chance."

"I'll give you an example of recent coincidences," he said. "I was on my way to meet a client when he cancelled. That was the first coincidence. I wanted to see this exhibit so I took a chance on getting a ticket. It would be one in a million because this morning they were sold out. But just as I got to the box office, a spot for the three o'clock slot had opened. Now if that wasn't a coincidence, what would you call it?" Both his eyebrows lifted, one crookedly.

She smiled. "I would call that destiny."

"You mean, divine intervention, kismet, fate?"

"Something like that."

He didn't answer for a moment and they changed the topic and continued to talk for another half hour. He had two more coffees, and she switched to peppermint tea. She learned he was fifty-eight years old, an inch under six feet, and wanted to be an architect after reading *The Fountainhead* when he was sixteen.

Funny that book popped into my head.

He had four sisters, all living in Truro, Nova Scotia, and his widowed ninety-one year old mother still lived in the original family home, close by one of her daughters and their family.

Cynthia relayed bare statistics about her family—that her father and stepfather were dead, but not that her mother intended to snatch her house from her. That she had two sisters, but not that she was born the ugly duckling. She glanced at her watch and snatched up her purse. "I have to go." She was ten minutes late meeting Sara Jane at the car.

"Do you have to?"

"Yes, but thank you for the new taste sensation and the gelato lesson. Both were delightful." She stood up.

He did too. "Will you go to a movie with me sometime?"

She hesitated for a fraction of a second. "Yes."

He punched her phone number into his cell and gave her his card. After he paid the bill, they walked down the curved aisles to the front door.

"I'll call you," he said. "And that's not a line."

She trembled standing so close to him. She wanted to kiss him.

"Are you ok? You have a funny look in your eye."

"I'm fine." She shook her head. *Whatever got into me to think such outrageous thoughts? It's like I'm someone else.* He was standing so close to her. "Gotta run."

She bolted out of the cafe, down the stairs, out the door and around the corner. Pulling her jacket tightly around her, she hurried down the street to the parking garage.

Chapter 9

Sara Jane was sitting on the hood of the car when Cynthia arrived. She slid off with a wave. "How was the exhibit?"

Cynthia pulled out her keys and clicked the doors open. "Great. Amazing paintings. Sorry I'm late."

"That's okay." She put her hands on her hips. "So what happened?"

"I didn't keep track of time and before I knew it—"

"I don't mean being late and, by the way, I just got here." She squinted. "Somethings changed. What's happened to you?"

"Nothing's happened."

They got into the car and Cynthia maneuvered it out of its spot and headed down the circular ramp.

Sara Jane stared at her. "Your aura is as pink as a Grade One Valentine card."

Cynthia hit the brake to let an insistent car in. "My aura? Don't tell me you read auras?"

"Not really. I only see them if they're extremely bright. And, right now, yours is leaping off you."

Cynthia continued down the cement spiral. "Okay. So what does a pink aura mean?"

"That you're an artist or you recently fell in love. Oh, m'gosh. You met someone." She slapped a hand on her knee. "Tell me everything."

"Can I not have any secrets from you?"

"Of course not. I told you, we're soul sisters. From a long time ago."

Cynthia pulled up to the exit booth. *Maybe she's right.* She paid and pulled into traffic. "Where are we going? Do you still want to eat out."

"Yes. I'm starving. It's five-thirty and the Gardiner and 401 will be crawling. We can go up Spadina to Dupont. The food at the *Live* restaurant is definitely something to live for."

"Don't people usually say something is to die for?"

Sara Jane lifted her eyebrows. "People who don't know the power of words do."

Some people thought Cynthia was way out, believing in reincarnation and having crystals on her window sills, but she was in kindergarten compared to Sara Jane. She turned onto King Street. "So this restaurant is actually called 'Live'?"

"Yup. Great philosophy, brilliant flavours and splendid atmosphere. The sign on their window says: 'To eat is a necessity, but to eat intelligently is an art.' I thought it would be a fitting place to eat after the Art Gallery."

Cynthia turned off King and onto Spadina. "You like quotes."

"It's a pithy way to get a point across and sometimes makes one think. But let's get back to your pink aura. Are you an artist or did you meet someone?"

"Maybe both."

"You are a sly one."

"Okay. I confess. I did meet someone."

"I knew it." She slapped her knee again.

"It was no big deal." *Yes, it was.* "We talked about the paintings and we went for coffee."

"Why do I get the notion that it *was* a big deal. When are you going to see him again?"

"We exchanged numbers. We might go to a movie."

"You will. And a lot more."

"So now you're psychic. I don't want to know anymore." The traffic lightened up after Bathurst and soon they reached Dupont and found parking on the street a block from the restaurant.

At six o'clock it was crowded but after a short wait were shown to a table. While they waited for their food, they talked about men in general and soon a certain architect crept into the conversation.

"Do you think I'm mad to go out with him?" Cynthia asked.

"I'd think you'd be mad not too."

"I haven't had much luck with men."

Sara Jane laughed. "You should try women."

"A woman did kiss me once at a party. On the lips."

"What happened after that?"

"Nothing. I was too surprised to react and she was too drunk to know if I was a man or a women. Anyway, I never saw her again."

"Well, I think everyone is bi-sexual, given a chance."

"What do you mean?"

"Sex is in the head, not the genitals. And that's one of *my* quotes. When you love someone, the body parts are incidental. Love is love. No matter what goes where."

Their food was delivered and both started into their salads.

After several moments, Sara said. "I told you I had an affair with a woman." A chunk of lettuce hung from her fork. "Thirty years ago. If we'd been allowed to marry, we would have."

"What happened?"

Sara Jane stared at the dangling green leaf. "She died. Quickly. Cancer." She put her fork down. "I was with her when she took her last breath." She blinked rapidly, picked up her glass of wine and held it high. "To old loves. And new ones."

They clinked glasses and drank.

Sara Jane continued. "I was married for three years to a priest."

"What? How could you marry a priest?"

"He wasn't a priest then. He left the order so he could f—"

"Stop! Don't say it."

"It's only a word, for heaven's sake."

"You're the one who said words have power. And that one is not to be uttered from polite women's mouths." *God, I sound like my mother.*

"Who said I was polite?"

"Tell me about your priest husband."

"He was a dear. Great in bed but he prayed too much. All that praying made my head ache. He cheated on me and left me for a younger version, even though I was only twenty-six at the time."

"Were you devastated?"

"No. I wanted to put my libido into my art. He was also possessive and I can't stand that. Have you ever been married?"

"No. The intimate relationship thing wasn't for me. My father held Victorian views and was much older than my mother. He disapproved of his three daughters having anything to do with the opposite sex."

She laughed. "He threw the paper boy out on his ear once because he winked at Patricia. She was thirteen."

"That didn't stop your sisters. You told me they were both married with kids."

"Sensible Patricia left home when she was seventeen. Joined the Air Force at nineteen and when she was twenty-one married a flyer. Mischievous Madison ignored our dad's dire warnings. She had tons of boyfriends in High School like any normal teenager."

"And what happened to Scintillating Cynthia?"

Cynthia grimaced. "More like Sourface Cynthia. To me boys were a foreign species. Maybe if I'd had a brother, it would have been different."

"But surely you dated after you had Stephanie?"

"Here and there, but not much. I made her my life. Which I learned wasn't the best thing for her."

"What about sex?"

"What would you ladies like next?" said a perfectly modulated voice attached to a drop-dead handsome young man. Probably an actor or musician between gigs. He waited patiently while they discussed their choices.

Sara Jane studied the hot drink menu and ordered *100 Mysteries*, a rooibos with coconut and Cynthia chose a cup of *Beautiful Foolishness*, a white tea with exotic fruits.

When he walked away, they laughed.

"Do you think he heard?" said Cynthia.

"So what if he did. Anyway, he could be my grandson. So what about sex?"

"It makes me nervous. I get the shakes."

Sara Jane's eyes grew wide. "Are you telling me you haven't had sex since that one forbidden night at your mom's second wedding?"

"I nearly did. Once at a party I'd had too many gin and tonics, but he couldn't perform and I fell asleep."

"My god woman. You're practically a virgin. You could be a nun."

"Keep your voice down."

"Well, I hope at least you pleasure yourself."

The gorgeous waiter hunk had arrived with their hot drinks. "Here you are ladies. Enjoy."

Cynthia blushed as he walked away. "What must he think?"

"Who cares? It doesn't matter what anybody thinks." She picked up her cup of *100 Mysteries* and took a sip. "What matters is what you think."

Cynthia tasted her *Beautiful Follishness* tea. "So what's your next art project?"

They left the restaurant at eight-thirty. Cynthia's one glass of wine was well absorbed and it was an easy drive at that time.

She turned off the 401 Highway at the Mohawk Raceway and on to Guelph Line. Sara Jane dozed as thoughts jumped in and out of Cynthia's mind.

That was a unique birthday.

She passed the casino's crowded parking lot.

At least I didn't think about losing my home.

The full moon made driving easy.

Was I crazy to agree to go to a movie with a man I'd just met?

A sports car overtook her and sped on.

When he phones, I won't answer.

She stopped at the traffic light.

Why would he want to go out with me anyway?

The light turned green and she drove on through the night.

I'm fat. I'm ugly. I'm old.

Chapter 10

She pulled into the back lane behind their houses. She had left her back porch light on and Sara Jane's backyard twinkled with a stream of solar lights, making an irregular path to her back door. She sat for a moment. *Some lives are straightforward and others twist and turn.* Sara Jane opened her eyes and stretched."Are we here?"

They got out and Sara Jane pushed open her gate. "Night," she mumbled, still half asleep.

Cynthia followed the flagstones to her back door. When she opened it, Minou darted out between her feet. She flipped on the inside light, walked through the laundry area and into the kitchen. The phone was blinking. The first message was from Madison with a simple *Where are you*? The second, a perfunctory birthday wish from Patricia, and the third was Madison again, saying she'd left a surprise for her. She had a key and often dropped things off.

A long white florist's box lay on the coffee table in the living room. "You shouldn't have," Cynthia said aloud. It was the kind in which long stemmed roses were delivered. She read the sign taped on the top. *Don't go by the box*. Cynthia smiled. In earlier frugal days, their family habitually used discarded boxes for gift giving, and it was not unusual to find a sweater in a toaster box, a tie in a sock box, or a scarf in a chocolate box.

She lifted the lid. A card lay on top of a long metal stake with newspaper wrapped around one bulbous end. As she pulled the newsprint off, a wing peeked out. A butterfly? No. A dragonfly with a solar light embedded in its back. The card said: *Thought this would be perfect for your herb garden. Tons of love, Maddy.*

Madison, who collected dragonflies, didn't know about the one Cynthia had found at the market last Saturday. Madison's house was alive with them. A group flew on her living room wall, a couple on the garden fence, plus three winged night lights placed around the house. Earrings, necklaces, plaques, mugs and a dishtowel rounded out her obsession. What was it with all those dragonflies? And what had drawn Cynthia to the old beat up one at the market, compelling her to buy it?

Minou scratched to be let in. "Well, Minou. I am not going to be a dragonfly collector. One in the family is enough."

Ten to ten. Too late for coffee. She made a cup of camomile, took it upstairs and sat in her wicker chair by the window. The Art Gallery's spectacular paintings, dinner with Sara Jane, and the long drive home had taken her mind off her house problem. But another thought lingered with her—meeting the man named Arthur Richardson. *It was so smooth. Did I really chat so easily to him a— for over an hour?*

For years, her disfigurement had kept her from thinking about boys and men and that she might ever have a real relationship. She had been busy raising Stephanie and had reconciled herself to a life of bookkeeping and the status quo.

Now, this man appears and turns my insides out.

Her thoughts whirled, her stomach churned, and a shiver rippled through her body. She took a sip of tea.

A spear of moonlight glanced over the quartz crystal on the sill. Like a searchlight, it moved to the dragonfly brooch before it blinked out behind a cloud.

Maybe it is my time to fly.

Minou jumped up on her lap. "Fifty-three isn't that old."

The next day, she hunkered into tax papers. She had Mr. Sutherland's and Charlene's Coaching Service to do. Both of them kept pretty good records so it was simply a matter of data entering and crunching numbers.

After lunch, Sara Jane phoned. "Has he called?"

"Who?"

"Don't be coy. You know who I mean."

"He hasn't called and he probably won't. And who's waiting, anyway?"

"He'll call. Let me know when he does."

They hung up. A hollow corner in Cynthia's stomach woke up, but it wasn't hunger. It was that old empty feeling of not being good enough pushing itself out again. She thought she had buried it. "Come on, Minou. Let's not dilly dally. There's work to do."

She dove into a scurry of numbers and at four o'clock closed off Mr. Sutherland's file, stretched her arms over her head and leaned back in her chair.

Why am I still a bookkeeper? Two new people in my life have recently asked me that question. Maybe it's time I answered it.

She went downstairs, put the kettle on and took the solar dragonfly stake to the backyard. For the last couple of years, she had been nurturing a modest herb garden. Simple kitchen plants: basil, rosemary, thyme, dill and three kinds of mint. Circles of rocks outlined the different plants and strategically placed stepping stones made it easy for weeding and harvesting. She stuck the stake in the middle where it would collect sun and give off an evening glow. "There you go dragonfly. And you're the last. Two dragonflies are enough for me."

After her break, she opened Charlene's file, stared at the computer and closed it. *That's enough torture for one day.* She glanced at the Art Gallery brochure with the Pollock painting covering half the front. *Wasn't there a movie about him?* She turned on the TV and opened NetFlicks. *Yes. "Pollock" with Ed Harris.* She'd missed it when it was showing at the Galaxy.

"No time like the present." She made a gigantic bowl of hot air popcorn, melted a huge chunk of butter and grabbed a can of club soda. Her comfy chair in front of the TV tucked into the alcove off the living room waited for her. She placed the oversized bowl, which Stephanie had made specially for her, on her lap. Minou allowed her to share the foot stool.

Two hours and two minutes later, she clicked off the TV. Hugging the greasy bowl to her chest, she stared at the blank screen for several long minutes. Visions of Jackson Pollock (via Ed Harris) flinging paint around sizzled in her brain. A surge of energy bubbled up from a deep and hidden pocket inside her.

She leapt up, and dumped the empty bowl and salt shaker in the kitchen. "Where did I put those old paints?'

She dashed upstairs to Stephanie's old room, now her hobby room. A chest with seasonal clothes filled the lower half of the closet. Craft kits teetered on the shelves and a plastic see-through bin held balls of wool. She slammed the door shut. *Why the heck do I start so many projects?*

At one end of a four-foot work table, an embroidery hoop, with a half-finished picture of a sleeping cat, leaned beside a pile of art magazines. At the other end, an unfinished stained glass plaque rested next to a stack of small squares of material waiting to be quilted. On a book shelf, a second-hand blender and two small screens with wooden frames were jammed beside each other ready for paper making.

A variety of plastic boxes with beads, stickers, lace, old coins, feathers, and other found objects filled the bottom shelf. On the floor was a stack of *how to* books on watercolour painting, drawing, acrylics, knitting, and sewing.

"I know I have some paints around here somewhere." Her grandmother's old Singer sewing machine sat in the corner, the top folded down to make a table. Piled on it was a stack of watercolour paper her neighbour, a printer who lived on her other side, had given her. Beside that sat a paint set that Madison have given her about ten birthdays ago.

It had three pans for mixing colours and next to that a row of squares of dried paint. And not an ordinary red, blue and yellow. Oh, no. These were real artists' colours with enthralling names, carrying you to other realms. Visions of romantic, mysterious, and unbidden images filled Cynthia's head. "Cadmium Scarlet"—*That has to be a naughty red.* "French Ultramarine"—*A handsome gendarme in a bright blue uniform.* "Naples Yellow"—*The bright sun of Italy.* And lastly. "Renaissance Gold"—*Kings, Queens, and master painters.* Each name a whisper of mystery and magic, and one had only to add a drop of water to make it spring to life and flood into its full glory.

She pushed aside an embroidery ring and a chipped cup full of crochet hooks and placed the paint box, its lid open, on the table.

"Now where are the brushes?"

On the floor beside the sewing machine, a clay jar held a mixture of pointy things: knitting needles, chopsticks, rulers, a backscratcher, and three paintbrushes. She snatched the brushes and added them to the table.

"I need water."

She removed three balls of wool from the plastic water bowl and ran to the bathroom to fill it. The paper her neighbour had given her was a good size to start with: nine by twelve inches. Nowhere as big as Pollock's huge canvases but she had to start somewhere. She closed her eyes. Jackson Pollock had flung the paint, dripped it and dragged it as he urged and coaxed it to flow, bounce or spin into shapes, textures, and a kaleidoscope of colours.

Do I dare attempt it?

The rules of watercolour flitted through her head. She should do an under drawing and mask off the parts where the white of the paper would shine through. Or start with a flat wash, layering and letting each dry completely. Or do a graded wash, lightening the saturation of colour with each wide strip. Or she could sponge over wet paint for a blurry, moody effect, or do dry brushing for rough textures. *So many rules. Dare I ignore them?*

She took a deep breath, dipped her fingers into the bowl and splattered water over the small squares of dried paint.

She wet the brush and slashed a vibrant streak of naughty Crimson Alizarin across the pure white paper. It screamed, 'look at me.' At the bottom she swathed in a thick layer of chocolate brown, so rich and inviting she had to stop herself from tasting a finger full. She swirled her largest brush—dwarfed by Pollock's house painting brushes—into the French blue and covered the top section until it shone like a cloudless summer sky over the Seine. She flicked droplets of clear water over the paper making colours run together in wild abandon.

She slid that sheet to the side and picked up another. Stripes of Lemon Yellow and Burnt Umber Brown fought each other for attention, like an angry bumble bee. On a third, she covered the whole page with a muted green and while it was still wet she dribbled dots and splashes of watery pale yellow here and there.

Minou strolled in when her mistress, wielding a flashing paint brush, yelled, "You go there. And you there. Oohh, that colour is like sparkling red wine." The cat, splatters of black, white and orange herself, crept under a chair.

An hour later, ten sheets of paper lay strewn about—six on the table, four on the floor—in various stages of drying. Paint splashes covered the table and the palette was the colour of mud. The water bowl a murky sludge, and her hands looked like contestants in a paint fight. However, one benefit of water colour was that even when it had dried, it was easy to wash off skin, clothes, table, floor and cat fur.

She sashayed to the bathroom and glanced in the mirror. A woman with a red streak in her hair and a goofy smile on her face looked back at her.

"Hello there, crazy woman," Cynthia said. "Time to wash up."

As she scrubbed the naughty crimson, the sunny yellow and the lip-licking chocolate from her hands, arms, and face, she couldn't stop smiling.

"Well, mirror. That was fun. More fun than I've had in a long time. I think it's time to give away my wool, and needles, and craft kits, and buy more paint."

Her smile grew. "And brushes too–big ones."

Chapter 11

Cynthia woke early the next morning and glanced at the bird clock on the wall opposite her bed. Patricia had given it to her two years ago, but within the first week Cynthia had turned off the hourly chirping and cheeping. *I wonder why Patricia and I have never gotten along? Even when we were kids, she would act like my mother, copying her words and frowns.*

The room smelled of fresh spring air from the half-opened window. She took a big breath and threw off her blankets. Minou stirred and opened one eye. Cynthia grabbed her robe, slid into her slippers and instead of going downstairs, went down the hall and stood in front of the closed door of her hobby room.

After the wild painting session yesterday, she had closed the door, gone downstairs and had dinner while watching a taped hour of an old *Doctor Who* with David Tennent, her favourite doctor. It would be fun to travel through time and space. To go anywhere and anywhen.

She opened the door. It looked as if a kindergarten class had gone wild. Crazily coloured papers lay on the floor and the dried puddle on her watercolour palette resembled left-over minestrone soup. The table top displayed a psychotic rainbow. She picked up a curled sheet of paper from the floor and flattened its edges, exposing a splash of muddy streaks and splotches.

"Abstract painting is harder than it looks." She picked up another sheet. Smoothed it out. A flash of red poked around a dark blue patch. "That yellowy-orange bit at the top's not bad." She picked up another and another. Each sheet a mass of confusion. Swirls of desperate dumping, streaks and dashes of wild expression with no harmony, no balance, no contrast.

"What was I thinking? I can't paint." She strode out and downstairs.

Minou joined her in the kitchen. "It was fun but I sure proved I'm no artist." She spooned the last of the coffee grounds into the filter, poured water over it and fed the cat. Instead of her usual smoothy, she scrambled two eggs with some left-over potatoes.

She still had three accounts to finish and had promised her clients she would upload their returns by six that day. "I shouldn't have played hooky yesterday. It was silly to watch a movie on a working day." She took a bite of potato, crispy on the outside and soft on the inside. "And sillier to waste time mucking about with paints."

Her wild foray into art had at least taken her mind off a certain person phoning. *He probably won't.* After breakfast, she put the dishes in the sink, had a shower, dressed and hunkered down in front of her computer.

At ten-thirty the timer buzzed. She jumped up, put the kettle on and scribbled a note to buy more coffee. Waiting for the water to boil, she drummed her fingers on the counter. "I should clear up that shambles I made yesterday."

She wrangled a garbage bag from a newly opened box, and took it upstairs. Puckered sheets of paper lay higgledy-piggledy over the table top. She scooped up three and tossed them into the black bag. One by one she pushed them in but stopped short at the last paper—the first one she had painted. In the top left corner, part of a swish of pure red disappeared into an oncoming slice of Cerulean blue which converged into a deep purple ridge. *I like that bit.* She folded the paper in half and gently ripped it apart. She took the half-sheet and folded it again. This time, with a small paintbrush, she wet the fold from the muddy water still sitting in the bowl from the night before. The water soaked into the fold, waking up the colour it touched. She smoothed the paper flat, spread her palms on each side and coaxed it apart, ending with the top left corner of the original painting. Along the edges, where she had ripped it apart, tiny threads waved like silk antennas.

The kettle shrilled from the kitchen. With the mini painting clutched in her hand, she ran down and stuck it on the fridge door under a cat magnet next to her shopping list. "My first Pollock."

A thrill of excitement rambled around inside her, like a hive of bees tending to their queen. She took her tea and sat on the back step. Fragrant patches of white and purple hyacinths grew alongside the flagstones, and the tulips and daffodils were budding and ready to pop. She loved her house and garden. *My mother can't take this away.*

Out of nowhere, a brilliant idea popped into her head. Numbers swirled inside her brain. *Maybe I can buy my house.* Her retirement fund of ten thousand dollars could be a down payment. But there was a BUT. A big one. *How would I approach my mother?*

Heat-embossed memories of narrowed green eyes and angry snarls flashed in front of her. The back handed swipes never stung as much as her mother's sharp tongue. Her mother had stopped swinging at her but her scathing sarcasm remained in full strength.

Cynthia went inside, added her cup to the sink and headed to her desk. Her mother slept late so it would be no use phoning her until noon. She opened Charlene's file, took a receipt out and clicked Car Expenses. An hour-and-a-half later, her stomach rumbled for lunch. *I should phone her before I lose my nerve.*

With a deep breath, she hit a number on speed dial. Three rings. Her mother never answered with a *hello.* Today it was a curt, "Have you started packing?"

"About that. I want to ask you something."

No response.

"I have some money saved and I was wondering if you would consider selling me my—the—house?"

"Sell you *my* house? Why would I do that?"

"For one thing I've lived in it for twenty-eight years."

No answer.

"And I am your daughter."

"Patricia is my first daughter and her daughter needs a house. You can live in the condom."

"I don't want to live in any condom—condo!"

"Don't be silly. I know what's best."

Cynthia sighed. *You've never known what was best for me.* A clatter of bracelets, a bang, and loud buzzing sounded in her ear. She stabbed her phone off and jammed it back in its holder. It fell over and she slammed it in again. "Stay put." She stomped to the kitchen and threw together a grilled cheese sandwich, banging frying pan, knife, plate and fridge door. *Maybe Patricia will listen to reason.* "Fat chance." Or *maybe I should call a lawyer.* "I must have some rights" She flipped the hot sandwich onto the plate and plunked herself at the kitchen table. She stared at her plate as if wondering who had put it there. Bubbles of golden cheese pillowed out the sides of the toasted bread. Her stomach churned and heart thumped. She took a deep breath. "What the hell is happening to me?"

She had long ago perfected stuffing her feelings, never allowing anger or rage to bubble up, flow over or spew out. But here she was acting like a two-year-old demanding her rights as a human being in a world of giants. *If feels good but strange.* Scary, but not anything she couldn't handle. She shivered. *It's as if I've been given permission to be myself. Whoever that is.* She lowered her shoulders a little bit and relaxed into the new feeling.

She ate the sandwich slowly, relishing every bite. Each swallow seemed to fill recently vacated spaces. It was as if she had more room inside her. As if some inky patches had broken apart or fallen away or as if an old and buried corner had been ripped off, its ragged edges now rippling and fluttering in a new light.

She finished eating, washed the dishes, made a cup of tea and brought it back to her office. She sat down and stared at her closed computer. In the last few weeks her life had changed. Was it because of her mother's announcement that she was going to take her beloved house? *Or was it when I rashly bought that ancient dragonfly brooch?*

Since she had bought that dragonfly, a number of unsettling events had happened. There was her quirky neighbour who rattled her mundane life. The momentous meeting of Arthur Richardson. And now here she was letting her feelings erupt like some unruly teenager.

Charlene's taxes needed attention, however. She put her tea aside and opened the computer.

At four o'clock, the front doorbell chimed and Madison called out. "Time to quit. It's Friday Happy Hour time and I happen to have a bottle of Merlot."

Thankful for the rescue, Cynthia closed her computer. She could finish Charlene on the weekend.

Madison had inherited their mother's red hair, but Maddy's was a rich chestnut, not the early carrot red of their mother's. Madison had long given up trying to control it, so she wore it short, and every six weeks her hairdresser camouflaged the stray grays.

"Look at you, big sister," Madison said, with a big hug.

"What about me?"

"I don't know. You look—sparkly or something."

"It's never too late to change."

"What do you mean? What's changed?"

"I'm not sure. I'll let you know when I figure it out."She took the bottle to the kitchen and poured two glasses of wine.

Madison took a glass. "So tell me about your new neighbour. You said you went to the art show with her?"

"Yes. Well no, she had to bail but we had dinner after."

"So what's she like?"

"Hard to describe—"

The phone rang and Cynthia jumped up and went to her office. *I should get a cell phone.* A few minutes later she returned.

"Who was that? You look discombobulated."

"That was Arthur Richardson." *He actually called.*

"Who?"

"A man I met at the Art Gallery. He—he asked me out on a date." *He really did.*

"A date? You? You're kidding."

"I'm not kidding. We're going to the movies tomorrow night." *Is this all a dream?*

Maddy's mouth dropped open.

Cynthia picked up her glass from the table and, still standing, drained it. But her legs, now made of rubber, wobbled, and she grabbed the back of a chair. Her world had tilted and she was about to fall off.

Chapter 12

Maddy finally closed her mouth. "I can't believe you're actually going on a date!"

"Honest. Pinky-swear." Cynthia plunked her glass on the coffee table and sat down. "Am I nuts? I don't even know him. He could be an ax murdere."

"I wouldn't worry. Ax murderers don't usually frequent art galleries. Trust your instincts."

Cynthia groaned. "I don't have any instincts about men."

"Oh, for heaven's sake. Anyone would think you're a nun the way you avoid the opposite sex."

"I don't avoid them. They avoid me."

"Go and enjoy yourself. It's no big deal."

"Easy for you to say. You were so popular."

"Well, when you were sixteen you went to the movies with that freckled-faced kid." Madison frowned. "What was his name? Ralph something."

"Ralph Myers. I put three layers of concealing cream on my cheek."

"Your face blemish wasn't as bad as you thought."

"Mom called it the Mark of Satan."

"I'm sure she didn't mean it. She was probably mad at Dad when she said that."

"Dad used to say it's where God kissed me."

Madison smiled. "He did have a soft spot for you."

At least one of my parents did. Cynthia lifted her glass. "Any more of that wine left?"

Madison poured it out and Cynthia took a sip. "Do you know what our mother said to me one second before I went out the door on that first date?"

Madison shook her head.

"Don't worry. Nobody's going to look at you."

"Mom said that to all of us. She had that British sense of humour inherited from her own mom."

A knock sounded on the front door. It opened and Sara Jane, in a Hawaiian muumuu, poked her head around. "Oops. Didn't know you had company. I'll come back."

Cynthia motioned her in. "Come in and meet my sister, Maddy."

Maddy took her hand. "Pleased to meet you. Would you like a drink?"

"Love one." She sat on the love seat.

Cynthia went to the kitchen for another glass and and when she came back Maddy and Sara Jane were rollicking with laughter.

"Well, you two have sure hit it off. What's so funny?"

Maddy wiped tears from her eyes. "We were exchanging memories of our most embarrassing moments."

"And you're laughing at them?"

Sara Jane held her stomach. "If you don't laugh, you're lost."

They ordered pizza and lifted their glasses. Cynthia smiled. "Here's to sisters and new friends."

She slept in the next morning until nine-thirty when Minou pounced on her. "Okay, okay." Cynthia pushed away her cover and a dream about swimming in an ocean full of fish.

It was D-day. Date Day. Was it only last Wednesday since she'd met Arthur Richardson? Several times she had thought of calling him to cancel. "I should have arranged to meet him at the movies," she said to her cat.

Minou answered by jumping off the bed. At the doorway, she looked back at her mistress as if to say, "Are you coming?"

Cynthia rolled out of bed and followed the meows downstairs, where she fed the cat and put on coffee. She leaned on the counter, and held her chin in her hands. *What am I going to wear? I don't have any date clothes.*

When she was eight she had been invited to her best friend Shirley's ninth birthday party where Shirley and all the other girls would be wearing pretty dresses.

"We can't afford a new dress." Her mother scowled. "Take one of Patricia's."

Patricia had tossed her an armful of pink, with the remark, "I've outgrown this old thing."

The sleeves gaped on Cynthia. Layers of material mushroomed at her waist and sleeves took turns falling off a shoulder. Holding her back as straight as she could, she slowly walked into the living room.

Her mother lifted her head from her paperback romance and snickered.

Cynthia froze.

Her mother shook her head, "Nothing looks good on you." She went back to her book.

Don't cry, Cynthia had told herself. It was too late to change and she had nothing else to wear. Maybe the others wouldn't laugh.

But they did. All the girls laughed, even Shirley who she thought was her friend.

That was the year she started biting her nails.

I'm not eight anymore and no one is laughing at me. She finished her breakfast and headed upstairs. *Madison and Sara Jane are right. It's only a date and my face is clear now.* She threw on a track suit and hunkered into finishing Charlene's account. That would keep her mind busy. Maybe she would go for a long walk later.

But later, she puttered around, vacuumed, gathered up old magazines, and cleaned out her desk junk drawer. She looked at her hands and groaned. *I'm too old to be chewing my fingernails.*

Her birthday card from Stephanie leaned against the napkin holder. *It's only a movie.* The clock chimed six. She had an hour to get ready. She threw the dishes in the sink and ran upstairs. A quick bath relaxed the kinks out of her back, but not her mind. *If only I wasn't so fat.*

When she was a child she was a skinny wee thing and her father would give her thick cream and extra servings of ice cream which made Patricia jealous. She didn't drink cream now, but was she still living her childhood legacy of trying to fill herself up? It was as if she had been born empty. Scarred and empty. Chocolate bars helped, but the bottomless hole remained and before long, the gnawing would begin again. That indefinable wanting that nothing would fill.

She climbed out of the tub, dried off, and with a towel wrapped around her, stared at the row of hangers in her closet. She turned away and put on her underwear, blow-dried her hair and went back to the hangers. She unclipped a navy skirt, pulled it on and wrestled with the tight button. The clinging material hugged her hips and bulged out in front. *Good Heavens. I look pregnant.* She sucked in her stomach and on the third try, the recalcitrant button let go, freeing her from her prison.

The first year after her father had died she couldn't eat enough to feel full and had never lost those ten to fifteen tenacious pounds she'd gained. She squished the skirt off, threw it at the bed and took out her favourite pair of black slacks. "Thank you, Kathryn Hepburn." A silk blouse and a below-the-waist blue linen vest completed her outfit. *Nuns had the right idea wearing shapeless robes.*

"It's only a movie," she reminded herself for the eight-hundredth time. *If he doesn't like me, so what?* After three years of therapy, modern laser technology, and four shelves of self-help books, she knew it was up to her to like herself. *So what if I'm in the fifth decade of my life. Chronological age isn't logical. It's how old you feel that counts.*

The door bell rang. She slipped into her low heeled shoes and hurried downstairs. *What's the difference? I'll probably never see him again.*

She stood at the front door, took a deep yoga breath and reached for the handle.

Chapter 13

She had forgotten how good looking he was, especially his eyes. "I'm ready," she said. *Am I?* She reached for her jacket at the top hook of the standing coat rack and gave it a yank. The whole rack careened toward her. A straw hat bounced to the floor, while the jacket, a cardigan, and her English Fog mac rained over her.

Arthur grabbed the slanting coat tree. "Whoops."

"I'm such a klutz." *Yikes. Did I say that out loud?*

"It could happen to anyone." He righted the swaying object and picked up the hat.

Cynthia smoothed her hair, carefully lifted her jacket off and threw it over her arm. "Shall we walk? It's only about ten minutes."*He must think I'm ditzy.*

In two blocks they were at the back of the city's landmark, The Church of Our Lady, now Basilica of Our Lady Immaculate. Its twin spires pierced the sky like two exclamation marks.

Arthur stopped at the end of Dublin Street and looked up. "Impressive Gothic Revival."

"I can see it from my bedroom window." *Why did I mention my bedroom? What will he think? I'm such an idiot.*

"Did you know the Gothic style first appeared in France? Notre Dame in 1160 and Chartres Cathedral in 1194."

"I didn't know that, but I know my mother was married in this church."

"I thought you said your family lived in Toronto."

"Her second marriage."

"Oh yes, and you told me your stepfather was also a relative."

Did I tell him all that? Whatever possessed me? "Er, yes. He was my uncle before he was my stepfather."

"Do you have any more uncles?"

She didn't want to get into a discussion about uncles. Her heart was beating so fast, she thought it might fly out of her chest. She had to say something. Her throat was dry. "I have one or two other uncles. In England." She pointed to a pair of stained glass windows. "You might be interested in those." She straightened her jacket over her arm to hide an inch of seam that had come unravelled.

Arthur stared at the windows. "Beautiful."

They walked along the side of the huge structure. Arthur trailed his hand over the bumps and grooves of the granite blocks and gazed at the ornate windows. "Outstandingly beautiful."

Opposite the carved oak doors at the front, a flight of stone steps led to the lower street level. Half way down, he stopped, and pointed up. "The arches and towering spires were to direct humanity's vision upward. Most medieval people were illiterate so the church used symbols in their architecture."

I won't have to worry about making conversation.

When Cynthia was born, the doctors suspected she had a hole in her heart. And when she was a little girl, she thought love drained out of it. Now, as she walked down the stone steps with Arthur toward Quebec Street and the Bookshelf Cinema, a warm spot blossomed in her chest and crept over that empty space.

It was a short few blocks to the cinema where a re-run of The Music Man was playing. He pulled open the front door, and the smell and sound of popping corn drifted down the stairwell. To the left was the entrance to the book store and behind that, a restaurant.

"Want some popcorn?" he asked as they walked up the stairs.

She did. "No thanks." *He probably thinks I'm too fat anyway.*

"One large, please. You can have some of mine."

They sat down and as his arm touched hers, that inexplicable sense of knowing him before—a long time before—rose again. *But that's impossible.*

He held the bag of popcorn between them and a couple of times, they bumped hands as they both reached for it. The feel of his skin on hers was like a coded message, eager to be read.

After the movie, they shuffled up the aisle behind the slow moving crowd. He suggested coffee, and she nodded yes.

At the bottom of the stairs, they turned right into the book store and toward the restaurant. They slid into the last empty booth. A painting of a Victorian house hung on the wall. Not her house, of course. Not her house of twenty-eight years. She shoved house thoughts to the far side of her brain.

He straightened the napkin holder. "What would you like?"

"Tea. Peppermint." She curled her fingers, under hiding her nails and shivered. Not from the cold but from a strange wave of energy that rolled through her body. *Who is this man? Where and when have I seen those dark eyes before?*

He ordered tea for her and coffee for him. "How did you like the movie?"

She let her breath out and lowered her shoulders. She could talk about movies forever. "I love Ron Howard movies. They remind me of Frank Capra's."

Arthur nodded. "*It's a Wonderful Life* is my mother's favourite Christmas movie."

Cynthia sipped her tea. *He must be gay. Gay men are so easy to talk to.* "I watch that every year. I get cozy in my pjs, fill my biggest mixing bowl with popcorn dripping with butter, turn off the phone and hunker into my overstuffed chair."

"Maybe this Christmas we can do it together."

Cynthia's cup rattled as she placed it on her saucer.

"I didn't mean to be forward. I feel comfortable with you." He grinned. "You remind me of my youngest sister, June."

"I do? How?"

"She was born with Down's Syndrome and is often judged as being less than who she is."

Cynthia gulped. "How—why do I remind you of her?" That old refrain of 'you'll never be good enough' coursed through her.

"You want to trust people but you're afraid they're not going to accept you."

She raised her hand to her right cheek, lowered it and grasped her tea cup in both hands.

"I didn't mean to get all psychological on you, but you are a bit of a mystery. You're a beautiful woman and you act like you're not."

She stared at her tea cup, blinking back tears. *He's lying. He's making fun of me. I have to get out of there.*

He reached across and touched her hand. "Are you all right?"

"Fine. I have to go to the bathroom." She rushed off.

She splashed cold water on her face and told the image in the mirror to stop being such a baby and grow up. She recited, "All is well, all is well, all is well, all is well for what seemed like a hundred times before she went back to the table.

"Do you want to walk back?" he asked. "Or take a cab?"

"No. I like walking."

They left by the side door of the restaurant and stepped into the cool April evening. Cynthia mentally recited another litany of positive affirmations, pushing away the last remnants of her knee-jerk reaction. They strolled along Norfolk Street and up the stone stairs to the cathedral. With each step she did her best to bring herself into the present moment. *The past is the past.*

As they neared the huge construction, his conversation moved to flying buttresses, ribbed vaulting, and pointed arches. "Did you know the great abbey churches built by the Benedictines outnumbered all others in England?"

"I didn't know that."

"They built in towns, but the Cistercians built in the remote countryside."

She had passed the imposing structure too many times to count but Arthur's eyes gave her a new perspective of the magnificent building and something else to think about. Halfway through the parking lot, he took her hand and held it all the way to Glasgow Street. By the time they reached her corner, she had let go of old fuzzy memories. She was now holding a real live hand. The warm hand of Arthur Richardson.

They reached her house nestled protectively between two identical ancient clones. The pang of losing it hit her again. How could she leave her beloved house? The light over the front door shone on the porchless stone slab entrance. *Should I ask him in?*

Her door key had again disappeared into the bowels of her purse. She scrambled through notes, receipts, Kleenex, comb, wallet and lip balm.

Arthur said, "I hate it when that happens."

She patted her hip pocket. "Here it is." She pushed the door open, took a step in and rotated her body half way around, like a person imitating a corkscrew. "Ah. Good night. Thanks for the movie. And the tea."

"That was fun. Let's do it again." He bent forward, brushed her hair aside and kissed her lightly on the right cheek. On his way to the curb, he turned and waved.

Cynthia, still standing in her twisted statue pose, slowly lifted her hand and wiggled her fingers in the air. As he drove away, she touched her right cheek. No one had ever kissed her there.

She unwound herself, closed the door, and hung up her jacket. The phone rang and on the third ring, she picked it up in the living room. When she hit talk, her mother was well into her first sentence.

"—so there's no way I can sell you the house."

Cynthia's shoulders slumped. *I should have let call answer take it.* "Can we not at least talk some more about it?"

"No." A jangle and crash of bracelets followed.

Her mother often banged the receiver into its cradle. The clash of copious bangles and bracelets only added more sound effects .Josephine Marshall, although left-handed, insisted on wearing her watch and bracelets on that arm and when Cynthia explained to her that people wore them on their left because they were right handed, her mother would sniff and waggle a clanging wrist at her.

Cynthia pushed the off button and set the phone in its holder. Her mother's harsh words and the jangle of bracelets reverberated in her head. She turned off the hall light and headed upstairs. "Well, mother. You are not going to spoil this evening for me."

With each step, she belted out the opening lines of Mamma Mia, and by the time she reached her bedroom, she and Pierce Brosnan had perfected a sprightly dance.

Her cat looked up. "Don't worry, Minou. I'm not giving up. I'll think of some way I can keep my home." She did a little spin and the cat skittered away.

"Tomorrow is another day."

Chapter 14

On Sunday afternoon Arthur phoned and suggested dinner the next week.

"Dinner? Next week?" *I sound like a parrot.*

"How about Wednesday? I could pick you up at seven."

"Wednesday? Seven?" *Get yourself together girl. It's only dinner. He's not an ax murderer.* "Seven is fine." She hung up. "What am I doing? I don't have time for him—for any man—in my life right now." She went to the kitchen. "I have to worry about my house and moving and living in a sixth floor condom." She picked up Minou. "Might as well laugh. As Sara Jane said, 'crying never helps.' Or something like that."

She set the wriggling cat down and opened the back door to let her out. "That's a good idea, Minou. It's a beautiful day. I think I'll go for a long walk." She already had her Meandering Mauve spring track suit on so she grabbed her runners.

On Tuesday afternoon, Madison popped in. "I was over at mom's after my dental appointment."

"I'm ready for a break," Cynthia said. "I'll put the kettle on."

Madison followed her to the kitchen and pulled a chair out. "I talked to Patricia about your house. How're you doing?"

"How do you think I'm doing? I'm being kicked out of my own home."

"Yeah, that stinks. I tried talking to mom, but she won't listen."

She looped her handbag over the back of the chair. "She says Sharon and Mike need a house and you don't need it anymore."

"How does she know what I need?" Cynthia plunked three boxes of herbal tea on the table. "Take your pick."

"Do you have any coffee?"

"That's a great idea. I happen to have some fresh beans."

"When did you change from a chamomile girl to a fresh 'grind your own coffee beans' woman?

"I'll have you know I've been drinking it for nearly a month."

"Wonders never cease."

Cynthia took the bag of coffee beans from the fridge. "If you ask me, our mother wants to get on Mike's good side. With him being a professor at the University, she probably thinks he has some influence to get her name on a building or something." She pulled the seed grinder from the back of the counter and clattered some beans into it. "As if that's going to make her somebody." She hit the top of the grinder until the rattling changed to a whine.

"That's a little harsh, Sis. You're not the only one with insecurities. Mom was raised by a strict mother and never had much education. If that makes her feel better, why not?"

"Why not?" Cynthia dumped the fresh grains into the coffee maker. "Because she's taking my house away, that's why not." She poured the water in and punched the button.

"Yeah. I agree that's a bummer. Bonnie thought it was a crazy idea too. I'll try talking to mom again, but I doubt she'll listen."

"She won't listen to me. She never has." Cynthia plunked herself at the table opposite her sister and stared out the window. Her perennial flower bed had begun to wake up. The daffodils and a few hardy tulips had bloomed. In the nearby herb garden, nurtured for the last twelve years, thyme and tarragon were poking shoots up through the hard earth. Cynthia looked back at Madison. "Daddy would never let her do this."

"You can't keep wishing Dad was alive. I know you think Mom hates you, but she doesn't. Your personalities clash and you set each other off."

Cynthia glared. "Every year on my birthday, she reminds me of how I nearly killed her."

"Your birth was a traumatic event for her."

"I'm sure it was for me too." She jumped up and took two mugs from the cupboard.

"I'll have another talk with Patricia. The funny thing is, I don't think Sharon even wants to move. I know Patricia doesn't want her to."

Cynthia looked out the window again. Even though she had planted the mint in large sunken pots, it was worming its way toward the lavender. Some things didn't know their boundaries. She made a mental note to build a stone wall around those persistent miscreants.

"Sis? Are you all right?

Cynthia jerked. "Yeah. I'm fine. Just hunky dory." She stood up and poured the coffee. "I have some cookies somewhere." She opened a top cupboard.

"None for me. Charles loves my spare tire, but I don't."

"I know what you mean. I've been walking a half hour a day." She put the cream out and sat down.

Madison reached for a cup and stopped. "I forgot. How was your date? I want to hear every detail."

"It was fine." Cynthia poured herself some cream, stirred and took a sip.

"Fine! That's all you have to say about your first date in—how many years? I thought you had given up men."

"I thought so too." Remembering her walk with Arthur and holding his hand warmed her insides more than the coffee did.

Madison lifted an eyebrow, waiting.

How could she explain those new stirrings? "He's—he's, well, different."

"Different? How different? What do you mean?"

"He's so easy to talk to and be with. And I'm going to see him again tomorrow night." She shivered. "I've never felt this way before. At least not in this lifetime."

Madison smiled, reached across the table and touched her sister's hand. "You go for it girl."

On Wednesday morning Cynthia woke with a start. This Arthur thing was happening too fast. *Do I want a relationship? What is pulling me to this man?*

Yesterday, she'd made an appointment to have her hair trimmed and she had written *false nails* on her shopping list.

At one-fifteen she sat in the hairdresser's chair. "Not too short," she said to Nancy, her regular cutter. *Maybe I should have it cut short. I don't need a blanket of hair to protect me from hurtful remarks. As if it ever did.*

In grade school, Billy Holder would point and yell, "Here comes ugly face" and Ricky Bracken would yell, "Didja fall on a hot stove?" Her friend, Irene, tried to help and gave her some of her mom's heavy makeup, but one day she overheard another girl say, "I'm glad I don't have a face like that."

Cynthia opened her eyes and stared into the salon mirror. "It's gone now, Cynthia. Get over it."

"What's gone?" said Nancy. "I only took a little off."

"Oh, nothing. Nothing at all." She gazed at her new image.

Twenty-five years ago her life had changed. Pulsed-dye laser technology had revolutionized the treatment of port-wine stains, especially on the face. The four surgical treatments over nine months were painless and the physical results spectacular.

Stephanie was three at the time and one morning after she'd climbed into bed for a hug, she stroked her mother's cheek and said, "Mommy, where has your pretty decoration gone?"

Cynthia had cried and thanked God for angels shaped as children.

After the hairdressers, she went to Shoppers and bought a set of false nails. She had tried the bitter tasting polish, but that hadn't stopped her from chewing on them. *Why do I still bite my nails? I'm not a kid anymore.*

At five o'clock she nibbled on cheese and crackers while her bath was running. She enjoyed a long soak, with green goo on her face and her hair pinned up so it wouldn't get wet and spoil Nancy's lovely blow dry. Another half hour to affix the nails and file them to a manageable length, fluff up her hair and get dressed. Her pale blue silk blouse matched her eyes and over that she put on a long tan vest. Walking every day was fine, but perhaps she should renew her membership at the Y. Maybe swimming would help smooth out her tummy and hips.

When the doorbell rang, the butterflies in her stomach woke up and bumped into each other. She took a deep breath and went downstairs.

They walked the same route as they did last time: up Cork Street, through the cathedral parking lot, and down the stone steps. She had suggested *Diana Downtown* on Wyndham Street, which served excellent Indian dishes.

As they waited for their order, Arthur said, "Did you know that Chicken Tikka Masala is now hailed as Britain's national dish over the iconic fish and chips?"

"That can't be right. My father was British and he said England's fish and chips were the best in the world."

They both had the special curry plate. "A little hot for me," Arthur said, wiping his brow.

"The butter chicken is milder. You could try that next time."

"I will." He smiled.

Did I just imply another date? "How many sisters did you say you had?" She knew how many, but it seemed like a good subject changer.

"Four. Two older and two younger. I prayed for a brother."

"Me too. My father said he wanted six children, three of each."

"And?"

"The three girls came first and that was it. I never did get my brothers."

"Was that your mother's choice or your father's?"

"After three daughters I don't think they—well, you know."

"Had sex?"

Cynthia grimaced. "It's weird thinking about one's parents that way."

"We know they did, so what's the big deal?"

She lowered her head. *I can't believe we're talking about sex.* She took a forkful of red curry, chewed, swallowed and took a drink of water. "You're right. This is hot."

She was tempted to get the Gulab Jamun balls. Her taste buds quivered at the thought of saffron sugar syrup, rolling over her tongue, but her inner voice screamed, *a minute on the lips, a lifetime on the hips.* "I'll have yogurt."

He had Kulfi, an equally sinfully rich frozen dessert and offered her some.

A teeny taste can't hurt. She took a small spoonful. It slid over her tongue. "It's like the gelato we had at the Art Gallery."

"There's so much more I want you to try."

Does he mean food or—what? "Seen any good movies lately?"

After coffee, they strolled past the library, along Paisley and headed up Cork Street. "It's delightful that you live so close to downtown.".

"Not for long."

"What do you mean? Are you moving?"

"I don't own the house. My mother does and she's giving it to my niece."

"That sounds ominous."

"You can say that again."

"That sounds ominous."

She laughed. He grabbed her hand and again held it all the way to Glasgow and her front door. She liked the feel of those fairy ripples dancing up her arm.

She invited him in, but he didn't stay for coffee or tea. He met Minou and when he crouched down to pat her, he also stroked the plank floor. "Great old boards." He stood and looked up at the original moldings and the oak staircase. "I can see why you don't want to move."

At the front door, he leaned down and kissed her briefly but firmly on her mouth. An electric tingle zapped through her body and the next second he was walking down her front path. Her heart thumped wildly as she watched him stop at his car and turn and wave. She stood like a store mannequin, her fingers lightly touching her lips.

He pulled away from the curb. She watched him drive up the road and out of sight. Willing her muscles to move, she stepped back, closed the door, turned off the hall light and on stiff legs walked upstairs.

Deep inside her, an ancient door cracked open and a sliver of light stole in.

Like an automaton, she changed into her pyjamas, put on her light robe, and sat in her wicker chair by the window. She pulled her knees up, wrapped her arms around them. The dragonfly, the crystal and the Angel Cards looked back at her from the sill. She brought her hand to her mouth. Her fingers lightly grazed her lips.

Snow White had been awakened with a kiss. *Am I ready to be awakened? Awaken to love? To love herself...and Arthur?*

She woke up at 2:15. The moon glinted through the curtains. She went to the window and stared out at the quiet night. "I've begun my fifty-fourth journey around the sun. What will it bring?"

She looked down at the dragonfly. *Is it asleep or simply resting? What is it waiting for?* She picked it up and stroked a wing. Scratched and worn. Its life hadn't been easy. What magic did it hold?

I think it's time for me to feel my wings. My turn to fly.

Chapter 15

The rest of the week passed quickly. Finishing up last minute tax returns, making sure Revenue Canada received the files, and waiting on inspiration for ideas of how she could keep her house, kept her mind from wandering back to Arthur and the fleeting kiss. Throughout the last few days, however, she often found herself smiling for no good reason.

On Saturday morning, Sara Jane dropped in for coffee and curled herself up in Cynthia's other armchair. It didn't take long before the conversation moved to men.

"Why would he be interested in me?" Cynthia said.

"Why not? You're an attractive woman—in her prime."

Cynthia laughed. "I would argue both points."

Sara Jane frowned. "Why do you put yourself down?"

"I don't. I —"

"Yes, you do. And stop it. I don't care what past crap has happened. It's over."

"What if something happened that you can't get over?"

"Like what?"

Cynthia furrowed her brows. "I think my life would have been different if I didn't have to quit school at sixteen and go to work to help support my family."

"What would you have done if you hadn't stopped school?"

"I would have gone to Art College and been an artist like my dad."

"You said he was a salesman."

"Not at first. He tried to make a go of it with his art, but had to give it up when that didn't work."

"Did you take art classes after work?"

Cynthia shifted in her chair. "No."

Sara Jane shrugged her shoulders. "So why do you keep blaming your parents or the situation."

"That's kinda harsh, isn't it?

"Is it? Everybody has had something to overcome. You never know what other people are going through or have gone through."

Cynthia was silent for a moment. "You're a philosopher as well as a weaver."

"I'm a kid from a large family and, as I said, two active parents. That gave me plenty of experience with all kinds of people coming and going in our house."

Cynthia grasped her coffee cup in both hands and stared into it for a long while. "I guess I have been holding on to that old complaint for a while."

"Ya think? Really, girl friend, time to let that old story go. You can be anything you want to."

"Do you believe that?"

"Absolutely. My dad never gave up with his inventions and my mother fought many injustices in vain, but she won a lot too."

"You had good models."

"Well, make up your own. There's always someone out there who's overcome great odds."

Cynthia nodded. "Yeah. I know what you mean. Thanks." She looked at the clock. "Not to change the subject, but would you like some lunch?"

"I'd love some, but—yikes. I have to go in five minutes."

"Well, before you go, at least leave me with some parting words of wisdom."

Sara Jane laughed, looked up at the ceiling and back to Cynthia. "I'd say, take your life in your own hands and recreate who you want to be. Only you can do that. Nothing or no one is stopping you but your own thoughts." She paused. "There's a quote in the Talmud I've always loved. 'If not you, who? If not now, when?'"

"I've heard that one, but I didn't know it was from the Talmud. Are you Jewish?"

"No. I But I read a lot.

"I wish I'd met you years ago. I worked in offices for nine years, changing jobs every nine months before the uselessness crushed me again. After having Stephanie, I took the bookkeeping course my mother paid for." She looked out the window. "Work has always been a burden for me."

"For a start, you might stop saying that. Tell me about the good stuff in your life."

"Well, I did keep my daughter against all odds. She was the light of my life and I did my best to raise her."

"Yeah. Appreciate what you have and let go of the should's or ought's or might-have-been's."

"I always wanted to be an artist."

"Then BE one!" The clock chimed twelve. "I have to go." She pushed her chair back. "When my brothers were fixing up their first house, which was ours, they gave me the job of scouting Salvation Army and Value Village for materials, furniture and other quirky things to give it character. That's when I learned I had a talent with fabric. And that has been a passion and a livelihood for me ever since." She sprang up. "Gotta run." And she was gone.

Cynthia gathered up the mugs and breakfast dishes and washed them as she looked out the window over the back garden. Red and purple tulips had opened and the lavender and sage were blossoming. An unexpected thrill ran through her body.

Is it possible for me to be whoever I want to be? The flowers outside her window bloomed so easily. They never got caught up in questioning their identity.

Could I change my thoughts—and feelings—about who I am?

Can I be an artist?

She picked up a dishtowel and dried the cups.

Could I have a loving relationship with a man named Arthur?

That evening, Cynthia curled up to watch a taped episode of *Downton Abbey*, when the phone rang. She hit pause on the remote. Her mother's number. She let it ring four times before she picked it up. "Helo."

"I have a proposition for you," her mother said. "About the Glasgow house."

"I'm listening."

"My brain waved at me and I had a thought that there might be a way for you to keep that old house."

"And what would that be?"

"I have to discuss it in person. Come tomorrow."

"Sunday? All right." Cynthia liked to have Sundays for herself.

"Come at two o'clock." Bang and a clatter of bracelets.

She clicked off her phone. *What did her mother have up her sleeve?* She picked up the remote and snapped *Downton Abbey* on. The second episode was a major tearjerker.

On Sunday morning, she woke with a start, a dream fading fast. Something about giant bangled arms, wrapped around her house. She groaned and rolled out of bed. After wrestling a slipper from Minou, she put on her housecoat and headed downstairs for a large mug of head-clearing coffee. "I shouldn't hope for too much." she said to the cat. "You know mother." She put the cat's food down. "I guess you don't." *It must be nice to be a cat.*

The last few days had bought a swirl of new sensations and ideas. At the top of the list was Arthur and what that might mean. And there was Sara Jane telling her to think differently and BE an artist. And now her mother's mysterious offer. Her head spun as thoughts tumbled on and off a fast moving merry-go-round.

"Time for a journalling session, Minou."

She had her first diary when she was twelve—a gift from her father. 'Your diary is your best friend,' he'd said. 'You can tell it anything and it won't answer back.' When she was eighteen, she called them journals and had been writing in them ever since. Not every day, but whenever something was bugging her, journalling would invariably uncover an agenda or some old belief.

Come to think of it, I guess I have been exploring my thoughts for some time.

She took her coffee, book, and pen to her comfy chair in the living room. *A fire would take the edge off the cool April morning.* She scrunched up pages of newspaper and put them on the grate and added a handful of kindling. Flames curled the paper into corkscrews and lapped at the sticks. After a few minutes, she put a fat log on top and waited for it to catch.

What should I tackle first? House? Arthur? Being an artist? She put her cup on the coffee table, picked up her journal and flipped to a new page. At the top she wrote: Men/Sex/Arthur. She stuck the end of the pen in her mouth and stared at the flickering flames. Her mother's voice echoed in her brain. *Men only want one thing. Stay away from them.*

"How come I believed our mother's words when Patricia and Madison didn't?"

Their father was a gentle man and Cynthia couldn't imagine him only wanting one thing. But he was over protective with his daughters, although Patricia and Madison didn't pay much attention to what he said.

Another thought surfaced from the cellar of her mind. *How come my mother married twice if she thought men were so bad?*

Cynthia's brain flip-flopped between her mother's dire warnings and her father's praise. Her sisters and girlfriends took it for granted they would marry, but Gloria Steinem and *Ms.* magazine assured Cynthia that women could make it on their own. It wasn't the dark ages anymore and one didn't *have* to get married. When she worked in offices, whenever a woman got engaged, an invisible crow flew over Cynthia's head, cawing, "Nevermore. Not for you!" while squeals of delight poured from the gathering of the circle for the *Ritual of the Left Hand.*

"Oooh," "Awww," "When?" "Lucky you," "Where?"

At first, Cynthia joined the magpies as they chirped and drooled over the glittering prize, but after a while, she would scrunch behind her computer at the first shriek.

An unhitched woman was either a spinster (a pinched, be speckled, rake-thin female with hair rolled into a tight bun) or an old maid (overweight and lumpy, sitting at parties with hands demurely folded over a flowered dress). Whatever its name, a woman without a mate was a third wheel in a two-wheeled world. Someone to call on a Saturday night to babysit.

Cynthia stared at the blank page of her journal. *I'm used to being on my own. Do I want to open that messy place of men and sex?* Her mind travelled back. It had been such a shock when she discovered she was pregnant.

Each week, her anxiety had grown, and four months later, still holding her looming secret, she had no plans.

Walking home from work one evening, she'd turned down Yonge Street for no reason and after a few blocks stopped in front of *The Roberts Art Gallery.* Large paintings with bold brush strokes and careening colours grabbed her attention and when she'd finally pulled herself away from the mesmerizing windows, a brilliant idea had jumped into her brain. She would legally change her name to Roberts, tell everyone she was married, and that it didn't work out and she was getting a divorce.

Cynthia took a breath and threw another log on the fire as she went to the memory of her mother's response when she'd told her the made-up story.

"You're what?" Her mother had yelled, "You? Married? I don't believe it? How could you grt married and not tell anyone?" She'd jammed her fists on her hips, "And now you're pregnant! What will people think?"

She had been afraid of that. As she had told Sara Jane, it may be no big deal now to be pregnant and unmarried but in her family, it was a gigantic no, no. A sin of huge proportions. A fate worse than death.

She looked down at her journal page. Still blank. She took the pen out of her mouth and shook her head as if to throw the memories out. "That's all in the past."

She went to the kitchen and refilled her cup. *I didn't even dare let Evan know.* And other than Madison, no one ever did, not even Stephanie. She went back to the living room and added another log, crossing it over the other. Two logs burned better than one.

She'd had learned from past experience to listen to that small voice inside and this time it was screaming at her to tell Stephanie NOW. Especially since she'd blabbed it to Sara Jane.

She sat down and tapped the pen on the heading in her journal: Men/Sex/Arthur. Four days after she'd found her dragonfly a new chapter of her life had opened with Arthur Richardson featured on page one. Would he be a poem? A novel? Or perhaps only a short story.

But another nagging thought demanded front row attention. *Before I can embrace the Arthur adventure, I owe it to my daughter to tell her the truth.*

She picked up the coffee cup and set it down again. Still too hot. It splashed on the table and she grabbed a Kleenex and set it under the cup. A brown blotch crawled across the tissue leaving a dark stain.

She snatched up her journal and pen and scribbled *Tell Stephanie!* across the page. As she slashed the exclamation mark, the paper ripped. She pressed a finger over the tear, but the edges wouldn't smooth down. Wouldn't cover the ragged hole she'd made. She banged the book shut and grabbed the phone. Voice mail answered.

"Stephanie. It's mom. Call me. As soon as you can."

The burning logs warmed her and a wave of empowerment flowed from her toes to her head like a veil being lifted.

Chapter 16

The clock chimed twelve. "Enough of all this past stuff." I going to enjoy some of the day before hearing my mother's new proposal. She put on some soup and ran upstairs to get dressed. After lunch she walked over to Exhibition Park and watched the kids play on the monkey bars and slides. Niggling thoughts wound their way in and out of her mind about what her mother might say. She walked back and picked up the car and at five to two pulled onto Stuart Street.

She clunked the lion head once and opened the door.

"I'm in the parlour."

Cynthia stepped into the living room where her mother had set out a selection of no-name cookies on a paper plate. The bag lay open on its side.

"Sit here, my dear." With a plastered smile and a jangle from her extended arm, she indicated the Morris chair. A lime green towel with brown puppy paws covered the seat. Tippy sat on her lap, intermittently yapping and commandeering the role of pack leader. Mrs. Marshall leaned across the barking dog and poured tea from her mother's porcelain tea pot.

Cynthia removed the towel and sat down. "What's this all about, mother?"

"First, a little mystery needs clearing up." She patted Tippy to the accompaniment of clanging bangles and her heavy charm bracelet.

The dog's barks changed to throaty growls, its beady eyes fastened on Cynthia.

Cynthia held her purse on her lap. "What mystery is that?"

"How come all these years I have never seen a picture of your husband?"

"My husband? What are you talking about?"

"I am talking about the mysterious man you up and married and who got you pregnant and left. I never did hear the whole story and whenever I bring it up you change the subject."

Why is she asking this now? "Really, mother. Is this necessary?"

"I think it's strange that you don't have one picture of him." She looked expectantly at Cynthia. "And you never told me any details about your wedding." Her voice rose. "In fact nothing at all. All these years, you have been side-stepping the issue."

"Mother, this is nonsense. It's old history and what has this got to do with me keeping my house?"

Mrs. Marshall folded her arms, bracelets rattling. "You want something from me? Well, I want something from you. Like a trade." She smirked. "Show me your marriage certificate and divorce papers and you can keep your house."

"Mother! That's blackmail."

"Hardly blackmail." She lifted her chin. "Unless you have something to hide and you don't have such papers."

The only legal documents Cynthia possessed were her change of name papers. First to Roberts and back to Marshall.

Mrs. Marshall shook a pointed finger at her stunned daughter. "I want proof you're an honest woman." Her scowl matched the dog's and she lifted her nose higher. "You don't have any such papers. Just as I suspected."

Cynthia found her voice. "What difference does it make? And what has it got to do with my house?"

"Trust you to sully the Marshall name." She jabbed the finger at Cynthia's face, bracelets rattling.

A freight train roared through Cynthia's head. "It was a Marshall who got me pregnant!" She slapped her hand over her mouth. *What the hell did I say?*

Josephine Marshall opened her eyes wide. "What! Who? Who was it?"

Cynthia bit her lower lip. "It doesn't matter." *How could I have said that?*

Her mother snapped her mouth into a straight line and stared into the distance.

Is she itemizing the Marshall men?

Her eyes were green slits. "I'll find out."

"It doesn't matter. I hardly remember him."

"You always were peculiar about sex."

Cynthia's face went ashen, except for a flared patch on her right cheek. "How can you say that? It was you who was forever reciting the taboos about sex. How many times did we hear that men only wanted one thing?"

The older woman sniffed. "Speaking of taboos. What about you and your father?"

"What about me and father?" *Whatever is she talking about?*

"He always had a soft spot for you." Her voice rose to a sharp point and bangles clashed as she rubbed the dog's back. "He loved you more than Patricia which wasn't right because she was the first born. He even loved you more than Madison.

"He was only making up for the fact that *you* never loved me." Cynthia's voice shook and her face flared crimson.

Mrs. Marshall shouted back, making the dog jump. "How could I love you when you took my husband away from me."

"What!" Cynthia leaned forward, bumping the table and making the cups rattle. "You were his wife, not I."

"Sometimes I wondered which one of us was the wife."

A sick feeling bubbled in Cynthia's stomach. She grasped the arms of the chair, her knuckles white.

Her mother spat more words at her. "He spent hours with you, playing chess and doing crosswords and whatever else."

Cynthia stared, open mouthed. *My mother is crazy.* "There was nothing untoward between Daddy and me. I can't believe you would even think that."

Her mother pursed her lips. "I don't want to talk about this anymore. I simply invited you here to ask for your marriage license." A smug look crossed her face.

"And what if I say no." *Lord, give me strength not to hit her.*

"No, you won't show it to me. or no, you don't have one?"

Cynthia stood up. "Good bye. Mother." She swung her purse over her shoulder, missing the tea pot by a breath.

Tippy's shrill bark followed her to the front door. She yanked it open, slammed it shut and stumbled down the steps to her car. *It would take less than two cents for me to kill that woman!*

She stomped to her car, crushing a tangle of weeds that had grown between the flagstones.

Chapter 17

She pulled out of the drive and took the first turn not caring which way she went. She continued to drive randomly, not thinking where she was going and by the time she had calmed down she was on Highway 7 heading toward Kitchener. The Belgian Nurseries' sign was just ahead. She slowed and turned in. Perhaps she'd add fennel and coriander to her steadily growing herb garden. *Oh, wait. I can't have a garden if I don't have my house.*

Maybe the spring colours would distract her. She parked and went inside. Tables were ladened with trays of cold-tolerant pansies. A hundred swaying faces waved at her. Were they laughing at her or with her? *For heaven's sake. They're only flowers.*

I should have told Stephanie a long time ago about her being born out of wedlock. Such an archaic term, portending some dire consequence.

She walked along another aisle of yellow and purple. *Was that why my inner voice was shouting at me to tell Stephanie?* Some part of her must have known her mother was going to raise the issue. *Are we all connected on some metaphysical highway? Like an invisible internet.* Stephanie hadn't called back. *I should get a cell phone.*

She walked up to the counter. "Do you have a public phone I could use?"

The teen-aged clerk looked at her as if she had asked where the dinosaur bones were buried. "Where's your cell?" she asked.

"I don't have one."

The young girl looked at her as if she *was* the dinosaur.

"May I use yours?It's a local call."

The girl punched in her password and handed it to Cynthia.

Cynthia tapped in Stephanie's number.

"Hi, mom. I've been up to my neck in clay this morning. What's up?"

"When's a good day for you to come for lunch? Or I can meet you half way."

"There's a potter in Guelph I've been wanting to visit. How about—Wednesday. If I can't arrange that with her, I'll call you."

"Okay. My treat. We can go to *Cornerstone*. They have great organic food."

"We usually have soup and sandwiches at your place. Aren't you too busy to go anywhere at this time?"

"I'm almost finished the taxes. Anyway, you're more important than work."

Stephanie laughed. "You're a great mom, mom. Someone's at the door. Gotta go. I'll call you right back."

"Don't do that. I'm not home. I'll see you Wednesday." She hung up and handed the phone back. *When she knows the truth, will she still think I'm such a great mom?*

She walked toward the herb section and stopped. *No use buying more herbs now.* She headed for the garden decors near the front and kept on going out the door. *Or garden ornaments.*

Stephanie phoned the next day. Wednesday wouldn't work for her, so they arranged for Friday.

Cynthia hung up. "Oh, well. After twenty-eight years, a few more days won't make any difference." She frowned. *Or would it?*

Her mother could be sneaky but surely she wouldn't dare phone Stephanie. A shiver went through her. Friday was five days away and her mother did not have a long attention span.

She forced herself to get back to work. *Worrying isn't going to help.* She open her computer and brought Quick Books up and retrieved the first file. Bookkeeping was always a chore, but that morning it dragged even more than usual. Her mind kept switching back and forth, pulling her from losing her house, to what to do about Arthur, to confessing to her daughter before her mother did.

She pounded on the keyboard, cursing when she'd hit the *caps lock* and had to redo half a page. In the next hour and a half she'd put a debit in the credit column, hit plus instead of minus, and entered a column of numbers in the wrong file. She made the corrections and slammed the lid of her laptop.

"That's it, Minou. I'm finished." She pushed her chair back. "Time for a break."

She took her coffee upstairs. The top of her bureau was crammed with moisturizer, hand cream, a half-filled journal, a small pink piggy bank, and a cracked mug filled with old pens. The two bookshelves overflowed with books and treasures found on walks (stones, leaves) or objects d'art from the second hand store (a bust of Beethoven, a miniature Monet painting). *Madison's right. I am a pack rat.*

She sat in her wicker chair and made a resolution to be neater. At least she kept her window sill tidy. The dragonfly, crystal and angel cards rested serene in their own uncluttered space.

Since she had found the dragonfly, her life had grown even more jumbled. She let the thoughts tumble out—the threat of losing her house, the secret about her daughter leaking out, and Arthur. He was the scariest of all.

She picked up the dragonfly. "What should I do about Arthur, dragonfly?"

She closed her eyes. Out of the mists of her mind, a disjointed movie swirled into view: a tall woman in black robes holding the dragonfly, a young girl sobbing, a child playing with it, buried in dirt, a hand polishing it, being held over a caldron, thrown into—. A loud ring burst the flow of images. She jerked and opened her eyes. With a shiver, she grabbed her phone.

It was Arthur.

After initial greetings, he said, "I'm busy all week, but what about lunch on Sunday, and maybe a drive in the country?"

"Sunday?"

"Yes, this Sunday. I can pick you up at 12:30."

"All right. See you then." She clicked the phone off still distracted by her daydream. Although she didn't have any answers about what to do about Arthur, she smiled at the thought of seeing him again.

Downstairs she filled the sink with sudsy water and cleaned off the counter. *How does so much stuff find its way here?* As she washed the dishes, she envisioned having lunch with Arthur.

"Wait a darn minute," she said, holding a dripping cup aloft. "This will be the third date." The infamous third date that her sisters talked about—the sex date. Any red blooded man would expect it. *Surely not on a Sunday afternoon.*

The next day, Madison swung by for lunch. Cynthia ladled out her homemade carrot soup.

"You think too much," Madison said. "You're not the only one with issues around men."

"What do you mean?"

"FYI sis, a lot of women have men issues." She lifted a spoon to her lips and blew.

"But I'm such a klutz around them. I thought you and Patricia had it all figured out."

"The trouble is you expect things to be like it is in the movies or a novel. Life's not like that. There's no 'happily ever after'."

"I don't understand men." She touched her right cheek.

"Not all men are shallow. You're an attractive woman and I wish you'd get it into your thick head that you're okay."

After soup, Cynthia brought out a gargantuan bowl of green salad.

Madison laughed. "You are the salad queen of Guelph."

"I like salad." She filled her plate. "But wait till you see dessert."

Madison lifted her eyebrows. "Golly gee. I can hardly wait."

"Don't tease me. It's our favourite. From Saunders Bakery in Rockwood."

"Do you ever think you might have sublimated your sexual needs into food?"

Cynthia pierced slices of radish and cucumber that had congregated at the bottom of the bowl. "Let's talk about something else."

"Okay. How's work?"

"Why did I ever become a bookkeeper? I hate working with numbers." She stabbed at the romaine. "The only interesting thing about bookkeeping is that it's the only word in the English language with three double letters in a row."

"I always thought you'd be an artist, or a writer from all your journal scribbling."

"Funny you should say that. Sara Jane mentioned something about me being an artist."

"Maybe you should." Madison took a bite of avocado.

"At least bookkeeping has provided me with a decent living. I suppose I should be grateful to mother for paying for the course." She speared another forkful of salad.

"She thought it was best for you."

"Yeah." She remembered that day, twenty-eight years ago, when her mother announced she had enrolled her in the local community college. "You can work from home," she'd said. Never mind she hated working with numbers. It was a repeat of her mother insisting she take the commercial course in high school when she wanted to take art. "You'd never get a job as an artist," her mother had growled. "Artists starve. Anyway, who do you think you are?"

She stared at the forkful of lettuce. *Who do I think I am? I wish I knew. Am I a fifty-three year old disgruntled bookkeeper? A frustrated artist? Or an overweight middle aged woman who, two weeks ago, went on a date?*

Madison tapped the side of her plate with her knife. "Earth to Cynthia."

Cynthia jerked and stopped her fork from falling.

Madison laughed. "You were out of it. Whatever were you thinking?"

"Oh, just some old stuff about things our mother said to me." She put the lettuce into her mouth.

"You've never given mom a chance. Maybe she was a little hard on you because she didn't want you to be disappointed the way she was."

Cynthia banged her fork down. "Don't compare me to her. I'm nothing like my mother."

They finished their salads in silence and Cynthia cleared off the dishes. "Let's have dessert."

"Speaking about dessert, tell me about this new man."

"Well—he's—" She slid the string off the white cake box and placed a large date square on a plate between them. "He's nice."

They picked up their forks and carved a chunk from each side.

"I think he likes me," Cynthia said. She took another forkful.

Madison did the same from her side. "That's good."

"What? The date square or that he might like me?"

She laughed. "Both."

"I'm nervous that he likes me."

"For Pete's say. Why?"

Cynthia took another bite and shrugged her shoulders.

"When are you going to get it that there's nothing wrong with you?"

"When I stop thinking about the past I guess."

"There's an easy solution to that."

"What's that."

"Stop thinking about the past!"

They met in the middle for their last bites, leaving nothing behind but crumbs.

Chapter 18

Friday morning, Stephanie phoned and cancelled again.

"Sorry, mom, but I am soooo busy. Was it something particular you wanted to talk about?"

Cynthia hesitated. *Only the most important thing I'll ever say to you.* "I just want to spend some time with you."

"I'm swamped getting ready for the spring pottery show. Maybe in a week or so?"

No. It has to be sooner. "Can't you make it any earlier?"

"Are you sure there's nothing special you want to see me about?"

I should just tell her it's important. Demand to see her. But fear had frozen her tongue. "Next week then. For sure. I'm so glad you're happy."

"Mark's the best, mom. And I love my work."

They hung up and Cynthia said to the cat. "It's okay, Minou. All is well." But her insides wobbled like jelly.

Her whirlwind neighbour was in Montreal for a few days so things were quiet on that side, and tax deadline was over. She had to do something to take her mind off meeting with Stephanie. It would be good time to attack those things she had hidden away in closets and under the bed.

She went upstairs, opened her wardrobe and stared at the jumble: two or three blouses shared each hanger, dresses and slacks squashed together, and on the top shelf a feather hat she never wore teetered on a pile of special events handbags. At the bottom: a crammed shoe rack, and behind that, a wicker picnic basket stuffed with Stephanie's grade-school projects.

She leaned in and pushed her head between a corduroy jacket and a ten-year-old suit to a tower of boxes stacked at the back. She pressed on the back panel of the cupboard, but it didn't budge. No gateway opened to a magical land beyond.

She reached for the top box and hauled it out. Photographs. Someday she would make a scrapbook. The next carton contained old art and craft supplies. On the top was an unopened box of chubby acrylic paints—a Winsor & Newton Six Tube set. She had forgotten all about them and hadn't thought about painting since that silly mad spree after the Pollock movie a couple of weeks ago. *When did I buy that little paint set?* It must have been three Christmases ago. *Didn't I also get a couple of canvases?*

She pushed aside a pair of winter boots that needed a new zipper and an overnight case she never used. Two 12" x 16" canvases leaned against the back panel. She wrestled them out, picked up the paints, and took them down to the kitchen. After stripping off the wrapping, she propped one of the canvasses on the table in front of a pile of overdue library books.

She filled a mixing bowl with water and lined up the pristine paint tubes in a row. Each with their own dazzling name filled with promise: Alizarin Crimson, Phthalo Green, Ultramarine Blue and Yellow Ochre.

Brushes. She ran upstairs to her hobby room. Watercolour brushes were sticking out of the chipped mug where she had shoved them after her last painting fiasco. She grabbed her largest brush, a half-inch wide and ran downstairs. An oval platter, which she rarely used, would make a good palette.

"I need a larger brush or—." She looked around the kitchen.

An earthenware saucer, sitting on the windowsill, held a jumble of seashells, an expired credit card, three river stones, a tangle of paper clips and a safety pin. "Perfect." She picked up the credit card and placed it beside the brush.

For a long moment, she stared at the empty canvas. In a rush, she snatched up the tube of Ultramarine, unscrewed its top and squished out a blob of blue custard onto the plate. With the credit card, she scooped up a corner of paint and dabbed dots onto the stark white space. The canvas bounced at her touch. She picked up a larger chunk of blue goo and swiped the dots into a wide arc of a smile.

A fat Yellow Ochre worm crawled onto the palette beside the blue and a thick Crimson stream wound its way in. The paint shimmered into life as it met the canvas. She grabbed a dishcloth from the stove handle, wiped the credit card clean and danced it through the paints, creating a concert of colour.

The top of the Titanium White refused to loosen, but after holding it under a stream of hot water it gave in and she pressed a snowy hill into the mix. A song of strokes emerged, through and around in a rainbow rhythm, thick and thin, smooth and bumpy, dark and light. She stood back and tilted her head. Finished. But what was it? Not like her early watercolour paintings of landscapes or daisies. She tilted her head the other way. But not a sea of mud either.

On the second canvas, she mixed red and yellow into a vibrant orange and covered the top half of the canvas. At the bottom, she added blue to crimson, producing a deep and dusty purple. For a lighter touch, she used her thin plastic library card. This made a softer effect as she swiped, scraped and dotted paint over the complying surface. Each stroke came alive. The bowl of water grew muddier as the canvas glowed brighter with its variety of shapes, textures, and vibrating colours. She stirred up a loose puddle of delicious Emerald Green and dribbled it into bumps and crevasses. Rivulets of thinned paint, acting like water colours, transformed the wet shade beneath while some trailed through ridges of dried paint and settled in grooves where they proudly sat like stones in a Queen's bracelet. She tilted the canvas to guide the meandering streams into newfound pathways. Her pine kitchen table could easily pass as a grade school art experience.

"Oh my god." She grabbed a tea towel, wet it in the muddy water and rubbed the table top. The dirty towel streaked the wet parts while the dried acrylic paint refused to budge. Her hands and fingernails were multicoloured, and her jeans and t-shirt looked like she'd come from a hippy tie-die party. Crumpled paint tubes lay pell-mell and a kaleidoscope of colour covered the oval dinner plate. Fortunately, the stack of library books had escaped decoration.

"Yoo hoo." A voice at her front door. called. "I'm ba-ack."

With the paint-smeared tea towel in her hand, Cynthia ran to the front entrance.

Sara Jane's eyes widened as she surveyed the red stripe highlighting Cynthia's fair hair, the blue spot festooned on her cheek and the splash of orange embellishing her forehead. "Wow. It looks like you've had fun."

"I've been painting."

"Now how did I know that?" Sara Jane closed the door.

"Come and see." Cynthia flipped the dish towel over her shoulder, snatched up her friend's hand in her painted one and dragged her to the kitchen. "What do you think?" She held her breath. *Are they a mad monkey's wild careening?*

Sara Jane stared at the storm of colour. "You did these?" She gaped at one canvas and the other and back again. "They're amazing."

"You think so? They're not an exploding mess?"

"Exploding, yes. But harmony and balance blended with raw, primitive emotion." She nodded. "A true expression of inner passion. I freakin' knew you were an artist."

"Well, I don't know about that, but—"

"Cynthia Marshall. Shut up. No more buts. It's time you got over yourself and admit who you are."

"Who am I?"

"You're a freakin' artist. Now get washed and changed. I'm taking you out to lunch to celebrate."

"Celebrate what?"

She plunked her hands on her hips. "Say after me. I am an artist."

I'm no artist."

"So you're deaf too. What the hell will it take for you to wake up?"

"Well, someday, maybe, if I work real hard, and practise and go to art school, and take a lot of lessons, maybe, someday, somehow, I might be—an artist."

"Golly gee. Ya think so?" Sara Jane shook her head. "In case you haven't noticed, you already are an artist."

Cynthia stared at her.

"You're a hard nut to crack but I never give up. See you in half an hour." She walked toward the door.

Cynthia pushed her hair off her orange forehead.

Sara Jane stopped, and walked back to the paintings. "I'm going to show these to a few people."

"What? You can't do that."

"Yes I can. I'll pick them up when they're dry." She spun around, and in a flurry of swaying skirts she was out the door.

Chapter 19

Skin is amazing. Even acrylic paint softens with a hot shower and lavender soap, however, Cynthia officially designated her paint splattered jeans and T-shirt as painting clothes. She changed into slacks, a blouse, and her ever faithful and forgiving vest.

They walked to Einstein's Cafe and sat on the patio where Sara Jane regaled her with stories of her Montreal trip, and how she had reunited with an old fling to have a new fling. She didn't say anymore about Cynthia being an artist.

"So you liked my paintings?" Cynthia asked.

"I told you I did, but no matter what I say, or anyone says, you won't believe it until you believe it yourself."

"But—"

"There you go 'butting' again. Stop with the buts. Change the 'buts' to 'ands' and you will change your life."

"But—oh. I do say that a lot."

"Yeah. So stop it."

"That was blunt."

"Yup. Let's order dessert."

That evening Cynthia was settled in the living room with a cup of tea, watching the Australian show, *Miss Fisher's Murder Mysteries* (now there's a modern woman) when her mother called.

Cynthia could hardly believe her ears. "You're actually giving me a month's grace on leaving my house?"

"You mean *my* house," she said. "Remember. July 1—unless of course, you can come up with those papers." The usual clatter of bracelets accompanied her hang up.

Cynthia punched the off button on her phone and banged it back in its holder. "Thanks, Mom, for the extra month. But it's still not fair, Minou. How can she do this to me?"

Minou twitched an ear but didn't budge from her curled up position on Cynthia's lap.

She hit the resume button but even Miss Fisher couldn't distract her from the tumult of thoughts racing around her brain. She snapped the TV off.

"I can't provide the papers she wants." She stroked the cat. "It looks as if we'll be moving." She reached for her tea mug and took a sip. "But it doesn't mean we have to move into her precious condo.There are other places in Guelph. Tomorrow I'll check apartments." She went to bed, and had a dream of being lost in an empty warehouse.

At eight-thirty the next morning, Sara Jane picked up the two paintings.

Cynthia frowned. "What if they don't like them?"

Sara Jane rolled her eyes. "Shut up, girlfriend." She opened the door and left.

I shouldn't have let Sara Jane take them. People will laugh at them. She went to the kitchen and gathered up her two string bags. A walk to the market would take her mind off it.

At eleven o'clock she was home and putting food away when the phone rang.

"It's Patricia. Are you busy?"

"Not really."

"I'm at mom's. I'm coming over to see you."

"I'll put the kettle on."

"Don't bother. I'll pick up a coffee at Tim Horton's."

While the water boiled for her own tea, Cynthia pulled a package of Patricia's favourite almond cookies out of the freezer.

In ten minutes, her older sister strode into the kitchen, and without a hello, tossed her purse on one chair and sat in another. Since her divorce she wore her hair pulled back in a serious bun. She pursed her lips. "You can keep your old house for a little while longer."

Cynthia nodded. "Yeah. Mom phoned and told me July 1."

"You have even more time. The tenant's house is not ready and they need to stay in the condo till the end of November."

"What about Sharon?"

Patricia nibbled at the edge of an almond cookie. "It works for her. She's due in September and wants to be close to me and the Kitchener hospital."

"A six-month reprieve is better than nothing." Cynthia sighed. "I still can't believe she' wants to take my house."

"She probably wants to get back at you."

"Back at me! For what?"

Patricia prided herself on her ability to secure inside knowledge. She would have made a great gossip columnist. "You reminded dad of his first love. She was blonde like you."

"How do you know this?"

Patricia continued in her smug way of displaying choice knowledge of family lore. "Mom told me in secret. She said every time she looked at you she was reminded of that."

"Well, it wasn't my fault our Dad had an old love."

Patricia shrugged her shoulders. "Well, as you know, our mother was always warning us about how bad men were."

"What was all that all about? What did she have against men?"

"You knew she had a bad heart since her bout with rheumatic fever when she was thirteen."

"Oh yeah, she goes on about her 'poor heart' enough, but what's that got to do with hating men?"

"She used to be a tomboy and loved sports and boxing with her brother. She even called herself Jo. But with her bad heart, she wasn't allowed to over exert herself and she became jealous and mad at seeing her brother so active."

"Why did she marry?"

"She didn't like working at Eaton's and she wanted someone to take care of her."

"That's a screwy reason to get married, but I still don't understand why she married a second time if she didn't like men."

Patricia nodded. "Our mother does have archaic ideas about men and sex but that wasn't an issue with Frank."

"What do you mean?"

"Frank was gay."

Cynthia spluttered tea down her front.

"He got married for a cover and mom got married for money." Patricia put the half-eaten cookie on the plate. "Who do you think designed the house and picked out the furniture?"

Cynthia mopped her chin. "I knew he did, but I thought that was his artistic flare coming out."

"He let his art out, but nothing else."

"He would turn in his grave to see the condition of his roses."

"I have to go," Patricia said. She stood up. "I wanted to be sure you were clear that Sharon didn't need the house until after the baby comes."

She actually said that as if she cared about me. "Thanks, Patricia." *Is my stiff older sister actually concerned about me having to move?*

Patricia swung around and strode out of the kitchen. Cynthia followed her along the hall. When they got to the front door, Patricia pulled it open, but didn't step out. She hesitated a moment and looked Cynthia in the eyes. "Mom doesn't hate you. Everyone's had some heartache in their life." She rushed out and into her car. She didn't look back as she pulled away.

Cynthia closed the door and returned to the kitchen and put the kettle on. She needed another cup of tea to absorb the thoughts that spun around in her head.

A spark of compassion for her mother crept over her. *She must have been resentful and frustrated to have been held back.* The kettle squealed and she made tea. *That must have been burden enough, but worse to think your husband was not only pining for a first love, but reminded of her by their middle daughter.*

It made a little more sense how her mother treated her. She took her tea and a cookie to the living room and sat in her chair.

But Uncle Frank being gay? That is an eyeopener. People often called her naive, or would ask her if she'd lived in a cave, after one of those 'everybody knows that' incidences.

She took a bite of almond cookie, tumbling her mind over Patricia's last statement. *And my all-efficient and organized older sister has her own heartache.*

The phone rang. It was her mother. She picked it up on the second ring.

"—just because you have six more months, don't think I'll change my mind."

"Hello, Mother. How are you?"

"And if Sharon doesn't want your—*my* house, it could be made into a student residence."

"Mother, it has two bedrooms and it's not that close to the University."

"Students like to live downtown. It will be perfect. No further discussion." Clang, clatter, dial tone.

Cynthia hung up. At least she had another six months. Six months more to enjoy her home and to find a place to live

Chapter 20

The next morning, Cynthia awoke early. Was it Sunday already? She rolled out of bed and ran to the shower.

Arthur was picking her up at twelve-thirty for their afternoon date. By twelve-fifteen she was dressed in black slacks and a long lavender blouse opened over a white cami. She sat on a kitchen chair, finishing her second coffee and swinging her leg.

She was no Audrey Hepburn, and he, no Gary Cooper, but she shivered, remembering their rendezvous in *Love in the Afternoon*.

At twelve-twenty-nine the door bell rang. She ran to answer it.

Right away, she said, "Why don't we drive to the restaurant and we won't have to come back for the car?"

"Good idea."

He parked in the municipal parking lot and they took the short cut to *The Aquarius Café*, a funky vegetarian eatery that served organic food. Ducking between the Royal City Church and the Bank of Montreal parking lot saved walking around the town's fountain statue of a naked man and woman holding up a naked infant. Cynthia smiled as she remembered her mother's reaction to it. Mrs. Marshall was scandalized when the Italian community had gifted Guelph with it.

Inside the restaurant, a bin of toys sat in one corner where a boy busied himself with Lego. At a nearby table, a young couple in tie-dyed shirts shared pita bread and humus. They gave their order and made their way to one of the well worn pine tables.

They waited for their lunch and after exchanges about the weather and latest movies, he said, "You're quiet today. Is anything bothering you?"

She didn't want to talk about her mother's request for nonexistent papers and she wasn't about to discuss her drunken one night stand that produced Stephanie. She lowered her head. "My mother and I have issues."

"You said she was taking your house from you?"

"That's her plan."

A girl with a pony tail and a ring in the side of her nose, brought their food.

They both dug in and after a few bites, Arthur said, "Could you buy it from her?"

"I've already tried that. She refused."

"Is there no other way?"

She shook her head. "How do you like the vegetarian lasagna?"

"It's good. Did you know that Pythagoras, da Vinci, Einstein, and Schweitzer were all vegetarians?"

"So are Demi Moore, Dustin Hoffman, and Richard Gere. I'm in good company."

They finished their meal and walked back to the car. He opened the door for her. "Where would you like to go?"

Cynthia had Googled and suggested the hamlet of Glen Williams a fews miles from Georgetown, where three converted mills housed the working studios of over thirty-five artists.

Forty-five minutes later they arrived at the Glen Williams art complex. The original stone walls and wide beams of what used to be a saw mill, a woollen mill and an apple-processing factory interested him as much as the art within.

They walked from booth to booth, eyeing a mix of abstract and realistic painters and everything in between. Cynthia took extra time at one booth with large abstracts. *Could I ever paint like that?*

"A penny for your thoughts? You look so intense."

"Oh, nothing. Just silly imaginings."

"Einstein said that imagination is more important than knowledge. I agree with him."

"I've heard that quote."

"Do you believe it?"

She looked back at the rampage of colour on the canvas in front of her. "I think I do."

After seeing all the exhibits, they walked into the sunlight, and up the road. A smattering of houses, one corner store, a church, and a river made up the main part of town.

At the bridge, they leaned on the wide stone railing and peered at the river below. They looked up at the same time, and before she knew it, he was kissing her.

On the mouth. Hard.

He pulled away and she stared at him—too stunned to speak or move.

A pair of bicycles zipped by, followed by three more which swished by and then four. All riders wore brightly coloured, tight-fitting costumes.

"Must be some kind of bicycle marathon," she said. She turned and walked toward the parking lot.

On the drive home, Cynthia kept her head turned to the side window, staring at the passing landscape. *What did that kiss mean? What else did he have in mind?* She wouldn't mind being kissed like that again, but kisses lead to—. They passed the *Welcome To Guelph* sign.

"Where do you want to eat?" he asked.

"I—I've made plans for later. My daughter's coming over."

"I didn't mean to presume."

"I've been trying to see her for some time now and…" Her voice trailed off. It even sounded hollow to her own ears.

Neither spoke after that and it was four-thirty when they reached her house. He pulled to the curb and before he turned the car off, she jumped out. "You must want to get going. Thanks for a great afternoon." She slammed the door shut, and scampered up the walk.

She had her key already and she shot through the door. Without looking back, she closed it firmly and leaned against it. She had told a lie. Stephanie was not coming.

Her lower lip trembled as she waited to hear his car start up and pull away. She stood for several minutes. No sound. What was he doing? She went to the window. He was just sitting in the car.

She thought of their walk around the art exhibits. Him so close, brushing his arm, feeling his breath, and there was that amazing kiss on the bridge. *What am I afraid of? Why does a part of me want to run away and never see him again?*

Finally, the motor roared to life and he pulled slowly away from the curb, up the street and out of sight.

And another part of me wants to hold him and never let him go?

Chapter 21

On Monday, Cynthia immersed herself in busy tasks: entering a new client's data, clearing out emails, updating her address book and cleaning out her kitchen junk drawer which had taken an hour.

She had made it to five o'clock. "Time to make soup." She pulled out an onion and garlic.mThe onion was particularly strong; they didn't usually make her cry that much. She threw them and the garlic into the heavy saucepan, stirring briskly. *Phew, those onions are strong.* She wiped her eyes and set to chopping carrots.

After supper—she'd made enough soup to feed an army—Cynthia washed the dishes, froze four containers of soup, and sat in front of the TV. Minou jumped up beside her.

Cynthia patted her. "There's got to be something worth watching." After a few dozen clicks, the phone rang.

It was Arthur.

She stared at his name on the little plastic screen on the phone. It rang again. *What would I say?* "Don't be such a coward." She picked up the phone and squeaked out a hello.

"I'd like to see you. How about Wednesday?"

Her chest tightened. "My daughter's coming to town."

"I thought she was there last night?"

"Last night? Oh, yes. She—cancelled." *Damn it. This lying stuff is hard.*

"How about the weekend?"

That's too soon. "I'll have to let you know."

A long silence. "Okay. I'll phone you Friday."

"Ah—if I'm out, leave a message."

"I'll do that." He hung up.

Cynthia stared at the buzzing phone. *What the hell am I doing? Am I nuts? Why am I pushing this incredible man away?*

Her mind spun in circles. She had long reconciled to being alone but since Arthur had appeared in her life, old thoughts had been snaking their way to the surface, demanding to be looked at, addressed. And her body was sending out new messages. Messages of wanting to be held and touched and…more.

She banged the phone on the cradle and stabbed the TV sound on, bringing up Netflix. Nothing interested her. She turned it off and ran upstairs.

Reading always took her mind off things. She picked up the latest library book, but even that didn't distract her spinning mind and churning stomach.

On Tuesday she had a late breakfast and sorted out another cupboard in the kitchen. She set up the ironing board and ironed three cotton shirts that didn't need ironing. Clients' monthly inputs had to be done but maybe she should wax the floor.

She stopped and put her hands on her hips. "Okay. Minou. What's up with all this?"

The cat stared up at her, sauntered into the living room and jumped into a soft chair. Cynthia followed and sat in the other one. "Eventually, I'm going to run out of activities and I'll have to face my thoughts—and my fears."

At least two of her worries had lessened. She now had a six months reprieve on losing her house, and her mother had not asked again for paper proof that she was an honest woman. However, two major items still loomed. Both of them spluttered and bubbled in the background of her mind: Arthur and painting.

"With Arthur, I'm scared and confused. With painting, I'm scared and wondering if I'm any good."

She went to the kitchen and put the kettle on. *The planets or stars must be in some sort of crazy alignment to have so many challenges coming to a head.* She'd had a few years of therapy and had read enough books to be a psychologist herself.

She poured out a cup of Licorice tea and headed for her office. Maybe work will take my mind off my blasted fears.

She opened her computer and clicked on Quick Books. After an hour of entering monthly totals, she pushed her chair back, stretched and stared at the column of numbers in front of her. "I need a cup of coffee."

Since it was lunch time she also had a sandwich. She sat at the kitchen table with her hands around the hot mug and stared out the window but looked inward. *Why am I so afraid of intimacy? I'm a grown woman. So what if I haven't had much experience with men?* It had taken alcohol and a willing shoulder to cry on to temporarily break down the barbed-wire barrier of sex. And from that half-forgotten night of sin, her life had purpose. She had Stephanie to love and to love her. *I don't need anyone or anything else?*

When she was a teenager, on most Saturday nights, Madison and Patricia would be on their dates, their mother visiting Mrs. Pefferlaw next door, and she would play chess with her dad.

Arthur reminded her of her dad. He was gentle and loving and looked at her with affection. But last Sunday, on the Glen Williams bridge, Arthur was nothing like her father. And she wanted to be kissed like that again—and to kiss him back.

So why am I pushing him away? Maybe she should go back and see that psychiatrist again. She finished her sandwich and drained the last drop in her mug. "Back to work, Minou."

After ten minutes at the computer, she glanced out the window. May buds sprouted on the lilac bush. In a week they would be in full bloom, filling her office with their sweet and heady aroma. Lilacs had always been her most favourite spring smell and five years ago, she had planted the soon to be flowering bush right outside her office window.

She turned back to the computer screen but in another ten minutes looked out the window again at the lilacs buds ready to burst. It was no wonder perfumers used that scent.

At two-thirty, she shut the computer. "That's enough."

She took her dish and cup to the kitchen. A clean oval plate sat at the back of the counter. On it was a credit card and a single paint brush. Crumpled beside it was a balled up dish cloth, streaked with a jumble of dried paint.

She picked up the cloth and threw it in the garbage. She slammed the lid shut. Who did she think she was flinging paint about with such wild abandon? Sara Jane was wrong taking those two paintings away. Who would ever buy them?

She picked up the brush and felt the bristles. Clean and waiting. She picked up the credit card. Expired but a great paint tool. *Who cares if no one likes what I paint?* "The art store is open. Maybe I'll buy one more canvas."

The phone rang. She groaned. She could let it ring, but her mother would only keep pestering her until she answered.

"Hello, mother."

"You're a sly one."

"What do you mean?"

"Stephanie was not early as you told everyone."

The words, and something in her mother's voice, made Cynthia's stomach drop. The tiny hairs on the back of her neck quivered to life. She took a deep breath and said, as calmly as she could, "What on earth are you talking about?"

Chapter 22

Cynthia held the receiver tightly. *I shouldn't have answered it.*

Her mother continued. "I made a little trip to Women's College Hospital in Toronto and after paying a small fee to the records department, I received some interesting information about the birth of a one Stephanie Roberts."

Cynthia's heart doubled its beating time. "How dare you. That's none of your business."

"Indeed it is. Stephanie is my granddaughter and a grandmother has some rights"

Cynthia face grew hot and her hands clammy.

"The records stated a full term baby."

"So what?"

"So what?" her mother yelled. "You said Stephanie was born a month early. If you add a month on, that was exactly the time of my wedding to Frank."

Cynthia gripped the phone even tighter. .

Her mother's domineering and accusing voice, pulling on Cynthia's puppet strings, continued. "I thought back, and you weren't dating anyone then. As if you ever did. And I don't remember any Evan Roberts, who you named as the father."

Cynthia gasped. She should have left that blank.

"Who is this Evan Roberts?" A long silence. "I am beginning to think that this so-called *husband* of yours was a phantom.

Cynthia's mind scrambled to find the words, any words.

"Wasn't there an Evan at my wedding?"

Cynthia said nothing.

"Yes, I believe there was. An Evan from England. A relative of Frank's."

Cynthia prayed her mother wouldn't put two and two together.

"I remember now. Evan was Frank's brother, so how could his name be Roberts? Did you make that up?"

Cynthia held her breath. *Don't go any further.*

"Well, say something," her mother commanded.

The blood thundered in Cynthia's ears and her hands trembled. "You seem to have it all figured out, Mother. What can I say?"

"You can admit that this Evan person is the father of your child." She gasped and her voicer rose. "Oh, no. That can't be. The Evan who came to the wedding was your uncle."

Cynthia sank into a kitchen chair, her legs weak.

"Tell me there is another Evan—a real Evan Roberts, even though I never met him." Her voice sounded desperate.

I could lie. I should lie. I should say there was another man named Evan Roberts. That I met him after the wedding while they were on their honeymoon. She said nothing.

"What have you done?" her mother half screamed. "How could you? It's like sleeping with your father!"

Cynthia had to speak. To say nothing implied the truth. *But it is the truth.* Her mouth was so dry she doubted she could speak.

"Does Stephanie know?"

"No. And do not tell her."

"She is entitled to know." Her mother's callous, conniving, 'I told you so,' voice was back.

Cynthia's head roared, her heart raced and her hand cramped. She released her hold on the telephone and in one red instant, she knew why most homicides were domestic violence. Through clenched teeth, she said, "Do not speak to my daughter about this."

"We'll see about that."

"Mother—"

With a crash of bangles, Josephine Marshall hung up.

The buzz in Cynthia's hand turned to a repetitive beep. She slammed the receiver in its holder, and slapped both hands over her mouth as if to trap forbidden words from ever being uttered. But they had. The one person who should never know, did.

She put her hands on each side of her head and squeezed, trying to push her mother's words away.

She stopped. "I know you too well, mother." She yanked the phone receiver out of its stand and hit the speed dial of her daughter's number. "Damn, damn, damn. I should have told her years ago." *Voice mail. Damn it. I can't tell her in a message.*

She tried to make her voice sound normal. "Hi, Steph. Can you come over for dinner tonight? Or I can go to your place. I need to see you."

She hung up. *I should have calmed down first. Stephanie can read my voice.* Surely, her mother wouldn't dare tell Stephanie.

She stood up and paced back and forth. "That's exactly what she would do, Minou. Damn it. I'll drive to Aurora. Right now."

She ran out of the kitchen and grabbed her purse and keys. At the front door, she stopped. "What if they're out?" *Don't go off half cocked. If you drive in this condition you could have an accident.*

She stood still for several long moments, taking deep breaths.

The phone rang. She grabbed the living room one. It was Stephanie.

"Hi mom, what's up with the urgent invitation."

Cynthia sat down in her chair and took another deep breath. "Not urgent, but important." She didn't want Stephanie to panic. "I'd like to seen you as soon as possible."

"Sounds mysterious but I can't tonight. Mark and I are on the way to Collingwood for two days."

Cynthia gulped. "Collingwood? For two whole days."

"There's a pottery show I want to see and we thought we'd take another day to chill. We'll be back Thursday morning so how about lunch then?"

Cynthia thought fast. It was Tuesday and she was sure her mother didn't have Stephanie's cell number so she couldn't reach her by then. "Thursday. Okay. I'll come to you."

"That's a long way for you, mom. I'll come to Guelph and I can pop in to see Aunt Maddy after lunch."

"Okay. See you at twelve. Sharp."

They hung up and Cynthia went to the kitchen and poured herself a tall glass of wine. "Too bad I don't drink the hard stuff. I could sure use it now."

She took her glass upstairs and sat in her chair by the window. The sun caught the crystal, making rainbows over the dragonfly.

Cynthia picked up the dragonfly. It's wings shone yellow and blue.

She tilted her hand back and forth, making the colours flicker and dance over it. "Dear Dragonfly. Give me strength."

A half hour later, calmer and the glass empty, Cynthia went downstairs. The paint brush and the credit card still lay on the while oval dish. She wanted to call Arthur. To cry on his shoulder and have him say that everything was all right. She took a deep breath. That wasn't going to happen.

She put down the glass and picked up the brush. Twirled it. Put it down and walked to the front hall where she grabbed her purse and keys.

At the Wyndham Art store she chose four stretched canvases, each two by three feet, and a couple of wide brushes—a two inch and a four inch. The acrylic paint also came in a larger size and she picked out several to replace the used tubes. She also added: Magenta, Phthalo Green, Raw and Burnt Umber, Payne's Gray,

Mars Black, and Renaissance Gold: names that made her spine tingle. She didn't look twice at the amount when he rang it up.

It took two trips to bring the canvases and art supplies into the house and stow them in a corner of the kitchen. It would be easier to clean up if she were closer to water, and the bathroom was too small to paint in.

It was now supper time and she was exhausted. Her stomach churned. Was she hungry or emotionally drained?

She didn't feel like painting or eating. She ran a bath, poured two cups of Epsom salts into it, put on Mahler's Fifth Symphony and immersed herself in a hot tub for an hour. She kept adding hot water and letting out the tepid, until her fingers tips were crinkled like overused tissue paper.

On Wednesday morning when she was in the shower, Arthur phoned and left a message. 'How are you? Phone me. '

She did want to. And she would. Right after she'd talked with Stephanie.

She moved the canvases to the laundry room off the kitchen, leaned them against the washing machine and went to her office. After the April rush, things had quieted down but there were her regular client's data to input. Painting would also have to wait until after her visit with Stephanie the next day.

What should I say? "By the way, your father is your uncle?"

She slammed the computer shut and went to the kitchen. She'd already had her morning coffee so she yanked down a mason jar of dried mint leaves from her garden, crumbled a handful into a blue pottery mug, and plugged in the kettle.

When Stephanie became a teen, Cynthia had not wanted to parrot her mother so she never told her that sex was bad or that boys only wanted one thing. But old irrational fears still slipped out when Stephanie became interested in the opposite sex.

"You want to go to a dance?" Cynthia had said, her voice rising. "But you're only fourteen."

"All the girls are going. It's a group dance."

"But—" She should have warned her about boys.

Ten years later came the serious romance.

"You're moving in with him!" Again, said in that rising voice of incredulity. "But—but—"

"Mom, we're engaged. I love him. I'm on the pill. Don't worry."

Cynthia had no reasonable argument to offer, only the craziness from her haunted past. And her daughter had turned out all right, but would she understand about her father?

She turned her attention to the steaming kettle and poured bubbling water over the leaves, stirring them before they sank to the bottom. Years ago she had gone to a tea leaf reader. One of those silly things you do with your girlfriends. The reader said Cynthia was going to meet a past love. Cynthia had snorted at that. She had no past love. At least not in this lifetime.

Sitting in her kitchen now, she stared at the spoon as she stirred it around and around in slow circles.

Years—decades—centuries fell away. A weird sensation of growing larger and taller spread over her. From a far height, she looked down at the shrunken kitchen counter and at her giant hand holding the tiny spoon. A rush of lightness filled her body and ribbons of joy streamed out through the top of her head. As the spoon continued its mesmerizing spiral, a far away voice echoed from an endless tunnel, *You will have your true love. For eternity.*

With a jerk, the spoon flew from her hand and clattered to the floor. In that instant, she was her normal size again.

Did I hear a voice?

On wobbly legs, more stunned than scared, she took her tea to the living room and set it on the coffee table. The reflection of the curling steam and blurred blue mug descended through the glass and intersected with the *Cineplex* magazine on the shelf below. Two realities overlapping.

She sat down and Minou jumped up on her lap. "Hello there, cat. You're real."

She sipped her tea and stroked the purring animal. *Am I going crazy? Or senile?* She looked around the room. A flagstone hearth, the Victorian love Seat, Van Gogh's sunflowers on the wall, drapes she'd made from Indian cotton bedspreads.

She was here in her house on Glasgow Street in Guelph, Ontario, Canada. *All is well.* She shook her head, flinging cobwebs and hallucinations away.

She drained her cup and got up. "Excuse me, Minou. I have to make my special chilli for tomorrow. I have an important meeting with my daughter."

Chapter 23

By twelve-thirty on Thursday, the chilli was hot, salad out, and the table set, with a crusty loaf on the bread board. Cynthia had also washed her breakfast dishes, tidied the counters, alphabetized her spices and checked her email three times.

At a quarter-to-one the door opened and slammed with a bang making the windows rattle. Stephanie's voice easily made its way to the kitchen. "Why didn't you tell me!"

Cynthia threw the dish towel on the counter and raced from the kitchen. *Surely my mother wouldn't have—* When she saw her daughter she knew she had.

Stephanie threw her purse at the hall table, sending envelopes and pens scattering. With hair flying, her face red, and shoulders heaving with every breath, she stomped into the living room and stopped dead in the centre of it.

"Stephanie, I—" Cynthia stepped toward her.

"Don't Stephanie me, and don't touch me." She stepped back and with eyes blazing, cried, "I had to hear it from my grandmother that I'm illegitimate. And that my father is a—a relative!" She yelled the last word even louder. "How could you not tell me?" She folded her arms across her chest as if trying to stop herself from flying apart.

Cynthia gasped. Her knees turned to rubber and she stumbled into the nearest chair. The love seat. *How dare she. I will kill that woman!* "Your grandmother told you?"

Stephanie thrust her arms wide. "Yes, she told me." Her eyes were still on fire. "*She* told me. I can't believe this. All these years, you've been lying to me!" Her piercing yes demanded answers. "How could you betray me!"

A sharp pain stabbed Cynthia's heart. She breathed in sharply and slapped a hand to her chest. *It would serve me right if I drop dead right now.* She opened her mouth to speak but Stephanie raged on.

"She phoned me three times over the last two days to come and see her. She said it was important so I went before I came here." She took two hard steps to the fireplace, swung around and faced her mother again. "But I guess it wasn't important to you," she snapped. "Wasn't important enough to tell me—your own daughter—the horrible truth about my birth."

A sick feeling in Cynthia's stomach joined the ache in her body. "Of course it was important to me. Your grandmother shouldn't have told you." She put her hands on her head trying to hold the guilty thoughts at bay. "Steph. I'm so sorry. I should have told you a long time ago. I meant to." She patted the seat beside her. "Sit down."

Stephanie lifted her chin. "I'll stand, thank you." Her voice was cold. She folded her arms again and her frown deepened. Her chest rose and fell with rapid breathing.

Cynthia took a deep breath. The knives in her heart made her catch her breath. She had dreaded this moment and here it was. "I—I..." She covered her hand with her mouth. She never meant to hurt her beloved daughter. She would die for her and yet she had caused her all this pain.

Stephanie's eyes flamed. "Well, is it true?"

"It—it happened at your grandmother's wedding."

"Yeah, Grandma told me that."

"She shouldn't have told you anything."

"Well, somebody should have." The glare never left her eyes

"I was going to tell you. I wanted to so many times." Her stomach twisted as if it were gathering speed to throw up.

"Yeah, well, she beat you to it."

Cynthia picked up the cushion beside her and pressed it against her chest. "The time never seemed right." How could she explain? She had lived the lie so long, she had half fooled herself that the public story was the truth.

"For my own sanity, tell me how close the relationship is between you and my father." She poked her head forward like an angry bird ready to peck an enemy.

"Didn't your grandmother tell you?" How could her mother have been so spiteful?

"She said she wanted to give you the pleasure."

Cynthia frowned. "I bet she did."

"I don't want to get into the crazy relationship you have with your mother. Just tell me the truth. I need to know." She threw herself on the chair opposite, swung one leg over the other and crossed her arms again. Her top leg swung rapidly up and down.

Cynthia took a deep breath. "Remember Frank? You were only five when he died."

Stephanie's eyes bulged. "Grandpa Frank? You slept with Grandpa Frank?"

"No, no. Not Grandpa Frank."

"Well, why did you mention him?"

Cynthia looked her daughter straight in the eyes. She owed her the truth, no matter what. "Your father is Grandpa Frank's brother." Relief washed over her on hearing the long held back words come out of her mouth.

Stephanie's forehead creased. "My grandfather's brother is my father?" She looked away for a second. "But that means he's your uncle. Is that true?"

"Yes." Cynthia whispered, and pulled at a loose thread which hung from the seam of the pillow she grasped. It remained stuck.

"Pardon?"

"I said yes."The fierce ache in Cynthia's head thumped louder filling her whole skull.

"But that means my father is also my—uncle. My great uncle?"

Cynthia didn't speak for several moments. "I'm afraid so."

It was Stephanie's turn to slap her hand over her mouth. Her eyes flicked from side to side. "Isn't that too close? Like sleeping with a brother or a father?" Her voice broke and tears welled in her eyes.

"You've turned out all right."

Stephanie slapped her hands onto the arms of her chair. "But what about *my* babies? Did you never think I might want children?" She stifled a sob. "That Mark and I—" Her eyes flamed again. "You should have told me before I married. This is terrible. How can I ever tell Mark?"

Minou jumped up on Stephanie's lap and pushed her head against her arm. Stephanie released one hand and patted the cat. She yanked a Kleenex from a nearby box. "I can't believe you've done this to me."

They sat in silence.

The cat purred.

The clock ticked louder.

Stephanie blew her nose again.

Cynthia's heart ached for causing her daughter such agony. "I'm so sorry. I was selfish and ashamed to tell you the truth."

The cat purred loudly as Stephanie's shaking hand moved over its back. In a strained voice, she said, "I can't think anymore. I feel sick." She got up and the cat jumped to the floor. "I have to go."

"Don't go. I made lunch. We have to work through this." Cynthia stood up and reached out a hand.

"I'm not hungry and I don't know how I can ever forgive you for not telling me."

Cynthia's held back tears fell over her cheeks. "Please. You're my daughter. I love you. I didn't mean to hurt you."

Stephanie backed away and strode into the hall. "I can't talk anymore. I can't even think." She grabbed her purse, flung open the door and stomped out.

Cynthia watched her get into her car and pull away. Her heart ached as if it were being wretched from her chest. A hollow place dropped into her stomach and futile words crammed her head, tumbling over each other, trying to find new ways to explain the unexplainable.

She closed the door, her whole body aching. The phone rang and she blinked through wet eyes. Arthur's number. She reached out with a shaking hand.

She wanted to talk to him. To hear his voice. She needed to talk to him. To tell him her daughter would probably never speak to her again.

Her heart lurched and she drew her hand back and walked into the living room. She sat down in her chair, yanked out a Kleenex and wiped her eyes. After five rings, voice mail clicked in.

Would her daughter ever forgive her? Would she ever forgive herself?. *I should have told her the truth. Years ago.*

The cat jumped up on her lap and settled in. The hollow place inside Cynthia swelled, filling her with more emptiness. She was a balloon stretching more and more, soon to burst into a billion pieces and spread throughout the universe. No one would ever find her. Not Stephanie. Not Arthur. Not Maddy. No one she loved would find her. She wouldn't even find herself.

She stayed in that floaty, nowhere space for a time that didn't move. The clock struck without meaning. Her fingers touched the cat's fur with feeling it.

In the far distance a constant dinging sounded. She shook her head. What was that? *The chilli! I left it on low.* In a semi-stupor she walked to the kitchen, turned the timer and the burner off.

She stared at the chilli pot. Chilli she had made for Stephanie. She wasn't hungry. *I suppose I should eat something.* Like a marionette, she ladled out a half scoop. The cayenne pepper was on the table and she shook it over her bowl. She forked some wilted salad onto a side plate.

She picked up the serrated bread knife and pressed down on the thick crusty loaf, nicking the side of her thumb. "Ow." She dropped the knife and it clattered to the table.

A thin line of blood seeped out. She wasn't full of nothing. She could still bleed. Maybe she could feel again. She stuck her thumb under the tap, wrapped a Kleenex around it and secured it with a strip of masking tape. She sat down to eat.

The chilli made her eyes water, the salad was soggy, and the bread had spots of blood on it. She grabbed her bowl, salad plate and utensils and tossed them into the sink. She went to the freezer and pulled out a pint of chocolate gelato.

With a soup spoon clutched in one hand and the cold carton in the other, she stomped upstairs to her bedroom and fell into her wicker chair.

"I was going to introduce Stephanie to Italian ice cream," she said to her dragonfly. She flipped off the lid and dug the spoon in. "She's probably tried it already."

She thought she had no tears left, but each watery spoonful of gelato tasted salty and the wet Kleenex on her thumb kept slipping.

She finished the gelato. Her gut ached and her head pounded. The make-shift bandage fell off and fresh blood oozed from the cut. *I should put a bandaid on that.* She stuck her thumb into her mouth.

The downstairs clock chimed three. *Who cares what time it is? What difference does it make? What difference does anything make?*

She sat for several moments looking at nothing, her mind incapable of thought. Her body made of straw. Dried and empty stalks with sharp ends piercing every pore.

She took her thumb out. The thin pink line grew red again. She grabbed another Kleenex. "I guess I'm still alive after all."

On stiff legs she went downstairs to the kitchen and a sink full of messy dishes. She put the lid on the chilli and shoved the whole pot into the fridge. Holding the wrapping on her stinging thumb, she stared at the spotted bread and the serrated knife beside it.

A tiny part of her whispered from far away. "Leave all this now. Go to sleep."

Tomorrow is another day.

The small voice whispered again. "*And put a bandaid on your thumb.*"

She found some bandaids in her newly organized junk drawer, however, none was big enough to cover a ripped heart.

She pasted one on her thumb, went upstairs, crawled into bed fully dressed and pulled the covers over her head.

Chapter 24

She woke at two a.m., stumbled to the bathroom and changed into a nightgown. Her body ached as if someone had punched her in the stomach.

When she awoke again at seven she lay in bed for a long time. Thoughts whirled around her head. *It's happened. Stephanie knows the truth. The horrible, shameful, unforgiving truth had been ripped out.* Like when her father had died it was as if a piece of her had been torn away leaving broken tentacles undulating inside her gut, reaching out to touch something real.

She got out of bed and walked woodenly to the shower. She stood under it for a long time. If only water could wash away a lifetime of holding so tightly onto her dreadful secret. *But was it, or is it, so dreadful?* Yes, it was that she hadn't told Stephanie, but as Sara Jane said, it's not big deal now to have a child without the sanction of a legal union.

She dried herself off, put on a track suit and went downstairs where she made a pot of coffee. Two cups later, she was still sitting at the kitchen table staring out the window at the spring growth bursting into life. *Plants die and come back. Can I?*

Her gaze moved from the window to the table top. A mucky mess of salad lay flat and forlorn at the bottom of the large bowl. She picked up the bowl and opened the small compost bucket on the counter. It was full so she took it and the limp salad out the back door and emptied them both into the large green drum.

Coming back through the laundry room, she passed the four new canvases leaning against the washing machine. She took a step back and stared at them.

Am I an artist? What does that mean anyway?

Sara Jane had said she was. "A freakin' artist," Cynthia said out loud.

She put the bucket and bowl down, picked up a canvas and brought it into the kitchen. She shoved the salt and pepper aside, and laid it on the table.

"I could pretend to be one."

She moved two kitchen chairs off to the side, took the new tubes and brushes from the Wyndham Arts paper bag which was still sitting on the counter and placed them on the table.

"Who cares anyway? I'll paint something just for me."

She went upstairs, gathered up her half-used tubes and her largest paint brush and detoured into her bedroom. At the window sill, she picked up the dragonfly. "C'mon, my friend. Let's paint." *I need something to take my mind off whether my daughter will ever speak to me again. And what difference does it make now where I live.*

She leaned the dragonfly against the pepper mill and pulled out a wooden spoon and plastic spatula from the jug sitting beside the toaster.

She squeezed a thick dollop of Alizarin Crimson in the centre of the white expanse and with a slash of the spatula, swished a stain of angry red across the surface. *I know I should have told her sooner.* With each swipe of paint, another thought darted through her mind. *But I didn't.* She slapped a thick glob of dense Mars Black against one ragged edge. *Well, it's not the end of my life.* A swipe of Payne's Gray—a bluish gray that made great shadows, landed on the other side. *It's time for me to come out of the shadows, wake up and stop feeling so damn guilty or inadequate.*

She dropped the spatula and picked up the credit card. *So, I made a mistake. A big one. But I am human aren't I?.*

"I'm sick of feeling like a victim." She splashed on another streak of Mr. Payne's shadowy gray.

"One mistake and I've been hiding out ever since."Scrape, went the credit card.

"Hiding from men." Stabs of serious navy blues and dark browns hit the canvas.

"Hiding from life." Slashes of deep reds and bright yellows swiped through.

"Hiding from myself." A puddle of green writhed its way in like a startled snake.

"Enough is enough. This is my life and I'm going to live it."

In a flurry of pouring, dribbling and throwing paint, the shapes grew, slid, formed and reformed. Large and threatening one instant, and in the next, rivers of blood and cowering valleys of putrid green.

She stopped and stared at the frenzied slashes of colours and streaks of midnight black. Minou had long ago fled.

"What do you think, Dragonfly?"She tilted her head and grimaced. "Okay. I guess I don't have to take it out on the canvas."

She set that one on the stove top and fetched another from the back room which she placed on the table. Arthur's face drifted across her mind's eye. She picked up a tube of soft blue and with her new two inch brush, stroked gentle waves across the canvas. Next came clouds of pure white and flecks of deep green. Small splashes of pinks, emeralds and jade, dripped and wound through the blues and whites.

She stepped back and looked at that one. *Are you finished?*

She tilted her head one way and the other. *Maybe.*

She picked it up carefully and laid it on top of the counter.

I'll revisit you later.

On the third canvas she danced the loaded spatula and the wooden spoon across the bouncing canvas, letting the painting tell her where it wanted to go.

The colours called to her. Pick me, said the bold Burnt Umber. No, me, hollered a saucy red. "Everybody will get a turn," she promised as she added a dash of soaring sky blue. Each colour sang their own song, while a touch here and there of Renaissance Gold suggested treasures hidden within.

A concentrated fifteen minutes later, she set that canvas on the other counter and returned to the Arthur painting. *I thought you had more to say.*

With the edge of the credit card, she cut in gold and red spears —or were they spires? Yellow curves, white burbling waves, blues, greens, gold, repeating, overlapping, growing and exploding in bursts of colour.

After twenty minutes, she put it on the dryer in the laundry room and shut the door. Minou loved to sleep on a warm pile of clothes on top of the dryer and Cynthia didn't want kitty paws added to her masterpiece.

The first wild painting lay on the stove, its fierce slashes yelling at her. She picked it up and tilted it back and forth.

"Are you a disaster or what?" *I'll have to sleep on that one.* "Figuratively, of course."

She took it to the laundry room and placed it on the washer. *Who cares what Sara Jane or her friend thinks? Or if anybody likes them.*

She picked up the last one from the kitchen counter and put it on the ironing board. Before she closed the door for the last time, she looked at the remaining blank canvas leaning against the washing machine. *Another day for you.*

After screwing on tops and washing the spoon, spatula and credit card, she put water on for coffee. While it dripped, she gathered her paints and tools and put them on a shelf in the laundry room beside the soap.

She poured coffee into her dolphin mug and took it and her dragonfly upstairs to her wicker chair. Her sitting chair, she called it. A place to sit and think. To be. She set the mug on the window sill and her dragonfly in its place beside the crystal.

After that wild and furious painting session, she was strangely relieved, as if a great load had been lifted—no—wrenched from her insides. The tearing exposure of her dastardly secret still hurt, but now it was more of a dull ache. A queer sort of empty feeling. She had been vigilant for so long in keeping her scandalous secret hidden but now the guards to her inner chamber had been released from active duty and were happy to get on with their lives.

Her birthmark has been gone for twenty-five years. Her dreaded secret about Stephanie had been revealed. She had no more to hide. No more to run from. No more excuses.

She picked up her mug and took a drink of coffee. Her jeans and shirt were a designer's nightmare. Dried splotches and splashes. Streaks and spots. Reds, blues, and greens darted through folds and creases, creating their own story.

"Looks like I have another set of paint clothes."

She sipped the hot liquid. Outside the window, clusters of purple flowers blossomed on the lilac bush.

She put her cup back on the sill and lifted the window open a crack. A gust of cool air brought in the sweet and exhilarating smell. She closed her eyes as she breathed in. An old memory drifted over her. A special memory from long ago which warmed her heart.

Her brain drifted, remembering…looking inward or backward —seeking and sifting. A seed of a sensation settled inside her and fluttered to life. It started at her toes and crawled up her legs. It crept up her backbone, gathering momentum at her solar plexus.

When it reached the top of her head, a gush of joy erupted in an overwhelming epiphany. A great light filled her and she drew in a deep breath allowing this new self to settle in. A new self of relentless courage and everlasting confidence.

Her eyes flashed open and she snatched the dragonfly from its resting place on the sill. "Okay, my beautiful dragonfly. Enough of being old scared Cynthia." A waft of lilac air brushed by her. " I am not her anymore." And with a smile as wide as the Cheshire Cat, she said, "I'm going to change my name."

She lifted her chin and raised the dragonfly high. "Thea. I am now Thea." She stood and lifted her arms. "No more Cynthia. No more Cyn in my life. Time to let go of the shame."

"I now declare myself a new woman." She held the dragonfly to her heart for a moment, letting a new self settle in.

"Thank you, dragonfly." She placed it beside the glittering quartz crystal. "I think I'm going to like Thea."

She smiled. "Thea Marshall. I like the sound of that."

She would not tell anyone her new name yet. She wanted to hold it to herself for a little longer. Grow into it. Savour it. Be it.

Chapter 25

The next day, Cynthia—or was it Thea?—awoke with a scramble of feelings vying for attention.

The elated part wanted to scream from the rooftops that she was free, while another part wept for her daughter's pain .

She glanced at the clock. Too early to try Stephanie again. Yesterday, Cynthia had let voice mail take the incoming calls but today she would answer the phone.

After a shower and quick breakfast, she punched in Stephanie's number. It went immediately to voice mail. She left a massage to please call.

She continued to jump from being a new Thea—or wanting to —to being a distraught Cynthia about her daughter's angry distance. It was harder than she thought to let go of Cynthia. *If only I could talk to Stephanie.* She hadn't even responded to emails.

Arthur had not called again either but Cynthia/Thea did not want to talk to him until she had sorted out the mess over Stephanie. His last message was to call him when she was ready. So why would he call again? He sounded fed up. A Cynthia spear of anxiety pricked at her. *Why am I ignoring him? Am I insane?*

She put the phone down. *Perhaps it's better this way.* What would he think when he found out she had been living a lie? He might not want to ever see her again.

It was going to take some practice being Thea and the elation of yesterday's painting session slid into a black hole of oblivion.

Right now, Stephanie was uppermost in her thoughts and she pushed her feelings about Arthur into a back corner. As she recalled Stephanie's reaction, the dull ache elbowed itself forward in a sharp and relentless stabbing.

Of the double barrelled sin, it wasn't the unwed part that's the most devastating but who the father is. Can she be put in jail for that? *I've got to check that out.*

Law or no law, how could she be Thea with her daughter hating her? And Arthur too when he finds out. Her stomach churned and the fist, holding her heart captive, tightened.

Arthur will never see me again and my daughter will hate me.

She banged the arm of the chair. "I could kill my mother for opening this can of worms." She jumped up, darted to the kitchen, and splashed cold water on her face.

She hung over the sink for several moments, tears and tap water dripping off her face. *Get hold of yourself.* She grabbed a towel and buried her face in it.

She poured another cup of coffee and took it to her office. On automatic pilot she opened her lap top, clicked Quick books, selected a client and immersed herself in setting up a file. Downloading documents and tediously inserting data kept the black thoughts that threatened to overwhelm her at bay.

Somehow the day ended. Did she even have lunch or supper? She fell into bed exhausted and sleep finally took over, fading the constant seesawing in her head into oblivion.

The next morning was no better. A step forward was immediately followed with a step back, which kept her at dead centre—stuck in a mire of confusion and desire.

Maybe a walk to the market will help.

She arrived home at mid-morning and was depositing produce on the kitchen counter when the phone rang.

Arthur? Or Stephanie? She ran to it and grabbed it up.

Stephanie was short and abrupt. "I'll be there in an hour-and-a-half."

Cynthia dumped the apples in the crisper, put salad greens away, hung the string bags on the door knob and grabbed the coffee beans. Keeping her hands busy left her mind free to go over Stephanie's phone call. Her voice had been neutral. Not angry but not forgiving. *Okay, Thea. We can handle this.*

She had not mentioned anything to her sisters about their mother's discovery although she suspected her mother had already filled them in. Madison, of course, had known the truth from the beginning, but Patricia's response would be the same as her mothers. *What will people think?*

Now that Stephanie knew the truth, Thea didn't care what anyone else thought.

That wasn't true. *I do care what Arthur would think.* But she couldn't dwell on that now. She put on the coffee. *What if my mother tells the authorities, I could be imprisoned for fourteen years.*

Her mother would not, could not, keep a secret. With a shaking hand, she poured water into the pot. Sara Jane's sister was a lawyer. Maybe she could help.

Stephanie arrived ten minutes early. She rang the bell, stepped inside and stood in the hallway.

Thea hesitated, took a step toward her. "I'm so sorry, Stephanie." She held her breath. *I don't blame her if she says she never wants see me again.*

Stephanie put her purse on the hall table. "I can't believe you waited so long before you told me."

Thea clasped her hands together. "I should have. There never seemed to be the right moment." *Dammit. Why didn't I tell her when she was sixteen like I planned to?*

Stephanie took off her sweater and hung it on the coat tree. "We've always been so close. That was a mighty big secret to keep from me."

"You're absolutely right. I don't blame you for being angry."

"I was angry at first. Shocked and angry, but—"

Thea didn't move. *Will she forgive me?*

Stephanie stepped toward her mother and put her arms out.

With a catch in her throat, Thea returned the embrace.

They were the same height for a comfortable and easy hug. "Maybe I wasn't ready to hear it when I was younger," said Stephanie.

Thea swallowed a sob and hugged her daughter harder.

When they finally let go, Stephanie looped her arm in her mother's. They walked into the living room and sat on the love seat. Minou jumped up onto Stephanie's lap.

Stephanie held her mom's hand and petted the cat with the other. "I've done a lot of thinking over these last three days."

Thea grabbed a couple of tissues from the box. "I'll answer any questions you have."

"First, I have to say, how smart it was of you to change your name and pretend you were married. You must have been in a panic of what to do. Especially with your mom being so strict."

Thea blew her nose. "I did have some terrifying moments. Sometimes the humiliation is worse than the sin."

"Times sure have changed. It's no big deal now to have a baby before you're married."

Neither of them spoke for several minutes before Stephanie said, "Have you seen my father since?"

"No." *I will be honest from now on.*

"Grandma said the name Evan Roberts was on the birth certificate."

"Yes. I made up the Roberts, of course."

Stephanie tilted her head. "I don't remember when your last name was Roberts."

"I didn't keep it for long. I wanted my dad's name back for me and for you, so I took Marshall back when you were two."

"Is he—Evan—still alive?'

"I don't know."*I should have kept in touch with him.*

"Where does, or did, he live?"

"Twenty-eight years ago, when you were born, he lived in England."

Stephanie's forehead wrinkled. "Does he know about me?"

"No."Cynthia frowned. *Was I wrong in not letting him know?*

"Why didn't you tell him?"

Cynthia shifted in her seat. "I was too ashamed and scared. Not ashamed of you but ashamed of not being married. I also worried if him being an uncle was too close a relationship."

"Did you ever wonder if I would be—all right?"

"That's a good question. Whenever I did wonder, I would sit quietly and ask if you would be okay, and I always got a resounding yes."

"You mean you heard a voice?" She wrinkled her forehead.

"Not a real voice. Kind of like a voice within and from a far-away place in the mists of time."

"That's weird."

"Maybe. But it comforted me and gave me strength to go on."

They were both quiet again. Stephanie stroked the purring cat for a long while before she lifted her head. She straightened her back. "I'm going to find my father."

Cynthia lifted her eyebrows. "But—where—how—."

"Mom. I have to try."

She gulped. "Of course you do." *It was natural that Stephanie would want to meet her father.*

Chapter 26

Stephanie stayed for lunch—an egg salad sandwich and the inevitable gargantuan green salad. After coffee, Cynthia filled the sink with hot soapy water and slid the dishes in.

"Let me wash, mom."

"I was going to let them soak."

"I like to wash." She went to the sink. "Remember when I was four and I would stand on the step-stool? I'm sure I made a mess."

"The floor usually got a good wash. And you too, up to and beyond your armpits."

"I felt so grown up." She finished the dishes and dried her hands. "What's that?"

Cynthia looked to where she was pointing. "Oh, that. That's a painting." The one that had lived on the stove for two days was now leaning against the wall.

"I can see that." She went over and read the signature in the bottom corner. "Thea Marshall. Who is Thea Marshall?"

"Well—that would be me."

"You? You painted this? You are Thea Marshall?" This time her eyebrows lifted.

"Yes, to both questions."

"When did you do it and when did you become a Thea?"

"Not Athea. Thea." She laughed. "It kinda happened at the same time. After you left and I thought I'd lost you—well, something cracked and out spilled a painting demon named Thea."

"Mom!" She threw herself at her mother, and pulled her into a crushing hug. "Finally! You broke through the wall."

Tears, laughter, more hugs and screams from Stephanie of "no way," "really" and "I can't believe it" followed.

Thea fetched the other painting from the laundry room and as soon as Stephanie saw it, she yelped and grabbed her mother again in a another bear hug which turned into a zany dance.

Ten minutes later, they sat in the living room, hands on their aching stomachs. "I don't think I've ever laughed or cried so much," said Thea.

"Me too," said Stephanie.

"By the way, what did you mean by, 'you broke through the wall?"

"You've always had a stone wall around you. Never letting your creative side out and not letting anything resembling a man in. In fact, It's a miracle I'm even here."

Thea huffed. "Every baby's a miracle."

"That's not what I mean. With your crazy ideas about sex, I'm surprised you ever indulged in the crass act."

"I don't remember much about that night."

"What do you mean?"

"I'd had quite a bit to drink and I wasn't used to drinking."

"You mean I was conceived in a drunken stupor. Mother!"

Thea looked up. Stephanie was not outraged.

She was laughing when she reached for her mother's hand and said, "Well, if it took that to bring me into this world, that's okay."

"I never drank a drop while pregnant." Thea patted her daughter's hand. "And never touched hard liquor since that night."

"Maybe you should. And touch other things too." She winked. "Maybe I would have had siblings."

"Well, it's too late for siblings. Thea shifted in her chair. "But not too late for your mother to have romance."

Stephanie opened her eyes wide. "What do you mean? Have you met someone?" She slapped her knee. "Have you done it with him?"

Thea slapped a hand to her chest. "Stephanie Marie Marsh—Watson. That is none of your business whether I have done "it" with him or not. I am not about to discuss my intimate life with you."

"You can say the word, Mother. Sex. It's natural for Homo sapiens."

"Stop teasing me."

"So tell me about this guy. Who is he? Where did you mean him? And when?"

"We met a couple of weeks ago. On my birthday actually. At the AGO."

"You met a man at the art gallery?"

"Don't be so surprised. I am human."

"I used to wonder."

They both laughed and Stephanie said, "So that's what's melting your walls."

"Well—maybe."

She shook her head and grinned. "My mother. Seeing a man. Now I can believe anything."

Thea frowned. "There's something else."

"You sound serious. What else can there be?"

Thea hesitated, looked away and back at Stephanie. "I could go to prison for fourteen years."

"What? No way. Whatever for?"

She explained the Canadian incest laws and Stephanie said, "Are you sure that old law is still in force?"

"I googled it but couldn't find any dates."

"I'll check it out. Besides, no one has to know but us."

"You forget that your grandmother knows."

"Oh." She narrowed her eyebrows for a moment and brightened. "But surely once Grandma realizes the consequences it could bring to you, she would keep quiet."

Thea snorted. "On the contrary. Once she knows the consequences, she will shout it to all who would hear, a second before she races to the authorities."

"Oh, yeah. You two have this thing going." Stephanie made a steeple with her fingers. "You are *not* going to jail. There's probably a statute of limitations. We'll find the best lawyer and fight this."

"My neighbour's sister is a lawyer. Perhaps she'll help."

Stephanie shook her head. "You are full of surprises. What can happen next?"

Chapter 27

Stephanie left at two. After the roller-coaster of emotions which had swept Cynthia back into feeling like Thea again and fear into forgiving, she needed to engage in some mundane and thoughtless activity to let things settle in. With everything else on her mind, she hadn't thought about her house situation and it was a warm May day. Time to attack last year's dried stems and twitch grass. If she had to move, she wasn't going to leave the garden in a mess. *No more messes in my life.*

She changed into a faded track suit, pulled on her gardening gloves and had her hand on the back door knob when the phone rang.

Arthur's number blinked at her.

It had been a whole week since they'd talked. A whole week since she'd run inside like a startled deer and slammed the door on him.

The second ring.

Every day since, she had wanted to call him. She had picked up the phone numerous times, but never tapped in his number.

A third ring.

She had planned to call him that evening. After letting her reconciliation with Stephanie settle in.

Fourth ring.

She snatched it up, and hit the talk button. "Arthur, I—"

"Do you have five minutes? I'd like to see you."

"You want to drive all the way here to see me for five minutes?" *Is he crazy?*

"I'm already here."

The doorbell rang.

With her phone at her ear, she ran to the front door. *How can he be here? He is crazy.* She opened it as he was returning his cell to his pocket.

She lowered her phone and backed up. She tapped off her handset. "C-come in." She set the phone on the hall table, pulled off her gardening gloves and flopped them on top.

He stepped in. She didn't move. *He's so close—and smells delicious.*

"I only have five minutes."

Her stomach roller-coastered and roared into impossible flip flops. *How could I have ever run from this man?*

"I'm on my way to the airport."

"Isn't this kinda out of your way?" *Where's he going?*

"Do you want to see me or not?" The scar above his right eye allowed only half his eyebrow to lift.

Thea stepped forward, put a hand on each side of his face and kissed him. He grabbed her and kissed back. Her lips parted and she let him in. She pressed against him, her hands moving behind his head, his shoulders, his body, holding him to her, falling into him, becoming him.

A breathless moment later, their mouth's parted but not their bodies. He held her tightly and she didn't leave. She held onto him just as tightly. Another hard and urgent kiss. She pushed into him like an escaped animal broken from its bonds. Seeking, reaching, rushing to freedom.

"I guess that answers my question," he said, breathing hard. "I wish I didn't have to catch that plane."

"Do you have to?" Thea said. Cynthia was definitely gone.

"I'm afraid so. My mother fell and broke her hip. There are complications, andI have to go to Halifax for at least a week." A honk sounded from the waiting car at the curb. He stepped back. "I'll phone. I'll email. I'll Skype. Do you have Skype?"

"I'll get it." *What the heck is skipe?*

He grabbed her and kissed her again. And again, she melted into him, holding and grasping. He broke from her and ran down the walk and jumped into the car.

Thea held onto the side of the door frame. Her body tingled and her thighs quivered. Her heart thrummed and her mind spun as a burgeoning new thought pushed its way up through her brain.

Neurons wriggled their way past hollows and grooves, scrambled over fences, breached iron doors, leapt over mountains and wiggled through gullies until, at last, the new thought came to rest in the front of her mind. *What is that feeling?*

Her heart opened wide and stayed that way and for the first time in her life, she had forgotten she was ugly.

She closed the door, glided upstairs to her bedroom and fell into her chair. *I'm really, honestly, truly okay. Maybe I always have been.* She didn't move or speak or think for a long time.

The dragonfly brooch stared at her from the window sill. She picked it up. "Dragonfly. You were here when Thea emerged. Now I really am her."

She took a deep breath. She could lose her house, she could go to jail for fourteen years and only see Stephanie on visiting days. She could lose Arthur and become a public outcast. Even if all that happened, she was still okay. She was whole. She was here. She had made the choice to step forward. To pick up a paintbrush. To kiss Arthur like there was no tomorrow. *Yes. I am Thea. And I am Here.*

Her heart thumped wildly. She jumped up. "Dragonfly. I need your help to fight this. I've come this far and I won't give up."

There was nothing she could do at the moment. Would her mother raise the alarm or not? *I'll be ready if she does but meanwhile, I have to get on with my life.* She kissed the dragonfly and replaced it on the window sill. *I'm not going to mope around and feel sorry for myself.*

She ran downstairs, grabbed her gardening gloves and raced out the back door. *Those weeds aren't going to pull themselves.* She kneeled at the edge of her herb garden and yanked out a handful.

Perhaps it was the pressure on her knees or the angle of her body or the smell of mint leaves, but a weird sensation enveloped her. It was as if she were part of another person—or a person was a part of her. A person who had done this a thousand times. A long, long time ago. Her fingers, encased in the fat canvas gardening gloves, interlaced themselves and she bowed her head. This other person inside her or around her was praying. Praying to be reunited with her loved ones.

Thea shook off the strange impressions that had come over her. *How bizarre.* The sensation passed but she paused before she grabbed another handful of dried stalks. Funny that she had been reunited with her loved ones.

Stephanie and now Arthur. I must have been identifying myself with some lovesick character in a movie.

She grabbed another thick bundle of stems and yanked. In half an hour she had pulled every dead and encroaching weed from the herb and flower garden, filling three garden bags. One by one she hauled them to the back lane. She was leaning the last bag against the others, when Sara Jane drove in.

She opened her car door. "Looks like you've been busy." She wore a pair of strappy heels and a slim black dress with a silk Chinese stole slung over her shoulders.

Thea peeled off her gardening gloves. "Wow, and it looks like you're somebody else."

"Sometimes, you have to dress the part." She yanked off the shoes and latched them over her purse strap. Peeled off her knee high nylons and, swinging them in one hand, walked bare feet to her gate. "Do you want a coffee?"

"Perfect timing. I've finished cleaning out old dead growth and a bunch of rude weeds who think they can take over."

Sara Jane lifted her eyebrows. "What's gotten into you?"

Thea opened her own gate. "It's what's gotten out. I'll put the water on."

"Can't wait. See you in five." She walked up her path.

Thea called over her fence. "Make it ten. I need a shower."

In fifteen minutes, the coffee was done, Thea had showered, and she and Sara Jane sat in the living room with their feet up. Sara Jane now wore a full skirt, peasant blouse and bare feet.

"My friend likes your paintings," said Sara Jane. "She wants to see more. Bigger ones. Can you manage that?"

"As a matter of fact, not only can I, I have." She got up and brought out one of the canvases she had recently painted. Slashes of wild red, glossy black and vibrant green fought for attention.

"Great God in Heaven. You did this?"

"Yup."She lifted her head. "I did."

"It's better than the first two." She squinted in the bottom corner at the signature. "Thea. I like it." She looked up with a smile. "Yes, you are a Thea."

"I am."

"Do you have any more of these? This painting looks like you're on a roll."

"Yes. Two more." She fetched them from the laundry room.

Sara Jane squealed when she saw them. "These—you—are amazing. I knew there was something inside you panting to get out, but I never—"

She stepped back and tilted her head one way and the other. "What do you call them?"

"You mean I have to name them?" Thea pointed to the one with waves of soft blue, emerald greens, and highlights of gold spears bursting through. "I was thinking of Arthur when I painted this."

Sara Jane winked. "You could call it Love Unrequited."

Thea smiled. "No. I'm going to call it 'Love Found'." Her thoughts jumped back to the hot kisses at her front door. She shoved them aside before her face turned red.

Sara Jane pointed to the next. "And this one?"

Thea turned to the last one she had painted with its gold patches peeking through. *This is fun being Thea. I never know what I'll say next.* "How about 'Undiscovered Treasures'?"

Sara Jane nodded. "I think you've discovered one."

"I think so too, S. J."

Sara Jane lifted her eyebrows. "Why did you call me S. J?"

"I don't know. It just popped out. Why?"

"The first boy I kissed called me that. We went steady from grade seven to grade ten. He was my first love."

"Oh, sorry. I won't call you that."

Sara Jane grinned. "I'd like it if you did. He was an odd ball like you."

"Gee, thanks."

"You're welcome." The clock chimed a half hour. "You do realize I complimented you?"

They both laughed. "Let's order pizza," Thea said.

Sara Jane nodded. "With everything on it."

"Even anchovies?"

"Why not? Let's go for the works."

Thea agreed. She could scrape away the sausage, pepperoni and ham. And if she got a mouthful, what the hell. It wasn't going to kill her. "I'll get the wine. You phone."

Chapter 28

An hour later, pizza finished and the paintings stowed at Sara Jane's, she waved a quick good bye. Thea opened the back door ready to put the pizza package in the recycling bin when the phone rang. It was Arthur. It had taken him longer to get from Oakville to the airport than the two hour flight to Halifax, not counting the hour and a half detour through Guelph. She grabbed the phone.

"We've just landed."

"I miss you."

"I miss you too."

"When are you coming home?"

"As soon as I can. I'll Skype you in the morning."

"Good thing I know what that means." She had googled it and had already signed on.

He laughed. "I *really* miss you."

"See you tomorrow in cyberspace."

The next morning, Thea was up and dressed by seven o'clock. Halifax was only an hour later than Guelph, but he hadn't said what time he would call. Last night she had downloaded the Skype software and emailed him her contact name.

She finished her coffee, one ear on her computer, listening for the ring tone announcing an incoming Skype. By nine she had done the dishes, tidied the living room, swept rather than vacuumed, and sorted a pile of papers on her desk.

"May as well start work." She sat down and clicked open a file. "I know it's Sunday, Minou, but since I'm sitting here I might as well catch up." Her change of name hadn't changed her aversion to entering columns of numbers, sending client invoices and paying their bills. Thea hated it even more than Cynthia did. "There's got to be a better way to earn a living."

The cat, curled in her usual place in the out-tray, didn't respond.

At nine o'clock, Sara Jane phoned. "Letting you know, I'm off on another trip. A week or so."

"Where are you going?"

"The city to beat all cities. New York."

"When do you leave?"

"In about half-an-hour. I'll give you a shout when I'm back." Click.

Thea looked at the buzzing phone. "And when will that be?"

At ten o'clock, her Skype alert rang and she hit the icon at the bottom of her screen. Arthur's image came up and she said, "I feel like I'm in a some futuristic Star Trek episode."

"The future is now. By the way, who is Thea? When you sent me that contact name, I wasn't sure it was you."

"Did I forget to tell you I changed my name?"

"You changed your name?" One eyebrow went up. "Why?"

She smiled. "Cynthia didn't fit me anymore. I've grown into a Thea."

"Althaea was a Greek goddess, and Athena was the goddess of wisdom—"

"Stop. It's just plain Thea."

"Not so plain, I would say." He wiggled his eyebrows and twiddled an imaginary cigar, a la Groucho Marx.

Over the next two days, they chatted each morning for a half hour or more. He had lots of news to tell. He had drawn plans to add a room to his mother's house with an ensuite so she could sleep on the ground floor.

On another call, he said, "We're going to renovate the kitchen—well, redesign the whole house, so my sister, and her family can move in."

"What does your mother think of that?"

"She loves it but she's terrifically independent and said she could manage the stairs but when I showed her my drawings with the windows facing the garden, she acquiesced."

Thea touched his face on the screen. "I miss you."

"You see me every day."

"It's not the same as in person."

"I cannot wait to see you in person."He leaned forward and his whole face filled the screen.

"Me too." A shiver leapt down her spine. *Yes, scared Cynthia has definitely disappeared.*

There had been no more threatening phone calls from her mother, and Stephanie had promised to be discreet in her inquiries about her father.

The next day, four days after Stephanie had discovered the truth about her parentage, she phoned. "Mom, I found my father."

"You what!"

"Well, I haven't talked to him but I know who he is and where he is."

"Good heavens, that was fast."*Am I ready to hear this?*

"Mom, you'd better sit down."

Thea's heart turned over. "I am sitting."

"My father and you are not related." Stephanie's voice sounded jubilant.

"What?" Thea's brain went fuzzy. The words did not compute. *That can't be.*

"It's true. I spoke to Grandpa Frank's brother, John, in England. Don't worry. I told him I was researching my ancestors, which was true."

"But—"

"Will you listen? Grandpa Frank and your father had two brothers, Harold and John."

"John? My dad never mentioned a John." *But he didn't mention Harold or Frank either.*

"Well, John was a brother."

"But he didn't come to the wedding."

"No, he didn't. He couldn't get away at that time."

"So who is Evan?" Thea's brain ran in circles, trying to sort out the brothers.

"That's what I've been trying to tell you. Evan is NOT a brother. When he came with Harold and Harold's wife, Meghan, everyone assumed that he was the other brother."

"But that's crazy. He must have been introduced."

"You know how it is with weddings. So much going on. He is a brother though."

"But you said he's wasn't a brother."*I am going crazy.*

"He wasn't your father's brother. Evan is *Meghan's* brother."

Thea took a moment to let that sink in. "But if he's Meghan's brother that makes him—"

"That's right. He's Grandpa Frank's and your father's, brother-in-law *by marriage*. Evan's not a blood relative at all."

It took several minutes for the information to reach the cognitive area of her brain.

"Mom. Did you hear me?"

The room spun and her stomach churned. "I heard you." She closed her eyes, and when she opened them, the wall had steadied itself. "I can't believe it. All these years I thought I'd committed a mortal sin." Her mind darted in and out of one-way passages, leap-frogged over bramble bushes and bounced off paper mâche walls.

"I have his address." Stephanie waited a beat. "Mom, why don't we go to England together?"

"England?" Thea's stomach surged and her heart couldn't make up its mind whether to beat faster or to stop all together.

"I want to meet my father."

"I—I don't know. It's all so fast. So new. So—"

"Well, I'm going. With or without you. Mark will come with me."

Thea gulped. "I can't believe it." *All the hiding—the shame—and the guilt.* She grasped the phone as if it might jump out of her hand. *All these years, I've let my shame keep my daughter from ever knowing her father.* "Stephanie. I am so sorry."

"Mom. You did your best. You were scared."

"But—"

"Don't start butting yourself. Sure I missed having a dad, but it had its plusses as well. Remember, we used to stay in the park long after all the other kid's and their moms had to go home to make dinner."

Thea, or maybe it was Cynthia, gulped.

Stephanie continued. "And if you had told me earlier that my dad was too close a relative to be a dad, that would have hurt me more then."

Thea/Cynthia couldn't speak. Her throat had shut and the tears wouldn't stop.

Stephanie had more to say. "You've been a good mom. I'm happily married and I've found out the truth, so stop feeling guilty or whatever the heck you're feeling."

Thea finally found her voice, although hoarse. "I don't know what I've done to deserve you. Will you ever forgive me?"

"There's nothing to forgive. I'm all right and I like myself. It's time now, mom, for you to like, no love, yourself."

Thea blubbered again.

"I'm going to hang up now, mom. It seems you need to have a good cry. I'll call you later."

They hung up and Cynthia went upstairs on shaky legs. She walked to the window, picked up her dragonfly and fell onto the bed. Grasping the dragonfly to her chest, the sluice gates opened and she cried away twenty-eight years of a shameful lie that had woven itself deep into her being. Torrents of tears washed the blame and the guilt out of her pores, out of her brain, out of her body as pockets of pain opened and dumped their contents into a flushing river.

Much later, she fell asleep with the dragonfly pressed to her heart.

Chapter 29

The next morning she awoke from a dream of standing under Niagara Falls. *I'm surprised I wasn't washed away.* She placed her dragonfly back on the window sill. "Thank you, my friend." She threw off her wrinkled day clothes and stepped into another shower. As the water washed over her, she let go of the last remains of guilt, shame and fear. "I am Thea," she shouted. "I am free. The past is the past."

She turned off the shower and stepped out. *If I do go to England, what will I say to Evan? Remember that ugly girl you slept with twenty-nine years ago? Well, you have a daughter.*

"Stop it right now," Thea said. She grabbed a towel. "That's old Cynthia talking. Not you." She stared at the mirror. "No more of that talk. Never say those words again."

She dressed and went downstairs and made a fruit smoothy. After that, she had coffee and two pieces of toast with peanut butter and blueberry jam. She hadn't eaten that much for breakfast since—never. *I'm hungry for life and ready to take it all in.*

"Okay, Minou. Today I tell my family about changing my name and being a new me." She finished her first cup of coffee and poured another one. "Well, maybe not the new person part."

When she did call, it was easier than she'd thought.

She phoned Madison first.

"My nutty sister," Madison said. "Why not? Thea it is. Can't wait to meet the new you."

Madison always was supportive.

Patricia said, "Such nonsense. What's gotten into you?"

"It's not what got in, it's what got out."

"Whatever," she said and hung up.

Her mother's response was, "Why in the world would you want to change your name? Cynthia is a perfectly good name." She sniffed. "I named you myself, after an old aunty who lived to ninety-five and never married."

"I'm Thea now, mom."

"Why don't you change your last name too? If the truth gets out, the Marshall name will be mud."

"Mother, people don't worry about things like that anymore. Some women even choose to have babies without getting married."

"How many of them have babies with their uncle!" She slammed the phone down with the usual clanging sound effects.

Thea grinned. She would wait a bit before telling her that Evan was not a Marshall. "Let her stew for a little longer."

She picked up her pen and message pad, and scribbled. Thea Marshall. Then she wrote, Thea Richardson, with a flourishing curl on the R. She liked the look of that one.

She jumped up. *I haven't told Maddy that I'm not an incestophile.* She punched in her sister's number and Maddy was as dumbfounded as Thea had been at the news.

"So why don't you go to England with Stephanie?"

"I'm thinking about it, but I'm still processing it. Everything's happening so fast. There's Arthur, packing, moving, and I want to keep painting."

"It's all good, sis. Relax and take it all in."

Arthur Skyped later that morning, and announced he was staying another week, maybe two. "Oh, no," she said. "I was so looking forward to seeing you again—in person."

"And me, you."His big smile turned into a frown. "But I have to get the contractors and builders organized."

They said their goodbyes and Thea stared at the blank screen for several moments. Had it been only five days since she'd kissed him with such passion and ready, nay eager, to fling off her clothes and crawl all over him? A chill stole down her back. *Why do I feel as if I know that man. A lifetime ago. And so intimately.*

She shook her head to stop the twirl of time from winding her back to some fuzzy past. *This is now. He is Arthur and I am Thea. How will I feel when I see him? What if I don't feel the same?*

"Shut up, Cynthia," said Thea.

The next day Patricia phoned and invited herself over. Ever since her ex-husband and son had moved to Australia five years ago, Patricia doted on her daughter, Sharon, now pregnant.

Patricia plunked herself into Thea's favourite chair, folded her arms and glared. "I don't want tea or coffee. I want to know about this Evan Marshall business."

Thea sat on the love seat. "You've been talking to mom."

"How else am I going to get news?" She smoothed her perfectly coiffed hair. "You are my sister and you didn't tell me."

Thea straightened a pile of magazines on the coffee table.

Patricia continued. "I can't believe you had the nerve to name your child Stephanie after our father, when you slept with our uncle. That's unspeakable."

Thea sighed. "He wasn't—isn't our uncle."

"What do you mean? Mom said—"

"Mom doesn't know everything." She told her sister what Stephanie had discovered.

"Well, I never." Patricia sniffed and glanced around the room. "I suppose this house might suit Sharon. The neighbourhood seems all right."

"I thought you were on my side."

"What can I do? It's our mother's wish. Besides, Sharon and Mike are only renting. They need their own house now."

"Why mine?"

"For one thing, it's not yours and it's in Guelph. Since Mike is a professor here—"

"Exactly. Mom hopes Mike will use his influence to get her name on a building at the University. As if that's going to make her somebody."

Patricia shrugged. "You know the story of how she struggled through school with her dyslexic thing going on. If it makes her feel better, then why not?"

"Why not? Because she's taking my house away, that's why not."

"Get over it, Cynthia. Being dad's favourite isn't going to help you now."

"My name is Thea."

"Whatever. I have to go." She snatched up her purse and stormed off.

The next day, after market shopping and putting her groceries away, it was eleven o'clock. Her mother must be up by now. Thea phoned to let her know she was coming and drove to Stuart Street. Maybe she could persuade her mother to put off the move until spring. She knocked the lion's brass circle twice and before she touched the handle, the door flew open.

Her mother stood there, holding a yapping Tippy to her bosom. "Tea in the kitchen," and she marched down the hall.

Thea closed the door and hung up her jacket. When she reached the kitchen, her mother was sitting at the table with Tippin still in her lap. The plastic red checkered tablecloth fought with the yellow crocheted napkins and the orange Mexican floor tile.

Thea pulled out the plastic chair. *Why did her mother ever buy this hideous thing?* She sat down.

"Bonnie's out shopping. She bought you some of that herbal tea you like. It's in the cupboard." She waved her hand. "You get it. They make the print so small these days I can't tell Earl Grey from English Breakfast."

Thea got up and opened a beveled glass door. Photos, jammed in the edges, flapped over each other: one of Tippy, two of Patricia, and a magazine picture of a teacup dog.

"While you're there, the sugar bowl needs refilling. The bag's on the top shelf."

Thea reached up. Beside the sugar bag was a blue box, emblazoned with a skull and crossbones and at the bottom, in large red letters: RAT POISON.

"What is rat poison doing here?"

"What do you think? It's for rats."

"You have rats?"

"That or big mice. Bonnie bought it."

"You shouldn't have it on the shelf next to the sugar. One of you could make a mistake and fill the sugar bowl with it."

"It's blue for heaven sake, nothing like sugar and it's handy for when we need it." A single stray bangle slid down her arm, joining the nest of others at her wrist.

Thea picked up the box of poison, bent down and opened the door under the sink.

"Don't put it there. Tippy might get it." The dog growled. "There, there, my baby." She stroked its back, dragging the dangling charms across it. "We can't let anything happen to you."

Thea shook her head and dutifully replaced the box, with the bright red letters on it, back on the top shelf right beside the bag of sugar.

Chapter 30

Thea topped up the sugar bowl, and took out a Lemon Ginger teabag. She must talk to Bonnie about relocating that box of poison. "What tea are you having, mother?"

"My regular Lipton's. What else?" She stroked Tippy on her lap, the clacking bracelets rattling up and down her arm.

The kitchen window looked out onto a once meticulously landscaped garden. Buttercups and crabgrass grew in wild abundance and a runaway ivy climbed over the granite fountain. A stone cherub stared glassy-eyed into the dried-up basin.

Thea poured boiling water into the flowered porcelain teapot and over her teabag in the matching cup. After trying for several years, the Marshall girls had stopped giving their mother a choice of assorted mugs. She even turned down one with a dog on it.

"No thank you," she'd say and if anything larger than a teacup made its way into her house it would be immediately passed on to Goodwill. Her one claim to refinement was "tea tastes better in proper china cups."

Thea stretched the crocheted orange and red striped tea cozy over the pot and set it and the cups and saucers on the table beside a plastic doily. *Has Patricia told her about Evan?*

Her mother pointed to the wooden breadbox at the far end of the counter. "Bonnie bought cookies."

Ginger snaps. Thanks, Bonnie. She placed them on a plate and sat down, ignoring the dog's low throated growls.

"You forgot the milk."

Thea got up, picked up the milk pitcher and sat down.

Bangles clinked down her mother's arm. "So, what do you want?"

"What do you mean?"

"You never invite yourself over unless you want something."

Thea dipped her tea bag up and down. "I was wondering if you would ask your condo tenants if they would be willing to postpone their move until spring."

"Why on earth would I do that?"

"Winter moving is difficult. It's cold and there's snow and ice."

"Nonsense. You hire a truck and they do it."

She let go of her tea string, picked up the tea pot, and tilted it over her mother's cup.

"Not yet. It has to steep. You know I like it strong."

She replaced the pot on the table, took the tea bag out of her own small cup and left it on the side of the saucer.

"Okay. You can pour me one now."

"You said it has to steep more."

"Well, it has."

Gritting her teeth, Thea picked up the pot.

"Wait. The milk goes in first. You should know that by now."

Thea grimaced, picked up the milk, poured it and then the tea.

Mrs. Marshall added sugar and noisily stirred for several seconds. "The tenants' new house closes November 30."

"The condo will need cleaning and painting."

Her mother glared. "That will only take a week."

"That's getting close to Christmas."

"What's wrong with moving at Christmas?"

"Oh mother. You're impossible." She stood up. "I have to go."

It was no use even trying to reason with her. She and her mother had never been on the same wavelength.

"You haven't finished your tea."

She gulped down the last mouthful, threw the soggy tea bag in the small compost bucket on the kitchen counter and put her cup in the sink. "Good bye, mother."

"You didn't finish your cookie."

"Give it to the dog." She grabbed her purse and stomped out. A jangle of bracelets and a round of sharp yapping followed her all the way to the front door.

On the drive home she complained loudly about her mother. When she arrived, she continued her tirade. "Why do I let her get to me, Minou?"

The cat didn't answer and Thea was tired of hearing her own voice.

The next day, after a long Skype session, Arthur announced he'd booked his flight home a week Tuesday. "I'd come home Monday but it's Victoria Day and my mother's planned a family day."

"Give me your arrival time. I'll meet you."

"No. The office car is picking me up. I'll be whisked to meetings and I have a ton of work to catch up on."

"When will I see you?"

"As soon as possible. I promise you." He leaned into the screen and mimed a kiss.

They signed off and Thea's spine did that funny little shiver. She pushed her chair away from her desk. "Well, Minou. It's Sunday. My day to do what I want." She still had that blank canvas waiting in the laundry room. She ran upstairs and changed into her painty T-shirt and jeans. "No use messing up another pair."

She grabbed her dragonfly and ran downstairs. "Come on, my friend. We're going to paint." She propped it on the counter safe from flying paint, fetched the canvas from the laundry room and set it on the kitchen table. Another trip to get paints and painting tools and she was ready to go. She should clear off the table in her hobby room and paint there, except she had to be near a water source. If she didn't wipe acrylics up before they dried, the floor or the table or wall would end up unintentionally decorated.

She opened the tube of Alizarin Crimson, which was quickly becoming her favourite colour and squished a thick vein onto the virgin surface. A swipe with the credit card left a racing red streak screaming toward the far edge. Another tube leapt into her hand and with the spatula she sliced in a yellow ray making orange somersaults. The unmixed reds and yellows looked like Ketchup and mustard. *So what? I don't have to prove anything.* It wasn't brain surgery although that red streak did look suspicious.

A few minutes later, the soft and shadowy blue of Payne's Gray had subdued the rowdy condiments. Her instinct whispered that the top quadrant needed a touch of Renaissance Gold and she listened when the Titanium White begged to be spread along the inner sides of the smokey blue paths which wound their way through, hills and valleys, peeking around corners as they went.

"What do you think, Dragonfly?" It was silly to be talking to a chunk of pewter shaped like a dragonfly, but it gave her confidence and she had always been good at imagining. *Maybe too good.* However, reality had been raising its head recently and it was a challenge to keep up with it. *There's Evan and Arthur and here I am acting like I'm an artist.*

The clock chimed noon. Her stomach growled. She smiled and placed the wet canvas on the stove top. "I like you."

She dumped a container of frozen chilli into a saucepan on low. It took her half an hour to tidy and wash up—herself included— and put her art supplies away. She scrubbed the half dried paint off the ceramic tile. *I must use a drop cloth next time.*

After a salad, two bowls of chilli and toasted garlic bread, she took her coffee to the living room. What was it about painting that whipped up her appetite? Maybe it had something to do with feeling free and having no rules about what she should or shouldn't eat.

The front bell rang. The door opened, and a cheery voice hollered, "Anybody home?"

"Sara Jane! You're back." Thea jumped up and was greeted with a kiss on each cheek. "You've gone Italian on me."

"It was a wonderful trip."

"There's fresh coffee. Help yourself."

Sara Jane went to the kitchen.

"I thought you went to New York?" Thea shouted.

"I did." She came back with a steaming mug and sat in the love seat. "A fantastic city. You have to go."

"So what did you do there?"

"What didn't I do?"

For the next hour, Sara Jane entertained her with the highlights of Broadway shows, art galleries, food to die for and a fabulous reunion with an old lover. "But I've left the best till last," she said.

Thea lifted her eyebrows. "After all that? Do tell."

Sara Jane drew in a breath, holding a dramatic pause. "One of my friends is interested in your paintings."

"What! How?"

"She lives in Manhattan and I showed them to her."

"But how did she see them?"

"I had them shipped to New York before my trip."

Thea's mouth dropped open. "You did? And she might buy one? Her stomach flipflopped.

"Didn't I tell you, you were an artist."

"I think you said 'freakin artist' but—"

"I also said to lose the *buts*."

A voice and image stirred inside Thea. *Who do you think you are? You'll never be an artist. Artists starve.* She furrowed her brown and in her mind's eye, she took a paintbrush and covered her mother's face with a wide strip of Cobalt Blue. "You're right." Her toes tingled and a rush of energy rolled up her body and out through the top of her head. "I *am* a freakin artist."

A round of hugs and cheers ensued, followed by a bottle of Beaujolais. They toasted art, New York, love and chocolate.

"I have something else to celebrate," Thea said.

"Have you finally hooked up with that man you've been so secretive about?"

"I haven't been secretive. You've been away and, no, not about him."

"Well, do tell, girlfriend." She took a sip of wine.

"Remember I told you about Stephanie's father and I thought he was my uncle?"

"I do. And what do you mean, 'you *thought* he was'?"

"That's what I mean. He's not." After she related the whole story, they clunked glasses, toasting sex, men, and lovers.

"And chocolate," Sara Jane shouted.

Thea's mouth made a large O. "Speaking of chocolate, I happen to have a package of those thousand calorie double chocolate muffins from Costco."

"No! They're fabulous with red wine."

"I know." Thea ran to the kitchen and brought back two meal sized muffins on a wooden platter.

"Now this is what I call 'love in the afternoon'."

They laughed and both took a large and decadent mouthful.

The taste of red wine and chocolate and the unique feeling of being an artist permeated Thea. In that spacious moment, gratifying sensations filled her body, thoughts, and emotions, leaving no room for any anxiety about moving, facing Evan, or where her relationship with Arthur was going.

Chapter 31

The week sped closer to Arthur's arrival. It was Saturday already and Thea arranged to meet Madison at the indoor market at nine. She downed a quick smoothy, grabbed her string bags and walked past the cathedral to town. Her sister was at the front door, chatting to the guitar player. They went in and wound their way along a busy aisle—past the egg man and the candle lady, past the table with the handmade greeting cards to the snack bar at the end. Thea spotted a couple of seats at one of the picnic tables and went to save them while Maddy got their coffee. A few minutes later Maddy arrived with a cardboard tray, holding two paper cups and a croissant and a donut. She sat down. "Take your pick."

"Croissant is fine."

Kids ran back and forth, people hugged greetings, lifted a hand in a wave, or yelled hellos.

Maddy took a tentative sip of the hot drink but put it down to cool. "So how does it feel to be without Cyn?"

"I think there's too much made of this sin stuff. How can anyone take religion seriously when they tell you it's a sin to play cards or wash your hair on Sunday?"

"I think those are the minor sins. The major ones are more serious, like murder or disobeying your parents."

Thea laughed. "And what about the mother of all sins—sex."

"What about it? Do you still have a hang up about sex?" She took a bite of the cherry doughnut.

Thea glanced to her left but the man beside her was busy tending to a rowdy child who had spilled his juice. She said in a low voice. "I haven't had much experience that's all."

"It's time you did. By the way, speaking of sex, when am I going to meet your mystery man?"

"Soon. And there's been no sex."

"What are you waiting for? Sex is fun."

Thea took a sip of the hot drink and a bite of croissant. "This is no place to talk about sex. There are kids around."

"You're a funny one."

Thea gazed off. "Do you remember that day when we learned boys were not only different from girls but bad?"

Maddy frowned. "No. "

"I was eight—oh, yeah, you were only four. It was a hot Sunday in July and we all trekked to Sunnyside beach to cool off."

"I remember the screeching, clattery streetcars.'

Thea nodded. "Patricia carried the picnic basket and I had the blanket."

"What did I carry?"

"Nothing. You sat on mom's lap. You were her darling."

"Don't get into that."

"I didn't mind you were her favourite. I only wished she'd liked me a little more."

"She did like—love you, but you never saw that."

Thea took the last bite of her croissant.

"So finish your beach story. What happened?"

"It was one of those sweltering days when families swarmed to Lake Ontario and we barely found a spot on the sand. Mom spread the blanket out and was taking your dress off while Patricia and I yanked off our outer clothes. We wore our bathing suits underneath."

Madison nodded again. "I remember that part."

"Next to us a woman had undressed two small boys around two or three-years-old and they were soon running around naked."

"Oh, sheesh. I can imagine mom's reaction."

"I have never seen our mother's eyes get so big and her mouth so rigid. She yanked your dress back down, nearly knocking you over, and yelled like an Army sergeant for Patricia and me to, 'Get dressed. We are leaving right now'."

"I do remember I cried because I wanted to go swimming."

"Patricia and I begged to stay but all she said was, 'We are not staying here with these depraved people.' I didn't know what depraved meant, except that it had to be something terrible about those naked boys."

"How ridiculous."

"We hardly got a peek at the offensive appendages before we were snatched away from the wicked sight."

"So did that scare you away from penises?"

"Maddy!" Thea looked around.

"Kids hear that all the time. It's not a dirty word."

Thea stood up. "Do you want another coffee?"

"Sure, but I thought we were going to buy vegetables."

"Plenty of time for that. Sometimes talking is more important." She brought back two coffees and two date squares.

"Oh, aren't we being daring," said Madison.

"Shut up and eat."

"So it seems you're in a talking mood. What's up?"

"Arthur's coming back on Tuesday and I'm a little nervous."

"What about?"

She took a bite of date square. "You know."

"No.Oh. You mean." She leaned in and whispered, "Sex."

"Don't make fun of me."

"I'm not. I thought you didn't like boys when you never went on dates when you were a teenager."

"They didn't like me."

"That's not true."

"I was the ugly sister."

"Nobody thought that."

"Oh, yeah? With that great red blotch the shape of Newfoundland on my face?"

"I never noticed it that much."

Thea blinked back tears. *How could anyone not notice it?* "I couldn't believe that I had to bring your attention to the lack of it." She gazed into her coffee cup. "Like when your husband shaved off his moustache and no one noticed, and when Patricia lost thirty-five pounds and was annoyed when no one remarked on it."

"When you love a person, you don't notice stuff like that."

Thea didn't know whether to laugh or cry. Was wearing a red map on your face 'stuff like that'? She straightened her shoulders. "Anyway, that's all past history. I'm a new person now."

"You have changed since you became Thea."

"I'm working on it. Let's get groceries."

They joined the stream of shoppers.

A half hour later, they stood outside with bulging bags. "Do you want a ride home," Maddy said.

"That would be great. Will you stay for lunch."

"Why do I get the feeling you want to talk more."

"You always did know me best."

Maddy parked in front of the house. "How's Sara Jane doing?"

"Fine. She's back from New York and I have something to tell you about that."

Maddy took one of the string bags and they walked in. "You are a bit of a mystery these days."

Thea unpacked and told her about Sara Jane showing her paintings to someone who was interested in one of them.

"I'm so happy for you. Dad would be too."

Thea grinned. "Yeah. He would. It's kind of unbelievable."

"I'm glad you gave me the latest scoop on Evan. Mom phoned and told me all the *shameful* details she had discovered from the hospital records. I pretended I didn't know."

"Why didn't she take out a full-page ad in the *Mercury*?" Thea ripped off a handful of romaine leaves. "I'm surprised Patricia hasn't told her by now. She dropped by the day after I told you.

"Oh, wow. What did she have to say about it?"

Thea took other salad makings from the fridge. "You know Patricia. She changed the subject."

"That sounds like Patricia. So have you thought anymore about going to England to meet him?"

Thea chopped up a stalk of celery. "No. What would I say to him?" She threw the salad together and put it on the table. "I don't even know the man."

Madison took a forkful of salad. "Well, you knew him in the biblical sense."

"I hate that biblical knowing thing."

"You hate anything about sex. For heaven's sake. Get over yourself. Sex is natural. Sometimes, you act as if men come from another planet."

"They do. They come from Mars."

Madison laughed. "Yeah, I read the book too."

"I guess it was mom always harping that 'men only want one thing'." She opened a goat brie and an old cheddar and put them and a multigrain baguette on the breadboard and set it on the table. "She always implied it was something disgusting and horrible and to keep away from it at all costs."

"It's a good thing we didn't believe her."

"Well, you and Patricia didn't."

"Why the hell did you?"

"I've asked myself that a million times." She sat down.

"So do you like this Arthur fellow?" She cut herself a chunk of cheddar.

"Yeah. I do. A lot." Thea hoped her face wasn't turning pink.

"Maybe you and he knew each other in a past life."

"Don't laugh. I thought that when I first saw him."

"I'm not laughing. I believe in reincarnation. I'm sure I've known Sara Jane in a past life." She helped herself to salad. "Do you remember when you used to call me Sara?"

"I remember pretending you were my baby. Until you went to Kindergarten." She looked away for a moment. "You're right. I did call you Sara. But how did you remember that?"

"Patricia told me when I mentioned the name of your new neighbour, right after she reminded me that Sharon was moving into your house."

"Don't spoil a good morning talking about that." Thea grabbed another piece of bread and cut herself a triangle of brie.

"I hear mom is sticking to a December move. That sucks."

"You can say that again."

"That sucks."

Thea did a double take. "Sara Jane did that too."

"Did what?"

"Took me literally and repeated what I said."

Madison laughed. "I guess that proves we knew each other in a past life."

Thea snickered. "I don't think it would stand up in court, but it does make you think."

Chapter 32

Thea spent most of Victoria Day immersed in the traditional activity of gardening. After pulling out clumps of twitch grass, she attacked a patch of gout weed, digging deeply underground to demolish its nefarious root system before it could wend its way another foot and pop to the surface.

"Can't catch me," it would yell, waving its three green leaves.

You couldn't simply pull it out. Oh no. You had to seriously burrow and follow every sneaky root to its end or one warm day, you would go out for a sprig of Rosemary and three gout weeds would welcome you with their cheery little smirks.

That night, after the last Skype with Arthur she had a long soak in an Epsom salts bath to relive her gardening muscles. She didn't want to be hobbling around like an old lady when she saw him but since he was being picked up and taken straight to the office, she'd have another day or two to recover. Also, with a haircut scheduled, Arthur would see the new Thea right off.

At noon, he phoned from the office, saying he would Skype that evening.

"No, don't." She didn't want him to see her new hairdo on a computer monitor.

"Why not?"

"I mean I want to talk to you but my Skype program is down."

"Okay, I'll phone. Gotta go."

After lunch she drove to the hairdressers.

The receptionist greeted her. "Nancy's sick today, so Susan will take you."

"But I've always had Nancy. She knows my hair." *Maybe I should cancel. It's a sign I shouldn't have my hair cut. Or is it a sign that I should?* Her stomach did a flip flop.

"Come on in," said Susan. "I'm pretty good at blunt cuts. Nancy tells me you don't want it too short."

Thea sat down and took a deep breath. "I—I want a different style today. Short." She pointed to a picture "Like that one."

Susan lifted her eyebrows. "That is short. Are you sure?"

"No, but let's do it." A whole family of butterflies woke up and fluttered all the way to her throat.

She left the beauty parlour and glanced at her reflection in every window she passed. *Is that me?* She turned her head and no swish of hair fell to hide her face. *They don't call it the pixie cut anymore, but maybe I am one.* She bounced past the naked statue in St.George's Square.

Half way up Macdonell Street on the way to the Cathedral steps, she stopped. "What am I doing? I drove here." *Where the heck did I park?* She retraced her steps and found her car on Quebec Street opposite the hairdressers. She climbed in and adjusted the mirror which didn't need adjusting. She smiled again. "Hello, new Thea."

After supper, Arthur phoned."How would you like to go to a movie.?Tomorrow night?"

"A movie?"

"Yes. You know, where twenty-four stills go flashing by every second making it look like a moving picture."

Thea laughed. "I know what a movie is." Her butterflies woke up and flitted to and fro. *But what about after the movie?* Especially after that passionate kiss before he left for Nova Scotia.

"Well? What about it?"

"Okay." She paused. "Do you mind if my daughter Stephanie comes? Wednesday is her day to visit me." *What are you doing? I thought you wanted this man?*

"Great. I'd love to meet her."

She pressed off and stabbed at Stephanie's speed dial button. It was true that Stephanie often came on a Wednesday, but no plans had been made for that particular Wednesday.

Stephanie picked up. "Tomorrow is a busy day for me. How about next week?"

"Arthur is coming over and I'd like you to meet him."

"In that case, I can change a few things. Can't wait to meet the man that is unfreezing my mother."

"Behave yourself, young woman."

Stephanie laughed and hung up.

The next evening, Thea, Stephanie, and Arthur went for pizza before catching a rerun of *North by Northwest* at the Galaxy. They had both remarked on her new hair cut and how much it suited her.

Arthur went to buy the tickets and Stephanie squealed in her mother's ear. "Mom, he's adorable. Definitely a keeper."

"Oh, Stephanie, don't be silly. I hardly know him."

"Well get to know him. He likes you."

Thea looked away.

"Mom, it's your turn. A new name, a new hair cut, and a new man."

It was late when the movie ended and Stephanie stayed over. Arthur said a polite goodbye at the door and, with Stephanie in the background, left Thea with a gentlemanly peck on the cheek and a whisper, "I love your haircut."

Early the next day, he phoned. "She's a delightful young woman. You must be proud of her."

Thea beamed. The two people she loved liked each other.

"What about Saturday? " He waited a moment. "Dinner?"

She couldn't use Stephanie as an excuse again. "Okay. How about I make reservations at La Cucina*?"*

"An Italian kitchen. Sounds fantastic. I'll pick you up at seven-thirty. Gotta run."

She hung up and told her butterflies to settle down. It was only dinner and she was a mature woman. *It's time I acted like one.* She took a deep breath and headed for her computer. A slew of numbers would distract her.

The next morning, Sara Jane breezed in with a quick report that Thea's paintings were getting some attention. "No sale yet, but I feel one coming. I love your hair, by the way."

"What do you mean, getting some attention. I thought you said you showed them to a friend."

"Oh, didn't I mention she owns an art gallery?"

Thea found her voice."What? But—"

But Sara Jane had already dashed out the door.

In the afternoon, Thea's mother phoned. "I need some manure. Bonnie says I should feed the roses."

It will take more than fertilizer to bring that garden back. "I have some errands to do later. I can get you some then."

She picked up a couple of ten pound bags at the nursery and dropped them on her mother's back deck. Tippy yapped and her mother called out. "Who's that?"

"It's only me. I have your manure for you."

Her mother opened the door and peered out. "What have you done to yourself?"

Thea touched her head. "Do you like it?"

Her mother grimaced. The dog yapped. "First you massacre your name and now your hair. You're becoming a different person." She slammed the door, making the seashell wind chimes rattle like dried bones.

"That's the idea," Thea said to the door and the yapping dog behind it.

On Friday, she caught up on work and—too soon—it was Saturday. Since Arthur had arrived back from his trip, she had had several stern talks with herself to let go of all her mother's dumb remarks. The rants and diatribes that sex was bad and that good girls never let a man touch her. Her body was ready for her to be a bad girl. *If only my thoughts would catch up.*

She rose early, had a quick breakfast that tasted like sawdust and was home from the market by ten thirty.

Arthur phoned at noon. "I cannot wait to see you."

She didn't trust her voice to agree with him. Instead, she said, "You'll love La Cucina and it's on Macdonell so we can walk if you want."

"Walk, drive, swim, fly. I don't care. As long as I see you."

After Thea hung up the phone, she stuck her fingers in her ears and recited, "La,la,la,la," over and over to obliterate—to yank out —the weeds of her mother's dire warnings of what was sure to befall her that evening.

It took several minutes but finally her mind and body relaxed. She was not Cynthia anymore. Not that scared and scarred teenager. She was an artist with a new hairdo. Anything could happen that evening. *I am ready for it.*

She ran upstairs and cut off the price tag from the lacy bra she had purchased that morning.

Chapter 33

At six o'clock, Thea was soaking in a hot bath with avocado on her face, cucumber slices on her eyes and Josh Groban singing *You Raise Me Up*.

At seven o'clock she stood under the tulip-shaped bathroom lights and fiddled with eye liner and mascara.

One of the three outfits spread on her bed was her usual slacks and vest ensemble. "What do you think, Minou?"

Minou was no help. Thea glanced at her dragonfly on the sill. It was no help either. She picked up the flowered dress next to the slacks and put it on. "Too summery and too tight."

Basic black won out. A simple dress with stretchy material and three-quarter sleeves. She added a blue and orange East Indian wrap and low heels.

At a quarter after seven, after ten minutes of pacing from kitchen to office and back to living room, she sat down on the edge of the love seat. At twenty after, she ran upstairs to the bathroom —again. At seven thirty, the door bell rang.

She ran down and opened the door. An armful of yellowy-pink roses hid his face.

She peeked around them. "Is that you behind there?"

He swung the bouquet aside. "Tis I." He moved toward her and she stepped into the delicious scent of roses and him.

After a long and satisfying kiss, she pulled away. "The—the roses need water." *And I need to catch my breath.*

"And I need *you,*" he said leaning forward.

The second kiss made her knees melt and her butterflies broke into an Argentine tango. "Flowers. Water." She broke away, walked to the kitchen and turned on the tap. She took a deep breath to balance herself and stared at the most beautiful roses she had ever seen. A flush of pale yellow started at the base of each plump petal and ended at the top in a soft satin pink.

Arthur had followed and stood close behind her. He stroked her back, while a trembling Thea placed the roses in the sink, tightened the stopper and turned off the tap.

"I can find a vase later." She turned to step away but he was right there and she was in his arms again. Kissing seemed to be the most natural and easiest thing to do. Breathing could come later.

After several long and delicious moments, Arthur said in a husky voice, "I guess we should get going."

"Yes, we really should." Thea's voice was a bit of a croak and her legs shook. "After all, we do have a reservation."

"And we wouldn't want to miss that." He held her to his chest.

She relaxed against him, as if she had done it a hundred times before. So safe. So secure. So familiar. *I could stay here forever.*

Minou jumped up on the counter and with a loud meow, butted her head against Arthur's arm. He laughed. "It seems someone objects."

"I must have forgotten to feed her." She stepped out of the warm circle of his arms and took down a can of cat food.

It was a short walk to the restaurant and they sat outside in the covered Il Terrazzo. With the music and the lights shimmering on the stone walls, they could have been in Italy. A bottle of merlot went well with ravioli for Arthur and vegetable pasta for Thea. They lingered over coffee and at ten-thirty, unclasped their hands from across the table and said their goodbyes to their gracious host.

The evening air was warm, perfect for walking and Arthur described his new office project with child care facilities, an arboretum and a sunny cafeteria."

"Sounds exciting."

"It is." He squeezed her hand. "But not as exciting as you."

Cynthia loomed inside her head, and Thea told her to go away.

At her front door, she fumbled with her keys, finally getting the door opened. "Do you want coffee?"

"Just you." He kicked the door shut with his foot as he pulled her to him and kissed her hard and long.

Shivers shot up her arms and her thighs were on fire. When he let her go, she nearly fell over. "Whoops. It must be the wine." She stumbled to the living room and fell onto the love seat.

He followed and sat beside her. "Are you all right?"

"A little dizzy." She lowered her head and held it in two hands.

He put his hand on her back. "Do you want to lie down?"

She looked up, startled. "You mean upstairs in bed?"

"Don't look so scared. I'm not going to attack you." He took his hand away. "I thought you wanted—."

"I do but—"

"But? But what"

"I—I don't know. I feel like a fifteen year old on her first date."

"You don't kiss like a fifteen year old. What's wrong?"

"I'm just being a ninny." She stood up and took a wobbly step. "Let's go upstairs right now and no matter what we'll make love." *That sounds better than 'having sex'.*

"Whoa, there. You make it sound like a chore."

Her mind raced in circles like a mad monkey.

He guided her back to the love seat and sat her down. "Why don't I get you a cup of coffee?"

"No, I've had enough coffee. Water is fine."

He brought back two glasses of water and sat down beside her. "Is it okay if I sit here?"

She took a glass from him. "Of course." She took a big drink "I don't know what's the matter with me. I couldn't wait for you to come back, and now that you're here—"

"I'm here to stay so stop your fussing. I'm in no rush. Well, I am, but I want you to want to as well."

"Part of me does but it feels as if there's a jailer inside me with a black-robed judge and twelve contorted faces screaming obscenities at me." *Cynthia was back in full force.*

Arthur lifted his eyebrows. "Good God, woman. Do you belong to some strange sex-hating cult or religion?"

She half smiled. "Anyone would think so."

He laughed and gave her a quick hug. "We can work with that. I'll woo the part of you that wants to while you slaughter the judge and jury."

She nodded. "That's a deal."

He leaned over and gave her an innocent peck on the cheek. "I've experienced the part of you that wants to and it's my bet that she wins."

"I darn well hope so."

They sat quietly for a few minutes slowly sipping water.

She put her glass on the table. "Someone may be interested in buying one of my paintings."

He lifted his crooked eyebrow. "I never knew you painted."

"I didn't either. I did a little watercolour a few years ago but recently I got the urge to paint again." She looked into the distance. "I feel transported when I paint." She looked back at him. "And I love it." The urge to throw herself at him surged within her. She took another drink of water.

You have a funny look on your face. "Are you all right?" He took her hand.

She squeezed it. "I seem to be doing a lot of new things lately.".

"If you're up for new things, how would you like to join me at my company's annual Gala Dance? It's in two weeks."

"A dance? I haven't been to a dance in—a long time." She'd never gone to a dance.

"Well, would you like to go? It's at the Royal York."

The Royal York?

"We'll probably stay over."

"Stay over?" *I sound like an echo.*

"We could have separate rooms if you like. So will you come?"

God in heaven woman. You adore this man. "Yes, I would love to go. And maybe we won't need separate rooms. I mean—"

"Don't worry." He kissed her lightly on her cheek. "We don't have to decide that now." He jumped up. "I should go. Long drive."

"Are you okay to drive?"

"Absolutely. Coffee and the walk disbursed the wine."

At the doorway, they kissed like people who would definitely not want separate rooms. When they parted, Arthur shook his head. "You certainly are an enigma. A wild tiger one moment and a spooked rabbit the next."

At the moment the tiger was present so they kissed again, long and hard and when he let her go, her knees buckled.

He put his hand under her arm. "Steady there, girl."

"Maybe the rabbit part just hopped out of me."

"Let's hope so." He opened the door, and walked to his car.

She leaned against the door watching him go. Her lips hummed from his kiss and her legs quivered, wanting to run after him.

He turned on the motor, pulled away and up the street.

She closed the door and leaned against it. Thea was back in charge again and nodded her head. "We definitely won't need separate rooms."

Chapter 34

Thea stood on the edge of the Grand Canyon, took a step off and woke with a jerk. She bolted upright and slapped a hand to her thumping chest. "Whew. That was close."

Still in her pjs, she made coffee, took her mug to the living room and set it beside the vase of roses. She sat down, closed her eyes and breathed in their sweet scent, remembering the night before. The sweet and urgent kisses. The see-saw of desires.

Sunday morning was usually her journal writing time but that morning she wanted to think. Or maybe she thought too much. The phone rang. "S.J. What's up?"

"Can't a friend phone a friend on a Sunday morning?"

"Of course, but you don't usually phone this early."

"Early? It's eleven o'clock."

"What?" Thea looked over at Grandfather clock. Its black hands looked like eyebrows frowning at her.

"Are you sitting down?" Sara Jane continued.

"Yes."

"Two of your paintings sold."

"What?"

"She loves your work and wants to see more."

"I don't believe it."

"You will when you get the cheque."

"Oh my god. She actually bought my paintings?"

"*She* didn't. A customer did. For two thousand dollars."

"Two thousand dollars?" Thea's brain went fuzzy.

"For each, less commission."

"For each?"

"Stop repeating me."

"I think I'm going to faint."

"The gallery will send you a cheque."

"A cheque?"

"Yes. I gotta go." She hung up.

Thea held the buzzing phone for several minutes before she clicked it off. She started at her cat. "Minou. Can you believe it? Two thousand dollars—for each. That's four thousand dollars—less commission."

The cat twitched an ear.

"Someone liked my paintings. Enough to pay—ye gods. Two thousand dollars?" *Are they crazy or am I?*

She tapped one finger after another. "That'a a lot of hours of bookkeeping to earn four thousand dollars?" She stood up. "I need to do more paintings."

She ran upstairs and got dressed. "It was probably a fluke. No one will buy anymore, but what the heck, I love painting so why not give it a chance. It sure beats counting numbers."

She threw on a light jacket. "Anyhow, I can't sit around writing in my journal or worrying about sex when I've got painting to do.

Fifteen minutes later she was in Wyndham Art Supplies staring at a rack of stretched canvases. She picked out four, and with two under each arm, headed to the front counter.

Chris was at cash. "Looks like you've caught the bug."

"What bug?"

He reached for the canvases. "The painting bug. Can I take those for you?"

She didn't move. Wild thoughts flitted through her head.

"Is anything wrong?"

"I need bigger ones." She smiled. "And one of those easel thingys that attach to a table."

Twenty minutes later, she pulled up to the curb in front of her house. She grabbed her purse, the easel and the bag of assorted palette knives and several tubes of new juicy colours. Four canvases, each two by three feet leaned on the back seat.

Ten minuted later, she screwed the easel to the kitchen table, positioned the first canvas on it, and laid in a background of soft beige. She set it aside to dry. On the next she applied a background of pure white with swaths of Hooker's Green. In the store, she had giggled at the name. She returned to the first canvas and added Ultramarine Blue and Burnt Orange: crisscrossing, slanting, letting the colours play with each other, and settled any arguments with a good dose of Iridescent White.

On the Hooker's Green canvas (where did that name come from?) she played with violet and Renaissance Gold. The new palette knives skipped through the landscape: the egg-shaped springy one left dashes, the long narrow one traced curved roadways, and with a twist of a wrist, the serious triangle left spikes of exclamation marks, each crying, "Look at me!"

Except for a fifteen minute break to grab something to eat, her focus revolved around canvas, paint, brushes and any other tool or instrument at hand to achieve the right effect.

At four o'clock her cordless phone rang from somewhere under a sticky tube of Magenta, two wet dishcloths (now relegated to paint cloths), a green stained credit card and a bright red spatula.

With the back of her hand, the least painted part of her anatomy, she shoved things to the side and uncovered the phone. With the more or less clean handle of the palette knife, she poked the speaker button on. "Arthur," she cried.

"How are you?"

"I am fantastically fabulous! How are you?"

A pause. "What are you doing?"

"Painting."

"Wall painting? Furniture painting? Oh, that's right. You said you'd taken up picture painting."

"I don't know if you would call it a picture." She gazed at the one on the stove. Touches of yellow peeked around gasps of blue. "It's an abstract expression of I don't know what."

"It sounds as if you're having fun."

"I am. Delicious fun. I wish you were here."

"So do I."

"Well, come on over."

"Okay." He hung up.

Thea stared at the buzzing phone. "What just happened? She hit the off button with the palette knife. "He's coming over."

The kitchen was in chaos and her hands and clothes splattered with paint. She'd have about forty minutes to get cleaned up and look presentable.

Her stomach churned. *What do I want? I want him. I don't want him.* And she said aloud. "Would you and your body please make up your minds."

In twenty minutes, she had cleaned up the kitchen art space, stowed the two wet paintings in the laundry room and stripped off her jeans and T-shirt. *Damn. Another set of paint clothes.* One of the orcas on her t-shirt wore a yellow saddle and the other blue and orange spots. How did artists do it or was she unusually messy? *I need an art room. A big one.*

A good scrub in a hot bath softened and removed dried paint from her hands, arms, hair, face and neck. At four thirty-five, in clean jeans and a crisp blue blouse, the coffee was made and she was reaching for two mugs when the door bell rang.

Chapter 35

He stepped in. She stepped back and forward just as he did. An awkward hug. A brief kiss, not quite hitting square on the lips.

"How are you?" he said.

"Fine. I made a pot of coffee." They walked into the living room and she held the mugs aloft. "I'll go fill these."

He sat in the chair next to the love seat and she scampered to the kitchen, reminding herself she was Thea now. Not Cynthia— the scared rabbit.

She filled the mugs, returned to the living room and handed him a cup.

"Thanks. So you said you were painting."

"Yes." She sat down. *Yes, let's talk about painting. Don't let's talk about kissing or—.*

"Can I see it?"

"What? Oh, the paintings.

"You said your neighbour was showing your art to someone?"

"I'm still in shock. I can't believe it. Two of them sold."

"That's fabulous. You're a professional artist."

"I wouldn't say that." Things were happening too fast..

"I would. And don't be all shy and modest about it. I didn't know you were serious about your art."

"I didn't either but I love doing it."

"That's what makes it special. Don't hide your light under a bushel."

"I wonder where that saying came from." *Why did I ask that? Of course he knows.*

"The Bible. Both Mark and Luke advised not putting your candle under a bushel."

She laughed. "It could start a fire."

"Indeed. If you don't let your light shine, you burn up inside."

"You're a philosopher too."

"Too? In addition to what?"

The phone rang, saving her from admitting he was also a disturbingly sexy man who drove her crazy with confusion.

She jumped up and ran to the kitchen. Her mother's number. She put the handset back in its cradle still ringing.

When she returned, Arthur said, "I want to see your paintings."

She took a deep breath. "If I show them to you, you have to promise not to laugh."

"Why would I laugh?"

She shrugged. "They're still wet. Even the sides, so it's better if you go to them."

He followed her. One canvas lay on top of the dryer, the other on the washer. Sweeps of vibrant colours, swirled and zinged, screeching to halts or leaping over precarious ridges.

Thea held her hands behind her back to stop from biting her nails. He moved his head side to side, looking at one and the other, and after a long and excruciating pause, said, "These are amazing."

"Amazing terrible or amazing wonderful?"

"I'm not sure."

"Are they that bad?" *I knew they were no good. I'm fooling myself.*

"Not bad. Different." He backed up and peered at them. "I've never seen anything like it." He pointed to an area on the Naples painting. "How did you get that effect?"

"What effect?"

"Those swishes that sparkle and are partially hidden by those blobs that come and go."

"I don't know."

"What do you mean, you don't know?"

"Well, I can't remember exactly. It's kind of a blur."

"I like it."

She smiled. "I like it, too."

He folded his arms, shook his head and stared at her.

"What?"

"You are a woman of hidden talents. What else can I expect from you?"

"I—I don't know." She averted his gaze.

"I didn't mean—" He pulled her close.

He hugged her like she imagined a big brother would, and she stayed in that warm place, still and safe. Like she had come home.

A meow from Minou broke the bubble. "I need to get the cat out," she said, "or I'll have paw prints where I don't want them."

She picked up the cat and they left the laundry room.

"Are you hungry," he said.

"I am. I think I missed lunch."

"Where do you want to go?"

"Why don't we order in? Chinese?"

They settled on their choices and she phoned it in. He was standing at the window looking out and when she hung up he turned to face her. The butterflies in her stomach started to rhumba or was it the tango? She only knew it was a sexy dance and if he took one step toward her she would be lost.

She had to say something. "What shall we do while we wait?" Her voice shook. *What a stupid thing to say.*

"What would you like to do?"

His expression was neutral as if waiting for her to make the first move.

She stared at him. *I don't want my first love making with him to be while we're waiting for Chinese food.* "How about a cup of tea?" *In a crisis, make tea.*

He smiled. "I thought you made a pot of coffee?"

"Oh, yes, Of course." *He'll think I'm an idiot.*

"So did I tell you about the house renovations I designed for my mother?"

Thea let out a breath of relief. *Bless him for knowing I am all of a twitter.* "Not everything. Do tell."

For the next thirty minutes, over another cup of coffee, he drew sketches and talked about doorways, arches, and windows. Once his hand brushed hers and a shiver of sparkles danced up her arm.

The door bell chimed and while he fetched the food, she set out plates and utensils.

Forty-five minutes later, cardboard containers, packets of soy and plum sauce, and plates with left over noodles, fried vegetables and chicken balls covered the kitchen table.

Thea held her stomach and leaned back in her chair. "Who says you feel hungry after a Chinese meal."

"Well, scientifically—"

"Stop! That was a rhetorical question." She smiled. "Have you ever been on a Trivia TV show? You would win, hands down."

He shrugged. "I find facts and figures fascinating and I seem to have a good memory."

"Let's have our fortune cookies in the living room."

She sat on the love seat. He sat beside her.

"You first," she said.

He cracked it open. "Share your happiness with someone today." He looked at her. "That's easy. Already done."

She broke hers open and slid the narrow strip of paper out. "Money is on its way." She gasped. "Money is coming from my paintings." A smile. "I feel different when I'm painting."

"You look different when you talk about it. You shine."

She lowered her head but no comforting hair swished with it.

He put his hand on her cheek and turned her face to his. "You are beautiful."

Beautiful! She had been called many things but never beautiful. Her chin wobbled, her face screwed up and strangled tears fell.

He put his arm around her. "What's wrong?"

She leaned against him and he held her close.

"Everything's all right."

She buried her face in his shoulder and cried. Tears dribbled and flooded over the slide show in her head: a cheerless teen-ager, a scared mother and a lonely middle-aged, confused woman.

Arthur rocked her until her tears subsided. He held her for a long time. "You are a conundrum. Maybe that's why I love you."

She pulled away and gaped at him.

"Whoops, did I say that too soon?"

"No. I think I love you, too."

"Think! What do you mean, *think*? I confess my love to you and you *think* you love me." He poked scrabbling fingers into her side.

She wriggled away. "I'm just learning to love myself. Give me time."

"I have all the time in the world." He pulled her close and kissed her hard.

She responded in kind.

He broke off the kiss first and holding her shoulders pushed her a foot away. They were both breathing heavily.

"Arthur." Her voice shook and she leaned into him.

In one swift move, he let go and jumped up. "I—I have to go. Early morning tomorrow." He charged out of the room, through the front door and was gone. Thea didn't move from the love seat. Her lips tingled and her body screamed for more of him.

Chapter 36

She didn't move for a long time.   Minutes ticked by. The Grandfather clock chimed but she didn't count them. The buzzing in her lips lessened but her heart leapt about in crazy circles.

He said he loved me. I said I loved him. She stood up. *I don't know anything about love.* "That's not true. *I loved Stephanie the moment the doctor laid her purple streaked body on my stomach. Of course I can love.*"

She sat down. *But what about sex?* It was as if her body had a mind of its own. It wanted Arthur. It wanted that man on her and in her and all over her.

She stood up again, snatched the small plate with fortune cookie pieces off the table and stomped to the kitchen. "I am not a scared teenager anymore or a drunken bridesmaid."

A film reel of her mother pointing her finger and yelling that sex was a nasty duty a married woman had to endure flashed in her head. She slammed the plate on the counter making cookie bits jump off. "I don't believe you, mother. Sex is not dirty or bad."

She swept the empty food cartons off the table into a garbage bag. "And I can stop idolizing my father and thinking no man would ever be good enough for me."

She took the paring knife and cut the chicken balls in half and scraped them into the cat dish. "There you go Minou. Have a ball."

She straightened up, laughing. "It's time I had a ball. Royal York, here I come."

In fifteen minutes, she had washed and dried the dishes, cleaned cookie crumbs off the counter and tidied up the kitchen. She picked up her phone and listened to her mother's message.

"Bonnie's uncovered more of Frank's roses that need manure. Bring me another one of those big bags tomorrow."

Thea yelled at the phone. "Manure! You want manure, mother. I'll give you manure. I'll give you back all that you've given me."

She hit the erase button and continued yelling into the handset. "You're wrong, Mother. Men don't only want one thing. They want love too. And what the heck is wrong with *that thing* they want? Maybe I want it too." She banged the phone back in its holder.

The clock chimed a half hour. Seven-thirty. Too early for bed, anyway she was too riled up to sleep. Her PVR had recorded her favourite shows but she was too restless to sit. She picked up the phone and hit Sara Jane's number. It went to voice mail with the message that she was in Toronto for a few days.

She tried Madison. Charles answered and said she was out and had left her cell phone at home.

Stephanie's also went to voice mail. She was at a Craft Show. She sighed. "Is there nobody out there to talk to?" *Don't I have a couple of Costco's giant chocolate muffins left?* A quick search in the freezer produced a wrapped chunk which she placed in the toaster oven. She put some water on for a hot chocolate and ran upstairs to change into her p.j.'s and housecoat.

By eight o'clock she had cozied herself in front of the TV and placed the toasted buttered double chocolate muffin and a steaming mug of hot chocolate, full to the brim, on the coffee table. The touch of mint she had crumbled into the drink tickled her nose and tantalized her taste buds.

She clicked the remote. Over the familiar music of *Downton Abbey,* Highclere Castle came into view with Lord Crawley's white lab ambling toward it. *Which character would I be? The wilting violet of Lady Edith or the bold and haughty Lady Margaret?*

She picked up the dripping muffin. "I choose Margaret." She took a big bite.

The next afternoon she joined the Saturday shoppers at the nursery and picked up her mother's bag of manure.

She lugged it around the house to her mother's back deck where she flopped it down and rang the bell. The door opened and a yapping dog sprinted out and squatted on the lawn. Her mother's face poked around the door. "Oh, it's you."

"Who did you expect? I phoned and said I was coming."

She glared. "Did you shut the gate? I don't want Tippy getting out."

"Yes, mother." She nudged the bag with her toe. "Here's your shit."

"Cynthia Anne Marshall! You know I don't like that word."

And I don't like the way you spit out my whole name. "Calling a spade a spade, mother." She turned to leave.

"Won't you stay for tea?"

"No." She walked down the steps and at the bottom half-turned and said over her shoulder, "I'm busy." She continued around the path and through the gate.

Each night, Arthur phoned or Skyped. He was swamped at work and couldn't get away. On Friday's call, he announced he had to go to Ottawa for a few days.

He phoned from Ottawa the next night and they talked for an hour about buildings, food, family, reincarnation, art and painting. Of course he knew where the name Hooker's Green came from.

"William Hooker was a botanical artist and he wanted the right pigment for leaves so he mixed Prussian Blue and Gamboge. He lived in the late seventeen hundreds."

"How do you even know a word like Gamboge? I only just learned it myself."

"Architects have to know about colour combinations. Speaking of colour. What colour is your dancing dress?"

"My what?'

"The dress you'll be wearing to the dance next Saturday."

"Blue," she blurted. "Why?" She didn't have a dance dress but if she did, it would be blue.

"I want to match the corsage. What's your favourite flower?"

"Red poppy. But that would clash and it's hardly a corsage."

"I'll surprise you."

On Monday morning she phoned the art store and ordered three two-by-four foot canvases. "You are getting larger," Chris said when she ordered them.

"Larger and braver."

They were delivered the next afternoon. She moved the chairs and a table in the living room to the side, and placed a canvas on a bed sheet spread on the floor. In the movie Jackson Pollock walked around his paintings, trailing, dabbing, stroking and dancing the paint over the surface. Her canvases were small compared to his ginormous ones which filled an entire wall. Her small tubes weren't enough, so she had bought the most expensive house paint she could find. Three one-litre tins of the primary colours sat in a row. She pried the lids off, hammered nail holes in the grooves at the top and took a deep breath.

"Here goes, Minou."

The next two hours evaporated while she dribbled, splashed, dotted and streaked winding gashes of red, hills of yellow and banks of blue, creating a symphony of shades, tints and tones.

She left it where it was to dry, with strict instructions to Minou to keep off. Fortunately, the cat took one sniff and backed away.

Chapter 37

The next day, Madison picked Thea up and they went shopping. Thea insisted she could find a suitable dress in one of the consignment stores or Winners or Walmart.

"We are not buying you a formal dress from a consignment store or Walmart." She parked on Macdonell and they walked to the Old Quebec Street mall.

"Anyway, we don't want something suitable. We want something fabulous," Madison said.

"These stores are expensive."

"So? You're worth it."

Thea tried on three dresses in Crème Couture and when she walked out of the dressing room in the last one—a calf-length periwinkle blue—its skirt swirled in a wide arc. "I love the three quarter sleeves."

"It's perfect. It's you. You have to get it."

Thea flipped the tag over. "$400! I can't pay that much for a dress."

"Yes, you can."

"But—but—"

"There goes that *but* train again. Time to get off that caboose."

"But I really can't afford this dress."

Madison lifted her hand. "I will hit you if you say one more *but*. Now take that dress off and go and buy it. You can't afford not to."

On Thursday, Thea awoke, not with a dream, but a nightmare. She was in a large ballroom, in her new dress with Arthur holding her in dance position but her feet were glued to the floor. The music rang out and Arthur took a step and stamped onto her $87.50 left shoe. The right one cost the same. He stepped back, pulling her with him. She leaned forward from the ankles, looking like one of those intrepid contestants on *Dancing With the Stars*, where the pro sails backwards, pulling their stiff legged partner across the floor, pointed toes scraping behind.

Thea, wide awake now, sat up in bed. "I can't dance!"

S.J. would have been the perfect person to give her some dance lessons but she was still in Toronto and didn't say when she'd be back. After breakfast, she phoned Madison.

"It's easy," she said. "Step back with your left foot and follow his lead from there."

At 10:30 she got into the car and drove to Elora where Madison and she waltzed and foxtrotted around the living room.

Thea lowered her arms."What about the tango or rhumba?"

"They probably won't play any and if they do, sit it out."

"Let's do the waltz one more time," Thea said.

"You're fine. You can do it and it's lunch time."

After soup and a sandwich, Thea drove home, repeating "one-two-three" or "back-side-together."

On Friday morning, her painting was dry so she moved it to her craft room, rolled up the floor sheet and took the paint tins to the laundry room.

After lunch she walked to Sandy's Mani-Pedi Shoppe and had her first manicure. Somewhere over the past month or so she had stopped biting her nails, and her new dress was a whole size smaller. *Did shedding old baggage shed pounds too?*

At three o'clock, Sara Jane, back from Toronto, phoned and insisted they go shoe shopping. "You can't wear old shoes with your gorgeous new dress."

Downtown, Sara Jane steered her to *If . . Footwear Boutique* on Wyndham Street.

"I'm sure I could find something suitable in Payless or Walmart," Thea said.

"Shut up and follow me."

She bought an outrageously priced pair of shoes (coincidently the same price as her dream shoes) and a glittery evening bag with a long pearlized strap. *Dating is expensive.*

"Light, delicate, and practical," said the smiling clerk as she wrapped it in tissue paper and placed it in an initialed FP bag.

She awoke the next morning—Saturday, June 15, Gala Day—to a squawking blue jay arguing with a determined squirrel.

She showered, dressed, and brought her coffee back upstairs. "No market today, dragonfly." She touched a wing. "Can you believe it's been three months since I found you." The dragonfly didn't answer. "It feels like several lifetimes, my friend." She had stopped taking her dragonfly downstairs for her painting sessions after it had taken half an hour to clean the Prussian blue off its wings.

She had an early afternoon hair appointment even though she could easily wash and dry it herself. Nancy could make magic with the blow dryer and a touch of the curling iron.

By three she was home. Still four hours to go before the appointed time Arthur would pick her up. She would have started another painting as that made time disappear but she dare not risk getting her hands, nails, or hair dotted with Hooker's green or some garish mixture.

She put the kettle on for tea and the door bell rang. As she walked toward it, it swung open and Sara Jane swished in. "Darn, I'm going to miss the blow-by-blow review of your big night."

"I've got to get through it first," Thea said. "And where are you going now?" That woman travelled more than Phileas Fogg in his eighty day adventure around the world.

"I'm so excited. I met a fascinating woman in Toronto at a textile show, and before I knew it I was saying yes to my next trip."

Thea lifted her eyebrows. "But you just got home."

"It all fell together. You know, one of those destiny things," Sara Jane held her breath as if for a dramatic pause. "I'm going to Peru."

"Peru!"

"There's a fabulous group of women artisans who do traditional hand-spinning with alpaca wool they dye themselves. They even raise the alpaca. It's a chance in a lifetime to study and work with them."

"Sit down and tell me all about it. I'll make tea."

"Nope. Can't sit. No tea. I've got to pack. My plane leaves in —" She flipped her wrist over and glanced at her watch. "Oh, my God! I gotta run."

She raced to the door. "See you in three weeks—or is it four? I'll call you." She ran out but a second later it opened and her head popped around. "Have a supercalifragilisticexpealidocious evening."

And she was gone again.

Thea shook her head and went to the kitchen to make tea. She took it to the back step and sat for a half hour contemplating the herbs and flowers. She went inside, flipped through a magazine and watched a rerun of MacGyver. At five o-clock she fixed a plate of cheese and crackers to hold her till the late dinner. At six she ran a bath. At seven, she was dressed and ready, except for her new shoes. She stood before the wooden-framed, full-length mirror fastened to the back of the bathroom door.

"Is that me?" The silk dress fit perfectly—with a little help from a form-fitting foundation undergarment which took several agonizing minutes to squirm into. Her hair bounced and shone with natural highlights and her fingernails glistened with Moonbeam Silver.

The doorbell rang. After a final glance in the mirror, she ran downstairs.

Arthur, alias James Bond, stood resplendent in a black tux. His hands were behind his back. "You look fabulous," he said.

"So do you."

A lovely soft kiss on the lips. "Which hand do you want?" he asked.

She pointed. "That one."

He unwrapped his right arm to reveal a clear plastic corsage box. A white orchid with a whisper of pale pinky-yellow at its centre nestled within. *The prom flower.* "It's gorgeous." She blinked rapidly, hoping the mascara was waterproof. "Thank you."

"Don't you want to know what's in the other hand?"

She looked up from the plastic cover and he whipped his other hand to the front. A large bouquet of California red poppies bobbed their crepe paper heads.

"They're beautiful." She took the armful. "I'll put them in water."

In the kitchen, she turned on the tap and put the poppies into the sink. He opened the corsage box and she lifted out the flower and held against one shoulder and the other.

He reached for it. "It's a wrist corsage. See?" He turned it over. A rucked fabric bracelet was attached underneath. "You don't want to put pins in that beautiful dress."

She slid it over her left hand, where it lay on her wrist like some fragile creature. "Orchids are so special." She tilted her arm back and forth. A special flower from a special man.

He grinned. "The ancient Greeks associated it with virility and the Aztecs were said to drink a mixture of the vanilla orchid and chocolate to give them power and strength."

She stared at him.

"But you don't want to know about that now, do you." He held out his arm. "Let's go."

"I need to get my shoes." She ran upstairs, slipped them on and fetched her evening bag from the window sill. Comb, lipstick, tissues. She grabbed her dragonfly and popped it in. "C'mon, Dragonfly. We're going to a party."

Chapter 38

During the hour's drive to Toronto, Thea stole several glances at her flowering left wrist. The traffic slowed at Highway 427 and again entering the Gardner Expressway, but he easily wound his way up York Street to the formidable Royal York Hotel.

The valet whisked the car away and Arthur ushered her through stately doors. She did indeed feel like Lady Margaret. Even with all the new and fancy hotels in Toronto, nothing surpassed the reputation of the Royal York. And here she was, attending a ball in the "grand old lady."

The ballroom sparkled with lights, mirrors, high arches and glistening chandeliers. Round, white-draped tables, each set for six, were set before a live band and ample space for dancing.

With smiles and handshakes, Arthur introduced her to his colleagues as they moved to their table and joined two of his coworkers and their spouses. Thea lifted her glass with the others to toast the company's success.

Six glasses, three couples—one of which she was a half. Her stomach butterflies settled down in pairs.

French Onion soup in pottery bowls started the meal. Thea dug through the thick layer of melted cheese to reach a steaming spoonful. She sipped carefully, letting its sharp flavours linger in her mouth. The waiters brought plates of Chicken Breasts around. *Oh, well. Eating chicken for once isn't going to kill me.* However, another waiter appeared and placed a different dish in front of her.

One whiff told her it was curry. She looked up at Arthur who smiled and winked. *Bless him.*

She took a large mouthful and an explosion of flavours burst forth. Rich Indian spices danced their hot trail over her tongue, shocking taste buds to a new experience. She swallowed and reached for her water glass.

"Bread is better," her neighbour said, holding up the bread basket.

"Thanks." Thea blinked back tears, while molten rivers coursed through her sinuses. The bread did soak up some of the fire, but on the next piece she slathered butter on it. Perhaps it would help calm things a bit.

"If it's too hot, we can send it back," Arthur said.

"No. It's delicious, but a surprise." *I hope this undergarment has strong seams.*

After a few more mouthfuls, interspersed with bread, her system had adjusted to the heat and she finished the whole thing. She also had a good share of the Sauvignon.

Conversation moved briskly. When the couple opposite brought up politics, she chatted to the man on her left about the latest exhibition at the art gallery. By the time dessert came, her stomach was battling a determined undergarment. *I am not passing up dessert, so steady down you elastic armour.*

Two tantalizing dishes were brought out. Thea gasped. "How can I decide between Caramel Häagen-Dazs and Molten Lava Chocolate Cake?" Dark chocolate dripped tantalizing rivulets onto the plate while on another, thick gooey caramel dribbled over a melting scoop of ice cream.

Arthur saved the day. "Why don't we have both and share?"

Everyone at the table agreed that was a splendid idea. The six servings were divided, slid from one plate to another and slowly savoured.

Coffee, tea, and liqueurs came next and the band's repertoire changed from dining music to a sprightly waltz. Thea took Arthur's hand and they walked to the dance floor and took their position. *Back-side-together* hummed through her head.

After the first three bars of music, she lowered her shoulders and breathed normally. He held her firmly and she easily followed his lead.

She smiled. "You're a good dancer."

"It comes from years of having four sisters drag me around."

She managed the foxtrot, and thankfully, the band never played a tango or a rhumba. With the help of concealed water cylinder, her corsage remained dewy fresh throughout the evening.

At one-thirty, the other couples at their table said their goodbyes, although the younger crowd were still going strong.

Arthur lifted an eyebrow. "What do you think?"

"I'm stuffed and a bit dizzy. I'm ready to go."

Arthur tracked down Mr. Parker, the Senior partner who said, "You're welcome to stay over. We have rooms available for the out-of-towners."

When Thea heard Mr. Parkers' invitation, her slightly inebriated butterfly family perked up their ears. *Do butterflies have ears?* She had been rehearsing all week for what she would say, when Arthur asked her if she wanted to stay over.

They wove their way around tables and chairs, nodding and exchanging good-byes as they made their way to the lobby—a large Victorian sitting room with flowered stuffed chairs, soft lamps beside discreet sitting arrangement for two or four, and a gigantic pot of fresh flowers. A large clock, high on the wall, presided over the scene.

Arthur pointed to it. "This used to be a popular meeting place during World War II. Canadian soldiers promised to meet each other under this clock after the war."

Thea stared at the ticking clock. She wasn't thinking about soldiers.

He turned to her."So, do you want to stay over?"

Cynthia poked her nose in and Thea pushed her away. "Yes, I'd like to."

"We could have separate rooms."

She'd been separate long enough. It was time to join the human race. "One room would be fine." She didn't look at him. *And you shut up Cynthia.*

He took her hand. "Come."

Did people still pretend to be married these days? It didn't even come up.   Arthur signed in and they walked to the elevators. "We're in room 1414," he said.

They were alone in the elevator looking at the numbers lighting up. At 14, the doors opened, and the moment they stepped into the hall, Thea's babble switch turned on and words scrambled off her tongue. "Did you know the fourteenth floor is really the thirteenth? Of course you do, you're an architect." They passed door 1404.

She prattled on. "I'm glad we're on the thirteenth floor. Thirteen is not bad luck, you know." *Shut up. You're talking too much*. But the words kept spilling out.

"The Chinese and Ancient Egyptians considered thirteen good luck but because it represented femininity it was maligned by the founders of patriarchal religions."

Room 1408.

"Who's the trivia expert now?" he said.

"I took an evening course in Feminism. Thirteen was revered in prehistoric goddess-worshipping cultures because of the lunar or monthly cycles and the Wiccan Coven is made up of thirteen. Witches were feared in the middle ages." *Shut up*, she commanded again but her mouth opened and the words shoved against each other, jostling to get out.

"The patriarchy was threatened by women's powers and declared thirteen bad luck. But it's good luck." She stopped and caught her breath.

Room 1414.

On the first swipe, the green light lit and he opened the door. He flicked the wall switch, lighting up a large L-shaped room. She froze at the doorway and gawked at the sage green settee and the two matching chairs that made a semi circle in front of an oval coffee table.

"Are you coming in?" Arthur took her hand.

"Er, why yes. Of course."Her knees wobbled as she took a step forward.

A soft light glowed from table lamps set in front of beige and pale green patterned drapes. A wall mounted TV screen and two gold framed art prints completed the arrangement.

She shivered. *My god. I'm actually here. And I'm acting like a teenager from the 1950's.*

Arthur smiled and led her further into the room.

She gazed around. A movie set waiting for actors. They took three more steps. In an alcove on the left was a king-sized bed covered with a blue-and-white duvet and three matching pillows. The bevy of butterflies inhabiting her stomach fluttered against restricting walls. "I didn't bring my toothbrush or my nightgown," she blurted.

"You won't need one. I mean, there'll be complimentary toothbrushes and—it is a warm night."

"Of course." She feigned the look of a sophisticated woman who was used to spending a night with a man in a hotel room. Her knees quivered.

He put his arms around her. "Everything is fine." And he kissed her. A long and gentle kiss that gradually grew deeper and more lovely. It ended with a long hug, just holding and being.

The scent of his after shave, or perhaps it was his natural male smell, made her tingle. Or maybe it was being held so close for so long. The longer he held her, the more she wanted more. "You smell delicious," she said. "Good enough to eat." *I am being the bold one.*

He pulled back. "Versace. A classy fragrance created in 1986."

For weeks, she had hyped herself up for this and here she was, sexy and available—at long last—and he's about to tell her about men's colognes. *That's the last thing I want to hear now.*

"This particular scent contains lemon, basil, pimento—"

"It sounds like salad dressing." *Why are we talking about salad when we're standing so close? In a hotel room ready for . . .*

"It's Versace's personal l'homme's signature male fragrance. It also has cinnamon and vanilla and—"

She placed her mouth on his which he readily accepted. *My mother was definitely wrong. Men don't only want one thing. Here we are in the perfect setting to make love, and he's talking about perfume that tastes like food.*

The kiss deepened with no more thought of salads or cologne. On her left wrist, a orchid with creamy white petals surrounding a pale pink and yellow centre lay fresh.

Chapter 39

He smelled and tasted of alcohol and her head swam from the wine, the meal, the hour, and the passionate kiss.

He pulled away. "Would you like a drink?" He moved to the side. "There'll be something in the bar fridge."

"No, I've had enough to drink." *I need to catch my breath before I fall down.* She took a step toward a stuffed chair but he was back and swooped her into his arms again.

"And you, my love, are enough for me to drink in."

Her lips still throbbed from the last kiss but she welcomed more and more came. Her body flamed with desire, ready to be propelled into the unknown. Now she knew why characters in a movie, after one kiss, would madly rip off their clothes. *Am I ready?*

Oh, my god. "Wait." She pushed him back. It was hard enough getting into the confines of the slim-line body garment and she cringed at the thought of him peeling it off her. Not the foreplay she had anticipated. "I—I—"

"Don't you want to?"

"Oh, I do. I do. I have to take care of something first." She ran to a door off the bedroom. Thank God it was the bathroom and not a closet. She slid the orchid over her hand and placed it beside the sink. No use it getting crushed. She lifted her dress and slid her thumbs into the top edge of the thick elastic band under her bra. Pushing, grunting (softly so he wouldn't hear) and wriggling like a hula dancer, she inched it down her midriff. A short rest at the waist and centimetre by centimetre, over the hips. Was there a saint of getting out of tight places?

With a final shove, she was free of its clutches and it dropped to the floor. She held onto the sink for a moment, lightheaded from wine? lack of oxygen? or the dizzying aroma of the man on the other side of the door?

A light knock. "Are you all right in there?"

"Coming." She smoothed her dress over her rounded tummy and unsquished hips and opened the door to a barefoot man in a white terry towel bathrobe.

He smiled. "Thought I'd get comfortable." He held a large plastic covered package in one hand. "There's one for you too."

She took it from him and held it in front of her with both arms wrapped around it. "Great idea." In two steps, she was back in the bathroom. She hung her dress on a hook on the door, slid easily out of bra, panty hose, and panties which she folded and added to the wrinkled undergarment tucked at the back of the wide counter.

She walked out thoroughly ensconced in the sumptuous terry towel robe. The only lights in the room were two small lamps, one on either side of the bed.

He was under the covers, leaning back against a propped up pillow. He smiled and patted the other side of the bed. "Lots of room." He was not wearing his bathrobe. "Oh, and I wish to be a gentleman. Will we need this?" He opened his palm, revealing a small plastic envelope.

She stared and feeling her face getting hot, mumbled, "Er, no. It's—that is, I—no. That's not necessary."

"Right." He slipped the object under his pillow and interlaced his hands across his chest.

She took a deep breath. "But I have to do one more thing."

"Another thing?" He lifted an eyebrow.

She walked to the side of the bed and pulled out a section of the top sheet from its tucked position. She made her way down the side and along the bottom, yanking the sheet loose. She stopped at the beginning of his side. "Do you want me to do yours?"

"Why not?" He grinned and put both hands behind his head as she continued up the edge of the bed.

"There." She stood with her hands on her hips, looking at the freed sheet.

"Are you planning to get into bed sometime soon?"

"Of course. I just can't stand tight sheets holding me down." She turned off his lamp and scurried around to the other side of the bed where she turned off hers. Before anyone's eyes had time to adjust to the dark, she threw off her housecoat and slid under the covers.

Arthur cleared his throat. "What shall we do now?" His voice held a hint of laughter.

She let out her breath. "Well, I don't want to talk about Versace or tight sheets or—"

Her words were cut off by his mouth landing softly on hers and his arms around her. Another long and soft kiss, and with his naked body pressed against her, her own body had ideas of its own.

He held her close as if that was all he ever wanted to do. Her shoulders dropped an inch, and her muscles gradually relaxed.

She leaned into him like a marionette with its strings untied and after several moments, she couldn't tell where her body ended and his began. Her breath slowed and a deep sense of peace enveloped her.

He stroked her back, her breasts, her stomach and her thighs, so naturally and smoothly, she effortlessly and easily yielded to his gentle touch. Bodies were amazing. Let them alone and they knew what to do. Their bodies fit as if they had done this many times before. She wasn't Cynthia. She wasn't Thea. She was Eve.

They moved together in the ancient rhythm of love making. Her body knew what to do. It knew what it wanted and it was opening to it and receiving it—fully and completely without censure. Without shame and without fear.

They lay in each others arms, exhausted, depleted and full at the same time. His limp penis lay harmless against her sticky thigh while she floated in an awakened fairyland of bliss.

She didn't know how long they lay there, limbs entwined, half covered with the loosened sheet but a few minutes after she opened her eyes, he opened his.

"Hello there," he whispered. "You're one mighty fine lady."

"You're not so bad yourself." Was this the shy woman who had been so afraid of sex? The seal of shame was broken and there was no going back.

He smiled and lay back on his pillow, one arm still around her. In a few moments, his regular breathing indicated he was asleep while Thea's body buzzed from rich food, too much wine and unsurpassed sexual delights.

She lay for several minutes when something prompted her to slide out of bed. She tiptoed to the bathroom and splashed water on her face.

Her mirror self said, "So you're not a nun after all."

'I never said I was."

"Well, it sure seemed so for a long while." A grin. "Until tonight."

She stared at the normal—one might even call pretty—face in front of her. A face of a woman who had experienced some extremely satisfying sex. She and the image nodded their heads.

She tiptoed out and walked toward the bed, passing the mirrored doors of the closet. The moonlight, stealing through a slit in the drapes, revealed a determined, naked woman. She stood sideways and sucked in her tummy. *Not a bad body.*

Like a stranger in a strange land, she crawled into bed beside the bare-naked man. An image of a bizarre 3-D animated Technicolour movie in surround sound darted into her head. An arm, bracelets jangling, pointed a waggling finger at her nose. *Do you have no shame? Running around with no clothes on! And what are you thinking getting into bed with a naked man?*

The bold lady in bed, attired only in her birthday suit answered, *None of your business, Mother. And get out of my head.*

The screen turned black and a freed Thea pointed her toes under the loosened covers, took a deep breath and fell asleep.

Chapter 40

Thea awoke, deliciously aware of the warm body spooning against her curved back. Puffs of air whistled over her cheek. His naked body was familiar, as if they had done this before. Arthur's arm shifted and she stiffened.

What now? What does one say or do after such a night?

With thumb and forefinger she picked up his wrist and lifted his arm from her waist. He didn't respond so she wriggled forward a couple of inches. Gingerly, she returned his arm to him, holding her breath when he snorted and changed position.

She slid out of bed, grabbed her bathrobe. *Will I ever get used to being naked in front of him?* Last night it had been dark and, in the throes of desire, who looks at bodies?

He hadn't moved. With his tousled sandy hair against the white pillow, he could be seventeen. Well, maybe twenty-seven. Thirty-seven at the most. She must ask him how he got that scar. Her eyes traced his biceps. He probably works out.

There was still so much she didn't know about him.

She took her purse and padded barefoot to the bathroom. She was Queen Guinevere leaving her King sleeping soundly in their love bed. She washed her hair with lavender-scented shampoo from one of the miniature bottles.

The hot water cascaded over her shoulders, down her stomach and between her legs to her toes. She let her hands roam over places so recently awakened and now appreciated.

Thank you body. As she rubbed herself dry, she couldn't help thinking it would be fun to shower with him. She wrapped a towel around herself and opened her purse. "Well, dragonfly, what do you think?"

She placed it on the counter and found a hair dryer to fluff up her hair.

A sing-song voice called from the other room. "Thea, where are you?"

She yanked off the towel, scrambled into her robe and took a deep *here-goes* breath.

Arthur, half-sitting up, leaned on an elbow rubbing sleep out of one eye. He smacked his lips as if tasting something unpleasant.

"Hello sleepy head," she said.

He groaned. "What did I drink last night? My mouth tastes like the armpit of a camel."

"You mentioned something about mixing wine with gin."

"How stupid was that?" He threw the covers off and stood up as if it were the most normal thing in the world to be naked before her.

Her eyes darted to his private parts and away. *Did he see me look?*

He stumbled to the bathroom, closed the door and the shower started.

She walked to the round marble table set between two red upholstered straight chairs. *This has to be a dream.* She stood up and flapped her arms but she didn't fly. *Nope, not a dream.*

When she was eight she had asked her dad if dreaming was real or was being awake really a dream.

He didn't laugh like her mother had. He'd said, "A wise philosopher once dreamt of a butterfly and he wondered if he was the dreamer or was the butterfly dreaming of him?"

It didn't answer her question but it make her think.

Arthur came around the corner with his bathrobe on, the belt ties flopped over loosely. "What would you like for breakfast?"

"Breakfast? You mean here?"

"It's part of the company's package." He picked up the glossy folder and handed it to her. "What are you smiling at? You look like the cat who swallowed the canary."

"I'm not used to this."

"You mean room service? Or this?" He bent over and kissed her full on the mouth.

When she could speak, she said, "Both, but mostly the latter."

"And how are you doing with the latter?"

"Fine." She wished her voice didn't sound like a little girl's. She looked into his eyes. Those lovely, kind, smiling eyes. It was as if she had known him forever, and last night was not only natural, but destined.

He put a hand on each side of her waist, drew her up in front of him and kissed her lightly on the forehead and on each eye. She lifted her face to him like a buttercup melting in the sun.

He kissed her with an open mouth and undid the double knot of her robe. He pulled his robe open and pressed his naked body against hers. Her lady parts throbbed. She never dreamed bodies could give and receive so much pleasure.

His hands slid down her back, latched onto her bottom and lifted her up to receive him. They moved in a steadily climbing rhythm.

Her roller coaster climbed higher and higher. At its tipping point, she cried out and a million ripples coursed through her. She began to shake.

He smoothed her hair. "It's all right, my sweet. I'm not going anywhere." He held her tightly and she clung to him. An image of her running into his arms, welcoming him back from a long journey. It was Arthur but not Arthur. The dark eyes were the same.

A dragonfly swooped down, picked her up, and carried her to a far corner of the universe. *It is you. You've come back to me.*

She took a breath and made a fierce vow. *We will never be apart again.* The dam burst and a volume of tears gushed out. She cried away the demons and the carcasses of years of bitter ogres: her mother's control, being ugly, and thinking sex was bad and wrong.

Arthur said nothing. He held her close and stroked her back.

Her cries turned to sniffles, sniffles to hiccups, and at last she was quiet and at peace. Home in his arms.

After a long moment, he said, "Welcome back."

She lifted her head. "Why did you say that?"

"I don't know. It seemed as if you went a long way off and came back home to me."

"I did."

"Let's have breakfast." He placed the order and before long they eagerly dug into scrambled eggs, home fries, English muffins with strawberry jam, and a pot of coffee.

Was it sex or releasing the past that gave her such an appetite?

They got dressed and on that bright Sunday morning, walked along Front Street and Queens Quay. She had left her restricting compression garment in the hotel wastebasket. It wouldn't fit in her purse and she could hardly tuck it under her arm.

A half hour later, they picked up the car and threaded their way north through the city toward the 401. As they neared the Bloor and Bathurst intersection, Thea cried, "Can we go to Honest Ed's?"

"We could but it's not there anymore."

"What do you mean, 'it's not there anymore.' That's nonsense. How could a block-sized store be moved?"

He grinned. "Honest Ed's is closed. It's torn down and there's a whole new building complex going up."

Her mouth dropped open. "But it was a city landmark."

He turned onto Bloor Street. Piles of earth, skeletons of buildings and huge machines sat idle on the place where Honest Ed's once stood. "I can't look," she cried. "Let's get out of here."

He passed Euclid Street and Thea said, "We moved here when I was fifteen."

Arthur turned his head left and right. "Here? Where here?"

"We passed it. We lived in an apartment over a store."

"Did you like living there?"

"It was weird after living in the country, but the best thing about it was Honest Ed's."

"Why was that?"

"We didn't have much money and you could buy almost anything from there. Ed Mirvish was a theatre buff, and the store's walls were decorated with old posters and signed photographs of actors, singers, dancers, and magicians."

"I don't think I was ever in Honest Ed's."

Thea's mouth dropped open again. "You missed a great experience. Signs announcing: *Don't faint at our low prices, there's no place to lie down, or Don't just stand there, buy something*"

"I guess you had to be there to appreciate it."

She gave him a poke. "Snob. I remember when I received my first week's pay from my first full-time job. Bell Telephone." She laughed. "Who hasn't worked for Ma Bell?"

"I haven't," said Arthur.

"I was sixteen and when I cashed my first cheque, I headed to Honest Ed's and bought everyone a present." She looked up. "Let's see. A green sweater for Maddy, a blue one for Patricia, a catnip mouse for Fluffy, a pipe rack for my dad and—" She stopped. "What did I buy my mother?"

The traffic moved easily along Bloor Street and Arthur asked, "So what did you buy your mother?"

"I don't remember. Probably something she didn't like."

"Do I sense some conflict with your mother?"

"I don't want to get into that now."

After another block, Arthur said, "I've been meaning to talk to you about something. My company closes for Christmas week, so —" His voice raised on the last word.

"So?"

"So, why don't we go to New York that week?

New York? Is he crazy?

"What do you think? We could catch a Broadway show, art galleries, the museum, the Met."

He means it. Her head and heart started an argument. *You love those things*, her heart said. *It doesn't make sense*, yelled her head. "Won't that cost a lot?" she said out loud.

"Not much more for two as for one. Anyway, I'm paying. My treat."

She stared out the window. New York would be fabulous but things were happening too fast. Her recent headlong plunge into the ocean of sex still reverberated in her body and mind and soul. *Am I ready to be with him for a whole week and to let him pay for such a trip?*

They passed Christie Pits. She and her dad used to go to baseball games and outdoor concerts there. *Central Park must have concerts.*

Over the years, she had worked at changing her attitude about money and her own self-worth. She had moved from 'never enough' to 'just enough.' *But am I ready to take the quantum leap to more than enough?*

She said aloud, "I'll have to think about it."

Chapter 41

Arthur stopped for a red light at the next intersection. "So what do you think about the New York trip?"

The light turned green and they moved forward. "I can't think that fast. For one thing it's expensive and—" She frowned. "I'm supposed to be moving in December. New York is impossible."

"I said I would pay for it and moving can be arranged easily."

She took a deep breath. *Easy for him to say.* She had been avoiding the thought of moving, hoping it would go away but even if her mother gave her an extension, letting him pay for such a trip would be not just immoral but downright wrong. It would cost hundreds, thousands of dollars, counting the air fare, hotel, eating out, Broadway shows, taxis, tips. "I'd love to but— "

"Thea, I have the money. It won't cost me much more than if I went alone. Consider it an early Christmas present."

She had never received such an expensive present in her life, Christmas or otherwise. Her chest tightened and the struggle between desire and fear stopped her tongue.

He glanced at her. "I'm looking forward to a whole week with you." He turned onto Dufferin Street. "Tell you what. Knowing your tendency for thinking too much, I propose we make a deadline."

"A deadline? You mean if I don't get to the line I get shot dead?" She wasn't smiling when she said it. It was enough to have her mother ordering her around al, she didn't need another 'boss.'

"Okay, so don't call it a deadline." He wasn't smiling either.

She wrapped her arms around her purse. "I'll give you my answer on Labour day."

"Does that give you enough time?"

"Are you being sarcastic?"

"Who me? Sarcastic? Never."

Three days after their Royal York liaison, Arthur stayed the night and they made love in Thea's single bed. The last chunks of the ice-queen's armour had definitely melted.

On Friday, she had a rollicking lunch with Madison. Besides sharing a history, a great thing about having a sister was you could be candid.

They placed their order at *The Cornerstone Restaurant* and Thea leaned over and said in a low voice, "I can't believe it, but I love sex. Arthur is amazing."

Madison slapped her thigh. "I can't believe you said that! Are you my same sister? The one who tells the joke about the woman who wears gloves to bed so she doesn't have to touch the nasty thing?" Her voice had raised an octave.

"Not so loud, Maddy."

Madison guffawed and Thea joined her. People at nearby tables looked up. Finally Thea caught her breath. "He's a fabulous lover —and so am I!"

They laughed till their faces hurt and stomachs ached.

Saturday night, Arthur stayed again, and after making love, they sat on the bed, he at one end, stroking the top of her foot with feather fingers. "So what's the big deal with you and money?"

"What to you mean?" She jerked her foot away.

"Don't have a hissy fit. You reacted so strongly about New York I wondered why you have such weird ideas about money."

She threw a pillow at him. "I don't—" *I do have weird ideas about money.* She grabbed the other pillow and hugged it to her chest. "It's funny how words have different meanings."

He slapped his naked chest and growled. "Like bare and bear?"

"No, silly. I'm serious." She tugged at the trim on the pillow case. "For example, does 'what you're worth' mean money or self-worth?"

"One's worthiness doesn't depend on how much money one has."

"I was brought up to think it does." She tucked the pillow under her chin and leaned on it. "My grandparents lived through the depression and believed in the Protestant work ethic of a never-ending struggle. Earning a living by the sweat of your brow and all that."

"A lot of people did at that time."

"My grandmother and great-grandmother and probably my great-great-grandmother were 'in service'—maids—in England and they passed on a servant mentality. My mother thought higher education was for *other* people." She scrunched up her nose. "Not for people like *us*."

Arthur returned to massaging her feet.

"If ever my sisters or I were proud of ourselves, our mother would yell, 'Stop that or you'll get a big head,' or 'who do you think you are?'" Thea shoved her face into the pillow as a vivid scene bubbled up.

She was five, clutching a broken doll to her chest. Her chin wobbled.

"You are a selfish little girl," her mother screamed. "Stop asking for things." Her face scrunched up. "And don't cry, or I'll give you something to cry about."

Cynthia ran from her mother's bedroom, gulping back tears.

Thea pulled her face out of the pillow, a nest of angry bees swarmed inside her. She'd had a breakthrough in painting and a sexual metamorphosis so why were old feelings of not being good enough still hanging around? *How dare they erupt again.* With a wild look in her eyes, she made a fist and smashed it into the pillow. "I'm sick of all this crap. I'm sick of feeling unworthy."

Arthur let go of her foot.

"My mother was wrong," she hollered. "I AM worthwhile." She gave the pillow a mighty whack. The seam split and goose-down tumbled out. Another punch tore it open and a mass of feathers exploded.

Arthur ducked, trying to avoid flying feathers.

Spluttering and spitting, she reached in, grabbed a fistful of feathers and tossed them into the air.

Arthur swatted at the flurry of white while yet another storm of feathers, released from bondage, cascaded over them.

"No more *shoulding* on myself," she cried. "I'm going to do what feels good."

She stretched an arm toward an equalling spluttering Arthur. "Let's make feather love." And they did.

Two days later, she was still finding feathers—in a slipper, under a book, or on a curtain. She left the one that had landed on the dragonfly's wing.

That afternoon, she was in her office, concentrating on inputting a column of numbers, when Madison phoned. "Do you want a queen-sized bed? I thought you might like it now that you're involved in nighttime gymnastics."

"You've been reading my mind again."

"Younger sisters know these things. Charlie's been wanting a king-size so you can have ours. It's like new."

It was great when one's idle musings were answered so quickly.

Madison continued. "You could get a new mattress if you like, but we had a thick cotton cover and a plastic sheet over it. It's in pristine condition."

"Why did you have a plastic sheet on it? Oh, sorry."

Madison laughed. "We're not incontinent. We like having tea in bed when we're watching Saturday Night Live and once I fell asleep with half a cup of cold tea in my lap."

"I'd love to have it. I'll pass mine on to Goodwill."

"Okay. Our king is coming tomorrow. I'll have the delivery people drop the queen off to you."

Thea hung up. Positive thinking did work but so did negative thinking. On days she decided she was going to have a good day, she did but if she started worrying about something, more stuff to worry about would show up. The idea of perceiving your world through a filter of beliefs was not new to Thea. One of her father's mantras was: "as you think, so you are." It did give one something to ponder but she often thought herself into circles or spirals of more thoughts.

Even after her feather throwing tirade, niggling thoughts of not being deserving or not good enough still poked at her. It was going to take more than throwing feathers around to dislodge her deep-rooted beliefs about money.

Chapter 42

She wanted to go to New York but if she went with a lousy attitude, it could ruin the whole trip. It was time to release that boring refrain of *not enough or just enough*. She closed her computer, made a fresh pot of coffee and took her mug, along with her journal and pen, to her chair in the living room. After a couple of sips, she opened the book to a new page.

At the top, she wrote MONEY and underlined it twice. She stared at it and then meticulously inked in the space between the lines making one fat one. No inspiring words came. No releasing thoughts. No enlightenment. Nothing. She needed a question to prime the pump. She stared at the ceiling.

"Why do I feel poor?" She waited. "Yes, that's the right word —poor." She was one of the poor people. Not only poor—but noble and poor. Her father had brought in a modest weekly pay cheque but he retained the struggling artist persona and put himself above such mundane matters as money.

She scribbled. *It's spiritual to be poor. I am proud to be poor. Rich people are stuck up and snooty.*

She stopped writing. The voice in her head changed to her mother's. *We can't afford that. Who do you think you are? Money doesn't grow on trees.* And a loud booming voice. *You're a selfish and ungrateful little girl.*

Her mother had said that to all of them, but suddenly a childhood memory filled her head. "My piggy bank!"

When she was six, she had saved nickels, dimes and pennies over months of collecting pop bottles and taking them to Stewart's General Store. Her piggy bank rattled with her precious savings of seven dollars and thirty-eight cents, the most money she'd ever had. Each night before bed, she'd pry off the rubber plug from the bottom of her pink ceramic pig and count the coins. One evening she picked up her piggy bank and it didn't rattle. Nary a sound. She shook it again. Silence. She pried the stopper out, stuck her finger in over the bumpy seams inside the pig. Empty. Every dime, every nickel, every penny and one quarter was gone. She ran to her mother, crying. "Mommy! Mommy! Patricia stole my money!"

Her mother frowned. "Your sister didn't take it, I did."

Cynthia's stomach clenched into an iron ball and her throat closed up.

"I needed money for bread and milk."

Cynthia's mouth wobbled. "But—it was *my* money."

A glare "And you ate some of the bread and drank the milk. You're a selfish and ungrateful little girl."

Thea stared at the word at the top of her journal as if seeing it for the first time—MONEY—underscored with a thick black line. The heavy ball in her gut shook, and the long awaited earthquake erupted. She dropped the book and doubled over, grasping her stomach. Burning acid rolled up her body, filling her throat. Rocking and moaning turned to crying and wailing. She grabbed a nearby cushion and beat on it with tight fists. She pounded as the pain coursed through her body, spewing like vomit. Old, stinking, putrid, vile, and poisonous, it sprayed out of every pore and every crusted crack of her being. The keening wails went on for minutes, hours, centuries before they changed to sobs, whimpers and gulps of fresh air. She pulled her knees up, curled into a fetal position and with a shuttered breath, fell into a deep sleep.

She awoke with a start, crunched in her chair. Her journal lay on the floor outlined in a shaft of light which shone through the front window from the street lamp.

She uncurled herself and picked up her book and pen.

"It wasn't about the money." She shook her head, opened her journal and shut it with a slam. *I don't need to write it out.* It's out. All out. The iron walls installed by a confused and frightened child had been dismantled.

She wasn't that helpless and disempowered child anymore. Like a Pavlovian dog, she had linked having money with being selfish and bad.

Minou meowed and pushed her head against Thea's ankle.

"You must be hungry. I have no idea what time it is and I don't care."

She went to the kitchen, not even glancing at the grandfather clock and opened a tin of Friskies and put water on to boil. Even though she'd missed her evening meal, she wasn't hungry.

She laughed. *I feel strangely full, like a big space inside me opened up and who I really am rushed in.* "I'm not sure what that means, Minou, but it sure feels good."

She poured boiling water over a tea bag and went to her office and picked up the phone. She hit speed dial for Arthur's number. It went to voice mail.

"Hi Arthur. I know it's not Labour Day but I've made my decision." She hesitated for a tiny second.

"I'd love to go to New York with you."

Chapter 43

Early Thursday afternoon, Thea had just opened her computer when the phone rang. Before she could say hello, a voice said, "I need a ride to the airport tomorrow."

"Hello, mother. How are you?"Thea's ears heard the same demanding voice, but it's daggers didn't cut through her the same. In a calm voice, said, "Where are you going?"

"Fort Lauderdale."

"You're going to Florida in June?"

"What's wrong with that? I can go whenever I want to."

It was just a question. A question Cynthia would never have asked. "Most people go in January or February. Are you going alone?"

"Of course not. I'm taking Tippy. I have his Rabies vaccination certificate and his special carry on."

"Tippy has a carry-on?"

"Don't be snippy with me, young lady. Tippy will be IN the carry-on."

"What time is your flight?"

"Four o'clock, but I have to be there two hours ahead."

"The traffic on the 401 is horrendous anytime of the day. Why don't you call the Red Car?" *Cynthia would never have suggested such an option.*

Her mother gasped. "You mean you're refusing to take your own mother to the airport? What's gotten into you?

Thea pictured her mother's astonished face that her daughter—this particular daughter—didn't jump at her command. "Those drivers know short cuts if there's a hold up on the highway." *This is fun talking back to my mother?.* "Where are you staying in Florida."

A huff and a puff sounded on the line before a sharp voice said, "With Janet, of course."

"Janet who?"

"Are you going senile? Janet Devereaux, my old whist partner from Toronto. She phoned last week. She's moved to Florida and we're going to celebrate Dominion Day and Interdependence day in her two-bedroom condom."

"It's called Canada Day now and it's Independence Day and it's not a—never mind.

"So are you going to pick me up or not?"

It wasn't a question. It sounded like a threat. *Maybe I need to give her a little time to get used to the new me.* "I can take you this time. I'll pick you up at one."

"Well, I should say so." A clank of bracelets and dial tone.

Thea stared at the receiver. *Enduring an hour's drive locked in a car with my mother will be a challenge.*

The drive took less than an hour and the whole time Thea kept the radio tuned to her classical music station.

Her mother stiffened. "How you stand that hoity-toity stuff?"

"I could switch to jazz if you like." *I am not turning off the radio.*

"No. Tippy hates that."

"Speaking of Tippy. He's awfully quiet."

"I gave him a valium."

"Is that wise?"

"They're from the Vet. I wouldn't hurt Tippy for the world."

Thea parked and took mother, suitcase and sleeping dog—in his wheeled carry-on—inside the airport. She steered them to a kiosk where she printed the boarding pass and luggage tag. "Now, go over there and follow those people."

"I won't phone. You know I hate long distance." Pulling her case behind and pushing Tippy in front, she marched off.

"And goodbye to you too," Thea said to the receding back.

On the drive home, Handel's spirited *Water Music* removed the last remnants of the *mom vibe* and reinforced Thea's new *I'm okay* space. She'd have two weeks being her new self without a nagging mother asking how much house packing she had done.

On Saturday evening, she and Arthur went to a movie, and afterwards they christened the newly acquired queen bed. He stayed all night.

Early the next morning, his voice woke her up. "What is that and how could I have missed it last night?"

"Wha—what's what?" she mumbled and blinked her eyes half open.

Arthur was leaning on one elbow, pointing over her shoulder. Her gaze followed his outstretched finger to a two-by-four foot blaze of colour leaning against the pine bureau. Yesterday, she had moved it from her craft room and placed it upside down to study it from a different perspective.

"That's a painting." She snuggled into the covers .

"I can see that. Did you do that?"

She poked out her head. "Yup."

"You amaze me more every day." He crawled over her and took a step toward it. "It's—it's—"

A little more awake, she sat up, swung her legs over the edge of the bed and giggled at the stuttering, naked man standing in front of one of her paintings. A few months ago, abstract art and naked men were light years from her world.

He stepped back, still staring at the canvas and lowered himself onto the side of the bed beside her. She, in a pink nightgown and he, in his birthday suit. "You are some wild woman."

She looked him up and down. "You aren't so tame yourself."

In a flash her nightie came off and they welcomed the morning in a style they were becoming used to.

He stayed over Sunday night and the next day after their nightly fireworks, they went to Riverside Park to see the Canada Day fireworks.

Later that week, Thea and Madison met for lunch at the *Bookshelf Café*.

"You seem perky today," Madison said.

Thea hesitated. *Now is as good a time as ever to spill the beans.* "Arthur and I are going to New York for a week."

Madison's mouth dropped. "You are the bold one! When."

"Christmas week."

"You know mom will be furious."

"I don't care."

"And are you going to let him pay for everything?" Both eyebrows lifted.

"Funny you should ask that. Yes, I am."

"What's come over you, Ms. Nobody-Pays-For-Me?"

"Let's just say I've worked out some stuff." She pierced a forkful of salad and before putting it into her mouth, asked, "Was I a wimpy kid?"

"You're asking me? I'm the youngest, remember. You should ask Patricia."

Thea laughed. "Remember when we were jumping on the bed and you fell off and hit your head on the pointy ears of that iron dog door stop?"

"There was blood everywhere." She made a face.

"Yeah and mom blamed me. She said I'd pushed you. I was the one who got no supper that night."

"I only remember her ripping up a sheet and winding it around my head."

They ate quietly for a moment before Thea spoke. "I can't have been that wimpy. I used to make a big fuss whenever mom made me eat meat." *It doesn't matter who you were as a kid. I'm a new person now.*

"That used to annoy mom to no end."

"I don't think mom and I will ever get along." *Why did I spend so many years trying?*

They finished their lunch and strolled across Quebec Street to the parking lot. When they were several feet away, Madison clicked the remote. "By the way, how do you like the new bed?"

"I love it. There's so much more room. And thanks for the sheets. Minou loves it too."

"I wasn't thinking of the cat."

Thea's face flushed.

Madison glanced at her. "Oh, it was that good, was it?"

"Sometimes I think I'm becoming a sex maniac. I love it so much. I didn't realize what I was missing." *And I love making up for lost time.*

"I've heard of late bloomers, but you take the cake." She opened her door.

On the other side, with her door half opened, Thea struck a Liza Minnelli pose, complete with an invisible long cigarette holder and definitely attitude. "You ain't seen nothin' yet, lady. This dame's headin' for the Big Apple."

They got into the car and Thea said, "And I don't care who objects."

Chapter 44

The next two weeks flew by and Thea was surprised when Janet Devereaux phoned with her mother's arrival time the next day. Thea phoned Maddy and Patricia but neither was available to pick up their mother.

That evening on the phone with Arthur he said, "When am I going to meet your mother?"

"Never?" suggested Thea.

Her mother's flight landed early afternoon so at least they'd miss the heaviest part of rush hour. Her mother, finally settled in the car, held a yapping Tippy and chattered incessantly. "We played golf, went on the Jungle Queen Riverboat for a barbecue, and sat on the Lanai—that's the porch—"

"I know what a Lania is, mother."

"And we went to a Polynesian Revue with real teepee torches."

"I think they're called tiki torches."

"I even went swimming in the ocean and did I tell you I played golf? We went to Butterfly World and saw a million butterflies, and a Japanese restaurant . . ."

Her voice droned over the bursts of dog yips, while Thea waited for the chance to bring up the subject of going away for Christmas. She had purposely not turned on the radio so when she brought up the subject her mother would hear her. Forty minutes later, with the Guelph exit coming up, she dove in, "There's something I need to talk to you about."

"I don't want to hear any more sob stories of you leaving your precious house." She pointed her finger. "There's our turn. Don't miss it."

Thea flicked the turn signal and curved onto the ramp.

Her mother went on. "I met the nicest woman on the plane. It had been her first trip to Florida and we talked the whole way."

Thea tuned out the ongoing monologue and pictured herself attending a Broadway play. After several pointed reminders from her mother that she wasn't listening, she pulled into Stuart Street, head aching. She dragged the suitcase and the empty dog carry-on to the steps.

Mrs. Marshall marched ahead, carrying Tippy. "I phoned Bonnie all the way from Florida to be sure she'd have a pot of tea ready. I hope she remembered."

Bonnie opened the door and Mrs. Marshall strode toward the kitchen. "Where's my tea?"

Thea bumped the suitcases up the steps. Bonnie, held the door open and Thea dumped them in the front hall.

Bonnie smiled. "Will you stay for tea, my dear?"

"Thanks, but I have to get going."

"Thank you for picking up your mother." She wrapped Thea in her plump arms with a quick hug. "I wasn't up for that drive."

"No problem." *Except I didn't broach the subject of Christmas.*

On the drive home, she turned in to Angelino's Market and picked up two large fresh baked pastries. The small white box on the seat beside her, along with the lack of chatter and yapping dog, eased her weary brain and by the time she pulled into the back lane, her head had stopped pounding.

Sara Jane's Mercedes was there. *I wondered when she was coming home.*

Thea wasn't in the house ten minutes when her doorbell rang, followed by an unmistakable, "Hello-o. I'm baaaaack."

A dervish in a whirling red skirt, a white cotton blouse and a multicoloured woven shawl sprang into the living room and swamped Thea in an engulfing hug. "So much to tell you."

Thea caught her breath. "I'll put the coffee on."

Sara Jane followed her to the kitchen. "You wouldn't believe the colours, the smells, the women, the air, the mountains." She stopped to take a breath.

"Sounds like you had a good time."

"Fabulous." She pulled off the shawl and shoved it at Thea. "This is for you."

"It's beautiful."

"I made it myself."

She lifted the soft material to her cheek. "You made this yourself?"

Sara Jane grinned. "Alpaca wool—which I also wove—shorn from a friendly alpaca who grazed a few feet from me."

For the next half hour over coffee and a pastry, Sara Jane regaled her with the sights and sounds of Sacred Valley, Cusco, and Machu Picchu. "One night a local shaman led us in a despacho."

"What's that? It sounds like a Spanish soup."

Sara Jane laughed. "A despacho is the traditional Incan ceremony of intention and letting go."

"I need one of those to shake off the last of my mother's claws."

"What's up?" Sara Jane licked the last drip of custard.

"My mother was away in Florida for two weeks. It wasn't long enough."

"You're always complaining about your mother. Tell her to eff off."

"Sure. As easy as facing a poisonous snake or a tiger."

"You're a grown woman, for heaven's sake. Get her out of your head."

Thea took a deep breath. "I thought I had but there must be more." *If I can overcome my hurdle with sex and money I'm sure I can handle my mother-stuff.* "Yes. I will. I'm a grown woman. I don't need her approval."

"Well, duh. Of course you don't."

"I'll tell her I'm going to New York for Christmas and that's that."

"New York. That's great. You can visit your paintings. By the way, the gallery wants more."

"You're kidding."

"Nope. Why don't I come and meet your mother?"

"What? You don't want to do that."

"Why not? Maybe I can soften her up a bit."

Thea stared at her friend. Perhaps this dynamic whirlwind might dislodge her mother's unbroken and sacred rule of her daughters being present for Christmas. "All right, but I want to tell Stephanie about my Christmas plans first."

The next day Thea phoned her daughter.

"You're what?" Stephanie squealed on the phone. "I can't believe it. You're actually going to New York for seven days with a man! Is this my mother speaking?"

"It's true. I'm not quite over the hill yet."

"That's for sure and it's about time you had a relationship. I'm happy for you. Arthur is a lucky man."

"I'm the lucky one. But I'll miss having Christmas with you."

"No, you won't. I'm sure Arthur is more fun to cuddle up with than me. Have you told Grandma?"

"No."

"I don't want to be around when you do."

"I wish I weren't as well."

A week passed and she hadn't told her mother. Another week and still not. Sara Jane phoned. "When are you going to arrange a meeting with your mother and me."

"Soon." She hung up. How was she going to tell her mother? Christmas was *the* mandatory obligation for the Marshall girls. Over the years, spouses came and went, grandchildren had been added, but Patricia, Madison and Cynthia, always sat at their mother's table on Christmas day. *But I'm Thea now*

It was the only time their mother loosened her purse, probably making up for her own bleak childhood. She and Bonnie would start plans in early November: food, decorations, presents for the grandchildren and a cheque for one thousand dollars for each of her daughters. It was the one time Thea felt equal to her sisters, however, once her mother hears her Christmas plans, she probably wouldn't even receive a card, let alone an enclosure.

It was the middle of August so that would give her a lot of notice. She hit her mother's fast dial button.

A week later, on a Sunday afternoon, Sara Jane in white slacks, a red top with spaghetti straps and her hair tied back with a narrow ribbon stood at the front door of Thea's mother's house. Thea wore a long sleeved summer dress and eyed Sara Jane's bare arms. *How does she keep them so toned?* "Now, remember," Thea said, "Do not mention Christmas to my mother. Let me do that."

Bonnie opened the door. "Come in, my dears. Tea is ready and I have a pan of lemon squares fresh out of the oven."

Mrs. Marshall swept along the hall, her hand held out to Sara Jane. "It's so nice to meet a friend of Cynthia's."

They sat in the living room and Sara Jane was her usual easy-to-talk-to self. Josephine Marshall was uncharacteristically civil. The conversation ranged from dog breeds to roses. Thea mostly just listened to the two of them talk.

Bonnie and Thea went to the kitchen to refresh the tea pot and lemon-squares plate. When they returned, Mrs. Marshall and Sara Jane were talking recipes. Thea put down the fat brown teapot. The spout and handle poked out of an orange and red knitted cozy.

Mrs. Marshall smiled. "Dear Sara Jane here has such good recipes that cost pennies to make."

Thea lifted her eyebrows. "Really?" Sara Jane had many attributes but she doubted economical meal planning was one.

"She gave me an excellent recipe for feeding eighty members of the Kennel Club at our annual convention. And for pennies a head!" She patted Sara Jane's hand.

Thea looked at her mother and Sara Jane. *I would swear they've met before.*

Mrs.Marshall nudged Sara Jane. "Tell them how to do it.'

"Okay." She looked off into the distance and recited. "Start with a big pot of water, add fried onions, parsley and garlic and to make it thicker, you add boiled and mashed barley."

Bonnie laughed."Wherever did you find that recipe?"

Thea was thinking the same thing. *She probably remembered it from another lifetime. Maybe from a convent kitchen?*

Sara Jane shook her head. "I have no idea. It just came to me. Funny. It feels as if I've always known it."

A shiver went down Thea's spine and a wild thought jumped into her head. *They have shared a lifetime—and I was there too.*

However, by the end of the tea party, no mention of Christmas was made.

Chapter 45

By mid-September, Thea couldn't put it off any longer. On one of Bonnie's days off, she phoned her mother. "I need to talk to you about something. In person."

"I don't want to hear any more about you not moving but if you have to come, bring that nice Sara Jane with you."

"It's not about moving and I'm coming alone."

"Oh, all right. Come at two." A noisy hang up.

Since the Royal York Ball in June, Thea's time and attention had been swamped with Arthur and painting. She hardly saw Stephanie who was also busy with summer shows and they hadn't discussed anything further about a trip to England to meet Stephanie's dad. Even losing her house had taken a back seat in Thea's mind. *Strange how your focus can change.* Well, right now she had to focus on confronting her mother.

At five after two, she stood at her mother's front door and clunked the heavy circle gripped in the lion's mouth. She opened the door and stepped in.

A holler sounded from the kitchen. "I already poured your tea. Herb for you and the real stuff for me."

Mine will be lukewarm. She walked to the kitchen and sat down. A plate with four cookies and the covered teapot sat on the table beside two china cups.

The tea bag filled Thea's cup. She took a sip. *Tepid.* Another mouthful drained the cup.

Her mother glared. "What do you want to talk about?"

"Can't I simply come for a visit?"

"You never come for a visit and you did say you had something to talk to me about." She glared.

Thea got up, added a little water to the kettle and plugged it in. "Yes, I do want to talk to you about something." She folded her arms and leaned against the counter. "About Christmas."

"Christmas? Bonnie and I don't start plans for another month."

"That's why I want to talk to you about it now."

Her mother held a cookie out to Tippy. He snapped off a chunk and she popped the remainder of it into her own mouth.

Thea grimaced.

The kettle whistled and she clicked it off, topped up her cup and sat down. "I've made my own plans for Christmas." Her voice cracked when she said it.

Her mother stopped chewing. "What do you mean 'you've made your own plans'?"

Thea cleared her throat. "A friend and I are thinking of going to New York for Christmas." She stared into her mother's eyes and lifted the thin cup to her lips. Her hand shook. *Damn it. I can do this.*

Her mother's mouth made a straight line. "Impossible. You and your sisters *always* have Christmas with me."

"I know mother, but I want to do this." *I should have said I will do this.*

Her mother's eyes narrowed to a slit. "It doesn't matter what you want. And who is this *friend*?" She sneered. "Madison said something about you seeing someone. What's this all about?"

Thea gingerly placed the translucent tea cup on the saucer. "His name is Arthur and I met him at the Art Gallery."

"You can't go to New York with a man you just met." She snatched a cookie and pushed it at Tippy who gobbled it down.

"Haven't you done enough to shame this family without prancing off to New York with some stranger." Her eyes shot daggers. "I forbid it."

"Mother! I am a grown woman. You can't forbid me."

Josephine Marshall's hand tightened on the dog's back. She stroked it furiously, her bracelets rattling and clanking. "We'll just see about that, young lady." Her bangles slid to a jangled heap at her wrist. "After Sharon moves into your house, I can rent the condom to someone else. Then where would you go?"

"I don't want to argue about this. You do whatever you have to." She stood up, and poured her steaming half cup of tea into the sink. She threw the teabag into the garbage and set the cup and saucer on the counter. "I have to go."

"At least pour me a cup of tea first."

Knuckles white, Thea splashed hot liquid into her mother's teacup. Rose buds and pale twisting leaves edged its fluted rim. When the last rose was drowned, she plunked the tea pot down, picked up her purse and strode down the hall.

A loud voice followed. "That girl always was ungrateful."

Chapter 46

A red and yellow October blew in. Thea hadn't started clearing clutter, sorting or packing. Madison called it denial.

Sharon, due any day, phoned on Monday morning. "Letting you know I'm not moving in December. With the baby coming it won't work. I don't know what mom was thinking."

Thea had no gripe with Sharon. She was a pawn to her mother, Patricia's, wishes.

"I don't know why Grandma ever thought I wanted your old house. She must be bonkers to think I would move anywhere with a new born baby. Especially into a hundred-year-old house. It will take us at least two months to renovate."

"Renovate?" *What are they planning to do?*

"If I have to live in an ancient house, it doesn't have to look like one."

"My house is beautifully refinished," Thea said. *How dare she —or was it Patricia who suggested renovating?*

Sharon continued. "I suppose if you move out at the end of February, that will give us time to renovate and move in by May."

Stop saying renovate. "I appreciate the extra time. And let me know if you change your mind about moving."

"It wasn't my choice. Some dumb thing my mother and Grandma cooked up. See you on Thanksgiving."

Thea hung up and stared at the buzzing phone. Her mind jumped from picture to picture in her head: moving, not moving,

Christmas with Arthur, her paintings in a gallery, a trip to England, "Stop." she shouted and took a deep breath. "This is now. Now is all there is. Live each moment."

It was the day before Thanksgiving dinner. Thea finished breakfast and took a minute to stare out the kitchen window to contemplate her day when the phone rang. "Hello mother."

"So you're going to ruin dinner too."

"What do you mean?"

"I don't want that man here gloating over taking you away at Christmas. Why don't you bring that nice Sara Jane over instead?"

"She's having Thanksgiving with her family and Arthur doesn't gloat. Besides, I want everyone to meet him."

"Well, if he can come for Thanksgiving, he can come for Christmas."

"We're going to New York for Christmas." The more times she said it, the easier it was.

"You absolutely cannot. I *always* have my girls with me."

"Things change, mother and I want to be with Arthur. Besides, we've already made plans—"

"Well, change them!" A crash of bracelets and the dial tone.

The next afternoon, Thea prepped Arthur in the car. "My family is inquisitive. I hope they don't ask you too many questions."

"They can ask away. Stop worrying. I'm a big boy."

"That's the problem. You *are* a boy. Well a man, of course." *This is crazy. I do want my family to meet Arthur. Except my mother.* She gulped. "We could call and say the car broke down."

"Thea. Stop it. It will be all right."

Too soon Arthur pulled in the last spot behind a curve of cars. On the front porch a collection of dried corn husks, a pumpkin and a squash had been arranged. No doubt by Bonnie.

Thea took a deep breath and grasped the door handle. *All is well. All is well.*

Arthur put his hand on her back. "It'll be okay."

The hall table had been decorated with a cluster of small gourds and clumps of red and orange leaves. They walked into the living room and curiosity and surprise rippled over faces.

Patricia was the first to grab his hand. She nodded sideways to a very pregnant Sharon. "This is my daughter, Sharon. I'm soon to be a grandmother."

Arthur smiled and took her hand. "I can see that."

Stephanie rushed up, hugged Thea and Arthur. She introduced him to her husband, Mark, and to her Aunt Madison and Uncle Charlie and their son who had driven down from Queen's University in Kingston.

Like a dowager duchess, Mrs. Marshall posed in front of the mantle, her chin lifted and hands clasped at her waist like Queen Elizabeth about to greet her subjects. She wore a high-necked floor-length navy dress. Quite a fashionable dress, however, a bright red, two-inch plastic maple leaf adorned one side of her bosom, and a feathered turkey brooch on the other.

Thea took a breath. "Mother, this is Arthur. Arthur, my mother."

Arthur extended his hand. "I'm honoured to meet you, Mrs. Marshall."

Josephine Marshall, Her bangles slid to a jangled heap at her wrist. offered a drooping left hand. Bangles raced down her arm, and in her best 'lady of the manor' voice, said, "How do you do?" Her marble eyes shifted to glare at Thea.

Bonnie hurried in, drying her hands on a dishtowel. She flipped it over her shoulder and stretched her arms out to Thea. "Cyn—Thea. Happy Thanksgiving." She hugged her, and whispered in her ear. "So this is your young man. Praise be to God, he's a looker."

Thea smiled and Arthur stuck out his hand. Bonnie threw her arms around him in a bear hug and stepped back with a big grin. "You are welcome here, laddy."

With a curt "dinner is ready" Mrs. Marshall led the way to the dining room.

Only one of Madison and Charles's sons came, fortunately making it twelve to dine, as her mother would have not accepted thirteen at the already extended table. Thea walked with Arthur into the living room. *If there were a terrible thirteen, who would her mother have banished from the table?* Its polished surface lay hidden under a bright orange bed sheet. A plastic faux lace tablecloth lay on top protecting the sheet and table from spills.

A twenty-pound turkey, several bowls filled with mashed potatoes, peas, carrots, squash, turnip, cranberry sauce and gravy, barely left room for plates and cutlery. Two kitchen helpers had worked the day before and all morning assisting Bonnie. Mrs. Marshall sat at the head of the table and Bonnie at the opposite end, nearer the kitchen. Bonnie leaned over to Thea beside her, and whispered, "I made tofurkey for you."

At each dinner plate, a handwritten name card, in Josephine Marshall's scrawl, had been propped up like a miniature tent. A dollar store sticker decorated each one.

On Arthur's, a baseball, and on Thea's, a thistle.

After the passing of food, filling plates and the perfunctory blessing, Madison's son, Craig, asked where Tippy was.

His grandmother pursed her lips. "I gave him a sedative. Too many people excite him."

This was a family who chatted while they ate—a time to catch up and share the latest news. With Arthur present, however, many questions came his way.

"What's it like being an architect?" asked Craig.

"Where did you meet Cynthia?" asked Patricia.

"What do you think of Guelph?" asked Mike.

"Give the guy a break," Madison said. "He doesn't need the third degree."

Arthur laughed. "That's all right. I like inquisitive people. I love being an architect. I met Cynthia—Thea—in Toronto at the art gallery and I find Guelph a charming city."

After that, everybody relaxed and chatter continued across and around the table with two or three groups talking at once. Cynthia overheard her mother asking Patricia how Sharon was doing. Sharon at the other end of the table was talking to her cousin about his courses at Kingston and Mark and Mike were discussing the latest scores of the current sports team.

Arthur leaned over and whispered to Thea. "Why were you so worried? Your family is great."

Thea didn't answer. She looked around the table at her family and Bonnie—now like one of the family. *Yes, they do look like normal, nice people. If you don't know them. Well, Madison is great. Bonnie is supportive. Mike is okay and Craig's just a kid. Charlie's a hoot. I like him. Sharon's a sweet girl too.* She looked at her mother and Patricia, heads bent toward each other. They looked like regular people too. Her mother looked up, caught Thea's eye and frowned. *It's not my imagination. My mother really doesn't like me.*

Bonnie fetched two large pumpkin pies from the kitchen and choices of ice cream or whipped cream were voiced.

Groans of "I'm stuffed, "I can't eat another thing," and "I won't eat for a whole week," followed.

Mrs. Marshall suggested they retire to the living room for coffee and tea. Patricia and Sharon went upstairs to the bathroom and Madison's husband and son went outside for some fresh air.

Bonnie took Arthur's arm. "This way." They headed off and Thea turned the corner toward the downstairs bathroom. As she came out, her mother cornered her. The elder Marshall had consumed several glasses of wine. The tilted turkey swayed with her.

She shook a finger in Thea's face. Bracelets rattled and clanked. She clutched the frame of the door with her other hand. "You cannot go to New York with that man. I won't have it."

"Let's not get into this now, Mother."

He mother shot a jangling arm out to the side like a traffic cop. "Yes, now," she barked. "You *have* to be here." Bangles and charms scurried along her arm.

"I thought you'd be glad to have me gone." Thea reached out, intending to gently push her mother's arm down so she could pass. However as she lifted her hand, Josephine Marshall swung her arm forward and collided with considerable force against the side of her daughter's hand.

Josephine's face crumpled. "My own flesh and blood. Attacking me!" She covered her face with her hands. Her white head bobbed above a shaking curved back.

Patricia hurried down the stairs. "What's happening? Are you two at it again?" She put an arm around her mother. "There, there, it's all right." She led her sobbing mother away while Thea held her throbbing hand that had slammed into the bundle of spinning bracelets. She rubbed her arm as she entered the living room.

Madison rushed up. "I heard some yelling, What happened?"

"We kinda crashed into each other."

Madison half smiled. "You mean physically this time?"

Thea ignored her remark. "I think mother was upset because— she looked around at the circle of faces. Because Arthur and I are going to New York for Christmas."She held her breath.

Charlie said, "Fantastic."

Craig said, "That's great, Aunt Cynthia—I mean Aunt Thea. It's about time you went somewhere."

The others grouped around, slapping Arthur on the back and congratulating Thea.

Sharon hugged her ."Don't worry about my mom ond Grandma. They'll get over it."

Arthur looked at Thea with a lifted eyebrow as if to say, *I told you it would be all right.* Thea looked a little dazed.

Bonnie entered with a silver tray of steaming teacups. "Coffee and tea are ready and there's leftover pumpkin pie." Arthur took the heavy tray from her and placed it on the sideboard. Soon everyone was busy pouring milk or cream, spooning sugar and picking up forks.

The phonograph blared out the strains of Frank Sinatra, and when his voice sang *I'll do it my way,* Thea glanced at Arthur. She tilted her head toward the door. He nodded and they got their coats. Again, a confusion of hugs and back slaps as they said their goodbyes.

"Don't be a stranger," said Charlie.

"Tell me more about architecture sometime," said Craig.

"Have a great time in New York if I don't see you before," said Mike.

"Call me tomorrow," Stephanie said to her mom.

They finally made it out the door and to the car. He backed out. "You have a terrific family. What were you worried about?"

"Most of my family is okay."

He drove onto Stuart Street. "A lot of people have issues with their mother."

"Yeah," said Thea. She crossed her arms tightly across her chest. "Tell me about it."

Chapter 47

Sharon went into labour that night and baby Claire made her appearance at eight the next morning. Josephine Marshall was delighted that her first great-grandchild was a girl.

With phone calls and emails passing back and forth among family members, nothing more was said about the alleged attack of Thea on her mother even though it was Thea who had ended up with the bruised arm.

Thea didn't talk to her mother for the rest of October. The proud Great Grandmother's attention was focused solely on the new baby, and she had Bonnie drive her to Kitchener at least twice a week. It was as if Thea didn't exist and Thea didn't mind a bit. It was a relief to not have to defend her decisions on every phone call. Meanwhile, Christmas and her infamous holiday was approaching in gallops. On December 1, when she picked up the phone, it took her a moment to recognize the voice.

Her mother didn't criticize her once. Didn't even demand she change her Christmas plans. She raved on about how beautiful Claire was and how Sharon was such a great mother, and Patricia the perfect grandmother. Thea hardly got a word in edgewise which was fine with her.

There was only one testy moment when her mother was winding down from the baby talk. "Are you still going away with that man at Christmas?"

"Yes," She held her breath for a verbal assault.

Her mother didn't speak for a moment. "It won't be the same."

"But you have baby Claire now."

"That's true. She is a lovely baby."

"Maddy and I visited last week."

"I have to go." Clatter, clank, dial tone.

Thea hung up. Was her mother becoming a little more tolerant after becoming a Great Grandmother? Or had Thea changed too?

The next day, Sara Jane popped in and when she saw Thea's latest large paintings, insisted they be shipped to the New York gallery at once.

"You amaze me," Thea said.

"What do you mean?"

"The way you make things happen."

Sara Jane smiled. "Like the Nike says, 'Just do it'."

The next day, UPS arrived and the brown suited man was wrapping them carefully in a blanket when Sara Jane poked her head through the door. "My treat," she quipped, and waved a credit card in the air.

"I can pay for it," Thea said.

"I know you can but let me get this one. You can pay for the next." With the transaction completed, the paintings were carted off. Thea watched them go. Her stomach turned over. *Is this really happening?*

December 25 was galloping closer. Since she had till February until moving, and with her mother a little more pleasant, and Stephanie not talking about an England trip, she got into the Christmas spirit. She set out three angels she'd made in ceramic class a few years ago. A two-foot nutcracker stood on guard in the front hallway and glittering silver balls and tinsel hung on her eight-foot-ficus. No use having a tree if she wasn't going to be there. Over the mantle, she draped a paper streamer that Stephanie had made in Grade 1. *This will be my first Christmas without her.* A lump in her throat made it hard to swallow.

She'd miss snuggling in front of a fire with a purring cat, seeing the display of a thousand lights in Riverside Park, and how the flock of plastic geese would be set up on the lawn outside of Rockwood. She'd miss hearing the carollers, the music in stores and the change in the air as people bustled about. *Stop being so maudlin. There'll be carollers and music in New York.*

A week before departure day, she prattled on the phone with Madison. "And of course, I *have* to go skating at Rockefeller Centre. Should I pack my skates? I haven't skated in years. I don't even know where they are"

"Are you crazy? You can rent them and what movie are you fantasizing about now?"

"None." Thea laughed. "I don't have to fantasize. This is better than a movie and *I* am the star. Imagine, *me* at Carnegie Hall, the Guggenheim, and the Met. And—ta da—Broadway!"

"Do me a favour and check if the lions are still in front of the main library. I had my picture taken on one when I was eighteen."

"Will do." She hung up. In spite of her love of reading, she probably wouldn't have much time for libraries.

Checking her list for the third time, she ticked off each item: her neighbours on the right would pick up the mail, feed Minou and water the plants. Sara Jane was in Italy and wouldn't be back until the middle of January. Turn the heat low, and if a deep freeze should happen, the neighbours would check her water pipes.

A flicker of nervousness zigged through her. *What will it be like to spend seven days with Arthur? What if we get sick of each other? And what about sex every night? Well, that might be okay.*

She picked up her expensive new Egyptian cotton nightgown and pushed her face into it. All through childhood, she'd worn Patricia's hand-me-downs and for most of her adult life, bought secondhand clothes. However, in the last few months, and especially since the Royal York gala she rarely went into Value Village or the other thrift stores.

What would her father think of the man who had crashed into her life and insisted on staying in spite of her being an ice queen? Arthur was her knight but she had been the one with the armour. His lance had not only penetrated her body, but also her heart. And he was so tender, buying her flowers and treating her like a lady. It was only in the bedroom he behaved like an animal.

She shivered and lowered the lid of the suitcase. Seven nights in New York, and they were at the best age to enjoy sex: no kids, no chance of pregnancy, no work stress.

She looked up at the ceiling. *What would it be like to be married and share your life with someone?*

"Husband," she said aloud. A foreign word in her mouth. "This is my husband." Or would it be, "This is *the* husband" as some men said, "*the* wife." Wife. Now that's an odd word. What's a wife? A life of strife? Or a life of togetherness, love and commitment?

The latter didn't rhyme but she would pick that one. The phone rang.

Arthur's name lit up. "All ready?" he said.

"I hope so."

"Our plane leaves at one-thirty so it will be an easy drive to the airport. I'll pick you up at eleven."

"Okay."

"I would come over tonight but I've got errands in the morning. We'll have lots of nights in New York."

She hung up with a flutter of being taken for granted. Like Ava Gardner, in *On The Beach*. As the mistress of Gregory Peck, she remarked that he took her for granted and after he apologized, she added, "Don't be sorry, it makes me feel like a wife."

Could I be a wife and still be me?

She snapped the suitcase shut. *For the next seven days, I will be half of a couple.* She gulped. *People do it all the time. Can I remain whole while being a half? Maybe it wasn't so much being a half. Maybe it takes two whole people to make one.* She snickered. Here she was a bookkeeper and she'd concluded that one plus one equaled one.

Bedtime. She leaned over to tap off her light. Her dragonfly lay on the window sill beside the crystal.

"Good night, dragonfly. See you in a week." With being so involved in painting and Arthur she had been ignoring her dragonfly lately. She tapped off the light.

A moment later, she tapped it on, slid out of bed, and went to the window.

She picked up the dragonfly. "You're coming with me." She dug down a layer in her carry-on and tucked it into the folds of her brand new, never before worn, light-as-a-feather, chiffon night gown. She patted the soft fabric.

"Rest easy, my friend. You and I are going on an adventure.

Chapter 48

They landed at JFK and jostled their way out, passing people dragging suitcases, skis and string-wrapped parcels. Canned Christmas music streamed through the concourse.

In the lineup, a young woman waited with two small boys. The woman smiled at Thea. The white tassel on her Santa hat bobbed with her words "This is our first trip to New York. We're visiting my mother."

"It's my first trip, too," Thea said. She was tempted to tell the woman that she was heading *away* from her mother but she kept that tantalizing tidbit to herself.

The flow of cabs quickly swallowed the waiting people and in a few minutes the yellow car they settled into tore away from the curb and headed downtown.

"I'm going to have a Manhattan in Manhattan," Thea said.

Arthur raised a crooked eyebrow. "That's a strong mix for someone who doesn't drink hard alcohol."

"There are some things one has to do."

"And I suppose you've had a Nanaimo bar in Nanaimo?"

"Yes. Two summers ago." She smiled. "With my friends Mary Ann and Sarah."

"What about French Fries in France?" Before she had a chance to speak, he added, "Although that's not what they're called in France. The name originated in Belgium."

Thea laughed. "Well, no matter where the name came from, if I ever go to France I will be sure to have some. And French toast."

"In France, French toast is called 'pain perdu,' meaning 'lost bread'."

Thea shook her head. I still don't get how you've amassed all those facts."

"When I was a kid, I used to drive my mom crazy asking questions so she bought me a set of encyclopedias. That was before the home computer became popular."

"You must love Google now."

He smiled. "One of my best friends."

The cab passed a McDonald's sign. "Did you know that hamburgers were not named after Hamburg?"

"I didn't know that." She waited for the inevitable statistic.

"The name originated in St. Louis at the 1904 World's Fair."

"Well, if I ever get to Hamburg I will definitely refrain from partaking in any phonily named food."

"Is *phonily* a word?"

She looped her arm through his. "It is now."

The taxi swerved to the curb at the Casablanca Hotel in the heart of the theatre district in Times Square. Along with the blaze of lights, a lightly falling snow welcomed them.

Thea stumbled out of the cab, lifted her head and stared at the walls of moving lights flashing from nearly every building. *I'm in magic land.* "This is incredible." She turned in a circle, taking in all the brilliance, the glare, and the impossible energy bombarding her.

Meanwhile, Arthur and the cabby got the cases from the trunk. At one corner, Santa clanged a swinging bell with every ho-ho-ho and near him a bundled up musician played *Deck the Halls* on a saxophone. People rushed past, no one returning Thea's smile. *People sure are busy here.*

Inside the Casablanca, Moroccan designs of red and burnt orange with snatches of indigo predominated in tapestries and murals. It even had a Rick's Café on the second floor.

"Can we go there?" Thea pointed to the sign.

"Absolutely. They have wonderful Italian coffee and snacks at anytime. But let's find our room first."

Inside the Queen room, Thea dropped her bags and ran to the window. *I'm in New York.* Below her lay the city, alive with lights, movement and a million dreams.

She flung her arms in a high V and sang, "New York, New York, a wonderful town, the streets go up and the avenues down."

Arthur set his bag on a webbed frame at the end of the bed.

She ran to him. "Oh, Arthur. Thank you. This is incredible."

He caught her with a tight hug. "*You're* incredible." He kissed her. "Where do you want to eat?"

"Mamma Leone's."

He raised his eyebrows. "Why did you pick that one?"

"I like Italian and it's famous." She didn't tell him that Madison had given her the name. "Let's go."

"Sorry to disappoint you but Mamma Leone's closed in 1994."

Thea's bubble burst. "So much for trying to impress you with my superior knowledge."

He laughed. "You've already impressed me with your other superior skills."

"Okay. Where can we go?"

"Well, if you want Italian, we could go to Carmines. It's in Times Square and has vegetarian."

"Sounds good."

New York buzzed and Thea's head swiveled. "I've been carried to another planet. A super energized one with a myriad of people. Maybe we'll see a celebrity."

"A myriad is ten thousand. The word comes from the Greek *muria*."

"Whatever you say, my walking encyclopedia." She smiled at everyone. Not only did no one smile back, no one hardly noticed her. She did not feel rebuffed as Cynthia would have. Instead, it was as if a weight lifted from her shoulders. *No one here knows me. I'm not a disappointing daughter, a shamed unwed mother, or a boring bookkeeper. I can be anyone.* She looked up and stuck out her tongue to catch a fat snowflake.

Carmines was huge and loud: filled with people, lights, hundreds of framed photos, a long bar and white clothed tables. They were led to what looked like the last empty one. As she sat, Thea glanced at the table next to them and raised her eyebrows. A plate, the size of a platter, held a layered tower of strawberries, cake slices and whipped cream, topped with a cone of more cream and sliced strawberries. *Who could eat that much?*

The waiters passed with huge steaming trays piled with enough food for two or three people. "Perhaps we should only order one dish," Arthur suggested.

She scanned the menu. "You'd be okay with vegetarian?"

"I hear the vegetable lasagna is as thick and delicious as any meat dish."

And it was. The noodles were al dente, and the sauce sizzled with perfectly cooked zucchini and mushrooms. The cut basil tasted and smelled as if it had been freshly picked from a sunny Italian garden. Red wine completed their meal as they toasted a launch to their week's holiday. Arthur volunteered another piece of information she couldn't live without. "Did you know it was the early jazz musicians who first called New York *The Big Apple*?"

Sufficiently stuffed, they dared not risk dessert since their main course could easily have fed six, they walked back to the hotel carrying a doggy bag emblazoned with the Carmine logo.

Thea unpacked, putting blouses, skirts, pants, and underclothes into drawers or on hangers. She snapped her empty suitcase shut and slid it under the bed.

"It looks like you've moved in," Arthur said as he hung up a suit. Everything else he left in his suitcase which lay open on the luggage rack.

"The stay seems longer when I'm not fishing things out of a suitcase every day." She placed her dragonfly on her bedside table. "There you are, my friend. Enjoy New York."

That evening, with her Dragonfly safety stowed in a zippered portion of her purse, they went to an off-Broadway play and as they walked back to their hotel the streets and sidewalks bustled with people. Time Square still flashed, even more spectacularly than Thea had seen on TV. She shook her head. "This place is mind boggling. A place that God would have built if she had enough money."

"I'm glad you're enjoying it so much. It is a vibrant city."

"I still can't believe I'm here with you and at Christmas."*A great time and place to be when you're in love.*

After a coffee and sweet bun in the Club Room (Rick's Cafe) they went to their room.

She had hardly put on her beautiful new Egyptian cotton nighty when Arthur stripped it from her. She did not object. *Did he even notice its fine weave? I could have been wearing my old flannel.*

After a delicious rendezvous, a satisfied Thea fell asleep.

Chapter 49

The next day was full with visits to the Art Gallery, the main public library (the two lions still guarded the stately entrance) and Central Park, where they rode on the Carousel. Hand-painted horses with red saddles, green bridles and garland-draped necks whirled around at a brisk pace to the merry tinkling of the calliope.

Arthur put up a hand for his lady to dismount. "That was fun. I haven't ridden a horse for a while."

"Nor I." She jumped down.

"Did you know in 1871, the first Carousel here was powered by a blind mule and a horse?"

"You're kidding." *How did he hold all that information in his head?*

"That's how the story goes. Apparently, they walked on a treadmill in an underground pit."

"That's awful. The poor animals."

"Others must have thought so too. At the turn of the century, they were replaced with steam."

They rented skates and joined the swirling circle in front of the ginormous Rockefeller Christmas tree with fifty-thousand shimmering lights and topped with a luminous crystal star.

At the site of the Trade Centre catastrophe, they silently bowed their heads.

That evening, Arthur surprised her with tickets to an opening night on Broadway. She wore her Royal York dress and her hand-painted silk scarf. Its marbled shades of reds and purples added a festive and classy air to her simple black cloth coat.

They had excellent seats in the centre of the fourth row. A woman in front and left of Thea, turned around to talk to someone. *That's Katie Couric.* She grabbed Arthur's arm and glanced along the row. On the far aisle seat, Harrison Ford bent his head, his ear close to Calista Flockhart beside him. There they were, waiting, like everyone else for the show to start. No fans or photographers swarming around them. Thea looked around. *Who else is here? Probably writers, producers, directors and other important people.* She peered past Arthur and caught the eye of an older woman staring back at her. *Does she think I'm somebody?* Thea lifted her chin and pretended to be a noble lady from another century.

After the show, they flowed with others, both famous and ordinary folk, up the aisle. At a nearby after-hours club, Thea ordered a Manhattan. One sip, and she wrinkled her nose and grabbed for the water glass. "Eww, it tastes like cough medicine."

"Well, at least you can say you tasted a Manhattan in Manhattan."

The next two days and nights tumbled by. Sightseeing, theatre, eating, walking, love making. On the third day, she suggested they take a walk along 57th street. Sara Jane had given her the address of the gallery where her paintings were.

"Why? What's there?"

"Well—" and she told him.

He stopped walking. "You have paintings hanging in an art gallery in New York and you didn't tell me?" He grabbed her hand, hailed a taxi and in a few minutes they were in front of the Sara Jane Jenkins Gallery.

"I don't believe it." Thea stared at the sign. "It's her own gallery." Her heart thumped and her throat went dry.

He paid the driver. "Whose gallery?"

They stood in front of an ornate wooden door. Plate glass windows displayed a large room full of paintings ar.d sculptures.

"Sara Jane's, that's who."Astonishment and confusion scrambled inside her. *She should have told me.*

"That's what the sign says. So what?"

"So what! She's a friend of mine."

"What's wrong with her owning a gallery?"

"She should have told me."She turned away.

"Where are you going? I want to see your paintings."

"They probably aren't even there. She was feeling sorry for me. I bet she bought the paintings herself."

He took her arm and swung her around. " I'm going in." He stepped toward the door. "Are you coming?"

She frowned. "All right, but don't ask if they have any of my paintings. I'm embarrassed enough."

They walked in, past sculptures and into another room where an installation of swaying fabric and threads formed a maze of colour and movement. A sign on the wall stated its name and artist: *Reality Transmigration* by *Sara Jane Jenkins*. They wound through the display, ducking under a rippling swath of shimmering material to another room. On one wall, all by themselves hung four of Thea's paintings. A large sign at the top announced in raised gold letters, *Thea Marshall, Artist.*

She gasped and her knees buckled. *My paintings. Hanging in full view.*

He put his arm around her. "Congratulations, my love."

Her brain searched for words. *She didn't betray me. My paintings are hanging in a New York Gallery. So what if it's hers.*

A young woman in black tights and a maroon tunic walked up. "This is a new artist Sara Jane discovered. We're all excited."

"I can see why," said Arthur. "They're striking."

They're talking about me! About my paintings! She squeezed her eyes shut and opened them. *They're still there.*

"And reasonably priced because she is still unknown. Only $2,000 for the smaller ones and $4,000 for the larger ones. Each of course."

"Of course," he said and held onto Thea who had swayed toward him. "Thank you."

"I'll let you browse," she said and walked away.

"Tell her who you are," he whispered.

"No. I can't. I'm going to faint." For a moment, an old insecure Cynthia peeked out. Thea took a deep breath. *I can wrestle her away again. I have no room in my life for her.*

He led her to a bench in the middle of the room where they sat down. After a few moments of staring at the four canvases that had been created in her kitchen, she nodded her head. "I am Thea Marshall and I painted those."

"I'm so happy for you. Now will you believe you're an artist?"

She smiled and let the thrill move from her solar plexus to her chest where it settled in her heart.

Arthur took pictures with his cell of Thea standing in front of them. After she touched each one, they left the room and zig-zagged their way through hanging threads, wool and ribbons to the front door.

That night she dreamed she was kicking her legs in a chorus line made of tubes of paints. When the music stopped, the sky opened and paint rained down in multicoloured drops. Gene Kelly slid up, took her hand and they tap-danced off under a twirling umbrella.

On the morning of Christmas Eve day, Thea luxuriated in a scented bubble bath. She stretched a leg out of the water, watching bubbles slide off. *Could my life be any better? Cynthia is gone and Arthur and painting are pushing my mother out of my head.*

She had told Arthur she hadn't married. She had been nervous telling him about Stephanie's birth, but when he didn't react, she'd relaxed and let the stale air out of another fear blown out of proportion. But after her confession, he had not offered any information about his own romantic or marital past.

After a continental breakfast in Rick's Cafe, they headed to Macy's. A line of children waited their turn to sit on Santa's knee.

"He's not Edmund Gwenn," Thea whispered.

"Hardly, *Miracle on 34th Street* was made in 1947 and he was in his seventies then."

The street signs of Broadway, Fifth Avenue, and Forty-Second Street further attested to the reality of where she was, as did the fabulously adorned store windows. The exquisite gold and red velvet-dressed characters among shining stars, twinkling lights, and magical music convinced Thea she'd been dropped into a wonderland of endless possibilities.

Arthur dragged her from the windows and into the store where she bought a necklace for Stephanie and a money clip for Mark. She closed the zipper on her purse, "Make yourself scarce. I want to buy you something."

"You don't need to get me anything. You're enough for me."

"I'll take that as meaning I'm spectacular but seriously, we're in Macy's. I have to get you something."

"Okay." He checked his watch. "Meet you back here in an hour."

She strolled through the store, soaking up the sounds and sights of last minute shoppers. Bells everywhere: Christmas bells, Salvation Army bells and elves with bells. *Each one melodious.*

She brought her attention back to buyings something for Arthur. *What do you get for a man who has everything? A gold toothpick? A pet rock? Another tie?* Nothing spoke to her, so she left Macy's and went to the next store and the next. She went from counter to counter, looking for that special something. When she saw it, she knew right away and had the clerk gift-wrap it.

The store clock showed she was ten minutes late for their meeting. *Where am I? I left Macy's, but where am I now? Okay. Keep your head. I can phone him. I should get a cell.* Public phones were scarce but in a far corner beside a door marked Maintenance a single black public phone hung on the wall. She pulled out a quarter, plunked it in and poised her finger over the dial. *What the hell is his number?* She'd coded it in months ago on her house phone and had no idea. She hit the return coins lever and the quarter clinked out. Worry gremlins gnawed at her edges of her mind. *He'll wait. I can find Macy's. It can't be that hard.* She fumbled with her purse, putting the quarter back. *What if he gets tired of waiting. What if he's gone back to the hotel and checked out and I'll never see him again*!

"Stop that!" she yelled. "Get a grip." She took a deep breath and walked to the nearest door. Out on the street, people scurried past. *I'll ask someone the way to Macy's.* Everyone she approached, rushed by but one person did help.

"Go back through the store and out the main doors. You'll see Macy's across the street, just on the right," Santa said. "Ho, ho, ho," he added.

She reentered the store and threaded her way around counters and people, apologizing as she banged against parcel-laden shoppers. Outside, she looked right. Across the street, the large lit up Macy sign beckoned. Glancing back and forth from the sign and the street, she dodged streams of yellow cabs as she crossed.

A loud snort sounded on her left and a huffing wall of chestnut reared at her. She screamed and her world went black. She didn't hear or feel a thing when her body hit the wet pavement.

Chapter 50

Thea opened her eyes and the world came into focus. She was lying in the wet street. A large chestnut horse attached to a hansom cab stood quietly at the side of the road.

"Are you all right?" a voice said.

She groaned and put a hand to her head. "I think so." Her elbow and both knees stung.

"Lay still, we'll call an ambulance."

"No, don't do that. Help me up." She reached for the hand of the young man bending over her. Her knees ached and right elbow throbbed. "If I could just sit down."

A young woman beside him looked worried and Thea reassured her and the hansom driver. "I'm all right. Really." She leaned on the young man's arm.

The girl carried her purse as they guided her to the sidewalk. "We'll take you into Macy's where you can sit down," the young woman said.

Once inside, the lad led her to a bench.

"What happened?" she asked. "Did I run into the horse or it into me?"

"A little of both I think. It looked as if you scared each other. At first, we thought you'd been hit but you must have tripped or fainted. It's a good thing we were right behind you."

Who said New Yorkers aren't helpful? The boy and girl looked about twelve but must have been in their early twenties. "Thank you so much. I'll be sure to tell the folks back home how helpful New Yorkers are."

The young man smiled. "Actually, we're from Iowa."

"Oh. Well, thank you Iowa. I'm feeling better now." The store loudspeaker crackled with a page for a Thea Marshall. "Oh, my gosh. Arthur." She leaned forward to stand up.

"Stay there. I'll get him." The young man hurried off and in a few moments he returned with Arthur.

He knelt down and took her hand. "Are you all right? You fell?"

"I'm okay. I couldn't find Macy's but Santa directed me and I was running across the road, looking up at the name on the—" Her eyes lit up. "Like Deborah Kerr and Cary Grant."

The young couple looked blank.

"*An Affair to Remember*," Arthur said to them.

They shrugged.

Thea chimed in. "A great movie. At least a five-hankie. You must see it."

"I think my grandmother has that one," the young girl said.

Is it that old? "Well, thank you for coming to my rescue."

"We were only too glad to help." They waved goodbye and left.

Arthur sat beside her. "Are you sure you're okay?"

"I'm fine. I banged my knees a little but I must have rolled as I fell." *Good thing I have some padding.*

He rubbed her knees and her hands and slowly the furrows in his brow smoothed out.

"Let's go," she said, "before we cause a scene."

"I think it would take more than seeing a man rub a lady's knees before New Yorkers would notice." They walked to the big doors and exited. He nodded his head toward the waiting horse and carriage at the curb. "How about a ride through Central Park?"

"That would be grand." Thea looked at the placid horse. "Better riding behind it than under it."

Arthur gave her a hand and when she stepped up, the carriage swayed and sleigh bells tinkled. With a clatter of hoofs, the horse moved through a movie-set Christmas Eve. Snow fell lightly and bells jingled as they clopped up Fifth Avenue toward Central Park. She snuggled close to him. They could be in Russia or England going to a Yuletide party where Dickens-like characters in long dresses and coats with tails greeted them.

"A penny for them,"he said.

"I was fantasizing about being in another place and another time."

"Where would you like to be?"

His lips were right there so she kissed him. "For a change, I'm happy being right here."

"But if you were to travel, where would you go?"

She'd always wanted to go to England. Now, with Stephanie's request, she had a reason. And her father's ancestors were from Wales. "If I had my choice, I would go to England and Wales."

"Why don't we?"

"Why don't we what?"

"Go to England and Wales."

"You're serious?"

"Yes. Let's do it. We can go in the spring. How about April?"

Pros and cons skittered around Thea's head. *It has been a colossal venture to come to New York with him but across the ocean to another country? And what about going with Stephanie?* She stared at the back of the horse's bobbing head. "I'll think about it." They passed a spectacularly decorated building. "Ooh, look at that."

That evening, she used Arthur's cell to phone Stephanie. "Merry Christmas, darling."

"Mom! How are you? Where are you? What are you doing?"

Her daughter's cheery voice brought a catch to her throat. "I'm fine. We're in the Casablanca Hotel. New York is fantastic. Arthur is wonderful. We're having a great time."

"Mark and I are on our way to an open house. I'm so glad you called, I've been thinking of you."

"All good thoughts, I hope."

"Of course. Always."

"Well, you run off and have a good time."

"I will mom. You too. Love ya."

"Love ya." She held the buzzing phone to her chest, blinking back tears. She was happy her daughter was happy and happy that she was too. *No need to cry.*

The next morning, she woke to a bulging Christmas stocking lying on the covers at the foot of the bed. She had told Arthur about how she and her sisters had hung their stockings over the bottom bedpost and in the morning would find the lumpy stockings lying at their feet. How Madison and she would stretch their feet down under the covers and wiggle their toes against the heavy bumps to make rustling sounds. Then one of them would jump up, turn on the light and with Patricia in her bed, and they in theirs, they would rip apart packages with "just what I wanted" and "look what I got." And always, at the bottom of each stocking was a shiny red delicious apple, a large navel orange, and way down at the bottom of the toe, a shiny new penny. After the shouting and laughter, they would munch their apples and play with their toys. As teenagers, it would be apples and movie magazines.

Thea shoved her covers off and crawled naked over them to claim her prize. "I can't believe you did this," she squealed. She picked up the bulging stocking and held it between her breasts. "I didn't do one for you."

"I didn't expect you to. Go on, open it."

First she reached under the covers for her rumpled nightgown and pulled it over her head. Sitting cross-legged at the end of the bed, she unwrapped the first gift: an antique pewter hair clip. "I love it!" she cried, and poked it haphazardly into her sleep-tangled hair.

Arthur propped two pillows behind him and leaned back. Between paper ripping, laughter, and shouts of, "You shouldn't have" or "This is too much," came quick kisses or hugs.

Red and green tissue paper, gold foil and curly ribbons lay strewn over the covers among a box of organic herbal tea, a silver pen, a bottle of bubble bath, an out-of-this-world scented soap, a box of gold paper clips, and tickets to the Guelph Galaxy Cinema. Two round bumps remained at the toe of the otherwise flat stocking. Thea reached in and pulled out a red delicious apple and a gigantic orange. With one in each hand she closed her eyes and brought them to her nose. "You're amazing. You remembered my story."

Arthur grinned.

She tilted her head. "You didn't." She pushed her hand far into the rumpled stocking and pulled out a shiny new penny. Throwing herself at Arthur, she cried, "You did! Thank you. You're the most incredible man in all of Christendom."

"It's only a penny for goodness' sake and what's with the medieval talk."

She shrugged. "It popped out." She jumped up. "I have a gift for you." She scrambled off the bed and after a quick rummage in her purse, pulled out a package. "I hope you like it."

"I'll like whatever you got me."

She handed him a small box. The size of a ring box.

He peeled off the outer wrapping.

It *was* a ring box.

He lifted the lid. "A ring."

Thea kneeled on the comforter beside him. "It's a signet ring. I hope it fits."

He stared at it.

Does he like it? Oh, m'god, he thinks— "It's not a *ring* ring. It's a friendship ring." She pointed to the design. "See? It has a sword on it. King Arthur's sword." *This is going all wrong. I should have bought him a tie.*

His face cracked into a smile. It fit his baby finger and he held his hand up at arm's length, palm facing away. "I love it."

"Do you?" she gulped.

"I do. Now let's get dressed. Christmas is awaiting."

Neither of them was religious but they went to St. Patrick's Cathedral and slipped in at the back. Arthur kept elbowing her and whispering how magnificent the Gothic structure was with its soaring spires and stained-glass.

Thea was not Catholic but the drone of the priest and the choir's joyous singing sounded oddly familiar. She took Arthur's hand. Her fingers felt the bump of his new ring. *Good Heavens, I hope he didn't think I was proposing.* They tiptoed out before the service finished and walked up Fifth Avenue. Even on Christmas Day, traffic and people still surged by.

She thought of Stephanie and all the Christmases they'd had together. Now, here she was walking along a famous street in New York. She squeezed Arthur's hand. In two days they would be flying home.

The week had gone fast and she was getting used to having him around. It was so natural to eat with him. Sleep with him. Walk with him. Be with him. She grinned to herself at how easily she had listed the sleep part. *You've come a long way baby. I'll miss the regular bedtime events.*

Arthur steered her to another busy street. "Thought you might like to walk along this one."

She looked at the street sign—Madison Avenue—and smiled. Being with Arthur was so easy and right. *Unmarried couples live together these days. It's no big deal. But what about marriage? Isn't that the next logical step?* She stumbled over a piece of broken sidewalk.

He grabbed her arm. "Whoops, got you. You okay?"

"Yeah, I didn't see that bump."

They found a place for brunch and after eating went back to the hotel to watch *It's a Wonderful Life*. Last April, when she first met him, she never dreamed she would be seeing it with him so soon. They settled in with eggnog, mixed nuts and a box of *Ferrero Rocher* dark chocolates, and for the next hour-and-a-half watched and cried as the angel Clarence showed Jimmy Stewart that he had lived a valuable life.

The credits rolled and the final music played. They didn't move until the Dolby logo appeared. Arthur picked up the remote and clicked it off. Thea mused about her own wonderful life and crawled under his uplifted arm which he tightened around her. The silence was full and comfortable. Life was wonderful with him.

"Arthur, why don't we get married?" She sucked in her breath. *Oh my god! Did I actually say that out loud!* Neither of them moved. *What must he be thinking?*

She laughed. "That was bold. Forget I said that."

He turned to her. "Thea, I would like nothing more in the whole universe than to marry you—"

There was a *but* in his voice.

"I was going to ask you myself—"

The *but* grew larger.

"But—"

There it was.

"I can't marry you. I'm already married."

Chapter 51

"You're married!" She caught her breath. Her stomach spasmed and a tangle of thoughts crashed in her brain.

"I should have told you."

"You're married!" Her blood thumped in her ears and roared hot on her face. With stiff elbows, she pushed him away. "You've been leaving my bed to go into another woman's arms!"

"I can explain."

She sprang off the couch and plastered her palms to her chest, willing her lungs to work.

He stood up. "It's not what you think."

"You don't know what I think." She drew her hand back. With her best Barbara Stanwyck swing, she smacked him across the face.

He grabbed her wrist, wrapped his other arm around her and held her in a tight embrace.

She thrashed, straining to pull herself free. To get away. To run where she could curl into a ball and hold her heart together to stop the pain from bursting out. "Let. Me. Go."

The words that came out of his mouth did not reach her ears.

"No," she screamed, twisting, and pushing at him. A smattering of his words trickled through to her.

"Listen to me, you goose. I love you."

And I loved you. I trusted you. Her body shook as it leapt from fighting to fleeing.

He held her tightly. "I'm not living with my wife. We married young."

The string of words didn't register on Thea's muddled brain.

More words came. "I don't see her. I don't even know where she is."

It was as if he were speaking a foreign language and she needed an interpreter to know what they meant. Slowly, one word and another became English and the screeching inside her subsided.

He guided her to the couch where they sat down, his arm still around her. She shivered and jerked and snuffled while he stroked her back.

"I married thirty-seven years ago. I was twenty and didn't know what I was doing. She was pregnant and—"

Another bomb. "You have a child?" She swivelled to face him.

Arthur didn't look at her. "We did. He died before he was a year old. Cheryl never got over it, but the marriage had been finished long before that. After the baby died, she left and went back to her parents in Cornwall."

Her logical brain filtered through. "That's not far. Cornwall's three hours away."

"Cornwall, England. We kept in touch for a while, pretending it was a trial separation, but over the months the letters and phone calls petered out."

"Why didn't you divorce?" She blew her nose Her heart had settled back to its rightful place, doing its best to beat in a more orderly fashion.

"At first, I didn't care. I didn't want to get married again and I figured if she had wanted to, she knew where I was." He shrugged. "Time passed and I never heard from her."

"Did you ever try to find her?"*I can't believe we are having this conversation.*

"I did. Fifteen years ago I lived with a woman and we talked about marriage. I wasn't sure, but I thought I may as well take preliminary steps and get a divorce."

"What happened?" *What else don't I know about this man?*

"I wrote and phoned her parents' number, but they'd moved. I even hired an agency to track her. They discovered her parents had died and she'd moved to London—England—but after two addresses, the trail went cold. It was as if she didn't want to be found. No driver's license, no passport, no insurance."

"So what happened with—your live-in girlfriend?"

"She wanted to be married and when I couldn't find Cheryl to get divorced, she left." He paused. "A year later I heard she'd married."

"How did you feel about that?" *I must stop watching Dr. Phil.* At least she had calmed down.

"I liked her but I didn't love her." He looked at Thea.

His eyes were soft.

"I didn't know what love was until I met you." He wiped her wet cheeks. "I was a fool. I should have told you about Cheryl sooner."

"I wish you had. You scared me. I thought I was having a heart attack."

He kissed her forehead. "My heart did a jump too. I was overjoyed when you asked me to marry you. I've been wanting to ask you for weeks."

She touched the sword on the ring she had given him and closed her hand over his.

He tightened his arm around her. "I never want to lose you. You fill all the crannies, corners and empty spaces in my heart." He pulled her to him and it was as if she were coming home from a place far, far away. They melted into each other as one, breathing in unison. After several moments, they released their holds.

His voice cracked. "Three months ago I renewed my investigation to find Cheryl. So far, dead ends."

"I remember a novel I read where the character had the same problem. After showing the court he did due diligence of trying to find his wife, he got something called a Final Judgment of Divorce." She looked up. "I think it was called Divorce by Publication."

"I know. I looked into that too." He frowned. "I may be old fashioned but I need to have closure on it for myself."

They sat in silence for several minutes before she spoke. "Maybe when we go to England we can do some searching."

Arthur's eyes widened. "You mean it? You'll come to England with me?"

"Why not?I've experienced a roller coaster of emotions with you and after today I can manage anything."

"From now on, whatever we do, we're in it together." He looked into her eyes. "Don't ever leave me. When I found you, I found myself. I like me more when I'm with you."

Her heart was close to erupting. "Every day, I thank all the Gods and the Universe that we found each other."

They sat interlocked in each others' arms for a long time with no need for words.

Chapter 52

Arthur sucked in his breath. "I didn't give you your gift." He unwrapped himself and leapt from the couch.

"You gave me the Christmas stocking."

A moment later, he returned with a small white box. It had the Apple logo on it. "It's not a ring."

"I can see that."

"It's not a romantic gift so I didn't wrap it."

She opened it. "A cell phone. I've been thinking of getting one but this one looks fancy. I'll need lessons on how to use it."

"I can show you in a couple of minutes." He tapped it and an array of colourful icons sprang into view over a blue sky.

"It's beautiful. I love it. Thank you." She kissed him lightly on the mouth. And harder. They moved to the bed, where she deposited her new iPhone on the side table, and they got involved in a more interesting and exciting way of communicating.

Thea awoke hours later, her body resonating with the memory of hearing the impossible from the man she loved. She had finally, after so may years, opened herself to love and a giant pickaxe had landed in the centre of her chest. She looked at Arthur asleep beside her. *I have not been betrayed. He does love me.*

She had been afraid of losing herself in this man. *But I found myself. Maybe romantic love isn't about sacrifice and compromise. Maybe it's about acceptance—of myself and my partner.*

She rolled over and peered at the clock. Its pale light showed four-thirty p.m. Lunch had been chocolates and salted nuts and her stomach rumbled for green and leafy. She slid her feet out from under the warm covers, removed the rest of her clothes and headed for the shower.

When she was scrubbing her hair dry, a hand snaked around her waist. She jumped.

"Didn't mean to startle you." He kissed her neck. "How about Christmas dinner?"

"Great idea. I'm starved."

While he showered, she finished dressing and picked up her new phone. *It can't be that hard to make a phone call.* She wanted to talk to her family on Christmas day and here it was half way over. Their three o'clock Christmas meal—Madison and she took turns calling it linner or dunch—should be over by now. The Marshall clan would be in the living room, sitting around the ladened fir tree with its popcorn and cranberry strings and paper-looped streamers—every third one popped open from dried-out mucilage and scotch-taped together. There would be the misshaped ornaments they had made in kindergarten a hundred years ago, and on the top, the bedraggled angel that she and her sisters insisted on keeping. Over the last three years, Bonnie had restitched the fallen halo, straightened the cellophane wired wings, and with the tip of the iron, carefully pressed the organza skirt.

She hit the phone icon and with another tap, a keypad popped up where she could enter the number.

It rang once. Would her mother even answer? It rang again. *She's probably still mad at me for missing Christmas.* Another ring. *With all the people and the noise there, will they even hear it ringing?*

Another ring. *Pick up. Somebody pick up.* She wanted to talk to Stephanie and Morgan at least.

On the sixth ring, a cheery voice answered with, "Merry Christmas."

"Bonnie, it's me."

"Praise be to the Lord, it's our Cynthia—Thea."

"Merry Christmas, Bonnie."

"We've missed you, lass. It hasn't been the same."

"I've missed you too." An unexpected lump jammed her throat.

"Everyone wants to speak to you. "

Madison's voice came on next. "Merry Christmas sis, and speak up. It's kinda noisy here."

Background noises indicated a rousing game of Monopoly was underway and after talking to Madison for a couple of minutes, Stephanie came on. "Mom, I bought Marvin Gardens but Mark has cornered the railways."

"Glad you're having a good time."

"We are but it's not the same without you. Hey, my turn." And she was gone.

The phone was passed from one member of the family to the other and over the "Merry Christmases" and "how-are-you-doing" came shouts of, "How much is Park Place?" "Where's my two hundred dollars?" and "Who's the banker?"

After hearing from Mark, Patricia, Charles, Sharon, Mike, and two nephews, Madison came back on. "Mother had an urgent call to the bathroom. She should be out soon."

"Sure," Thea said. After another chat with Stephanie and a virtual hug and kiss, she hung up. Her mother still hadn't come out of the bathroom.

Arthur called from the bedroom alcove. "How's your family?"

"Stephanie bought Marvin Gardens and Madison owns Park Place."

"Did you know that Charles Darrow's wife and son handmade and distributed the first monopoly games?"

"I didn't know that." *I don't care if my mother won't talk to me. The most charming, beautiful man ever created is standing in front of me.*

He came toward her. Over his white shirt, hung a red tie smattered with small to large snowflakes. "And Marvin Gardens was misspelled. The place it was named after in New Jersey was spelled with an 'e' not an 'i'."

"Are you wearing that tie?"She loved that he would be brave enough to wear something so outrageous.

"Absolutely. It's my traditional 'eat your Christmas Dinner in' tie." He smoothed it over his shirt. "My sister, June, gave it to me and I promised her I'd wear it every Christmas."

She kissed him lightly. "Let's eat." She smiled to herself. *I forgot to tell Stephanie I was calling from my own cell phone.*

The hotel phone rang and Arthur picked it up, spoke a few words and hung up. "Our chariot awaits."

Downstairs, they were shown to a waiting limo. The driver opened the door and an astonished Thea stepped in, followed by Arthur. Once they were settled, the car pulled away from the curb.

He picked up a bottle from the small bar in front of them. "A glass of wine, my dear?"

Thea's mouth was still open and when she collected herself, said, "What is this? Where are we going?"

Arthur poured two glasses of wine and handed her one. "Sit back and relax. It will be a bit of a ride. But there is some fine brie and crackers here."

Thea took the glass, her eyes still open wide. She took a sip and gulped. "Where are we going?"

"Let's just say that it was impossible to find an eating place in all of New York City which served a traditional English—or British—Christmas dinner."

"Really?"

"I searched everywhere. Chinese food is what most people eat here on Christmas day."

"No!"

"Yes. But I did find a place, so lean back and enjoy the appetizers."

An hour later they were half way to Connecticut when the driver turned onto a side road for another half hour. Finally, the headlights showed a snow-plowed driveway heading toward what looked like a large stone farmhouse or inn.

"This is like a movie set," Thea said. "I bet *Christmas in Connecticut* was made here."

"'Fraid not. That was made on the Warner Brothers lot in Burbank."

The car pulled up to the front. Up close, Thea could see that the building extended on each side and looked more like a hunting lodge or large country home. In the foyer, they hung up their coats and exchanged their boots for warm slippers handed to them.

"Come this way." A tall elf with bells on his hat led them into a red and green ribboned festooned buffet room. A crowded Christmas tree, glittering with silver balls, silver streamers, silver icicles and silver sprayed snow, grazed the twelve foot ceiling. Strings of lights outlined the windows, and a miniature English Village nestled on the sills among puffs of cotton ball snow.

As they were seated, Arthur explained that the wife of the owner, born and raised in England, insisted on installing the traditional scene. Muffled couples, their skates glued to a circular mirror, held a frozen pose. A steepled church, gabled houses, a livery, a barbershop and green grocers sat side by side, each lit from within—the wires artfully concealed under wads of cotton batten. A trio of ceramic angels completed the tableau: one with chin in hand gazed out from a park bench, another with head tilted and staring aloft, teetered on a snow bank, while the third—wings and arms outstretched—stared down from the steeple of the non-denominational church.

Festooned decorations on the walls and dripping from the ceiling made with silver balls, twisting icicles, and gold streamers, vied for attention with the food and the unmistakable smells of Christmas dinner. Platters of turkey and ham, dishes mounded with stuffing and mashed potatoes, bowls of peas, carrots, squash, brussel sprouts, gravy, and cranberry sauce filled two long buffet tables. On the dozen individual tables, each covered with a white cloth, stood a pair of red or green candles. Arthur and Thea sat at a red candled table while the canned voice of Tony Bennet's mellow tones rang out with a medley of Christmas carols.

Thea smiled at the setting: the tree, the candles, and Arthur's sentimental tie. The perfect setting for the end of an almost perfect day. Santa-hatted waiters refilled wine glasses and whipped away soiled plates.

After several trips to the buffet and their plates taken away, Thea held her stomach. "I can't eat another bite."

At that moment, their waiter swooped over and deposited a flaming plum pudding in front of them. Other waiters were doing the same at each table. No doubt another requirement of the proprietor's wife. Blue flickering lights licked around the edges as a large dollop of thick English custard trickled down.

Thea picked up her fork. "Well, maybe one more bite."

After finishing off the whole pudding, they and the other guests were directed to an adjoining room where a large space for dancing had been set out with small tables on the periphery and a four-piece live band in front.

Plate glass windows looked out on mounds of snow lit up with outside lights.

Arthur held his stomach. "I need to sit awhile and let my stomach recover."

"I know what you mean." Thea groaned. *Thank goodness I didn't wear any form fitting undergarment. I would have exploded by now.*

They sat out the first two songs, then Arthur stood and held out his hand. "Shall we dance, m'lady?"

"Indeed. T'will be my pleasure."

They joined the other dancers and after a moment, he said, "You dance well, my dear."

"I love the waltz. It's so romantic." She closed her eyes. *I am a Vienna princess, in a buttercup dress with a billowing crinoline and white silk gloves dotted with pearls. My hair is piled high, and curls tumble down from my sparkling tiara.*

"Whoops, careful there," Arthur said, and grabbed a tighter hold.

"Sorry. I got carried away." Was it being so close to him of the whiff of his spicy aftershave that made her lightheaded.

After two Strauss waltzes, her calf muscles screamed to sit down. A Christmas cracker lay beside each of their plates. They toasted with newly filled wine glasses, pulled the crackers, put on the silly tissue paper hats and claimed their prizes. Thea's hat was red and Arthur's, green.

"You look like Robin Hood," she said. It balanced on top of his head, threatening to topple off, while hers drooped over her forehead and would have slid to her neck like a collar if her ears hadn't stopped it. She pushed it off her brow and they unwrapped their surprise novelties.

"I got a tiny paint set," Thea cried, holding it up.

"Wait till you see what I got." In the centre of his palm lay a yellow plastic ring boasting a gigantic Lucite diamond. "Two rings in one day," he said. "I wonder what that means?"

A woman singer in a long red velvet dress took the stand. After *White Christmas, Good King Wenceslas* and *Deck the Hall* the music changed to an old war favourite, *We'll Meet Again*. Thea eyes filled with tears on hearing the well known words sung in so many World War II movies. She could only imagine the pain of seeing a loved one off to war. *"We'll meet again/Don't know where, don't know when/But I know we'll meet again, some sunny day."*

She blinked tears away and looked across the table at Arthur— at the man she had met again. It had been a sunny day for her. *What is that strange look on his face?*

He stood, put a hand on each side of her chair and turned it away from the table to face him. He knelt on one knee, and took her left hand in his. "I don't have a proper ring, m'lady. Alas, this simple bauble will have to suffice."

Thea's heart pounded.

He held the plastic ring aloft. Its ridiculous bulbous diamond actually twinkled in the candlelight.

"Will you do me the honour, fair maiden, of being my wife?" He smiled. "Forsooth, will you marry me?"

Thea caught her breath as her mother's cynical voice slithered into her brain with its dire edict: *Who would ever marry you?* Thea narrowed her eyes, and with one well-placed shot from her imaginary cannon, she disintegrated the words into a withering mass of wriggling witchery.

He smiled. "That is, of course, when I have unburdened myself from a previously unfortunate covenant?"

Her hand—fingernails shining pearl pink—rested in Arthur's. She straightened her shoulders, looked into his face, and said, "Yes. I will marry you."

The ring was loose on her third finger left hand and no flurry of squealing office girls rushed up although people at nearby tables hooted and clapped.

They sealed their agreement with a kiss, while Arthur's paper hat slid to the floor and Thea's fell over her eyes.

Chapter 53

After a long ride back to the hotel they got ready for bed. Thea slid her plastic engagement ring over the dragonfly's head. If she could have gotten it past the wings, it would have made a fine saddle. She switched off the lamp and crawled into bed. Arthur's warm body was a most satisfying replacement for her down comforter. Outside the windows, a splash of shifting lights, staccato horns, and a steady swish-swish-swish of tires filtered into the room, rocking her to sleep.

On the next day, their last in New York, they went to the Guggenheim. It great white curves looked like a giant upside-down layer cake. While Thea gazed open eyed at the great skylight far above them, Arthur led her to an elevator which whisked them to the top. From there they would follow the sloping ramp down through the galleries. The open plan allowed them to view exposed multiple sections on different levels. The spiral building, in itself a work of art, was like walking through a nautilus shell as each space flowed naturally into the next. It was Thea's first time in a Frank Lloyd Wright building and when they passed an oval-shaped column she yanked Arthur's arm. "Look at that!" A moment later, she pointed to a Picasso. "Look at that! Can you believe all this?"

"It's entertaining coming here with you," said Arthur.

She spun around, arms stretched wide. "I can't wait to get home to do another painting. A big one."

He dodged a whirling arm. "Good for you."

After that they headed to the Museum of Modern Art and a retrospective of paintings and drawings of an upcoming American artist. From there to the Whitney for more Picasso.

Back in the hotel room, Thea twirled about, arms wide. "Did you ever see such glory? Such colour? Such originality?"

Arthur smiled and ducked out of her way. "When I was a kid I used to be teased for loving art over sports, and museums over hockey arenas."

"I'm so glad you love art." She ran to him and kissed him. "I have never been this inspired in all my life. Thank you, thank you, thank you."

They had an early seven a.m. flight the next day, and they enjoyed a quiet supper at the hotel. After that, Arthur packed while Thea soaked in a hot bath to soothe her burning feet and stiff legs. When her fingertips turned into wrinkled maps, she pulled the plug and climbed out. Arthur was snoring lightly when she put on her barely used Egyptian cotton nightgown and slipped in beside him. For the first time in seven days they didn't make love before going to sleep. *It's like being married.*

Around two a.m. she awoke to a hand sliding under her nightie. Half asleep, she lay like a possum and played the game of pretending to know not whose bold hand lay upon her breast. *How dare this stranger touch me? I mustn't respond. Only bad girls like sex.* Her nipples rose as his tongue tickled them awake. Feigning sleep, she resisted the rising impulse to partake. *I am an innocent maiden about to be taken advantage of. Oh, kind sir, be gentle.* However, her body couldn't lie and she happily accepted his invitation.

The next day at the airport, waiting to check in, Arthur whispered, "Who was that vixen in bed last night?"

"Who? Why dear sir, I know naught of what you speak."

"Must have been somebody else."

"Must have been."

They boarded and soon took off. Thea scanned the in-flight magazine and was halfway through an article on how cats don't always land on their feet, when the prepare-to-land announcement came through the sound system.

Light snow fell in Toronto but the roads were clear and in an hour they arrived in Guelph to her quiet street and her quiet row house. She made a big fuss over Minou, but the cat, with righteous demeanor, ignored her with its usual look of *How dare you go away for a week.*

"This is weird leaving you," Arthur said. "But I have a backlog of work and a stack of year-end reports."

The week had been a roller coaster: great food, great sex, the Macy's mishap, learning about Cheryl, more incredible sex, all ending with a marriage proposal.

"Catch you later," he said and plunked her suitcase inside the front hall. A quick kiss and he was gone.

She stared at the closed door, her mind swimming in circles. She fingered the wavering swirls of woodgrain remembering how she had coaxed it out from under two layers of lead paint. It had taken three pads of extra fine steel wool to rub in the best English wax to get that rich and permanent finish. She shook her head. "Why am I fixating on a dumb door? That's not going to help me deal with him leaving so suddenly." She stumbled into the living room like a person whose support had been yanked away and sat down before she fell over. *It had been so easy. So normal to have him around. Had it only taken one week to feel as if I have lived with him forever?*

The next day, she caught up on email, phone calls, and thanking the neighbours. "Yes, we had a great time." "New York was fabulous." "Yes, we went to Macy's and the Met and Central Park." She didn't tell anyone about her Lucite ring. It still lived on the dragonfly's neck—an incongruous match of pewter and plastic, looking like some alien insect.

Stephanie was happy for her mom's happiness. "It's about time," she said. "And don't forget, as soon as Mark's term's over in May we're going to England. I hope you'll come with us."

"I'm thinking about it." She didn't tell her that she and Arthur may be going for another reason.

She rang her own mother and left a message. They would never have a close relationship, but it didn't have to be hostile. Arthur phoned that evening, still swamped with work.

The next morning, she went to the laundry room and brought out the last two blank canvases. *Not big enough to paint New York.* She phoned the art store and yes, they could make up a canvas that big. *I suppose I should be thinking about packing instead of more canvases.* "But I can't see myself living in a condo," she said to Minou. The cat walked past still looking haughty. "I don't think you want to live in a condo either. Oh, well. I still have two months and anything can happen"

She unpacked, put a wash in, dusted and vacuumed while Minou gradually made overtures of being her old friendly self. She left a message for Arthur at his office.

When the phone rang, she grabbed it. It was her mother's number. *Let her rant or rave. I don't care.* She hit the talk button. "Hello, Mother."

"Was it worth leaving your family for?"

"I had a wonderful time. I hope your Christmas was good. "*I can at least be civil. She's not going to dent my happiness.*

"Have you seen the new baby?"

"Not since I got back. Madison and I visited before Christmas."

"She is such a dear. It will be so nice when they live closer."

Thea didn't answer.

"How is your packing going?"

"I haven't started yet."

"Well, you better." A rattling cascade of bracelets and a click.

Thea sat holding the phone, the dial tone humming in her ear. She hit the off button. The cat jumped up on her lap. "I guess I will never please her, Minou."

The phone rang again. "Arthur," she cried."So glad you called."

"You won't be after you hear what I have to say."

"What's up?"

"I have to go to Vancouver immediately. I don't even have time to see you before I go. I'm sorry."

"I am too."

"I'll make it back for New Year's Eve and I'll phone every night. Have to run. Bye. I love you." He hung up.

Wednesday slid around and New Years was Friday. Two days until Arthur was back. Lots of time for her to do the New York painting. She shoved a living room chair and the table to the side and laid out her plastic painting sheet on the floor. It was a short drive to Wyndham Arts but when she got there, she soon discovered the four by six foot canvas wouldn't fit in her car.

"No problem," Chris said. "You live in town and I have some other deliveries."

She picked up a spicy dhal from Diana Downtown, a few steps away, and at home, she put on brown rice. Thirty minutes later, Chris was at the door with her New York sized canvas.

"I like your easel," he said as he laid the canvas on the living room floor.

"At least it can't fall over."

She piled her Mexican bowl high with rice and dhal and, sitting cross legged on the floor, stared at four by six feet of white space.

Fifteen minutes later, she dropped the bowl and fork into the sink, and lined up the paint tins, brushes, spatulas, sticks and half crumpled tubes on the edges of the sheet surrounding the canvas.

"I'd better change, Minou. I have enough paint clothes already."

A few minutes later, she pried off the lids, picked up a large brush and closed her eyes. Images swirled across her landscape of vision: burnt oranges and yellows of the Casablanca, the red and green garlanded carousel, the Rockefeller Christmas tree, St. Patrick's Cathedral, the soaring skylight at the Guggenheim, the lions at the library—the lion in bed with her.

She opened her eyes and dove in. A dash of Ultramarine Blue. A slash of pearlized Mica for light and movement. A bulbous patch of Phthalo Green. Weaving trails of Burnt Sienna. The next hour disappeared. Hand prints decorated her backside, swipes streaked her legs and splashes spotted her shirt. *It needs Cerulean. Not too much. Perfect. Yes, like that. No, don't touch it.* She stepped back and tilted her head. Divergent textures, shifting shapes, dancing colours—but it needed more contrast. She mixed a thick pool with the oval knife, and wound rich blacks through the painting, bringing out its intrinsic light. The paints, the canvas, her hand were partners in love. She stepped back and stared at the blaze of colour. Finished. Is that New York? She didn't know, but she was certain of one thing. It was complete. There was not a trace of not-enoughness in it.

It took twenty minutes to scrub paint off credit cards, brushes, table, floor, arms and hands. After that, she made a mug of licorice tea and took it to her comfy chair. By now, Minou had totally forgiven her lapse of being an irrresponsible owner and curled herself into a cat muff on her lap.

That evening her mother called again and chatted about her granddaughter Sharon and Claire, her new great granddaughter.

She never mentioned Thea moving and neither did Thea. After Thea hung up, she sat for several minutes. *What if she has changed her mind about me moving? What about Arthur and me? When we get married, where will we live?* She went upstairs, washed, put on her nighty and sat in her thinking chair by the window. She slid the plastic engagement ring off the dragonfly and put it on her finger. "Well, dragonfly. I thought I would never say this, but with Arthur I would leave my house to live anywhere, in anything, with him. Cob hut or castle. Either will be fine."

December 31. She awoke with a start. *Arthur's coming back today in time for New Year's Eve.* The New York canvas still lay on her living room floor. It was almost dry and Minou had stayed clear of it. She would move it before he arrived to surprise him.

He was due back from Vancouver that afternoon. She had a quick lunch and waited for the phone to ring. One o'clock chimed. Two o'clock. Why hadn't he called? His plane was supposed to be in at two. He said he'd left his car at the airport and would drive to his house in Oakville, get changed and pick her up for dinner, dancing and New Year festivities.

She checked her cell phone. *Why hasn't he returned my messages?* By three-thirty the worry gremlins woke up, stretched their arms and kicked their legs. "Be still," she shouted. They retreated for a moment, but soon slid their slimy hands around her intestines and whispered a bunch of rasping and dire *what-if's*.

She sat on the edge of the bed, took a deep breath, closed her eyes, and made pictures in her mind. *Arthur getting on the plane in Vancouver—the flight attendant handing him peanuts—getting off at Pearson—driving home—having a shower—great body—getting dressed—phoning me—*The phone rang and she scrambled for it. "Arthur?"

"It's only me."

Madison.

"Is Arthur back?"

"No. He must be caught up in meetings or something."

"I wanted to wish you Happy New Year, sis."

"Same to you. See you next year." As kids, they'd giggle at their cleverness, knowing it was only the next day.

"Yeah, see you next year," Madison said. "Don't forget to kick father time out and welcome the new year baby in." Another family tradition.

"That might be hard to do from a ballroom or wherever we are, but I'll do my best."

Madison said "We're spending a quiet night at home so I'll do it for both of us."

They signed off and Thea checked if a new message had come in.

Nothing.

He was hours overdue.

"Arthur, where are you? Call me!"

Chapter 54

All of Thea's calls to Arthur went to call answer. Her grandfather clock gonged four bells. *Where is he?* Her tea had gone cold and when she was refilling the kettle, the phone rang.

"Hi, it's me."

She let out a heavy breath. *Thank you, Universe.* "Arthur, where are you?"

"Sorry, my love. The meetings went on and on and no cell phones allowed. Did you get my mental message that I was all right?"

Arthur was getting as weird as she was. "Well, I would have if I'd stopped worrying. Where are you?"

"Still in Vancouver."

"Oh, no. When are you leaving?"

"I have a two o'clock flight so I should be there by—"

"Two o'clock! But it's already—oh, yeah. You're three hours behind."

"We land at 9:10 Toronto time and home to change—I should get to your place elevenish."

"As long as you're here to kiss in the new year."

"Plenty of time. And I'll get you to the ball before your coach turns into a pumpkin."

"Thank you, my prince. I'll await your arrival."

She turned off the steaming kettle, made fresh tea and brought it to the living room. Her washed brushes and palette knives, weres till lined up on the paint-stained sheet beside the New York canvas She picked them up and took them to the laundry room. *An art studio would be awesome.*

She turned on her computer. "Okay, Minou, let's get rid of the trash on this." It took an hour deleting old emails and cleaning out her promotion and social media folder. She closed her computer and stretched her arms back. "See you next year."

Why does time seem to tick so slowly when you're waiting for someone? She heated up left-overs and ate in front of the TV, switching back and forth to the various programs featuring compilations of the past year. After that, *Josh Groban's* Christmas CD from Madison kept her company as she did the dishes while the clock hands crawled by in a lazy circle. *He's not due for another three-and-a-half hours.*

A long lavender bubble bath and a face masque was in order. While the water churned into soapy clouds, she spread green goo on her forehead, cheeks, chin and nose. She lit a sandalwood incense stick and put *Vivaldi's Four Seasons* on her bathroom CD player.

Minou sat on the edge of the tub while her mistress closed her eyes, rested her head on a pink plastic pillow and thought about resolutions: good health, prosperity, more incredible adventures with the wonderful man in her life, and—painting. "You know what, Minou?" She blew a bubble off her hand. "I *am* an artist."

The incense had burned down and the staccato strings of Vivaldi's winter came to a finish. Wrinkled fingertips and a stiff face also signaled time to get out. By the time she dried off and cleaned up it was still only nine-thirty—too early to get dressed for a party.

In her terry towel robe, she went downstairs and turned on the TV. Several channels were highlighting the worst and the best of the last year. She set the timer for ten-thirty.

At five after eleven she was dressed. The phone rang.

"Arthur, where are you?"

"I just got home. The flight was late and there's a storm in Toronto."

"You'll never make it here by twelve." *Who cares about a silly old New Year's kiss*

"I'll do my best. I think it's letting up a bit."

"If it's too dangerous, don't come."

"I'll let you know if I can't make it."

They hung up and she poured herself a glass of wine. Gulping down a mouthful, she shivered. *Everything is fine. It doesn't matter if he makes it on time. As long as he's safe.*

Her eyes flicked from the TV screen to the clock: eleven fifteen —eleven twenty-five— eleven forty-seven. *Why doesn't he phone?* She went to the window. Blowing snow and swaying branches whirled the bird feeder in crazy circles. She yanked the drapes shut. "So what if he doesn't come? It's only another night.

Eleven-fifty-five. The Times Square ball was poised to drop. She slipped her feet into her shoes. Eleven-fifty-seven. At least she would kick out the old year and welcome in the new. Eleven-fifty-nine. The TV countdown began. Ten—nine—eight—seven. She went to the door and grabbed the handle. Six—five—four—three —. The door flew open, knocking into her. Arthur rushed in and grabbed her.

"Happy New Year!" he yelled.

The bells of The Church of Our Lady pealed, the TV blared, neighbours hollered out their windows and before her brain could compute, cold lips met hers. He kicked the door shut, muffling wind and outside merriment. When they came up for air, he hollered above the blasting horns, bells and shouts. "Happy New Year, darling. I love you."

"I love you too." She gasped. "I had given up hope of you getting here in time."

"It was touch and go for a bit, but I kept seeing myself here with you at 12:00 o'clock on the dot."

"And on the dot it was."

With his arm around her, they walked into the living room. "I need to sit down for a moment."

They sat on the love seat as *Auld Lang Syne* rang out from the TV. In a weary voice he said, "Did you know that Guy Lombardo and his Royal Canadians played *Auld Lang Syne* for the first time on December 31, 1929 in New York City?"

"I didn't know that."

"It's been played every year since in Time's Square." He leaned back and closed his eyes. "We were in Time's Square."

"Yes, we were."

In a tired mumble, he said, "Do you want to go to Time's Square."

"Not tonight. In fact, we don't even have to go out tonight. I'm just glad you're here and safe."

He pulled himself upright. "But I promised you a New Year's date. I need to catch my breath and we can go out and dance the light fantastic—or something like that."

"What? No more relevant facts to regale me with?"

"Are you joshing me?" He leaned back again.

"A little. W hatever got you onto collecting facts and figures?"

He grinned. "I was about twelve and my youngest sister, June, was six. She would watch me do my homework and ask me to tell her something, so I started rhyming dates and facts from my history book or my new set of encyclopedias. It turned out I had a pretty good memory and every night before she went to bed she wanted me to tell her another fact." He shrugged. "So I started collecting them for her and never stopped. Of course she never remembered any and I used to repeat some of them." He closed his eyes again and his head slumped to a pillow.

Thea waited for several minutes before she got up and turned the TV off. She pulled his shoes off, lifted his feet to the couch, squished a cushion behind his head and covered him with a plaid throw. After a soft kiss on the forehead, she switched off the light and headed upstairs. *Having him safe is more important than any fancy New Year festivities.* She changed, washed and climbed into bed.

"Happy New Year, dragonfly." She cuddled under her comforter. The cat was already curled in her regular spot at the foot of the bed. "Happy New Year, Minou."

In the middle of the night, Thea awoke to a cool naked body hunkering against her flannel nightie. She put a warm arm over it and fell back to sleep.

Chapter 55

January brought snow drifts and below zero weather. Thea's bookkeeping business slowed and weekends were taken with Arthur. He was still catching up from work so had no time in the week to get to Guelph and although she missed him, she was glad to have the time to focus on painting. Stephanie was busy making pots for the spring shows and the weather was not conducive for long drives. But they kept in touch by phone or text. It was fun to be so absorbed that she would forget to phone her daughter. That was a first.

She phoned the art store and Chris delivered two more giant four-by-six canvases. She had stowed her first large piece, *New York*, in her craft room. She hadn't even shown it to Arthur, and Sara Jane wasn't due back for another week. *Wait till I tell her I visited her gallery. I bet she was the one who bought those first two paintings.* She stared at the white expanses leaning against her living room wall. *What did it matter?* She didn't paint to sell them, she painted because not painting wasn't an option anymore. The strokes, dabs, and swirls of living paint carried her to a land of light and fire, to that place of feeling full, of soaring with her other self, the self who expanded into a gigantic being who raced with wild abandon to the edges of the universe and back.

She pulled the paint splattered bed sheet from under the dining room table (now permanently in the far corner), spread it on the living room floor and lay the first canvas down. She retrieved her paint tins, brushes, palette knives and on the way through the kitchen, grabbed the pancake flipper. She changed into her paint jeans and t-shirt and selected a half dozen CD's.

Yellow first. She dipped a wide brush into the large opening of the gallon tin of acrylic house paint and with one bold stroke, created a fat diagonal sunbeam. From a puddle of Raw Umber she danced the dripping pancake flipper across the bouncing surface, making pathways of dark brown beats. Minou sat under the table, front legs folded under, surveying the peculiar activities of her mistress gone wild.

"What do you think, Minou? Blue?" She stepped back, and tilted her head. "You're right. Purple, not blue."

For the next twenty minutes, with the help of Chopin, Thea made love to the canvas, tenderly inviting each shape and colour to show themselves. Intermittently, and still holding a spattered paint knife, a kitchen utensil or a wet credit card, she'd stop and walk to the window and stare at snow covered branches or watch the chickadees darting at the squirrels around the feeder. One time Minou followed her, jumped up on the sill and made throaty noises at the flitting birds on the other side of the glass.

She would return with fresh eyes to a part that cried for a touch of brooding reddish brown of Burnt Sienna or a daring dab of Alizarin Crimson. By late afternoon, the natural light had faded and her stomach growled. She looked at the clock. Three-thirty-three. When she was doing bookkeeping, caterpillar minutes crept by, but with a pot of paint at her side, hours gleefully escaped their appointed confines.

She washed brushes and utensils, capped the paint tins and tossed a frozen veggie dinner into the oven. She set the timer for thirty minutes and went upstairs for a shower, shedding her clothes as she went.

The next day, she moved the Chopin painting upstairs and laid the second one out. She painted for a half hour and in the middle of Mozart, stopped. "That's enough for now, Minou."

She had learned not to push it. Not to force it. Not to touch it if it didn't feel right.

For the next few days, she and art continued their love affair. The spatula laughed as it slid over the surface. Her library card carved ridges and rivulets, while the triangular palette knife drew strings of Vivaldi into a network of expanding galaxies.

On Saturday afternoon, it wasn't quite dry so she left it where it was, taking up a large portion of the living room. When Arthur came in, he said, "Wow, do you paint here?"

She shrugged. "Nowhere else works."

'You need a studio." He nodded to the painting. "A big one."

A week later, Saturday flew in cold and snowy. She had finished her morning coffee and was thinking she should refill the bird feeder when her front door flew open with a swoosh.

A snowman stood in her front hall. Or was a Sasquatch? No, it was Sara Jane buried in a cloak of white fur. She shook her head and fuzzy tentacles of red hair poked out from under the all encompassing hood that surrounded her pink cheeks.

"Sara Jane! You're back. Come in."

She stamped her thick white feet leaving clouds of snow on the mat. "I walked from the market. I thought I might see you there." She shook her snowy shoulders, showering another mass of white to the floor.

"That's a fifteen minute walk. You must be freezing." Thea took the heavy cloak and hung it on the hall rack. "I'll get you a coffee."

Sara Jane pulled off her white furry boots. "It was invigorating. I'd forgotten how lovely snow is."

Thea went to the kitchen and brought back two cups of coffee.

Sara Jane was standing beside the painting that was laying flat on the floor. "You have gone big. My god, girl. You are amazing."

"I call it my Mozart." She handed her a cup. "*The Magic Flute* played while I painted. Well at least when I started. Vivaldi jumped in at the end."

"They would both be pleased." She walked around it. "Perfect for the gallery."

"Speaking of galleries. You didn't tell me it was *your* gallery you were taking my paintings to."

Sara Jane laughed. "The bank mostly owns it and my friend Ivana runs it. She's amazing at finding new artists."

They took their coffee to the soft chairs on the other side of the living room. "You mean those two sales were legitimate."

"Absolutely." She held one hand up as if swearing on a Bible. "I did not buy them."

"Wow." *Someone I don't know ought a part of me that I've only recently discovered for myself.* A shimmer of light filled her heart and flowed through her body, opening lifelines to the tips of her fingers and down to her toes.

"A penny for them."

Thea laughed. "It will cost you two thousand dollars."

"The *Mozart/Vivaldi* will bring n that, I promise."

"*Chopin* is in my bedroom and *New York* is in my craft room. Would you like to see them?"

Sarah Jane plunked her coffee down, jumped up and ran upstairs. First the bedroom and next she spun to the craft room. Bumping into Thea in the hall, she whooped, "My God, Kiddo. I'm so glad I moved in next door."

Thea laughed. "I am too."

She dashed back to the bedroom. "One of my passions is discovering new talent." She threw her arms around a startled Thea.

A quick hug and she scooted back to the craft room and before Thea could say a word, she bubbled over again. "You've caught the soul of New York." She stared at Thea. "I had a funny feeling when I first saw the ad for the house that I had to buy it. Now I know why."

"Why?"

"So I could meet up with you again."

"I must admit, I feel as if I have known you before too."

"I think we were sisters in a past life."

"I remember you said that the first time we met. In this life that is."

The mysterious smile on Sara Jane grew larger. " I don't mean blood sisters. I think we were nuns together."

"I can see me being a nun but not you."

"I was probably very naughty."

"That's probably when you learned to make soup to feed eighty souls."

They went downstairs where Thea threw a salad together and cheese sandwiches which they polished off with a bottle of Merlot.

January neared to an end and after Thea's three large paintings were shipped to the New York gallery, her mind skittered back to thoughts of moving. Sharon had said February but the baby was keeping her busy and she and Patricia hadn't mentioned moving when Thea had last spoken to them. Madison had told Thea the condo tenants had left and it was being painted so it sounded as if the February deadline was still on.

Her mother hadn't called all month, but on February first, she phoned. "Are you about ready to move? The condom will be ready on the twenty-eighth."

Thea sighed. "This is leap year. I have another day. Besides, I haven't heard from Sharon about when they're planning to move."

"Never mind about that. They're going to gut the whole place anyway and it will be months before it will be decent enough to live in."

"Thanks, mother."

"Are you being sarcastic?"

"I thought you were."

"Good grief, girl. You were an impossible child and still are." A rattle of clashing bracelets and a bang.

Thea held the buzzing phone in her hand. "Damn it all, Minou. I don't want to live in a condo." She jabbed the phone in its holder and marched to the laundry room. *I guess I've been denying this long enough. I kept thinking it would go away.* She grabbed the two empty liquor cartons she had picked up a few weeks ago and stomped upstairs.

In half an hour, she closed the lids of both boxes, crammed full of books from her bedroom shelf.

Chapter 56

Valentine's Day fell on a Sunday and by then, Thea had taken three. She'd also packed three boxes of kitchen stuff, leaving only a few essentials for daily use. In spite of the growing pile of boxes, she still couldn't believe she was moving. *What could possibly happen to change things at this late date?*

Early that evening, Arthur arrived with red roses and a box of Lady Godiva chocolates. In the morning, over coffee and croissants, they set the date for the trip to England.

"For a whole month?" said Thea. "That's a long time."

"We really need five weeks to do it right." He punched in some numbers on his phone. "I'll be sure we're in Wales on the 17th for your birthday." He looked up. "And remind me. Why do you want to be in Wales on your birthday?"

"I don't know. I just know I have to."

In two days it was her mother's birthday and Patricia had arranged for her and her sisters to take her to the Mandarin that evening. Their mother always insisted on not making a fuss and one year they didn't and their mother's long face lasted a month.

Sharon was vague about the date they would start tearing her house apart but assured her she didn't have to be out by the 29th. However, the next day she tackled the hallway closet. She didn't need three raincoats or her fat clothes anymore so she filled another couple of boxes.

The next day, after lunch, an itch to paint called to her. Their mother's dinner wasn't until six so she'd have plenty of time. She turned off the phone, gathered her supplies, and popped in a CD.

For the whole blissful afternoon, she worked alternately on two small canvases, smiling that she now considered a two-by-four foot size small.

Four bells chimed and she stared at the clock hands. "Four o'clock? Already?" She went to the kitchen to change her muddy water bowl and the message light was blinking on her phone. It might be Arthur and she was at a stopping point. She clicked the phone back on and was about to retrieve her messages when it rang. Her mother's number showed but when she picked it up, it was Madison, talking fast.

"We've been trying to reach you for the last hour and a half. I was about to come and get you. You'd better get over here right away."

"What's the matter? What's wrong?"

A scuffle and Patricia came on the phone. "Our mother is dead and it's all your fault."

Thea's heart kathumped deep in the walls of her chest. *Our mother dead! Impossible.* She forced her mouth to work. "What happened?"

Another scuffle. "Don't listen to Patricia. Just get yourself over here."

Thea yanked off her paint clothes and threw on the nearest slacks and sweater. With scrambled thoughts and paint-streaked hands she sped to Stuart Street. When she got there she didn't ring or knock. She charged into the living room.

A red-eyed Patricia leapt from the couch. "You broke our mother's heart. All this fuss about not wanting to move and going to New York for a week with a man AT CHRISTMAS!"

"Shut up, Patricia," Madison said.

Thea dropped her purse and sank to the edge of the stuffed chair beside Madison. "What happened?"

A tightlipped Patricia glared and jabbed at her eyes with a fresh Kleenex.

Madison spoke. "The doctor thinks it was a heart attack but they have to do more tests."

"Where is she now?"

Patricia jutted her chin. "At the morgue. Where do you think?"

Madison blurted, "For heaven's sake, Patricia, drop the attitude." She touched Thea's hand. "Bonnie found her at two-thirty. Mother insisted she take the day off but she had the feeling she should come home early. When she found her she called the doctor and he phoned the police."

"Poor Bonnie," said Thea. "Why the police?"

"We don't know why," shouted Patricia. "It's horrible."

"The doctor gave Bonnie a sedative," Madison said. "She's pretty broken up. The weird thing is—Tippy's dead too."

"What?" Thea looked from one sister to the other.

"Dogs can die from broken hearts too," Patricia cried.

The absence of Josephine Marshall and her yapping dog loomed large. An eerie quietness wrapped itself around the furniture and the three women. Thea went to the kitchen and made a pot of tea while a tearful Patricia phoned Gilbert & MacIntyre Funeral Home to start making arrangements.

Madison would stay with Bonnie that night and sleep in the spare room. Thea called Stephanie.

"Mom, I'll be right there."

"There's no need to rush over."

"Are you sure?"

"Yes, really. I'm okay."

Arthur's phone went to voice mail and she didn't want to leave the message. The rest of the day and evening passed in a fog and when she got home, she fastened the paint lids and wrapped up her painting utensils. They would need soaking in paint thinner now.

The next morning she awoke groggy and it was nearly ten when she pulled into the curved driveway on Stuart Street. Madison's and Patricia's cars were already there in front of a third car—a black one. She pulled in behind it.

Bonnie, with red eyes, met her at the door and crumpled into tears. "Oh, poor lass. I canna believe it."

Thea hugged her and patted her shoulder. Madison walked out. "We've been waiting for you before we started."

"Started?"

The three women, arms linked, walked into the living room.

"It's about time." Patricia voice dripped with icicles.

A short, rotund man rose from a chair and extended his hand. "Inspector Bailey. " He wore a rumpled brown suit and the first two fingers on his right hand were stained a dirty yellowy-orange.

Thea shook his hand. *Inspector?*

Patricia sat upright in her mother's straight-backed chair. Thea, with Bonnie crushing her hand, headed for the couch. Madison sat in one of the three stuffed chairs.

The inspector remained standing. "I wanted you all present to hear this." He took a pair of rimless glasses and perched them on his nose as if ready to read something.

"I don't know what the police have to do with my mother having a heart attack," Patricia said. She wore no makeup and the dark circles made her eyes look even more sunken. "It's enough having our dear mother gone without you and your men snooping around all morning."

"Well, that's the thing," he said. "We have strong evidence that your mother did not die of a heart attack." He laced his hands over his protruding stomach. "We have a strong suspicious that Mrs. Marshall and her dog may have died from unnatural causes." He tapped a forefinger over a straining button. "Possibly an overdose of some medicine or—poison."

Gasps erupted. A picture of the box of rat poison next to the sugar flashed into Thea's brain. *No!*

He continued. "We found an open box of rat poison in the pantry."

Thea put her other hand to her thumping heart. *It's my fault. I killed my mother. I knew I should have taken that box away.*

"We will know more once the lab results come in."

Bonnie wrung her hands. "I shouldn't have left her." She pulled a large handkerchief out of her apron pocket and hid her face in it, muffling her cries.

Thea hugged her. "It's not your fault, Bonnie."

The inspector went on. "We are checking out her medications. It's possible she took—" He raised his eyebrows and peered over his glasses at each of the women. "—or was given a lethal overdose."

A wide-eyed Patricia straightened higher in her mother's straight backed chair and Bonnie's sobs turned to a wail. Madison and Thea's eyes locked. Were they both thinking the same thing? Could their mother have actually taken her own life? And if so, why?

Patricia broke into sobs. "Poor mother."

The inspector walked behind an empty straight-backed chair and clamped his hands on the top. His gaze roved over each person. "Forensics is checking all the containers, plus the box of rat poison, for fingerprints. An officer will be coming by with a portable fingerprint kit to get all of yours."

"This is outrageous," Patricia cried. "Are you intimating that one of us—"

"My fingerprints are on the box of rat poison," a voice said.

All heads swivelled toward Thea.

Chapter 57

The inspector peered at Thea over his his glasses. "Your fingerprints are on the box of rat poison?"

"It was months ago. I was here for tea and Mother and I had an argument about where it should be stored."

"Go on," said the inspector.

"I was getting the sugar when I saw it on the shelf. I picked it up to move it but she was adamant I leave it there."

He pulled a pen from his pocket, opened a small note book, pushed his glasses up and began scribbling.

Thea shook her head. *This can't be happening.*

Inspector Bailey finished writing and looked up. "An officer will be here shortly to take prints.I'll see myself out."

The door closed behind him and a frowning Patricia stood up and walked back and forth across the room.

"Stop pacing, for heaven's sake," cried Madison.

She stopped in front of the fireplace, clasped her hands in front of her and lifted her head in her imperial Queen of England pose. "I have something to tell you."

Madison and Thea exchanged a quick glance before looking back at Patricia. Bonnie stared at her with her mouth open.

"As horrible as our mother's death was—" She took her signature pause for dramatic effect. "It was a blessing."

"I wood'na call dyin' of poison a blessin'." Bonnie scrunched the oversized handkerchief in her fist.

Patricia lifted her chin. "She swore me to secrecy." Another drawn-out pause. "On January sixth she was diagnosed with pancreatic cancer."

"What?" said Madison.

"The doctor gave her three months." Her voice cracked. "She refused chemo and radiation."

Bonnie unfurled her large handkerchief and covered her face with it. Madison went to the couch and put her arms around her. Thea got up and walked to the window. A bossy blue jay was lording it over the chickadees as they battled over scattered seeds.

Patricia glared at everyone hile Bonnie blubbered in Madison's arms. Thea watched the power struggle on the front lawn.

"Why didn't she tell us?" Madison asked.

"You know mother," said Patricia. "She didn't like being controlled by anything, especially some damn cancer."

No one spoke for several minutes. The air hung heavy with unspoken thoughts.

Between sobs, Bonnie muttered. "She wouldn't have taken that horrible rat poison or too many sleeping pills. She was a fighter. "

"I don't want to talk about it," said Patricia. "I'm going to make coffee." She strode from the room.

Thirty minutes later, officer Brandon arrived with a portable fingerprint scanner. No more stamp pads with messy inks. Ms. Brandon, an officious looking woman in her late thirties, instructed them to place their fingers on a glass plate. Then the CCD camera took a picture and filed a record of the print. After checking she had a clear image from each, she thanked them and left. It had taken less than twenty minutes.

At seven-thirty that evening, a weary Thea returned to her house. She hit her daughter's quick dial button and told her the latest news about her grandmother possibly taking an overdose of something.

"That's terrible. I can be over in the morning."

"Thank you, darling, but that's not necessary. Everything is chaos and there's nothing you can do right now." She didn't tell her about the rat poison and what that might mean.

"Are you sure? It's no trouble. I can drop everything,"

Thea sucked in her breath feeling the depth and strength of her daughter's love. "I know and thank you for that. I'm okay. I'll call you tomorrow and keep you up-to-date." Hopefully, not to tell her her mother was in jail. They hung up and she went to the kitchen, passing, but not looking at her two unfinished paintings. Her stomach rumbled and after staring in the fridge for several minutes, she shut it and stared at the half empty pantry. She picked up a tin of tomato soup, opened it and poured it into the pot.

The phone rang. Arthur. She hadn't told him.

"I've been thinking about our trip to England, and I have some great ideas."

His cheerful voice gave her a lift.

"Oh?" *Let the moment last a little longer*. She put the pot of soup on the stove and turned on the burner.

"We could start in London and once we've located Cheryl, we could sightsee. You and I that is. There's the National Gallery, the Tate and the British Museum, to name only a few.

Tiny bubbles plopped around the perimeter of the red liquid. "Sounds great."

"There's the Old Vic—you sound different. Are you all right?"

She took a deep breath and told him about her mother dying, not of a heart attack or cancer but from either an overdose of something or from poison, finishing with how her fingerprints were all over a box of rat poison.

"Do you want me to come over?"

"No, I'm alright. It must have been an accident and she got the rat poison mixed up with the sugar."

"That seems unlikely, although there is no set standard for colour-coding rodenticide. Do you have a lawyer?"

"Do I need one?"

"Your mother was in the process of taking your house from you, so you had motive, means, and opportunity."

"Arthur! I didn't kill my mother."

"I know you didn't. Calm down. I'm playing devil's advocate."

"I don't like you as a devil." She groaned. "This is such a mess."

"I can be there in an hour."

"No. Don't come."

"Are you sure? It's no problem. I can—"

"No, I'm exhausted. I'm going to bed—to sleep."

"I'll put a call in to my lawyer in the morning."

"Arthur! I didn't do it."

"I know, but things can get twisted. It's good to have a back up plan."

The next morning, Patricia phoned with a curt, "The funeral is Tuesday, two o'clock. That is if her body is released from that dreadful place."

Right after that, Bonnie called telling how the police had come back and searched the house again, taking a long time in Josephine's bedroom and the kitchen.

"What were they looking for? Did they find anything?"

"They already took all her bottles of medications, so I don't think they found anything else." She cleared her throat. "But I found something before they came."

"What was it?Did you give it to them?"

"Land sakes, no."

"Bonnie, what did you find?"*Do I want to know?Whatever it is, I should tell her to give it to the police.*

"I got the premonition to look in our secret message place."

"Your secret message place? What's that?"

"You know how people hide keys outside, well, your mother would leave messages for me in the onion bin."

Only my mother would think of that. "What did you find?"

"A blue sealed envelope."

"What was in it? What did it say?"

"Glory be to the saints, I didn't dare open it. I was afraid what it might say."

"Is there any writing on the outside?"

"Yes. I have it right here."

"Bonnie, what does it say,"

"It's not addressed to anyone. It's only written, '*To be opened after I am dead*'. What should we do? Should we open it?"

Thea's curiosity burned but caution won. "Even though it was in your private message place, it might be better if you don't. Why don't you phone Inspector Bailey and tell him you found it?"

Bonnie's voice shook. "But when did she write it? What does it mean?"

"I wish I knew." She clicked the phone off. She remembered the day she'd found the poison, leaving her prints all over the box and her mother demanding she leave it in the kitchen. So what had her mother written? Would she have gone so far to actually take poison and accuse her own daughter of poisoning her? Thea could never figure out why her mother was so down on her. It had to be more than a difficult birth and her birth mark. For Thea, that was so in the past now.

She headed for the shower, envisioning the headline in the morning Mercury: *Newly Discovered Artist Suspected of Murdering her Own Mother.*

Chapter 58

Thea had a quick shower, dressed and made a smoothy. Her stomach couldn't handle food and there was no use going to the house until the inspector called. Nothing to do for the moment but wait. She looked at the canvas on the floor—a work in progress. She folded her arms and stared at it. *Are each of us a work in progress? And do we ever get it finished? Or do we die before we reach our destination.* She went to the kitchen and poured herself a coffee. Maybe later she could paint her feelings, but not now. Right now, they were a mess of confusion. The moment she'd heard her mother was dead, a sense of relief had washed over her followed by guilt to feel that.

She took her coffee upstairs, sat in her wicker chair and stared out the window. From the reflection, it looked as if her dragonfly was perched on the snow outside her window sill. "I don't know what I feel, dragonfly." She looked past it to a world dressed in white. "I suppose I should cry or feel sad." The snow-covered branches lay still on that windless morning while an opaque sky shrouded a pale sun. She closed her eyes for a second.

A loud ringing woke her with a jump. She grabbed her phone, nearly knocking over the cold cup of coffee beside it. What time was it? Still daylight. She punched it on. "Hello."

It was the Inspector. "Please come to the Stuart Street house."

"I'll be right over."

"Tests showed your finger prints are on the box of rat poison."

"I told you they were. I picked it up to move it—"

"Mrs. Baxter has found a letter. Officer Brandon is taking prints from it now. You had better come over here."

"I said I was." She hung up. *Silly man.*

She parked behind the inspector's car. In the front hallway, she hung up her coat and took off snowy boots. Inspector Bailey was standing in the living room in front of the fireplace, holding a piece of her mother's blue stationary in one hand and an opened envelope in the other. Patricia, sitting in their mother's chair, ignored her. Bonne nodded and sniffled a hello from the couch and Madison, beside her, motioned for Thea to join them.

Thea grabbed Madison's outstretched hand and sat down. The inspector looked at the paper. No plastic gloves this time. He folded it in half, pressed the crease with cigarette stained fingers and replaced it in its matching envelope. He held it up by the corner. "Prints have been taken from this envelope and the letter."

Loud ticktocks from the Grandfather clock beat steadily into the room, echoing the thumps of Thea's heart.

"Your mother's prints are on the envelope along with Mrs. Baxter's." He brought the envelope to his forehead, holding it like a fake fortune teller.

Will he get on with it? Thea brought a finger to her mouth but remembered she didn't bite her nails anymore. .

"The prints on the letter," he paused, "were only those of Josephine Marshall's." He gave the envelope to Patricia and pulled the edges of his jacket together over his round stomach. The fabric strained to meet the button. "Only her fingerprints were on the empty bottle of sleeping pills found under her pillow. Chemical evidence clearly concluded she died from an overdose of those same pills. No rat poison was evident." He smacked his hands together. "This case is closed."

Thea gulped. *Had it ever been a case?* Madison and Patricia exchanged looks and Bonnie gasped.

"Good day, ladies." He turned to leave.

Bonnie jumped up and saw him out while Patricia took the inspector's place and stood in front of the cold fireplace. She stared at the envelope. Madison and Thea darted a glance to each other. Bonnie returned and sat in the stuffed chair beside them. Patricia, the newly appointed family matriarch, pulled the letter out and placed the envelope on the tree stump coffee table.

Thea frowned. *Does she know what's in that letter?*

Patricia picked up the blue paper, her fingers pinching the outer edges as if were poison itself. She straightened her shoulders. "I'll read it, shall I?" She never needed permission to do anything.

Madison said, "Yes, please do."

Josephine Marshall always wrote in one long sentence. Whether three lines or thirty, her words followed each other like a rambling herd of cows wending their way homeward. A liberal scattering of *ands*—mixed with a sprinkle of dashes—took the place of commas, periods, and question marks or any other punctuation that one might deem necessary.

"It's addressed: To whom it may concern." Patricia cleared her throat. "If I should die on my birthday, I want my funeral to be all white like I saw on Oprah with a white casket—Gilbert and MacIntyres have them—with white flowers and a white hearse and white limos and I want everyone in the family to wear white—the men too because Moores have white suits for rent—I checked on that to be sure—and I want to be dressed in my new long white dress which I bought for the occasion and is hanging inside the front door of my closet and dont forget my white shoes even though they wont show."

She looked up. "It's signed, Josephine Annette Marshall and there's a PS. If Tippy should die at the same time as me I want him buried with me in his new white collar which is hanging in my closet with my dress."

Bonnie resumed crying. Patricia sat down in the upright chair and placed the letter beside the envelope which rested on what Stephanie called 'the tree table.' Thea never liked it. It stretched three feet in diameter, its bark still attached and the whole thing was encased in multiple layers of polyurethane. She stared through the thick plastic surface at the golden wood trapped beneath. When she was eight she had counted its seventy-eight rings. How fitting that both the tree and her mother met their demise at the same age.

Madison's voice sounded loud after the prolonged silence. "I wish she had somehow said goodbye."

Patricia had regained her composure and set her head in its usual erect position. "She didn't want you to know she was sick and she wasn't going to suffer the pain or an undignified death."

"I realize *why* she did it, but what was all that stuff about the rat poison? It made Thea suspect." Madison said.

Thea shrugged. "Maybe she changed her mind about implicating me. And sleeping pills is an easier way to die."

Bonnie spluttered and crossed herself. "Poor Jo. A terrible thing. And on her birthday. Poor Tippy." She wiped at her eyes. "At least they're together. Praise be to God, Joseph, and family."

Two days later, a stream of white limos filed through Guelph's downtown streets toward the Woodlawn Cemetery, each carrying white-attired mourners. Family and friends assembled around the white coffin, with white roses cascading over it. Flashes of white peeked beneath black or navy coats. At final prayers, fat snow flakes drifted down and blanketed the gathering with a frosty topping. Even nature had complied with Josephine Marshall's last wintery wish.

Chapter 59

Immediately after the funeral, the family, plus Bonnie, gathered at the Stuart House for the reading of the will: Patricia, with Sharon, Mike and baby, Thea and Arthur with Stephanie and Mark, and Madison and Charlie and their two sons from Kingston.

Mr. Cecil Weatherbee, Josephine's solicitor, sat in the living room on a hard-backed chair in front of the unlit fireplace facing a semicircle grouped around the plasticized coffee table. First, he announced that the will had been drawn up two weeks prior and that Mrs. Marshall had been of sound mind.

Thea and Madison glanced at each other.

He shuffled some papers, smoothed the top one and cleared his throat. "I, Josephine Annette Marshall, bequeath eight hundred thousand dollars to the University of Guelph with the stipulation that a building be named after me."

Nods of approval and a smattering of murmurs.

"I leave a trust fund that pays a monthly sum of $1,000 to my dear friend and helpmate, Bonnie Baxter."

Bonnie brought a kerchief-sized handkerchief to her eyes. "Sweet Mother Mary and Joseph. God bless her."

"My house on Stuart Street and its furnishings are to be sold and proceeds divided equally between my daughters, Patricia Mae and Madison Joyce."

With gasps and whispers, heads turned to look at Thea. She kept her gaze straight ahead. *I didn't think she hated me that much.*

Mr. Weatherbee continued. "All my assets, stocks, bonds and current savings account are also to be divided between my two loving daughters, Patricia Mae and Madison Joyce. I leave the houses they are living in to each of them as well."

The whispering rose. Arthur squeezed Thea's hand. "The house which I own at 37 Glasgow Street North, Guelph, Ontario, I leave to my friend, Bonnie Baxter."

Bonnie drew in a sharp breath. "Glory be to all the angels." She clapped her hand over her mouth and darted a look at Thea.

Thea gasped. For nearly a year, she had been wrestling with losing her house and now here it was. The ax had fallen. *It seems it was not my imagination that my mother hated me.*

Patricia explained. "A month ago, Sharon told mother she didn't want the Glasgow house."

No one commented and Mr. Weatherbee droned on. "The condom (sic) in Royal Gardens subdivision, goes to my granddaughter, Stephanie Margaret Watson."

The boys snickered at their cousin being left a condom. Madison groaned and Stephanie bent close to her mother's ear. "Mom, I don't want or need a condo or a condom for that matter."

After the initial surprise, a weird sense of peace enveloped Thea. She lowered her shoulders and leaned back. *I may be an orphan. I may be disinherited. I may be homeless but—* She looked into her daughter's loving eyes and at the beautiful man beside her, holding her hand tightly. *—I'll be fine, thank you. Just fine.*

Cecil Weatherbee shuffled the papers back into his brief case. People shifted in their chairs, bent toward each other and talked in low voices.

Madison leaned over to Thea. "Don't worry. Patricia and I will work it out so you'll get a third." She looked at her older sister who had risen and was passing in front of them. "Won't we Patricia?"

"Won't we what?"

"Make sure that Thea gets her share."

Patricia's glance moved quickly past Thea and fastened on Madison. "That's the way mother wanted it." She lifted her chin. "Besides, it's the law and we can't change that." She strode to the hallway, catching up with Sharon.

Madison's jaw tightened. "We can and we will."

Thea touched her sister's arm. "I don't want any of the money." *I am not a victim and I will not beg for anything from my mother.*

"But—"

"No, Maddy. It's all right. Thank you, but I don't want anything."

Bonnie continued to live at Stuart Street and Thea would stay in her house until the Stuart residence was sold and its contents auctioned. Stephanie did not want to live in the condo and told her mother several times, "Mom, it's yours if you want it."

She didn't want it. Thea and Arthur, secretly engaged since Christmas, had no definite plans for marriage and had never talked about living arrangements.

Over the next few days, Madison doggedly tried to persuade Patricia to relinquish some of her share. She wouldn't budge, citing the law as binding and finishing with a righteous lift of her chin with, "Nothing can be done."

A week after the funeral, Thea walked up to the front door of the Stuart Street house. She entered without knocking and hung her coat on the hall rack. She started to remove her boots but froze when the familiar and foreboding sound of jangling bracelets came closer. Common sense told her it couldn't be—

Patricia, carrying a suitcase, turned the corner and Thea put her hand over her pounding heart.

Patricia dropped the case and reached for her coat. When she slid her arm into the sleeve, the clinking muffled. "There is nothing I can do."

"I wish we could have been closer but mom always seemed to come between us."

Patricia had pulled on one boot and held the other in her hand. "What do you mean?"

Thea finished taking off her boots and hung up her scarf."Mom always favoured you and never seemed to like me for some reason."

Patricia yanked on her other boot. "Oh, that's all in your head. You were too sensitive." She picked up the suitcase. "I have to go." She opened the door and walked out.

Stephanie, in jeans and a blue shirt, poked her head around the doorway. "Tea's made. Bonnie's upstairs with Madison labeling boxes."

The women were meeting to sort through Josephine Marshall's personal effects. Patricia had taken what she wanted and clothes had been put into separate piles. One for the thrift store, and the furs for auction. Thea hugged Stephanie and they walked into a fire-lit living room. Stephanie poured tea and set the mugs on the plastic tree table. She sat on one of the stuffed chairs with her feet tucked under her. Thea sat on the couch and put her feet on the table.

"Grandma would have your head for that."

Thea wiggled her red stockinged toes. "I know."

"How are you doing, mom?"

"I'm okay." She picked up her mug. "But there is something I want to talk to you about." The tea was too hot and she set it down. "I know we talked about going to England together, but— "

"You're going with Arthur."

She lifted her eyebrows. "How did you know?"

"I saw your passport on your hall table and since you hadn't asked me about mine, I figured it was Arthur you were planning to go with."

"Oh, Stephanie, I'm sorry. We talked about it in New York and —"

Stephanie leaned over and took her mother's outstretched hand. "Mom, it's all right. You deserve to get away. And you can check out Evan and prepare him to meet me when I go."

Thea gulped. She hadn't thought about how she would approach Evan. *Hello, how are you and by the way, remember twenty-nine years ago when you came over for my mother's wedding and—* "I'll do my best. I owe you that."

"Mom, you owe me nothing. I have a fabulous life. In fact, I have something to tell you." Her grin got bigger.

Thea glazed at her daughter's stomach. "No!"

"Yes! We're pregnant. Due in September."

Thea jumped up and hugged her daughter, letting tears flow. Being called Grandma was more than fine with her.

Madison walked into the room and deposited a packed box on the floor. "Okay, quit the blubbering. We have work to do."

"Madison," Thea cried. "Stephanie's going to have a baby!"

"Congratulations." Madison flung her arms wide and hugged her niece and her sister.

"Praise be to God, what's all the fuss about?" Bonnie came through the doorway, her arms piled high with linens.

After the news and more hugs, the sorting continued. The clothes (sans furs) and costume jewellery (sans bracelets thanks to Patricia) went to Good Will. Bonnie kept three cardigans she had knit for Josephine, and Madison took some linens. Stephanie wanted Frank's dance sculpture. Thea wanted nothing.

Madison rummaged around. "You have to have something of mother's."

"I don't want anything."

Madison lifted some things aside. "Here's the perfect thing." She held up an old book. It was a little larger than a pocketbook with a rusty-brown leather cover that flapped over like an envelope. A thin strap of leather wound around it, holding it shut. "I've never seen this before. I guess it's a diary." She handed the book to Thea. "It will be a challenge for you to sort out mother's long-winded sentences."

Thea stared at the book in her sister's outstretched hand. *Do I want to read what my mother wrote? Would it help me understand what made her tick and why she had it in for me?*

"Oh, for heaven's sake. Take it. It won't bite."

Thea frowned and took it. *Some words do bite.* She slid it into the outside pouch of her purse.

Am I up for the challenge to read what's in that old book?

Chapter 60

Hours later, Thea and Madison sprawled on the floor beside sealed and stacked cardboard cartons.

"At least everything is sorted," Bonnie said, flopping into a chair. "The auction people are coming on Monday and I'll phone Good Will in the morning." She looked at Stephanie who held a fat magic marker in one hand and a roll of packing tape in the other. "Can I ask you something?"

"Sure." Stephanie marked the side of the last box and stretched a strip of tape across the top.

"I was wondering if you would rent the condo to me. I've always liked it and I'm not much for living in old houses downtown." She glanced at Thea. "No offense."

Stephanie ripped the tape along the serrated edge of the roller, looked at Bonnie and her mother.

Thea lifted one eyebrow, smiled and nodded.

Stephanie put down the tape, walked over to Bonnie and took both hands in hers. "How would you like to trade the Glasgow House for the condo?"

"Trade?" She looked from Stephanie to Thea and back to Stephanie. "You mean—"

"You would own the condo outright. And I, or at least mom, would own her house."

"Praise be to our good Lord, what a grand idea." She grabbed Stephanie in a hug, "Of course, my dear, of course." She pulled back. "Oh, my. What would Josephine say?" A sly smile crept out and she lifted her chin. "I don't care what she'd say. This is my decision." She stuck out her hand and they shook on the deal.

Three days later, Madison phoned with news that Patricia had received a letter from the University of Guelph. "Wait till you hear this," she said. Her voice thrilled with laughter. "The funds will be used to build a wing on—get this—the student residence!"

"The student residence? But mom wanted something prestigious like a science or medical building."

"It will be named the Josephine Annette Marshall Coed Residence."

"Coed? Oh my," Thea said. "Poetic justice." Imagine her mother's horror of having her name on a building where males and females slept under the same roof.

"An oak plaque with her initials in gold will be installed at the front entrance."

"Well, mom would like that."

Madison held back a giggle. "On this big plaque in big letters will be written JAM HALL." She let the laughter out. "How eloquent is that?"

For the first time, a pang of sympathy rose up in Cynthia for her mother.

Now that she wasn't going to have to move, Thea unfolded the tops of the few boxes she had packed, mostly books and kitchen stuff. As she sorted through them she found herself putting most of it back into the box. It had been kinda nice haven't less stuff around. She had finished organizing one shelf of books in the bedroom that she couldn't live without when the phone rang. She put it on speaker.

Sara Jane's voice boomed out. "Hold onto your hat, my friend."

"What now?" With a friend like Sara Jane she could expect anything.

"Your New York painting sold. Drum roll please. For five thousand dollars!"

Thea's knees went weak and she sank to the floor. "What?"

"You heard me! Five thousand dollars which means three thousand for you. I told you you were a freaking artist. I hope you get it now."

"I—I don't know what to say." She slapped her hand to her forehead. "But I think I'm starting to believe it."

Sara Jane laughed. "Enjoy. I gotta fly but thought you'd want to know right away."

The phone buzzed for several moments until Thea hit the off button. She shook head, trying to rearrang her thoughts. *I wish I could go back in time and tell a young Cynthia that dreams do come true.*

When she was fourteen, she had begged her mother to let her take the art course at school.

"Art!" her mother had growled. "What use is that? You saw how far your father got with art." She spat out the word 'art' as if ridding herself of a bitter taste. "You'll take commercial. If you can type, you'll never go hungry."

Cynthia had become an excellent typist and from sixteen years old, she worked for nine years in offices: Bell Telephone, Hydro, Consumers Gas, Living Lighting and other assorted businesses. In one insurance company, she and twenty other women sat in neat rows, clattering on typewriters in what was called the Office Pool. She nearly drowned in it. Letters, invoices, and orders would arrive over anonymous dictaphones, audio tapes, and finally floppy discs. Never a face or a smile attached to a Mr. Samuels or a Mr. Burnaby. Later it became Ms. Jeffreys or Ms. Johnston but resulted in the same relentless tap, tap, tapping. Its endless monotony, albeit more subdued on computer keyboards, was Chinese water torture to Cynthia. By the grace of God, or too much alcohol and an equally willing "uncle," a surprise pregnancy had saved her from the nine-to-five office trap. And now here she was earning money —good money from her art. Minou jumped into Thea's lap. "What would mother think of that, I wonder?"

A cold March bristled in and with tax deadline rushing closer, Thea's weeks became fully occupied. Their flight to England would be leaving on the 29th, the day after Easter Monday and she would let her clients know that she wouldn't be available after that and refer them to a colleague.

Bonnie was settling into the condo and Stephanie was getting ready for spring shows. Maddy was overseeing the auction and final sale of the house, still trying to get Patricia to bend, while Thea reassured her again to not bother. Arthur also had extra work to finish before leaving for a month so with everyone busy, Thea was able to complete all her clients' tax returns. She closed her computer with a satisfied click. "No more bookkeeping for a whole month." When she got back she might even think about giving up working with numbers. She pushed her chair away from the desk and went downstairs to make tea.

In one week, she and Arthur would be leaving for England. *Do they have herb tea there?*

Her mother's leather covered book was still sitting on the coffee table where she'd left it three weeks ago. She still wasn't sure she wanted to read it. She had long ago reconciled that her mother and she were too different to ever get along.

She stared at the book. "Dare I see what she has written?"

Chapter 61

She made a cup of Moroccan Mint tea and brought it back to the living room. She thought of her own journals and the thousand pages of tears. "What tears have you shed, mother?"

Minou leaped up beside her and burrowed into the space between the cushion and Thea's thigh. Since the dragonfly and Arthur had come into her life, she was writing less and less in journals. Were journals only for sad times? She picked up her mother's book.

"Okay, Minou. No time like the present." She turned the book over. The thin leather strap was knotted tightly at the back. She jumped up, startling the cat, and marched to the kitchen to get a fork. Back in her chair, she coaxed the tong into the clenched knot and gently teased it loose. It finally let go and she unwound the strap into two long ties fastened to the back. She turned the book over and opened it to the first page.

Josephine Annette Turner

Today is my birthday February 18 1954

Thea turned the page.

Finally I am sixteen –my dad gave me this book and my mom gave me this pen–my sister gave me a scarf and my brother gave me a yellow band for my hair– I bet mom bought it for him –I hate being a middle child

Thea didn't know much about her mother's family. She knew there had been a brother but he'd moved far away and there were no pictures because of a fire when their belongings were in storage between moves. Her mother's writing style with no punctuation or capitals was the same then as in her recent last letter The next few pages went to the end of February about looking forward to quitting school in June and going to work. Next entry:

Feb 18 1956

Today I am 18—I hate work—its stupid—my sister Anne is two years older than me—shes pretty and all the boys like her—she works at Eatons downtown and she said why dont I apply—I think I will—it cant be worse than filling shelves at Honest Eds—mom and dad moved to Chatham and I have rented a room in a house on Bloor street around the corner from where Anne lives

The next few pages were empty before the next entry.

February 18 1959

I am 21 today and still working at Eatons—I am in curtains and I hate it—I have trouble measuring and when the curtains I have sewn are hung up they are crooked every time and I want to cry but good news—I met a man—his name is Stephen Marshall

Thea smiled at seeing her father's name. She knew her parents had met at Eaton's but not the details and never about how her mother felt about him. By the time Thea was old enough to notice, her parents were either arguing or not speaking.

February 18 1961

I am 23 and Stephen asked me to marry him and I said yes—we are getting married on June 23—he left Eatons and is working at some advertising place

Obviously, birthdays were the times she'd write in her diary. It was weird reading her mother's words. Like reading about someone she didn't know. She turned the page.

Feb 18 1962

I am 24 and Im going to have a baby—Im scared—I dont know how to look after a baby but now I can quit working at Eatons—at least I am not in curtains anymore—they moved me to notions where I package buttons and pins

The next entry was the first time the date wasn't her birthday.

August 6 1962

Patricia Mae was born three days ago—August 3 1962—Im home and my sister Anne has come to stay with us for a few weeks —she has babysat before and will sleep on the couch

Next Page:

October 1 1962

We rent the main floor of a house with three apartments—the girl upstairs moved out and Anne took her apartment—we still argue like we did when we were kids but she helps me with the baby—my brother lives in Australia so hes no help—mom and dad are getting old and they moved to Victoria—Stephen is working at maclean hunter in the advertising dept—he wants to be an artist but my mom says that artists starve

October 15 1963

I cant believe it—my stupid sister is pregnant—she has had lots of boyfriends but she told me no one serious and she only saw this guy once and had sex with him—he was from out of town and she doesnt even know his last name—its a good thing mom and dad live far away—she cant have a baby and be unmarried—she even had the nerve to say that we could pretend it was my baby—but I told her that was a stupid idea and one baby was enough for me—I don't want anymore and anyway I don't like sex much,my mom was right—sex is stupid

She often wondered why her middle name was Anne but her mother never talked about her sister. Just that she had died. *What happened to her baby? Probably died as well.* She had never met her uncle who'd stayed in Australia and her grandparents died a year apart from each other when Thea was three.

She turned the page.

April, 17 1964

When she saw the date, prickles stole up the back of her neck. *That's my birthday. Do I have a cousin born on the same day?*

Anne had her baby this morning at the womens hospital—Stephen will look after Patricia so I can go and visit—mom and dad still dont know—if mom ever found out it would kill her—anyway Anne said that she would give the baby up for adoption

April 17 1964 - 8 in the evening

Anne is not well—some kind of toxemia thing—the baby is scrawny and sickly and has an ugly red stain on her cheek

Thea's hand shook. She blinked and, holding her breath and the book steady, read the next entry.

April 18

My life is falling apart—Anne died in the night and Stephen insists we take her baby as our own—Dear God—when I asked him why would we ever do such a thing he said because the baby was his and he had already named her Cynthia Anne

Thea dropped the book as if it were on fire. It somersaulted to the floor and landed pages down. The leather tie, fastened at the back lay stretched out each side like two long spider legs. She stared at the leather tentacles, clutching her churning stomach with both hands. Her heart tripled its beats as she gasped for breath. *My mother is not my mother!* She struggled to catch her breath. *My aunt is my mother! And my dad! How could he?* The pedestal under her father wobbled.

This can't be true. She rocked back and forth, willing her stomach to stop rolling and her head from spinning. The room finally settled, and she leaned back in her chair and stared at the book on the floor.

Does anyone else know? Does Patricia know? Or Madison? Has anyone else read this?

Chapter 62

A scramble of thoughts tumbled through Thea's head, bumping and crashing into each other. Her chest tingled and she gulped in air, trying to take a full breath. *It can't be true. It has to be more lies my mother has made up.* But other words crept up from a deep place within. *It's true. It's all true.*

She continued to stare at the tented book, mesmerized by its power to turn her world upside down and inside out. *It would explain a lot. Why my mother hates—hated—me. And why daddy and she were always at odds with each other.* It's also probably why she didn't include me in the will.

She bent down, picked up the book and wound the leather strap around it. She tied it tightly as if to trap what was inside. "I can't believe my father would have been unfaithful." *Who knows what goes on in a marriage? And who am I to judge?* She straighten up in her chair. *I repeated the pattern. I also had a baby out of wedlock just like my mother—my real mother. How uncanny is that? I have to tell someone.* "Madison."

She set the book on the coffee table and went to the kitchen for her cell phone but reached for the coffee pot instead. *I have to think this through.* A rush of thoughts stacked themselves up as she put on the coffee. *Who needs to know? Who should know? Should anyone know? Stephanie. She should know.*

She sat heavily on a kitchen chair. In the nearby pot, fat drops of water plopped into the dark liquid below. "Dear God. My daughter doesn't know her father and the grandmother she thought was hers is really her great aunt." She jumped up and took a mug down. "Wait a minute. I don't even know my own mother myself." She banged the cup on the table. "Josephine Marshall is not my mother."

A strange sense of relief rushed through her and a whisper fluttered into her mind. *Maybe there was nothing wrong with me after all. And never was.*

She shook her head, poured herself a cup of coffee and returned to the living room without her cell. *I will tell Stephanie, but not right away. I need time to digest this.* She sat in her chair in front of the cold fire. *Will I tell Arthur? It would feel strange not to tell him. I want to tell him. He'll know something's up anyway.* Minou jumped up on her lap, settled in as Thea absently stroked her. "One should be careful writing in a diary, Minou. You never know who's going to read it."

She opened her eyes wide. and jumped up. The cat tumbled off her lap and indignantly stalked away.

"I don't want anyone reading my diaries and journals."

 She ran upstairs to the bedroom, and grabbed an armload of journals of the bookshelf. Blue, black, and red covers, covers with cats, and covers with pink poppies. She raced downstairs and threw them in a heap on the floor in front of the fireplace. Cold embers and a blackened log lay on the grate. The cat had retreated to her basket at the side. "I especially don't want Stephanie to read my sad tales of woe. Anyway, that is not who I am anymore."

She took a long match out of the holder from the side of the fireplace and sat cross-legged in front of the jumble of books. She picked up the nearest one and placed it on the grate.

"Good bye past." The flaring match met the edge of the book only to smoulder and go out. She yanked the book off the grate, ripped a fistful of paper out of it and tossed the loose pages over the dead log. The next match caught and blazed high. More tearing, bunching, twisting and screwing of pages into balls followed. One by one she fed the flames. Spidery red fingers crawled over bitter words, turning them black.

Page after page, book after book went in. The log caught and its heat now accepted a whole book. The cardboard cover glowed hot from underneath, looking like a seeping bloody wound, until it burst into flames, curled its corners up and succumbed.

Flaming tongues greedily begged for more. She picked up the last book and laid it open on top of the hungry log where an obliging fire waited. A brown stain blossomed through the inky lines. Red and orange flames broke though eating up paragraphs which turned black and, like all the others pages, fell into ashes to become nothing.

She didn't need to reread one word, one line or one sentence. It was over. A tale told of another person. She needed no reminders of who she had been.

She closed the folding glass doors and latched them snugly as the last page spluttered out.

She lifted her head and gazed at the ceiling. *Who am I now? With a new mother, I have the chance to reconstruct my life. To invent another one with a mother who loved me.*

She pushed herself up, sat in her chair and took a sip of coffee. Curling both hands around the thick cup, she welcomed the heat that travelled up her arms all the way to her heart.

A strange lightness encompassed her. Warm and caring, inviting her to be whomever she chose. She was not the ugly daughter. She was a love child.

She smiled and took another sip of coffee. The diary lay on the table, tied with Thea's new knot. What should she do with it? Patricia didn't want it and Madison had given it to her, so she didn't want it either.

She put her cup down and picked up the book. "Should I burn it too?" She ran her fingers over the soft leather and bumpy knot. *It's part of my daughter's history too.* She tapped the front of it. *I wonder what else she's written? What other dark secrets might be hidden within?* She undid the knot and flipped to where she had left off. Seeing the words of the last entry she had read gave her the shivers all over again.   *—because the baby was his and he had already named her Cynthia Anne.* She turned to the next page.

April 20 1964

We buried Anne today—mom and dad came for the funeral and mom cried and I did too but for a different reason—we told them Anne died from a busted appendix—they are still here sleeping in our bed which is fine with me—I never want to sleep with Stephen again—they go home tomorrow—we told mom and dad we wanted to surprise them that I had been expecting so they think the baby is mine—at least I think they do—who cares anyway—I feel sick and mad—how dare Stephen expect me to raise his bastard—he said to never call her that but this is my diary so I can—he made me promise I would love her like my own—I said yes to shut him up but I dont know how I can—she is ugly and every time I look at her I think of my pretty sister with Stephen—she could have any man she wanted—why did she steal Stephen from me—maybe the baby will die—I know thats an awful thing to say but I cant do this.

February 18 1965

Its been a terrible year—I will never get over being betrayed by my husband and sister—I could never talk to anyone about it except Patricia but she doesnt know what Im saying—the baby is sickly and has that red blotchy face but it wasn't me that gave her Satans curse—Stephen and Anne did that to her and every time I look at her I feel sick—I know I promised Stephen I would love her and I tried—but thats one promise I cannot keep—I cannot love that child.

Thea's eyes teared. A broken promise which left a baby lacking a mother's love. Her father used to say 'the truth shall set you free.' "Perhaps he was right."

It must have been hard for Josephine to have me around. She took a breath and read on.

February 18 1968

Happy Birthday to me—I am 30 today—sometimes I feel like an old woman—I should never have had kids—they are so much work—Patricia is 6 and in Grade 1 and Cynthia is only 4—another full year before she can go half time to kindergarten—Stephen is working part time at Barton and Barton and painting pictures in the basement—a waste of time and not much money and I can't work with having to look after two kids.

March 17 1968

Damn it all—I can't believe it—Im pregnant—Stephen sold a painting and he bought me some perfume and flowers for my birthday—he also bought some wine—damn that wine

Thea grinned. "So that's how Madison was conceived. I guess my mother—that is, Josephine—was human after all."

December 5 1968

Another girl –– Stephen wanted a boy but Im glad its a girl –– she can wear Cynthias clothes –– I had my tubes tied –– no more sex or kids for me –– Stephen dotes on Cynthia –– she is still skinny and sickly –– I feel sorry for her but I still cant get over that my sister seduced my husband –– he hasnt sold any paintings in months and is depressed –– so am I –– I hate being poor –– we are going to call the new baby Madison - I found the name in a novel

January 6 1986

Thea looked twice at that next date. "Eighteen years later? I wonder if she lost the diary or was she too busy to write in it?"

I found this old book looking for insurance papers—Stephen died three days ago—the funeral was today—he had a heart attack last saturday I heard a crash in the basement and there he was flopped over his easel—he didn't have much insurance so I dont know what I will do—I met his brother Frank at the funeral—he lives in guelph—I thought all his family lived in England

July 23 1987

A year-and-a-half later. She wasn't much of a diary writer.

Tomorrow Frank Marshall and I are getting married—I had to turn catholic—never knew Stephen was once catholic—my baptist mother would turn over in her grave but Frank has a lot of money and isnt interested in sex—thats perfect for me—Patricia is married and on her own—Madison is engaged and will be gone soon—Frank and I are going on a honeymoon—Ive never had one.

February 18 1988

Cynthia is pregnant—how did that happen—she told me she got secretly married and it didn't work out—she insists on keeping the baby but how is she going to raise it on her own—Ive tried to do the best for that girl but its been hard—it wasnt her fault and it wasnt mine that I never got over what Stephen and Anne did—she was branded from birth—poor thing

Thea slammed the book shut and yanked the ties around it. "Don't feel sorry for me." The cat's ears perked up. "I made it. I'm great now." She snorted. "If I'm so great, why am I shouting?"She took a deep breath. Shock, disbelief, anger, compassion, and confusion had coursed through her since opening that old leather diary. But it had answered a lot of questions she'd never asked.

Her coffee was cold. She went to the kitchen for a refill, taking the diary with her. She went upstairs, placed the book on the empty shelf where her collection of journals had been and took her coffee to the window seat. "What do you think of all this, dragonfly?"

She had one week to digest her new identify before she would be in England with the man she loved.

Chapter 63

Two days until departure day. Every morning she woke up feeling as if she had survived an earthquake. She pondered whether to take her mother's diary with her on her trip. Meanwhile it sat in the bottom drawer of her desk. *I need more time to let it settle and before Stephanie or Arthur learn the truth.* She would deal with it when she got back from England. Meanwhile, she'd let it simmer in the background of her mind.

She went over her check list: passport, ticket, money, credit card, names of B & Bs. Sara Jane or Susan, her neighbour on the other side, would pick up mail and feed Minou. *Is this happening? Am I going to England?* She had dipped into ancestor tracing online and the more she learned about Wales, the more affinity she had for the small country that had fought so hard for its independence. Arthur was busy that week, and in their daily phone call he added relevant facts about Edward the First and how he invaded Wales in 1277 and again in 1282. When he named those dates, a shiver passed through her as if an old memory of a real and intimate experience had surfaced.

Was Edward plagued with feelings of being not enough that he had to conquer another country? *How many castles would it take to be enough. Where did a person's self worth come from?* She had a father who doted on her and a mother who seemed to resent her. *Mother figure, I should say.* It still was still weird that the woman she had known all her life as mother, was really her aunt.

Knowing the truth about her birth explained a lot. *With my father feeling guilty and Josephine struggling to deal with me, it made sense that I thought there was something wrong with me. In addition to my glaring birthmark.* She shook her head. "Stop thinking about all that. This is now."

She finished her tea and cleaned up the kitchen. Arthur had the last address in England of his estranged wife that the detective agency had given him. Although his desire to get divorce papers signed had originally motivated their trip, Thea also had the Evan situation to deal with.

She had asked Arthur, "How would you feel if you discovered thirty years later that you had a daughter?"

He'd kissed her forehead and said, "After the initial shock, I would be proud and so will he."

"I hope so. I don't even know the man." Thea had furrowed her brow but didn't ask him her second question. *How would you feel if you found out your mother was not your mother?*

Departure day arrived and Thea awoke with butterflies in her stomach and her dragonfly packed in her new travel purse. She had found the perfect bag with a zippered section for a passport, another for tickets, several pouches to hold a variety of currencies, and a roomy central compartment for brochures and maps. There was even a place to tuck in a thin plastic rain poncho.

Arthur came in the back door "All ready, my love?" He'd parked his car \and they would take the Red Car Service.

"I hope so." A month was a long time to pack for.

They got to Pearson Airport in plenty of time and enjoyed a glass of wine in the lounge.

Thea had a window seat and after a quick stop in Gander, they would head straight to Heathrow in London. Flying through a fairy sky of cotton balls and rolling white dunes, she ate, napped, watched a movie and dipped into a paperback she had bought at the news stand. *I'm going to the home of my ancestors.* Perhaps she was related to someone famous—or infamous. At least her ancestors had not changed, since her birth mother and the woman who had brought her up were sisters. A wave of something akin to gratitude swept through her. *I could have been adopted and I would never have known my father or Madison and certainly not Stephanie. I have that to thank her for.* A small chunk of resistance broke off the rigid mold in which she had encased Josephine. She looked out the window at the swiftly moving clouds. *It must have been hard for her.* A clump of clouds broke up into trailing wisps of white. *She did the best she could.*

They arrived at Heathrow in the early morning to a misty rain and gray fog. Passengers deplaned directly onto the tarmac where busses waited to trek them to the main terminal. She followed Arthur down and the moment her foot hit the black surface, a wave of familiarity—of coming home—rippled through her.

She swayed and Arthur grabbed her arm. "Are you okay? You look like you've seen a ghost."

People stepped around her with "pardon me" and "excuse me Ma'am," as she continued to stare blankly. *I know this place: This Sceptered Isle of Edwardian Britain.* She took a deep sniff of misty air. "I've come home."

"It'll be your home for four weeks, my dear. Let's go." He put an arm around her shoulders and guided her to the bus shrouded in the rolling fog.

After a bouncy ride, they arrived at the airport where people flowed past arrayed in an array of styles: Sarongs, turbans, and scarf covered heads, ripped jeans, sequinned t-shirts and London Fog trench coats. Arthur pointed to the red circle sign of the London Underground. The Piccadilly Line took forty minutes and the Heathrow Express took fifteen to London's Paddington Station.

"Let's take Paddington. I want to tell Stephanie I've met Paddington Bear."

They changed their money and headed for the turnstiles. Arthur snapped a picture of her by Paddington Bear and, after Thea bought a miniature of it, they hopped into a cab to Piccadilly.

Thea lurched as the cabby took off. "Madison was right when she said a London cab ride would be an adventure."

The driver pulled into traffic on the wrong side of the road. She grabbed the hanging strap. Maybe their plan to rent a car later would not be a good idea.

Arthur had been to London, but in addition to the world famous art galleries, Thea wanted to see Charring Cross, Piccadilly Circus, Westminster Abbey and ride on a double-decker bus. The turban-attired driver (Josephine called it a turbine) careened crazily around cars. Thea shut her eyes and prayed.

Arthur laughed. "Wait till you drive."

She and braced for a crash. "We'll see about that."

They arrived safely at the hotel hungry and tired. From the abundant selections of of restaurants, East Indian won. Thea ordered curried lentils and Arthur had chicken. While waiting for it to arrive, Arthur added one of his customary tidbits. "Did you know there are more than eight-thousand Indian restaurants in Britain?"

She smiled. The man was a walking treasure chest of trivia. After finishing off with Chai and sandesh they walked back to the hotel. Madison had advised them the best way to avoid jet lag was to go to bed, no matter what the time, and sleep the clock around. It sounded like a good idea but it was a little too early to sleep and they were too tired to do any sightseeing. They did end up napping and after a light supper rolled into bed.

The next morning they awoke early ready to explore. Thea put on her sturdy walking shoes and they joined the tourists at Charring Cross, Tower Bridge, Westminster Abbey, and St. Paul's. They bypassed the Tower of London because of the long queue and ended the day with fish and chips wrapped in greaseproof paper and newsprint.

"My dad was right," Thea said between mouthfuls. "These are the best in the world."

That evening she fell into bed—legs aching, feet sore and a mind brimming with sights, sounds, colours and smells. Tomorrow they would contact the detective who had the last address of a Mrs. Cheryl Richardson. Thea looked at the name. "It's odd that after women's lib, women still take their husband's name." She looked at Arthur. "If they kept their own, it would make research easier on the female side."

"What about kids? Whose name would they take?"

"They could take both and hyphenate."

"But what about the next generation? If John Hadley-Smith married Mabel Johnston-Tyler, their kid would be Harriet Hadley-Smith-Johnston-Tyler and what about her children and—"

"Okay, I get it." She stroked her chin. "I know. The girls could take their mother's name and the boys, their father's. She smiled at her brilliance, however, she did like the sound of Thea Richardson.

The next day, the visit to Messrs. Willoughby & Smyth, Private Investigators, brought forth no new information. Cheryl's parents had died and she had left no forwarding address from her last flat in Bromley, a suburb of London. She had no siblings or aunts and uncles, but Mr. Willoughby offered one sparse clue. Apparently, she had mates in Liverpool, however, the helpful detectives had checked both her married name and birth name in that city to no avail. It was a slim thread to follow.

They spent the rest of the day touring London. So different from New York, but it had that same big-city's flavour of excitement and promise. First, the changing of the guard at Buckingham Palace, then a walk through Hyde Park where they paused at Speakers' Corner. Thea also had a bridge to visit. Ever since she'd seen the vintage movie, *Waterloo Bridge*, she had dreamed of standing on the famous span à la Vivian Leigh waiting in the fog for Robert Taylor. However, the day was clear, crowds of people, and the National Film Theatre and Cleopatra's needle stood out prominently. No mist and no mystery. Sometimes dreams trumped reality.

The next day, they took the train to Liverpool which gave them a good chance to see the countryside. Perhaps they would brave the driving later. Thea wanted to see Stonehenge, but not through a chain link fence. She had envisioned standing alone at midnight among the towering giants and seeing the full moon break through the ancient, ghostly spaces. Arthur said they would find plenty of standing stones in northern England and Wales dotted all over the countryside. Even in farmers' fields.

"This land is so ancient," she said. "Can you imagine living here eight hundred years ago?"

"You've seen too many movies."

"There's something incredible about walking into a building that's six hundred years old." She stared out the window. "No wonder it's called the old country."

They arrived at Lime Street station mid-afternoon. Arthur phoned the first Bed and Breakfast on their list but it was booked and, after three more calls, they checked in at the Crowne Plaza Hotel.

Arthur pulled off his shoes, stretched out on the queen-sized bed and clasped his hands behind his head. "Well, Detective Marshall, where do we start?"

"Let's see." She wrinkled her forehead. "You told me she was a hairstylist. That's a clue."

"But there are hundreds of hairdressers in Liverpool."

"Maybe the phone book has been updated since the detectives looked." Thea found a fat phone book in a drawer. "It's worth a try." First she looked at all the Richardsons, and the Grangers—Cheryl's birth name. There were no Cheryl's under the Gangers so she tried all the C's, but after getting a Charles, a Clarence, a Charlotte, a Cornelius and a Cornel, she closed the book. "What kinds of hair salons did she work in?"

"I don't know. She worked—wait a minute." He sat up. "She said she liked to do dead people's hair." He shrugged. "They didn't complain."

"I wonder if funeral homes employ hairdressers or hire from a local shop?" She opened the phone book. "I'll start with the largest ads."

She phoned a dozen funeral homes and Arthur took over. In half an hour they found three who employed a part-time hairdresser but none had heard of a Cheryl Richardson or a Cheryl Granger. Nearing the end of their list, they were ready to give up when Thea dialed one more. It rang several times before a young man answered.

Her ears were getting accustomed to the various accents but she still had to listen carefully to the Liverpudlian voice.

"We used to have a young woman in our employ some time ago. Maybe father will remember. I'll ask him."

She covered the speaking part with her hand and said to Arthur, "A young man answered. They used to have a hairdresser and he's asking his father if he knows—" She turned her attention back to the phone.

"No, father doesn't recognize either name. Sorry we can't be of more help, luv."

British people didn't rush like North Americans and even though she knew it was only a saying, it was nice to be called luv. The young man started to sign off when he stopped. "Wait. Granddad might know."

She held on for five minutes, seven, and when twelve minutes had passed, she was about to hang up when he came back.

"Sorry to take so long. Grandad is a wee slow. He did remember we had a Cheryl who worked part-time for us about seventeen years ago. A Cheryl Granger. Does that help, luv?"

Chapter 64

Thea gave a thumbs up signal to Arthur. "So you *did* have a Cheryl Granger working for you."

He handed her a pen and pad from the side table.

She scribbled down the details. "Thank you. You've been a big help." She hung up, dialled the number and frowned. "Not in service." She tapped the pen against the pad.

"Well, it has been seventeen years. People move."

"We have the address. Someone there might have known her."

He shrugged. "It's the only lead we have."

"We'll be Nick and Nora Charles, master detectives."

"Who?"

"William Powell and Myrna Loy? *The Thin Man*?"

"Must've been before my time. I think I remember my mother talking about them. Or was it my grandmother?"

She threw a cushion at him. "Fiend."

"I'd rather be Mr. and Mrs. Smith. Brad and Angelina are sexier," he said.

"They were assassins, not detectives." This time, she threw herself at him. "And speaking of sexier—"

Much later, they dressed and headed for a restaurant before starting their hunt for Cheryl. The British knew how to make a good cup of tea, always preheating the pot. Arthur had bangers and mash but when Thea learned that bangers were sausages, she had a bread roll with Stilton cheese and pickled onion.

They hailed a cab which took them south to Toxteth and an older block of a three-story apartment building. Two girls, about ten years old, turned a double rope while another one jumped back and forth over the slapping arcs. In the side yard, a trio of boys on skateboards flew up and over a home-made ramp.

Thea said to the skipping girls, "Where does the super live?"

Therope continued to slap, slap, slap. One girl, turning the handles, looked up and shrugged.

Arthur tried. "Where does the man live who looks after the place?"

Without missing a beat, both rope-turners shook their heads.

Arthur took Thea's hand. "Let's try the main entrance."

In the foyer was a bank of post boxes and a garbage can—dust bin—overflowing with flyers and unclaimed mail. A stick, wedged under the inside door, held it ajar. There was no Cheryl Granger and no Superintendent listed.

"Usually the super lives on the main floor," Arthur said.

A burnt orange carpet stretched the length of a central hallway. The smell of brussel sprouts hung in the air. They knocked on the first door. No response.

"They sleep all day," a voice at their side said.

A boy, about seven, wearing jeans and a John Lennon T-shirt, looked up at them.

"Pardon?" Arthur's ears hadn't caught up with the local accents.

"They sleep all day. Work at night."

"Could you tell us who manages this place? Who looks after things? Like if a pipe breaks or the heat doesn't work."

"Oh, that'd be Mr. Henderson. But he doesn't live here."

Thea said, "Who's the oldest person here?"

"That'd be ol' Mrs. Saunders. She's been here forever. She's a hundred years old."

A lot of people must look a hundred to a seven-year-old. "Where does she live?" Thea asked.

"One-ten." He pointed to the left corridor and ran off.

At apartment one ten, the framed name plate identified the residents as Saunders and Flynn.

Thea knocked. "Sounds like a vaudeville team." No answer. She rapped again.

"Maybe we could phone," Arthur said.

They left the building, nodded at the bouncing girls and noted no boys were bleeding after flinging themselves into space. A restaurant at the end of the block had a public phone, but there was no number for Saunders at that address. However, two Flynns were listed. He let the first number ring thirteen times. Thea phoned the second number. A woman answered.

"No, I've never heard of Cheryl Granger, but I've only been here nine years. Maybe mummy or Nana would know." She spoke with a thick Liverpudlian accent. "They live across the hall, but they nap until their soaps come on so you won't be able to talk to them until then. Come by just before three."

Thea said they would and Arthur glanced at his wrist. "Thirty-five minutes." His shoulders slumped. "Will we ever find Cheryl?"

Thea grabbed his arm and pulled him into the restaurant. "C'mon let's get coffee and a muffin."

They sat down. He ordered coffee and Thea, tea. She reached her hands across the table and took his. "We'll find her."

He squeezed her hands and smiled.

The muffins turned out to be tea biscuits and Arthur spread homemade apricot jam on his. "What if this is another dead end?"

"We can only hope for the best."

"You are an eternal optimist."

"Worrying only makes it worse."

"You mean the self-fulfilling prophecy thing?"

She smiled. "Something like that."

"Did you know an American sociologist, William Thomas, in the eighteen hundreds first used that term?"

"I didn't know that."

"It became more popular in the 70's when a teacher was given a list of students, indicated as poor, average or excellent. At the end of the year the students tested exactly the way they had been categorized. But the kicker came when the teacher learned the ability levels had been randomly assigned."

"She or he must have been upset. Or enlightened to learn the power of attitude."

The waitress came to their table. "Will there be anything else, luv?"

"That's all." Arthur looked at his watch. "If we walk slowly to the apartment complex, we'll arrive a few minutes before three."

Thea gathered her bag and scarf and at ten-to-three they knocked on apartment one-eleven. A plump, sixtyish looking woman answered. "Ah, there you are. Come in."

After introductions, Miss Flynn said, "Mummy and Nana love to watch their soap and I go over at four when it's finished to make tea." She motioned for them to sit. "They like to eat on trays in front of the telly."

"We could come back at four if you like," Thea said.

"Oh, no. You're here now. We can talk during the adverts."

Arthur sat on a nondescript brown couch with white crocheted doilies dotted along the back and Thea took the fat stuffed chair covered with an orange and red afghan. A basket of knitting sat on the coffee table. Thea had learned by now that four o'clock tea was not only cups of tea but thinly sliced cucumber or watercress sandwiches on white crustless bread. An alternative might be scones and jam to tide people over until a late evening meal which they called supper.

Miss Flynn continued. "They'll be all ready in front of the telly at three. We'll go over before their show starts."

After pleasantries about the weather and their trip, they went across the hall where Miss Flynn opened the door with a key. "Mummy, Nana," she yelled, "It's Moira." And to Arthur and Thea. "They're a bit deaf."

Two older ladies sat beside each other in the middle of a couch which looked as if it had come from a fifties movie set. A long knitted shawl with maroon and pink zigzagging lines stretched across both their laps. A variety of crocheted cushions, each with black trimmed granny squares of blue, red, yellow, orange, and green, filled the rest of the couch. The women stared at a large TV set, its volume on max.

Miss Flynn picked up the remote and pushed mute. She first introduced mummy. Thin white hair and a multitude of lines easily marked her eighty years. Moira's grandmother, Nana with a dried apple face and tufts of wispy white hair, did look a hundred. Heavy glasses dominated her face and corded hands gripped a puce and purple pillow. Two stuffed armchairs, also heaped with cushions, rested on their haunches at each end of the couch, their angled positions completing the semicircle in front of the TV. Miss Flynn gestured for Thea to sit in one and she fetched a kitchen chair for Arthur, which she squeezed between Thea and a china cabinet. She herself sat in the other armchair, moving an oversized cushion off.

The elder lady shouted, "Quiet! Program's starting."

With the press of a finger, the TV blared into life. Thea looked around. Knickknacks crowded each other on a bank of shelves and framed pictures jockeyed for space on every horizontal surface. The walls displayed a haphazard conglomeration of magazine photos, a kitten calendar, a tea towel depicting the map of England, several pictures of Queen Elizabeth at different ages, and a large wedding picture of Charles and Di. A brass coloured frame caught

Thea's eye and she leaned closer. It was a letter from the Queen two years ago, congratulating Bessie Saunders on turning one hundred. The seven-year-old was right. Nana was more than a hundred.

When the first commercial came on, Miss Flynn clicked the mute button and in a loud voice said, "These nice people want to know if you ever heard of a Cheryl Granger."

The older ladies took a moment to shift their thoughts away from the gripping lives of their TV families. The younger of the two creased her already wrinkled forehead. "Never heard of her." She yelled to mummy, "Did you know a Cheryl Granger?"

The wizened old lady stared at her daughter for an interminable moment. "Cheryl Granger," she repeated in a creaky voice. "Cheryl Granger." A long pause. "She did dead people's hair."

Arthur leaned forward. "Yes. That's she."

The TV blasted forth as the program resumed. It would be another eleven minutes until the next commercial. Thea hoped the old lady would remember Cheryl after immersing herself in the bittersweet lives on the small screen. And would she be able to answer the crucial question of where she was now?

The commercials—adverts—started again, which Miss Flynn graciously muted. They had four minutes to bring the topic back.

Arthur said loudly to the eldest lady, "You knew Cheryl?"

"Cheryl who?"

Arthur rolled his eyes.

Thea interjected. "You know—Cheryl Granger? She did dead people's hair?"

A pause. The crinkles beside the old lady's eyes deepened, "Yes, Cheryl. A lovely girl."

"Do you know where she went?" Thea yelled.

"Oh, Yes. It was the talk of the building." She must have had one eye on the screen, because she shouted, "Program!"

With the flick of a finger, actors' voices filled the room.

Thea smiled. *Old people don't give a wit what anyone thinks. At least the old lady knows where Cheryl has gone.* She squeezed Arthur's hand. He rolled his eyes again and shrugged.

Another eleven minutes dragged on before glorious silence descended. Would this four minutes be enough for the old lady to retrieve the information?

Thea leaned over, touched the papery hand and yelled, "Where did Cheryl go?"

The old lady smiled. Her eyes were blank behind her thick glasses.

Thea took a deep breath and hollered again. "Cheryl, the girl who did dead people's hair. Where did she go?"

Pause. "Oh, Cheryl." Another pause. "She was such a lovely girl."

"Yes. Where did she go?" Thea could be persistent.

The old lady looked at Thea as if seeing her for the first time. "You'd like Cheryl. She did dead people's hair. Do you know where she went?"

Thea smiled encouragingly. "No. Where did she go?" She held her breath.

"You'll never guess." The old lady's eyes glazed over for a long moment before a flicker of light returned. "She became a nun." Her shoulders shook and her eyes disappeared into the crinkles surrounding them. She chuckled. "She lives in a convent." She turned toward the telly and yelled, "Program!"

On the small screen, a man and woman exchanged heated words, while in front of it, another man and woman exchanged astonished stares.

Chapter 65

The two old ladies and Moira stared at the blaring screen.

Thea glanced at Arthur. From the look on his face, she guessed he was surprised that Cheryl had become a nun. *But what convent and where?*

Eleven more minutes dragged by. The next commercial included a station break, so they would have more than four minutes. Finally the advert came on and Miss Flynn pressed mute.

Thea leaned in and, in a loud voice, called to the deaf old lady, "Do you know where Cheryl went?"

"Who's Cheryl?"

Another eye roll from Arthur.

"Remember?" Thea hollered. "Cheryl Granger, the lovely girl who did dead people's hair."

The old lady looked vacant.

Thea yelled again. "What convent did Cheryl go to?"

Recognition sparked in the hundred-and-two-year-old eyes. "A convent. That's where she went. She's a nun." The old lady cackled at the joke.

Arthur tried. "What convent? Where is it?" he hollered.

Bessie Saunders rambled on as if he hadn't spoken. "We didn't expect that. She liked men." A bewildered look crept around her face searching for a place to settle.

Arthur crossed his eyes and the scar on his eyebrow twitched. Thea reached over and touched the old lady's thin hand which lay on the edge of a purple zigzag. "Mrs. Saunders, which convent did Cheryl go to?"

The old lady lifted her head and studied the ceiling. Arthur stared a red-and-yellow crocheted granny square. Thea waited.

The old lady opened her mouth, closed it and opened it again. "It was near Chester." The adverts continued flickering on the screen. "Mercy something." Her gaze returned to the TV. "Program!" She slid her hand out from under Thea's and stuck a bony figure toward her granddaughter.

"It's only the title, Nana," Miss Flynn said loudly.

"I like to hear the music."

"So do I," said Mummy.

Miss Flynn sighed and the signature tune blared out. Thea looked at Arthur and tilted her head toward the door. He nodded and they stood up, rescuing several escaping cushions.They hollered their thank you's and goodbyes while the two elderly ladies remained engrossed in the flashing screen of the telly.

Moira Flynn stepped into the hall and pulled the door closed. "I hope that was some help. You were very patient."

"It was a great help and such a pleasure to meet them," Thea said. "I've never met anyone over a hundred."

"Nana is a hundred and three." Miss Flynn grinned. "And still going strong." She grasped the door knob. "Tea time."

They returned to the Crowne Plaza to do a Google search for convents around Chester. Having missed four o'clock tea, they took advantage of the hi-speed internet in the lobby. Chester, they discovered, was an old Roman town close to the border of Wales with a church dating back to 660.

"Imagine a town more than a thousand years old." A shiver went through her body when she thought of Wales. *What is it about that country?*

"Look." Arthur pointed at the screen. "There was a Benedictine monastery in Chester."

"Interesting," Thea said over his shoulder. "But what about convents?"

Arthur clicked another link. "A convent was in existence, thirty miles west of Chester named 'Our Sisters of Mercy Convent'." He scrolled down. "It was built in 1157 and flourished as a convent until Henry VIII's dissolution of the monasteries and convents in the fifteen hundreds."

"Oh, no. It's closed?"

"Wait a minute. There's more. 'Our Sisters of Mercy Convent reopened in 1855 as a home for the chronically ill and in 1967, hospice services were added.'"

"How do you feel about seeing her again?" Thea asked.

"It was so long ago. We're other people now." He gazed at the computer screen. "I can't believe she became a nun. I thought nuns were not supposed to be married."

"Maybe she didn't tell them."

"You mean she lied? That's an un-nun like thing to do."

Thea laughed. "I'm surprised she didn't try to contact you for a divorce. She had your address."

"Probably it made no difference to her."

Arthur printed off directions to the small town of Mercyshire.

"Let's eat," he said. "The Albert Dock Riverside Restaurant is a two-minute walk."

Near their hotel loomed the impressive Royal Liver Building. Arthur nodded to it. "That was one of the first buildings in the world to use reinforced concrete and until 1965 it was the tallest building in Liverpool."

Thea looked up. "What's that sculpture on top? Birds?"

"They're called Liverbirds and legend tells us if they were to fly away, the city would cease to exist."

"Now that's more interesting than concrete."

At the restaurant, he asked, "So when are you planning to visit Evan?"

She didn't respond. *I should phone him. And soon.* She studied the menu.

Arthur reached for her hand across the table. "I'm not bugging you, but we have to make plans."

She gulped. "Let's first focus on finding Cheryl and getting your papers signed."

He squeezed her hand. "Okay."

"I'll phone right after that."

The next morning, they had crispy toast and milky coffee at the Crowne, later than they had planned, but before they got out of bed, a mutual distraction had arisen so it was nearly ten when they finished breakfast.

Thea's new pink iPhone rang..

"That has to be an emergency." She fumbled for her phone. "It's Sara Jane." After several "no way" and "I can't believe it," she turned the phone off and stared at Arthur.

"What?"

"The Mozart/Vivaldi sold."

"The what?"

"My painting. The one I did to the Magic Flute and one of the Four Seasons."

"That's great."

"It's bloody impossible. She lowered herself in a chair.

"What's impossible?"

"It sold for five thousand dollars!" Her eyes were as large as charger plates.

He grinned. "I guess that smashes your theory about you not being good enough.

Chapter 66

Arthur guided a giddy Thea downstairs to the rental car. The fog would add to the driving challenge and Thea's job was to help him stay on the right—correct—side of the road which was left. But she was in her own fog.

Five thousand dollars. Her head spun as she absorbed what that meant. *Now I will give up bookkeeping.* A voice sounded from her right.

"Remember. Keep a sharp outlook, especially when I make a turn."

"What did you say?"

"Remind me to stay on the left." He cautiously pulled into traffic.

"It's weird sitting here without a steering wheel," she said. She needed to focus, and repeated 'left' inside her head, ready to shout it out if necessary. Meanwhile, the needle on her self-esteem dial had gone off scale and she was ready to float up and through the roof of the car. She took a deep breath and forced herself to stare at the road ahead. *Left. Left. Left.*

They drove through the Mersey Tunnel and past Birkenhead before the road opened to countryside. Hedge rows or piled stones served as fences. In one field she saw a little step ladder on both sides of a stone fence which one could to take up one side and down the other. *Looks like something from a fairy story.*

Before long, a scattering of houses and the sign, Mercyshire, signalled a town ahead. A thousand years ago, travel must have been difficult. Probably horseback or Shank's Pony. She had first heard that term when she was six. She and her sisters were going swimming at Innis Lake, three miles away. Sometimes a neighbour would drive them, but that day, her mother said, "You'll have to take Shank's Pony."

"A pony!" Cynthia yelled. "We won't all fit on one pony."

"You stupid girl," her mother said. "Shank's Pony means you walk."

Her chin trembled. "No pony?"

Thea looked at Arthur. The traffic was light. "Where did the term Shank's Pony come from?"

"What made you think of that? I haven't heard that term for a long time."

"I was thinking what it must have been like eight hundred years ago. No cars. Just horses and walking."

"Shank's Pony means to hoof it on foot. It was first called *shanks-nag* or *shanks-mare* in an 18th Century poem by a Scotsman, named Fergusson. It derives from the part of the leg between the knee and the ankle."

"You mean the shin-bone?"

"Precisely."

A sign ahead took their attention from shanks and ponies. Underneath "Welcome to Mercyshire" hung a small painted sign. "Our Sisters of Mercy Convent. Long Term Care and Hospice" with an arrow pointing left. After several minutes along the dirt road, goose bumps crept up Thea's arms. *I know this road. But that's impossible. I've never been here before.* She looked at the map and its wriggling, crisscrossing lines. Arthur stopped the car and she looked up. A chill stole over her body. She knew this place.

Arthur got out. "This is it."

Ivy crawled over the low stone wall. A gravel path led to a half-opened iron gate.

Thea didn't move. Ice flowed through her veins.

Arthur leaned down and looked through the car window. "Are you coming?"

A ghostly cedar fence wavered in front of the stone wall. She blinked twice. Her shoulder bag lay at her feet. *All is well.* She shook her head, picked up her bag and patted it. *The dragonfly is safe inside. Why did I think of that now?* She opened the car door and stepped onto ancient ground. *Why is the gate open? It's always shut.* She took a step. *How do I even know that?*

Inside the entrance, a sign directed them to the Administration Centre. The instant Thea stepped into the courtyard, the air shimmered. She staggered.

Arthur grabbed her arm. "What's the matter? You've gone white."

"I—I feel strange. This place is so familiar. Like I've been here before."

"That's odd."

They followed the signs to the main building and the reception area. A young woman wearing a plain, pale-blue dress, sat behind the desk. A simple wooden cross hung around her neck.

Thea wrinkled her brow. *Why isn't she wearing her black habit? And her silver cross?*

"We've come to see Cheryl Granger," Arthur said.

"Is she a patient or a sister?"

"A sister."

"Do you know her religious name?"

"No."

"One moment." She attended to a computer screen. "Oh, yes." She smiled sweetly and motioned for another young woman who wore the same costume to come forward. "Sister Mary Miriam will take you."

After a glance at the computer screen, Sister Mary Miriam said, "Come this way." She headed down the hall several paces in front of them.

"They don't wear habits," Thea whispered.

"Most modern nuns don't," he whispered back.

"I thought maybe in the old country they would."

Arthur shrugged. They followed the Sister to a small waiting room at the end of the hall where she stopped and motioned to Arthur. "You'll have to wait here. She's in a restricted area."

"Oh, yes of course." He sat on a settee covered in fake leather in front of a stained-glass window depicting a seated Jesus and a group of children.

Thea bent down and whispered, "I'll tell Cheryl I'm your secretary." She followed the sister out of the room.

The two women walked to an outer courtyard. Thea stepped through the door, and a feeling of déjà vu swept over her again. Much stronger this time. She walked a few steps, stopped and looked around. She turned in a full circle.

The Sister stopped walking and waited.

"Where is the herb garden?" Thea asked.

"Pardon?"

"The herb garden." She walked toward a crumbling well. Broken stones lay at its base amongst a tangle of weeds. She stroked the smooth top edge, worn down by hundreds of years of rain, fog and human touch. "The herbs were watered from this well." She took a few steps to the right where a clump of tall weeds had recently been chopped. "And this is where they grew— mint, Lavender, and St. John's Wort."

The Sister frowned and shook her head. "I don't know. I believe there used to be a herb garden here a long time ago."

Thea scanned her surroundings and brushed a hand against the tall stalks. She pinched off a leaf from a straggly plant and rubbed it between her fingers. "Lemon balm."

The sister frowned. "Have you been here before?"

"No. but it seems there should be a herb garden here."

The sister took her arm. "Perhaps we should continue."

They passed a row of outbuildings. Some were made of ancient stones and looked as if they had been standing forever. Others had been rebuilt with timbers, adding to the mishmash of old and new. Thea tried to shake off the curious sensation which crept along the edges of her consciousness. They turned the corner.

"Here she is," the nun said.

Thea gasped and covered her mouth. Tears spilled out.

"Oh, my dear. I assumed you knew."

It wasn't the thought of Cheryl Granger lying in the field of white crosses that disturbed Thea. She was crying for her many dear friends buried there.

Chapter 67

Sister Mary Miriam patted Thea's shoulder and handed her a packet of Kleenex. Thea fumbled to find the opening and the sister took it from her and deftly slid a tissue out and handed it to her.

She blew her nose. *Why am I crying over worn white crosses? I don't know Cheryl or anyone here.* A whirlpool of thoughts spun in her head while a torrential wave of grief engulfed her again.

The nun put an arm around her and led her to a wrought iron bench. Thea sobbed again for several minutes. Finally she stopped shuttering, took a deep breath and wiped her eyes.

"Are you feeling better?" the young nun asked.

"I think so." A sense of familiarity hung around her like a phantom limb. *I know this place so well.* "Who is buried here?"

"Only the nuns who lived here. Patients who die here are looked after by their families."

"How old is the cemetery?"

"It dates back to the mid eleven hundreds when the convent was built. We have a smattering of records but most were lost when the convent was confiscated in 1540."

Church bells clanged and Thea jerked. "Those are Sext bells for noon prayers." Reverberating peals rolled over each another.

"Yes, they *are* noon time prayers. The sixth hour of the day."

Thea pointed right. "And the chapel is around that corner."

No line of black robed nuns appeared. The bells ceased but the sound in her ears echoed their insistent clanging.

"Our chapel *is* there. Are you sure you haven't been here before?"

"I don't know what to think." Thea shook her head. "May I rest here awhile? I'll find my way back."

The nun hesitated. "Of course. Stay as long as you want." She hurried to the right and around the corner to the chapel.

Thea fished into her purse for another Kleenex. Her hand bumped against the dragonfly. She lifted it out. *You have been here before too.* She held it to her chest, leaned back on the bench and closed her eyes. Thoughts and feelings crowded in on her, pulling her backwards in time. An image flew past her consciousness—too fast to catch, like a dream at the edge of awareness. Another and another: a flushed-faced nun yelling at her—a nun falling to the ground dead—sweet arms handing her a baby—and bells, bells, bells—kneeling, praying, crying—a kaleidoscope of sounds, shapes, scenes and emotions merged and melted through her.

A tap startled her and she opened her eyes with a jerk.

"Are you all right, Miss?"Another nun stood beside her. She also wore the modern garb of blue dress and wooden cross.

"Uh—" Thea looked around.

"Mr. Richardson's asked for you. He wondered if you got lost."

Arthur! She clasped her handbag and stood up.

"Is this yours?" The nun picked up an object from the soft earth and held it out.

"Thank you." Thea took the dragonfly, put it safely into her purse and followed the nun through the abandoned herb garden to the administration building.

Arthur jumped up. "Are you all right? Did you see Cheryl?"

"I'm fine. I did find Cheryl and I—I got distracted."

"What did she say? What took so long?"

"Let's sit down." They moved to the vinyl-covered bench by the wall opposite the stain-glassed window.

Arthur grabbed her hand. "I don't understand. Where is Cheryl? Why didn't she come out with you?"

"Cheryl is dead."

"What?" His voice raised a pitch. "Dead? Why didn't you come and tell me right away?"

"I should have. I was overcome with emotion."

"But you didn't even know her."

"It's hard to explain." She searched for words. "I wasn't crying for her. I don't know what happened."

"When did she die?"

"Who?" Thea's brow wrinkled.

"Cheryl, of course. Who else?"

"Oh—yes—who else? I don't know. I didn't even look for her grave. It would have been a newer one. It was when I saw the old ones that I— "

He squeezed her hand."You look as if you've seen a ghost."

"I think I have. Let's get out of here."

They thanked the nun at the desk and followed the forsythia lined path out to the waiting car. Thea's rubbery legs grew steadier as they walked. She went around the car and opened the door.

"Wrong side, sweetheart," Arthur said.

Her heart warmed at the familiar word's and casual inflection. She moved around to the passenger's side. Hr slid in behind the wheel and handed her a large brown envelope.

"What's that?"

"While I was waiting, I perused the gift shop."

She opened it, pulled out a single page and gasped. "Oh, my god, Arthur. Where did you get this?" Her hand shook.

"I told you. The gift shop. It's a copy of a page from an ancient illuminated manuscript. I think it will look great with the right frame and, look here." He pointed to three tiny figures drawn around the large initial letter.

Thea stared at the intricate drawing while Arthur's voice faded into the background. *I know this page well. I drew it.*

"Hello. Earth to Thea. Are you in there?" He touched her arm.

She looked blankly at the man sitting beside her. *Where am I? Who are you?*

"Thea, you look strange. Are you all right?"

"I—" She looked down at the drawing again: the swirls, the figures, the lettering. A vortex gathered in the pit of her stomach and swished up to her throat. She and the page spun in a spiral and the world went black.

Something wet and cool touched her brow. Thea opened her eyes. Arthur was leaning over her, holding a moist wipe on her forehead.

"What happened?" she said.

"You fainted."

"I fainted?"

"I was showing you a manuscript page I bought and you fainted." He handed her the brown envelope.

She slid it under the road map on her lap. *My manuscript page.* "Let's go from this place. I'm all mixed up."

"Are you okay to travel?"

"I'll be fine once we're away from here."

He turned the car around and drove away. She didn't tell him about the invisible hands pulling her or the silent voices imploring her to stay. She moved her gaze to ordinary, everyday things: the map on her lap, the dashboard, the keys dangling in the ignition and as they drove through Mercyshire, the passing bicycles, cars and hikers.

"Do you believe in reincarnation?" she said.

"That again. I haven't thought much about it. Why?"

"I've lived a life in that convent. I knew the herb garden and the cemetery and those bells. They rang right through me."

"Our memory can play tricks on us. Maybe it reminded you of Sunday School when you were a kid?"

"I'm not Catholic. How would I know about Sext prayers? I've never heard the word before. And I knew where the chapel was." She shook her head. "So many memories and it felt so real."

"You read a lot and see a lot of movies. Maybe it triggered something you didn't even know you knew."

"Something was triggered, that's for sure. Now that I think of it, it started when we landed at the airport. The instant my foot hit English ground, I knew I had come home."

"Uncanny." He slowed for traffic as they came to the stone wall of Chester. "Can you believe that the Romans started the building of that stone wall more than two thousand years ago—give or take a hundred years."

She smiled. *Bless him for changing the subject.* "I wonder what stories those stones could tell."

"Many, I'm sure. If stones could talk."

The conversation continued to turn her attention outward. "Of course they can. Can we stop?" *Maybe a long hike will help.*

Charmed by the ancient city, they took turns pointing to a building, a walkway, the river, or the cathedral. They continued along Lower Bridge Street to *The Bear and Billet Pub,* one of the finest frontages in Chester's black-and-white style, squished between two plain brick buildings. Arthur read from the plaque. "Built in 1664." He turned to her. "Are you hungry?"

"I am. Let's eat." She was ravenous, or ravished as her mother —er, Josephine—would have said. Her chest tightened and her stomach quivered as she remembered for a moment who her mother was. *Am I hungry? Or Empty?*

"There are over a thousand pieces of glass in this building." That is amazing. Glass in the 17th Century was expensive."

They went inside and Thea ordered a salad while Arthur had black pudding with chutney and onion rings. Over pints of English beer, he offered another nugget of information. "John Lennon's grandmother, Annie Jane Milward, was born here in 1873."

Thea's stomach had settled and she even sipped a beer. "How do you store all those facts in your head?"

"That one's written on the back of the menu."

She laughed and slapped his arm. "That's cheating."

"I get my data wherever I can." He took a swig of beer. "To change the subject, with you acting all weird back there, it overshadowed the reason we came to this country."

Thea lifted an eyebrow.

"To find Cheryl so I could get a divorce. Well, we found her and I'm a widower." He took her hand. "We can get married whenever we want to."

Thea stared at him. He was part of those strange feelings that had swamped her at the Convent. She wasn't sure she believed in soul mates, but she did know that the moment she met Arthur, she had known him before and with a bond stronger than marriage.

"You're so quiet. You do want to get married don't you?"

She put her hand over his. "Of course I want to marry you."

"Good. Glad to hear that. Now where do you want to go next?"

"We're pretty close to Wales, aren't we?"

"Those distant mountains we saw driving up are in Wales."

"Let's go there. I read about a castle I'd like to visit."

"You're the custodian of the map. Which way?"

She spread the map out and traced a line. "Here it is. We keep on A55 and across Four Mile Bridge. My castle is in Holyhead, in Anglesey." She pulled out a crumpled piece of paper. "It's called Castle Llewelyn."

Chapter 68

At 2:22 on the car's clock, they passed a sign: *Croesco Cymru.* "Welcome to Wales." Arthur had no trouble staying on the left side as they drove on the four lane highway from Chester.

"So much for a quaint roadway," Thea said as a huge truck (lorry) roared past.

"I was thinking the same. Can you find me a less busy road?"

She consulted the map and after driving around the roundabout three times, they found their exit for the coast road.

Definitely less traffic and when they came to a cluster of buildings, one a roadside pub, Arthur slowed down and pulled up to the Myddleton Arms. Close to Chester, it offered a convenient rest spot for travellers on their way to Wales or a farewell drink before heading back to England.

Inside, they ducked by a bushy-haired man poised to throw a dart and walked past the crowded bar to the tables. Three young men with ruddy faces, wearing bicycle gear sat at one table. An older couple, cameras around their necks, sat at another and a lone man sat in a corner one. They found an empty one and in short time, a smiling waitress who spoke English and Welsh recommended a mead honey drink.

He ordered a special beer and she chose the honey mead. While they waited, Thea said, "Don't look now, but that man in the corner keeps staring at you."

Arthur glanced over.

"I said not to look."

"Why not? My mother used to say, 'A cat can look at a queen.' "

"What does that mean?"

"I think it means something about being equal."

The waitress brought their drinks and a plate of crisps (potato chips.) They clinked glasses and took a mouthful

"I'm glad I ordered this one," He said. "This beer is kept in cool barrels in the cellar and served by pulling it up with a hand pump. It continues to mature after leaving the brewery so it's not pasteurized or filtered to remove the living yeast."

"That shifty-eyed man is still looking at you."

Arthur laughed. "You look pretty shifty-eyed yourself, sneaking looks at him. Maybe I remind him of a long-lost brother."

They finished their drinks and got up to leave. When they reached the front door, a voice stopped them.

"Excuse me, sir. Could I have a word with you?"

It was the man who had been looking at them. He was a cordial, but serious looking Welshman. His girth made up for his lack of height and with his short beard, he could easily have passed for Henry VIII.

"What is it?" Arthur said.

"We can talk outside. Come this way." He stepped forward and opened the door.

Thea moved after him but Arthur took her arm and stopped her. The man turned, reached inside his coat pocket and pulled out a laminated card. Arthur nodded and King Henry led them around out to a stone building with a Welsh sign on it. They stepped into an office with a wooden desk. Three mismatched chairs lined the wall under the window. A lamp curved over the desk, lighting up an irregular stack of files piled beside a coffee-stained blotter. Beside that, a three-tiered tray was stuffed with more papers.

"Sit here," his majesty commanded, pointing to the chairs.

Thea took Arthur's hand and they sat.

A few minutes later a uniformed man entered, sat at the desk and asked for their names and passports. Arthur gave their names and showed but did not surrender their passports.

The man said, "Where are you coming from?" He was taller than the King, but also sported a well-rounded beer belly.

"We've driven from Chester and before that Our Sisters of Mercy Convent. It's outside of—"

"I know where it is." He scowled, pulled a piece of paper from the pile, stared at it and up at Arthur. "Arthur Richardson, I am holding you on suspicion of murder."

"What! That's nonsense. I've murdered no one."

"A man of your description was reported fleeing a murder scene in the town of Mercyshire last night." He peered over his half-rimmed glasses and scanned Arthur's face. "There aren't too many sandy-haired men of your height around here."

"When did this murder take place?" Arthur asked.

Thea knew he was innocent, but her heart tripled its beat.

"Between midnight and four a.m."

"It couldn't have been me. We weren't there at that time."

"Can you prove that?"

"We were at the Crowne Plaza in Liverpool." He rummaged in his pockets. "I have the checkout slip here somewhere." He pulled out his wallet and flipped through bills and papers. No receipt.

The officer leaned back in his squeaky chair, folded his arms high on his chest and glowered at Arthur.

"Maybe it's in the car. " He started to get up.

"You stay there. The Missus can get it."

Arthur handed Thea the keys. "In the glove compartment."

She wrested with the office door, pulling instead of pushing, shoved her way through and ran out. She raced to the parking lot, dropped the keys once and scooped them up. All the cars looked alike. She should have paid attention to where he parked. *There's my scarf slung over the seat.* She shakily inserted the key and it opened right away. *Thank you key angels.* Arthur's travel booklet was in the glove compartment. Ticket stubs from the London Museum and a miniature map of the Underground poked out from the pages. Underneath the book was a pile of papers they had collected so far. She yanked them out and flipped through them. At last she came to an ochre-coloured slip with Crowne Plaza imprinted on it. She stuffed the papers back in and hurried off.

"Here it is." She thrust the paper at the first officer.

He smoothed it out on his desk blotter and squinted at it. He turned it over and read the back and the front again. "It says here you checked out at nine forty-five a.m. Were you there all night?"

"Yes. We slept the whole night there," Arthur said.

"I was with him the whole time," Thea said. She didn't correct Arthur that they hadn't slept the whole night but they were in bed.

The man looked from one to the other and back to the hotel receipt. "Where are you headed?"

"Anglesey. We're tourists, not murderers."

"I'll make a copy of this but keep it handy. You might have to show it again. All of Northern Wales and England are looking for a man who fits your description."

"It must have been a terrible murder," said Thea. Her curiosity had risen, now she knew Arthur was a free man.

"A labourer was stabbed in the chest on the front steps of the church." He shook his head. "A nasty business."

Arthur and Thea glanced at each other with a grimace and they left the building, fighting the urge to run to the car. She handed him the keys and looked back at the small stone building where two solemn faces stared at them walking away.

She said, "Didn't you think that first man looked like—"

"A spitting image."

"How do you what I'm going to say?"

"It's obvious. I could imagine the royal insignia hanging around his neck. Henry's father, Henry VII, was Welsh."

"You never cease to amaze me." They joined the stream of traffic. "Thank goodness we didn't go to Mercyshire last night. Let's change the subject. How far is it to Anglesey?"

"You have the map. How far is it?"

She unfolded it. "We should be there in half an hour."

Twenty-five minutes later, the Holyhead sign appeared and a huge stone castle loomed in the distance.

"It's beautiful," she said.

"Even from here, it looks massive."

"Can we go in?" She held her hand over her heart as a jumble of feelings crowded in on her.

"I'm pretty sure we can. Castles are for tourists these days." The great stone walls grew larger. "Imagine standing on those ramparts and shooting arrows or throwing boiling oil over."

Thea grinned. He didn't know everything. "It was boiling water they threw."

"I can't imagine living there with drafts and the plumbing none too desirable, not to mention hoping for a hot bath."

"They did have hot baths but it took many servants to carry pails of water from the fireplaces." *How do I know that?* An eery feeling slid over her.

"Give me good old Canadian plumbing any day."

They drove through Holyhead toward the great structure. The stone walls of Castle Llewelyn, one of the largest in Wales, rose before them. A section of ruins poked shadowy fingers skyward.

He pulled into the parking lot alongside a dozen cars. They stepped out onto a gravel path which led to an arched stone entrance. The unmistakable smell of ocean filled the air. When they stepped under the high stone curve, a tidal wave of déjà vu swept over Thea. "It's back."

"What's back?"

"The feeling I've been here before. It's so strong."

"You're not going to faint are you?"

"I don't think so. I feel bubbles of happiness in my stomach."

"Well, that's better than nausea."

They walked into a courtyard surrounded by various buildings. The main one near the edge of the sea looked like a castle itself with ramparts, slit holes and turrets. They followed the signs to this inner castle and to an outside curved staircase which led upwards to a walled walk. She grasped the chrome handrail cemented into old stones, and leaned over the edge. The Irish Sea stretched north and the wind billowed their clothes, tossed their hair across their faces and blew their words away.

"How are you doing?" Arthur yelled.

She held her hair out of her eyes. "I'm on top of the world."

They pushed into the wind and wound their way down to a quieter spot. Near the bottom, a entrance opened into the castle. Worn painted arrows led them along passageways over hard earth to a cavernous stone room, sparsely furnished—the great hall. Ten-foot tapestry hangings adorned two of the high walls. They stepped in and Thea shivered but not because she was cold.

Unaware of a half-dozen tourists, she walked to the centre and. Rooms encircled the top level like the mezzanine in a mall. She walked over to the eight-foot wide stone staircase and without hesitation ascended. Arthur hurried after her. At the top, she stopped, turned left and strode past two open doors. She paused at the third one and stepped over the stone threshold.

Lifting her hands and, holding them in front of her like a blind woman feeling her way, she walked to the centre of the room. She turned in a wide, slow circle. "This was my room. I lived here."

Chapter 69

Arthur stepped through the doorway. "What do you mean you lived here?"

"I know this room." She pointed to the left. "The bed was there with curtains around it to keep out the drafts. I had a table here with a big chair." She turned around. "And on this side was another table—a smaller one—with a wash basin, and—" She pointed. "There's the fireplace."

A folding fireplace screen angled in front of a dark hole. Arthur bent down and peered in. "It must have been a small one."

She did not seem to hear him as she stepped over to the leaded window. "I had that clear view of the sea and I grew herbs in pots all along a shelf that was here."

He stood up straight. "How do you know all this?"

She turned, with a faraway look in her eyes. "I don't know how I know, but I know. I see the whole room in my mind's eye."

He lifted an eyebrow. "You make it sound so believable."

"It's as if another room has superimposed itself over this empty one." She gazed around, glassy eyed. "I see ghostly images of the bed, the tables, the chair and the fire in the grate. They shimmer like heat waves rising from a hot road."

Arthur scanned the empty room and pointed to a wall. "All I see is that six-foot tapestry of a knight."

"We had tapestries but that one is new." She turned in a circle again. "I was happy here."

He reached for her hand. "Shall we explore other rooms?"

"I'd like to stay for a moment." She wandered around, touching a wall and gazing this way and that. *I'm in the same place but in two different times.* She walked to the empty fire place and stretched her hands over the screen as if to feel the warm fire. *I'm me, Thea, but I'm someone else too. It's weird but it feels so right.*

Arthur waited at the doorway, his arms folded. Finally, she took a deep breath. "Okay, we can go now."

They moved into the wide passageway, and he said, "You sure have a good imagination."

"Imagination or whatever. I only know what I feel and what I saw. It was like reliving an old movie or a novel."

"I'm sure that's all it was."

They stood at the edge of the stone balustrade surrounding the great hall below. "Can you imagine the banquets and feasts they had here?" he said.

"Yes, I can." They continued along the hall, in and out of rooms, admiring a banner in one, a four-poster bed in another, and an ancient trunk in yet another. At the end of the hall, a door opened into a large room on the right and when they stepped on the stone threshold, she gasped and stumbled.

He caught her. "Are you okay? You have that same look you had at the convent—as if you've seen a ghost."

"I think I have." She stepped into the room and into another time. "This was our room. You were here with me."*I can't believe I'm saying or feeling this. But it's so real.*

He stared at the bare stone walls and deep window sills. He looked up at the modern lights affixed to the ceiling. "All I see is an unused room in a gigantic castle."

She walked to one side and pointed. "Your desk was here. You did— " She took a sharp breath in. "We both did. We made illuminated manuscripts." She stared into space. "We were husband and wife." A shiver of energy shook her body as if an electric eel had wriggled down her back leaving ripples of memories behind.

He walked over and touched her arm. "If you keep this up, you're going to have me believing in reincarnation."

"I don't believe it, I *know* it. I can't explain it, but I've never been more certain of anything in my life." She kissed him.

"Oh, excuse, please." A Chinese woman with two children stood at the doorway. Her fingertips hid a smile.

"We're just leaving," Arthur said. And to Thea, "Are you sure you're all right?"

She took his hand. "I am more than all right. I'm—I can't explain it." She smiled as they walked along the wide hallway and down another flight of stairs. "I feel full, like every cell in my body is fatter." She laughed. "I'm full of fat joy."

"You are my mystery woman and although I don't understand you, I love you."

When they reached the kitchen area, Thea examined every inch of it, pointing and naming more unseen articles. "Pots hung here. A table there. The butter churn was near a stool."

Arthur looked around at the bare stone walls. "Can you actually see those things."

"Not with my physical eyes. It's as if I have another set which see beyond or through the physical room at another one. That sounds crazy but it's the only way I can explain it."

"Dr. Rhine did extensive studies on extra sensory perception at Duke University but the jury is still out about the veracity of ESP."

They left the kitchen and headed for the exit. "I don't care what any studies showed or didn't show," she said. "I only know what I experience."

They made their way through the central area toward the arched exit, their feet crunching on the stones.

"That's good enough for me," he said. "I like to gather facts but perhaps some things are unexplainable. A little enigma is good for the soul."

"You're the best. Thanks for not thinking I'm totally crazy."

They stayed at the Crossroads, a Guest House with a view of Holyhead Mountain, and the next day explored the town. As Arthur explained how Holyhead used to be a three-walled Roman fort, with the fourth wall being the sea, Thea nodded absently, her mind still on her strange experience at the castle. She bought a handful of postcards each depicting the castle and they took a packed lunch and hiked to a group of standing stones. Next they headed for Holyhead Mountain—Mynydd Tw'r or Tower Mountain the locals called it, which was the highest point in the county of Anglesey. Near the bottom, they passed an old stone quarry.

That funny electric feeling came over her again. "That quarry's new," she said.

"Hardly," Arthur added. "Seven million tonnes of limestone were taken from here in the early eighteen hundreds to build the breakwater which is the longest in the United Kingdom—two point seven kilometres"

"Maybe so. All I'm saying is that it wasn't here when I lived here." That dreamy far-away feeling enveloped her again. "The sea, the birds, the rocks, the yellow gorse and purple heather are the same."

At the summit, hundreds of gulls, guillemots, gannets, and puffins filled the sky, dipping down to visit the remains of a Roman watchtower. A Peregrine Falcon perched high up on her nest while the humans looked down on the castle and at the long S shaped breakwater winding its way through the sea. Thea held Arthur's hand, an anchor to physical reality. *My life is with him here and now.*

When they came to Ellin's Tower on the way down, Arthur related another choice nugget. "It's called a Victorian folly and was built by the Lord Lieutenant of Anglesey for his wife Ellin in 1868."

"How come you know that tidbit?"

He looked a little sheepish. "I googled it last night on my phone."

She slapped his arm but was glad to focus on something in the present. "Why is it called a folly?

"Because these costly and strictly ornamental structures had no practical purpose. There are plenty of them in England, built in large gardens or parks purely for whimsical or aesthetic reasons."

She relaxed into the security of one of his detailed descriptions. *All is well.* She squeezed his hand and when he stopped talking, said, "I like foolish and impractical things. Let's build a folly of our own somewhere."

The next morning, he tore her away from Holyhead and they headed back to England. As they neared London, he said, "I don't want to be a nag, but when are you going to phone Evan?"

"Soon," she said. "Soon."

When they got to the hotel, she let the phone ring six times. No answer and no invitation to leave a message. The next day, she tried again and admonished herself that she hadn't phoned from Canada. *I can't leave England without talking to him. Stephanie would never forgive me.* She tried her uncle Harold's number. "Is Harold Marshall there?" *He would know where his brother was.*

"No, this is Meghan, his wife. My husband died three years ago. Can I help you?"

"You probably don't remember me. I'm Thea—Cynthia Marshall. My—mother, Josephine Marshall, married your brother-in-law, Frank, twenty-nine years ago in Canada."

"Oh my. Yes, I do remember that trip. You're the middle daughter. You were single at the time, but you eloped, divorced and had a baby."

Thea gasped. *How does she know all that?*

"We're not great letter writers, but Patricia keeps us informed of family news in her yearly Christmas card."

Of course. Patricia would do that and not tell me. "I'm here in London for a week—"

"Oh, you must come by for tea. Is your daughter with you? Susan? No, it's Stephanie, isn't it?"

"Yes, Stephanie and no, she's not with me." She cleared her throat. "I'm with Arthur—my fiancé."

"Patricia didn't mention a fiancé in her last card. When can you come by?"

They arranged for a visit the next afternoon. Thea gulped. "By the way, it would be nice to see Evan again." *She must still be in touch with her brother.*

"Evan? Oh, yes, Evan went to the wedding too. He's not here right now. He's in Paris, visiting his daughter."

But she's in Canada. "Oh."

"I'm sure he'd like to see you, luv."

"I would like that." *Did that sound suspicious?*

Meghan gave her the address of the house and finished with, "See you tomorrow. Cheerio."

Cheerio indeed.

Chapter 70

They spent the rest of the day visiting art galleries, although they could have stayed a whole week at the National. Arthur gobbled up the architecture at the Barbican and Thea drooled in Chelsea's Sastchi Gallery. After hours of walking, and staring, she never once thought of her visit with Meghan the next afternoon.

On the taxi ride to Meghan's house, Arthur held her hand. "Run it by me again. How are they related to you?"

"By marriage only, thankfully. There are no blood ties." She turned to Arthur. "I told you all that when Stephanie found out about her father, Evan."

"It was confusing. I got mixed up about who were the uncles and who was married to whom."

Thea smiled. *He remembers every fact I told him, but bless , he's trying to calm me.* She took a deep breath. "At my father's funeral, my mother—that is, Josephine—"

"Well I do know that your mother is—was Josephine."

Thea didn't answer and Arthur stared at her. "Josephine was your mother, wasn't she?" He lifted an eyebrow.

The questioning look on his face waited for an answer. Thea sighed. "That's another story for another time."

"You never cease to amaze me. Living with you is going to be an adventure." He leaned over and kissed her lightly. "Okay, back to the story about Evan."

"At my father's funeral, Josephine met Frank, my father's brother, for the first time. We knew he had three brothers, but didn't know their names or that one lived in Guelph. And when he came to the funeral, Josephine latched onto him. He was a successful architect, financially secure and a year-and-a-half later they were married. Frank's relatives came over from Britain for the wedding. They were my father's relatives too, of course.

"Okay. I get that. And Evan was one of the relatives?"

"Yes. There was Harold, who was Frank and my dad's brother. He came with his wife Meghan—who we are about to meet now."

"Ah, yes. I do know that part."

Liar, liar, pants on fire. You know all of this. But it helps to talk it out. "Two aunts and Evan came. Everyone assumed that Evan was the third brother. But he wasn't. He was Meghan's brother. John, the third brother, was away at the time and couldn't come."

"I can see where it could have been confusing, especially since you had never met any of them before."

"We didn't even know they existed." The cab slowed and waited for a bicycle to turn off. "I was an emotional mess at the time, and everyone's nerves were on edge. And after I'd had a few drinks, I couldn't have told you my own name."

He laughed. "I wish I'd known you then."

It was her time to raise an eyebrow. "Oh, no. You wouldn't have. We met at the perfect time." She squeezed his hand. "However, if we had met then, you would have probably ended up being Stephanie's father."

"I wouldn't have minded that a bit."

They were silent for several moments.

She said, "This may sound crazy, but I'm sure we've had children together in another lifetime. Somewhere, sometime ago."

"You mean when you were a princess in a castle and I was your lionhearted knight?"

"Something like that."

"I love your imagination."

She leaned over for a kiss. "And I love you. Thank you." *Thank you for taming past demons of guilt and shame that had started peeking out of the shadows.*

The cab pulled up to a small brick house in suburban London. "Here we are, luv," the driver said.

The visit to Meghan and her family was like meeting strangers. Meghan's husband, Harold, had died three years earlier and Thea had never met her grown cousins—Edith, a matronly woman in her fifties, and Edward, a dour pipe-smoking chap, sat in a stuffed chair and quietly puffed. Meghan, a cheery woman in her seventies, put heaping spoonfuls of tea leaves into a large Brown Betty teapot. "We always enjoy Patricia's cards at Christmas."

"She never told me she was in touch with you," Thea said.

"Oh, yes. Every Christmas without fail, we get a long letter with her card."

Thea grimaced.

"I see you have the Welsh flag out front," Arthur said.

"Yes. My brother and I were born in Cardiff. When I married Harold Marshall I moved here. Evan moved a year later. His wife died in childbirth, poor soul." She covered the teapot with a quilted tea cozy and patted the top. "He never remarried so he only has the one daughter, Elizabeth."

Thea stared at the tea pot. *No. He has two daughters.*

Meghan continued. "Sorry you missed him. He'll be in Paris for another three weeks. Elizabeth—Beth, we call her—is a fashion designer and lives there."

Edith spoke up. "She is so talented."

His other daughter is creative and talented too. But out loud she said, "What does Evan do?"

"Oh, he's retired now," Meghan said. "He was an art dealer. Travelled all over the world buying and selling art. He still does a little consulting."

"Thea is an artist," Arthur blurted.

"I'm just a beginner."

Meghan placed two more teacups out. "Well, you must see Evan again. Would you like his phone number?" She reached to a sideboard and took out a well-used leather binder.

The remainder of the visit passed quickly as Meghan and Edith chattered on about relatives Thea had never met. Edward grunted in response when required while everyone devoured cups of strong tea and home made short bread.

Thea slipped her hand into her pocket. The scrap of paper with Evan's phone number scribbled on it was still there.

They said their good-byes and with a final wave, Meghan called after them. "Now you be sure to call Evan. He will be delighted to hear from you."

She gulped and took Arthur's hand. *I wonder. I hope for Stephanie's sake that he will.*

Chapter 71

Back in the hotel room, Arthur said, "I'll go down to the cafe."

"You don't have to go." She was about to add, *I have no secrets from you*, but bit the words back. He had probably already guessed there was something about Josephine that she hadn't told him.

"I'll be back in a jiff." And he walked out.

She picked up the phone before she could change her mind. Her hand trembled as she dialled Evan's number. *Maybe he'll be out. I should have rehearsed a message to leave him.*

A deep voice in a Welsh-English accent answered. "Hello."

Thea froze. Her knees wobbled and she sat down.

"Hello," the voice said again. "Who is this?"

"Thea," she blurted.

"Thea? Oh, you mean the Marshall woman? "

"Yes." She gripped the phone.

"Meghan said you might call."

She must have phoned him right after we left. "Yes, I'm visiting England with my fiancé and Meghan gave me your number."

"So she said. I'm sorry I wasn't in London to meet you."

Tell him who you are and that you've met before. "I—I—we actually have met." She gulped. "Twenty-nine years ago." Her voice came out in a croak.

"Oh, my. That is a long time. Were you over here for a visit?"

"No. It was the time you and Meghan and Harold and your two aunts came to Guelph for my mother Josephine and my Uncle

Frank's wedding." She held her breath. There was silence at the other end of the line.

"The Canadian wedding. Yes, I recall that trip now. We went to Niagara Falls the next day but I had such a hangover all I remember was the torrential pounding in my head."

"Do you remember the party after the wedding?" Her stomach did a flip flop.

"Let me see. I remember your mother making a big fuss at the reception over some seating arrangements."

Thea laughed. "Josephine did like to have things her way."

"You said 'did'. Has your mother passed?"

"Yes, last February."

"I'm sorry."

"She had five happy years with Uncle Frank."

"If I remember correctly, Josephine and Uncle Stephen had three daughters. Which one are you?"

He doesn't even remember me. Her voice cracked. "I'm the middle one. My name was Cynthia, but I've changed it to Thea."

A long silence. "Cynthia. You were the quiet one. Self conscious of—. Oh, I am sorry."

"It's all right. Yes, I had a birthmark that covered half my face. I had laser treatment many years ago and had it removed."

"I am happy for you. I remember you seemed quite sad."

Does he remember anything else? This is agony. I should hang up. She took a deep breath. "Do you remember our evening together?" She was glad she was sitting down.

A long pause. "I do remember now. I saw you to your room. I'm afraid I'd had quite a bit to drink."

"We both did."

"I do hope I was a gentleman. I was recovering from a broken relationship and feeling sorry for myself."

Oh, my God. Should I even tell him? "Well, that's the thing."

"What do you mean?"

"Ah—well, with both of us lonely and inebriated, one thing led to another and . . ." She let her voice trail off. *We had sex, we made love, we slept together*. None of those words left her lips.

"Oh, my dear. Are you saying we—."

He can't say the words either, but they both knew what they were. "Yes. We did and nine months later I had a beautiful daughter."

A gasp came from the other end of the line. "Oh, no. I never knew. This is a shock. I—I don't know what to say. After all these years. I have to sit down. Oh my—why didn't you tell me? I would have helped. I would have stood by you. I'm not a cad. I never knew. My God, I have another daughter!"

Thea couldn't hold back a rush of tears. The memory of going through it alone swept over her. It had been hard but she had been in such an emotional turmoil she could do nothing else at the time. She swallowed and tried to say something.

He spoke instead. "I remember now Meghan telling me that you'd had a child. I never dreamt in a million years that the child was mine. Oh, my dear. I could have helped."

She found her voice. "I should have told you."

His voice quavered when he answered. "What can I do now?"

"That's why I'm calling. Stephanie, my—our daughter, tracked you down and she wants to meet you." *'Our' daughter, sounds so strange. She's always been mine. I have been selfish.*

His voice still sounded shaky, as if he was having a hard time holding back tears. "I would love to meet her, and you again. I have another daughter. Beth."

"Yes. Meghan told me. I'm sure Stephanie would love to meet her too."

They were both silent for many moments. It was a silence full of questions about twenty-nine years of a child's life.

"Can you come to Paris? Beth lives here. It would be a good time for us all to meet."

"It's not going to work on this visit. Arthur, my fiancé, and I are going home tomorrow. I should have phoned earlier."

"I am sorry you didn't."

"I am too."

They both knew they meant much earlier—like twenty-nine years earlier.

A long silence. He said,"We can only do what we can do.'

She hung up and dried her tears when Arthur walked in.

"Are you all right?" He took her in his arms.

"Considering I have been dreading that conversion for most of my life, I feel better than I thought I would."

"And what is that feeling now?" They sat on the couch.

"Mixed. He sounds like such a nice man. He was shocked and moved knowing he has another daughter. And he wants to meet Stephanie. I wish now, for both their sakes, I had gotten up the courage to contact him years ago."

"We can only do what we can do."

Thea stared at him.

"What?'

"He just said the exact same thing."

"He must be a wise man."

She kept staring. *Now would be a good time to tell him who my real mother is.*

"Now what?" He tilted his head, waiting for an answer.

"Nothing." *Not yet.* "So much has happened and with all that weirdness in Wales and visiting the Castle." *I hate holding things back from him.*

"Weird or not. I love you."He hugged her. "And you'll tell me when you're ready."

Chapter 72

It was the day before Thea's birthday and their last full day of their trip. For most of the morning, they wandered through the Royal Academy of Art and could easily have spent the whole day there. At Whitechapel Gallery, Thea thought she'd died and gone to heaven when they came across a special showing of Pollock's.

At lunch, she said to Arthur, "I am gutted with art. I need time to digest it all. Would you mind if we go back to the castle?"

"What castle?"

She jabbed him in the ribs. "My castle, silly."

"Why not. I'm always up for more weird."

Late that afternoon, the ramparts rose in the distance and ten minutes later their feet crunched along the gravel path toward the arched entrance. "We missed something last time," she said.

"What was that?"

"The chapel."

"Is there a chapel?" He opened the guide book.

"Of course there's a chapel. All castles have a chapel. People were very religious in castle times." Ignoring other tourists milling about, she marched past the kitchen building and the stocks.

Arthur scanned the pages as they walked.

"It's over here," she called, three steps ahead of him.

The chapel was a gothic structure, far smaller than the magnificent cathedrals in London. It reminded Thea of St.

Patrick's in New York or the Church of Our Lady in Guelph. They entered as a chatting family exited. On the front altar, three tall unlit candles stood on a white embroidered cloth. Filtered light shone through the row of narrow windows along each side.

Arthur smoothed his hand over the curve of a darkened pew. "Did you know they didn't have seats until the fourteen hundreds? It was only when sermons became more popular, some lasting up to four hours, that they brought pews in. It must have been tiring standing."

"It was very tiring," Thea said.

At the front, a plaster crucifix hung beside a statue of Mary. Some of the stained-glass windows depicted nature scenes, and others, Stations of the Cross. They strolled up one side, looking at the glass pictures.

Thea walked over to a window set apart at the far end. On it, was a family crest of the Welsh dragon, scrolls, and a purple flower depicted in separate panels. She leaned closer to look at the semicircle of Welsh writing at the bottom. *What is it cradling?* She looked twice to make sure. "Arthur, come and look at this."

He joined her and she pointed.

"What's that picture at the bottom? Right above the words."

He bent down. "It's a dragonfly. What a coincidence."

"It's not a coincidence. It's *my* dragonfly! I *told* you I was here." She touched the glass outline of golden wings spread in flight. "My dragonfly." Her heart beat faster and her blood seemed to slide more easily through her body, reaching every cranny of her being.

A noisy group came into the church. They ooo'd and ah'd at the windows and walls and when they left, the silence seemed to fill that ancient space.

They sat down on the six-hundred-year-old pew where thousands of souls had sat before them.

He took her hand and looked at her as if for the first time. "Let's get married."

"What?"

"Let's get married. Right here. Right now."

"What?"

"These timeless walls can be our witness." He stood up and went to the altar. "Quickly, before anyone else comes in."

She went to the front and he took her hands in his.

"Thea Marshall. I, Arthur Richardson, do take you for my wife. To love and honour you no matter what crazy things you say or do. I love you."

Thea's eyes brimmed. She stared into the eyes of the man she had known for lifetimes. "I, Thea Marshall, do take you, Arthur Richardson to be my husband, my lover, my friend, forever and ever, my everlasting love. I love you." She couldn't have felt more married if a priest, rabbi, or minister had spoken the words over them. The front door banged open and a noisy group bustled in.

Still holding hands, they turned from the altar and walked down the aisle and out of the church. On the front steps, he stopped. "I nearly forgot." He pulled a small box from his pocket and flipped the lid open.

Thea stared at its contents: a glittering pear-cut diamond ring. He lifted it from its crimson velvet groove, took her left hand and slid it onto her third finger. A perfect fit. She tilted her hand back and forth letting the sun catch it. *The girls in the office were right. They do sparkle.*

On the smoothly rounded steps of a 13th century castle chapel, oblivious of tourists, they kissed as husband and wife.

Chapter 73

It was their last evening in Wales. Thea changed, washed, and climbed into bed. After fluffing the feather pillow, she propped it behind her and picked up her travel journal and pen. She scribbled a few lines, stopped and looked at Arthur.

He had removed his watch and was placing it on top of the high bureau. Next, he emptied his pockets: wallet, coins, keys and a scrap of paper. He glanced at the paper, smoothed it out and stuck it under the keys.

He started to unbutton his shirt but stopped and looked at her. "Why are you looking at me like that?"

"Like what?"

"Like you've never seen me empty my pockets or get undressed."

She paused and breathed in the moment of intimacy. "Because I love you and you make the ordinary special."

"You're the one who's special." He finished undressing, pulled back the covers and got into bed. "It's too bad you didn't get to see Evan."

"The phone call was hard enough but I hope Stephanie won't be disappointed that I didn't see him in person."

"She isn't."

Thea's brow crinkled. "What do you mean, 'she isn't'?"

"I spoke with her last night. She and Mark will be here the day after tomorrow."

"Here? What are you talking about? Our flight leaves tomorrow morning."

"Our *old* flight leaves tomorrow morning, but we won't be on it." He put his hands behind his head. "Hope you don't mind if we stay another week."

"But—but—"

"You sound like a rusty motor boat."

"But what about your work?"

"I arranged another week off. How would you like to go to Paris? I hear it's enchanting in the spring."

Thea's mouth and eyes opened even wider.

"Can you handle meeting Evan, and Stephanie meeting her father?"

She slapped a hand on her chest and sucked in a gulp of air. "I —I—" She slammed her journal shut. "Yes, I am ready."

"Good. I don't care how many people you are or whether you lived in that ancient drafty castle whatever many years ago or not, I love you forever and a day."

She leaned over and kissed his cheek. "And I, you, forever and forever, through past lives and future."

"Now there you go, being weird again." He smiled.

"And you love it."She placed her journal on the bed stand and laid the pen on top. "My dad never quoted the Bible much, but there was one saying he repeated often to me. "You will know the truth, and the truth will set you free."

"And do you feel free?"

"Almost. There is one last secret I need to tell you."

"You don't have to tell me everything."

"I want to tell you this." She looked down for a moment. "I think it might have been the truth my father was alluding to." She took a deep breath and told him about the contents of Josephine's diary—the woman she thought was her mother.

He was silent for a moment. "You never cease to amaze me. I thought I had the biggest surprise with Stephanie and Mark coming, but that beats all. Does Stephanie know?"

"Not yet. Of course, I will tell her."

"You're handling it extremely well."

"To tell you the truth, I feel relieved. It explains so much about my mother's—Josephine's—attitude and actions toward me."

"And what about going to Paris? Are you sure you're okay with that? I mean meeting Evan and having Stephanie meet him?"

"Absolutely." She lifted her chin. "And Paris is a great place to have a honeymoon." She leaned over and kissed him. "Thank you."

"You're welcome m'lady."

She lifted an eyebrow. "You have your thinking face on. What else have you dreamed up?"

"How would you like to live in the country?"

"The country? With you?"

"Nobody else I hope."

"You mean the country as opposed to the city?"

"I've been thinking about early retirement and I'd love to design and build a house for us." He stared at the ceiling. "A large art studio for you and an office for me—"

An art studio! She reared up and launched herself at him where she anchored his face in her two hands and splattered kisses all over him: nose, forehead, lips, chin, cheeks and back to nose.

Between the battery of kisses, he managed to say, "I'll take that as a yes."

With a huge smile, she snuggled her head into his shoulder.

They lay quietly for a moment before he spoke. "Even before I was an architect, I wanted to build ecological houses: domes, yurts, cobs. How would you like to live in a straw bale house?"

"Straw, sticks, or bricks. As long as it's with you."

Chapter 74

The next morning Thea woke before six. Her stomach churned. *Am I excited or anxious? Probably a bit of both.* Instead of heading home to Canada, they would be meeting up with Stephanie and Mark in London and fly to Paris together. But today was her birthday and she had to do something all by herself. She pulled her covers off and swung her legs over the side of the bed. Arthur turned over and buried his head under the blanket.

She splashed water on her face, brushed her teeth and put on her jeans and her new ecru fisherman's knit sweater. Arthur insisted he buy it for her when she raved over it in London. Tomorrow, she would arrange to mail it home, along with Paddington Bear, and a small but exquisite Van Gogh print she had picked up in London.

She grabbed her yellow rain jacket, handbag, and a bottle of water, and blew a kiss at the jumbled heap of bedcovers. She had one more thing to do before she left. On the pad of note paper, below the picture of the iconic red dragon, she jotted that she had gone for a walk.

Morning mist blotted out distant scenes, but she knew the way along the coastal trail to Holyhead Mountain. Flocks of raucous birds meant she was getting closer. On their last visit, many people had been about, but she was alone now. She picked up a walking stick that an intrepid hiker had left leaning against a pile of stones and started the long climb. Her endurance and leg muscles had grown stronger over the past three weeks. Half way up into cooler air, she put on her jacket and continued over hardened earth and ancient stones. *Who else has wandered over these paths?* She looked at the golden yellow gorse and the pinks, purples, and mauves of the heather. *Nature has a good eye for colour.*

She reached the top, and not having the capacity of the dragonfly with its visual range of nearly three hundred and sixty degrees, she slowly turned in a full circle to gaze at every angle of hills, rocks, mountain and sea. *Land of mystery. Land of song and story.*

She unzipped the outer pouch of her travel bag, pulled out her rain poncho and spread it over a patch of ground. Moist air and damp earth added to the morning smell of a new day. Wales had that old world, yet fresh smell of foreverness over its lush valleys.

She lowered herself to the ground and hugged her knees. Myriads of—yes, Arthur, there must be at least ten thousand squawking birds darting and swooping through the air.

A large dragonfly hovered into view. She smiled at how she and her sisters used to yell, "Darning Needle!" when one flew into their vicinity and woe to you if you did not open your mouth and eyes as wide as you could, spread your fingers and splay your toes like a startled lizard. There they would stand, like crazy people: feet apart, plastic man arms fully extended, with mouth, eyes, fingers and toes stretched to aching points.

The dragonfly rested on a stone in front of her about three feet away. It had been a year almost to the day since she'd found her dragonfly at the Guelph market. She reached into her purse and took it out. The old man's gentle words came back to her. *Pewter. It's made of pewter.* And the trill in the voice of the lady antique dealer whispering, *That's worth plenty.*

It may be worth plenty, but no matter how much money she might be offered for it, it was more precious to her than any remuneration. She cradled it in her hands. "Dear Dragonfly, if only you could speak. You heard my pain, you caught my tears, but most of all, you woke me up. Thank you, my friend."

Sitting on the hard ground, with birds soaring overhead and the Irish sea spread before her, a fresh idea nibbled at the corner of her mind. On that day, a year ago, she had bought the dragonfly on impulse, and on impulse she would let it go. *This is the perfect place to leave you, my dear friend, my totem. Here in this sacred place, in Wales on this peak of land, at this peak of my life.*

She looked around for the best spot. She rolled to her knees and gathered up the poncho. A flat rock with a pointed end lay nearby. She picked it up and scraped away the soil to make a shallow depression. Cupping the dragonfly in two hands, she engraved its image in her brain and kissed it for the last time before lowering it to the ground. "Part of me is screaming to keep you, but a deeper part is telling me that my time with you is over and to leave you for the next person." She stroked each wing. "I leave you in good hands, in the warmth and protection of Mother Earth. Bless you, my friend. I will remember you always."

She covered her talisman with fresh earth, scattered a few branches and stones on top and brushed off her hands. She stood up. "Time to go. Time to start living."

With a last long look over the misty valley and the never ending sea, she drew in a deep breath and slowly let it out. She slipped her handbag over her shoulder, tossed her poncho over her arm and picked up her borrowed walking stick.

Half way down, a small bent woman, stepping cautiously over the irregular stones, came toward her. Thea's heart lurched. The old woman lifted her head and Thea stabbed her stick into the hard ground to steady herself. Under a halo of white hair, a pair of sunken, watery green eyes met hers. The old woman nodded as she passed, but Thea stood as still as the nearby Roman stones.

"Wait," she called. She dropped her stick and in two paces, stood in front of the stationary old soul. A flash of Josephine's green eyes momentarily pierced into Thea's. Then it was gone and there was only an old woman staring back. Thea placed her hands on the rounded shoulders, leaned down and brushed a feathery kiss on each crosshatched cheek. "Thank you, mother."

I forgive you. I forgive me. It is over.

A perplexed smile quivered at the edges of the old woman's face. Thea stepped back, picked up her walking stick and headed down the mountain.

Back to sea level.

Back to a new life.

And as she walked, her feet tread lightly upon the earth.

Appendix A

If you've read *Book 1: The Hidden Vow,* in the Dragonfly Series, you may remember the characters. Have you guessed who these people are 800 years later in this book? Below is the list of the reincarnated counterparts.

The character on the left is from this book, ***The Broken Promise,*** and the one on the right is who they were in ***The Hidden Vow.*** The Dragonfly, of course, is the same Dragonfly in both.

Cynthia (Thea) Marshall = Margrett of Ussex

Arthur Richardson = Drew (Andrew) Silverson

Josephine Marshall (Thea's mother) = Mother Helwyska. (the Mother Superior)

Stephanie (Cynthia's daughter) = Bundy (Margrett's charge)

Madison (Cynthia's sister) = Lady Sarra-Emma, Margrett's daughter.

Sarah Jane Jenkins (Cynthia's neighbour and friend) = Sister Sarra, (Margrett's best friend in the convent).

Bonnie (Scottish Housekeeper) = Lucia (the manor house bakery cook)

Patricia (Cynthia's older sister) = Lady Ussex, (Margrett's mother)

Margrett, from *The Hidden Vow*, came to me in a dream and as I wrote the first book, I felt I knew her well. Was she a real person? Another me in another life?

"The same circle that sent you out
then gathered you back beyond all doubt
now sets you forth to live again
remembered by another name."
From *Unison of Circles* by Ruth Cunningham

Thank you for reading The Broken Promise
I hope you enjoyed it.

I would really appreciate it if you would leave a review at
amazon.com and/or amazon.ca

Book browsers rely on other readers' opinions
and I am thankful if you can take the time to write about
your experience of reading *The Broken Promise.*
I look forward to reading your comments.

I love to hear from my readers, so do email me at
gloria@gloriawnye.com or visit me at
www.GloriaWNye.com

The 3rd book in the Dragonfly Series, ***The Forbidden Path,***
will be launched in May 2021. This one takes place in England at
the time of the great fire in London in 1666.
More adventures await the reader and our new heroine as the
dragonfly comes into her life to help her overcome obstacles
and find her own power and true love.

Go to my web page at www.gloriawnye.com
to sign up for my author's Newsletter

About the Author

Gloria W. Nye is an award winning author, receiving several prizes and acclaim for her short stories from various writing festivals: Elora Writers' Festival, Eden Mills Writer's Festival, and Sharon's Words Alive Literary Festival. Several of her stories have been shortlisted at the Writers' Union of Canada Contests.

She is a retired special education teacher, living in Southern Ontario, where she writes and paints full time.

My heartfelt thanks to -

- my sister Alberta, for her constant encouragement, many cups of tea, and for diverting phone calls and other interruptions during my writing time, but most of all for her time and talent in making the book trailers for each of the Dragonfly books.
- Marilyn Kleiber, in my River Writers' Group, who offered valuable plot changes and editorial suggestions
- Marie Davis Zimmerman, my first editor. I still hear your voice whispering in my ear, "Cut that part and that and that."
- my beta readers, Debrah Gopsill, Barbara Heagy, Marilyn Kleiber, Alberta Nye, and Betty Radford Turcott for your helpful comments.
- our Abraham Group: Cathy Steffler, Alberta Nye, and Alice and Bob Trotter for over fifteen years of inspiration and appreciation
- the Rockwood Crones for their support and comments on my first book, *The Hidden Vow*. I hope you enjoy this one.
- my online teams: Mark Dawson, Joanne Penn, and Nick Stephenson for help with marketing
- my daughter, Melanie. Thank you for choosing me to be your mom. You have enriched my life.
- my three grandchildren, Rick, Jake, and Genessa. May each of you follow your dreams
- and thanks to baby Claire for coming into our lives and making me a capital G, Great grandmother.

www.ingramcontent.com/pod-product-compliance
Lightning Source LLC
Chambersburg PA
CBHW060341260626
47160CB00006B/2161